For almost twenty years Sally Bradfield has worked with the who's who of professional tennis.

She has travelled the globe working as a Communications Manager/publicist for the WTA Tour. She worked alongside Venus and Serena Williams, Maria Sharapova, Martina Hingis, Monica Seles, Anna Kournikova and hundreds more.

Subsequently she joined the men's tour as Brand Manager for the ATP. She ran major events with Roger Federer, Andy Murray, Rafael Nadal, Novak Djokovic and many other household names.

Wanting to leave the suitcases and hotels behind, Sally settled back in Australia with her retired tennis champion partner, Nicole Arendt. Together they live in the Blue Mountains in NSW running tennis and fitness businesses.

To find out more visit www.notquite30love.com

Not Quite 30-Love

Sally Bradfield

First published by Sally Bradfield in 2019
This edition published in 2019 by Sally Bradfield

Copyright © Sally Bradfield 2019
www.notquite30love.com
The moral right of the author has been asserted.

All rights reserved. This publication (or any part of it) may not be reproduced or transmitted, copied, stored, distributed or otherwise made available by any person or entity (including Google, Amazon or similar organisations), in any form (electronic, digital, optical, mechanical) or by any means (photocopying, recording, scanning or otherwise) without prior written permission from the publisher.

Not Quite 30-Love

EPUB: 9781925786736
POD: 9781925786743

Cover design by Red Tally Studios
The characters and events in this book – even those based on real people – are fictitious and any resemblance to real persons, living or dead, is purely coincidental.

This novel's story and characters are fictitious. Certain long-standing institutions, agencies and public office are mentioned, but the characters involved, are wholly imaginary. Where certain public figures appear, the situations, incidents, and dialogues concerning those persons are entirely fictional and are not intend to depict actual events or to change the entirely fictional nature of the work. In all other respects, any resemblance to actual persons, living or dead, events, or locales is entirely coincidental.

Publishing services provided by Critical Mass
www.critmassconsulting.com

To the players, WTA, ATP, Tennis Australia and all national associations, their staff (past and present) who continue to make this sport we love a spectacle.

KATIE COOK'S ADVENTURE

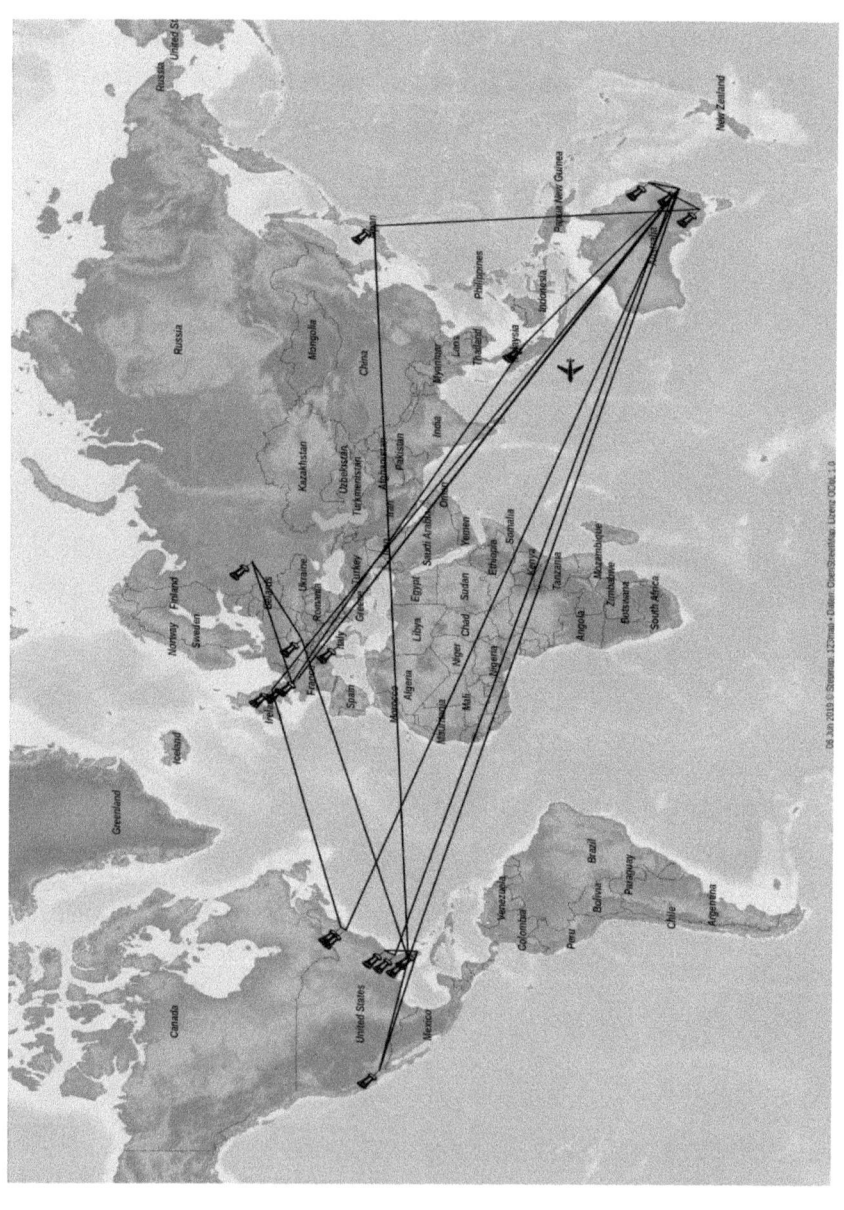

#Prologue, #BondiDreaming

The last sunrays of the day fell on the floor of my Bondi Beach apartment. Jen and I sat cross-legged next to a rug laid with cheese, grapes and bread. The brie was soft and the bread a little stale; our glasses were full. One empty and one depleted bottle of rosé sat on the floor within arm's reach.

'I have Facebook, why do I need Instagram as well?'

'Because you're going on an epic adventure – Instagram is how you document it. Everyone knows that.'

'Oh that's right. Everyone does it, so must I.'

'You're the bloody marketer, why do you have to be such a snob about it?'

'I love social media for work. I'm not so sure I want so many people up in my business.'

'Here lies Katie Cook. She had an epic adventure – I think, maybe, who knows?'

I smiled at Jen and downloaded the app onto my iPhone.

'Fantastic, now what should we call you?'

'Um, what about Katie Cook?'

'Are you fucking kidding me? You could just hang a sign around your neck that says "no imagination".'

'We could do that.'

'It has to be something to do with tennis. What about Advantage Katie?'

I indicated the need to vomit.

'Okay, what about LoveMatch?'

I mock projectile vomited.

Jen sat and visibly tossed ideas around in her head. Jen's a talk-thinker. 'I know, I know, it's brilliant. What about @NotQuite30Love?'

'No.'

'You don't get it. It's because you're twenty-eight and don't have a boyfriend. It's brilliant.'

'I get it, Jen. I'm just not sure I want to advertise it.'

'It's not as desperate as being on E-Harmony.'

'Which you're on.'

'Which I'm on and you should be.'

Jen was the same friend who goaded me into sleeping with that guy on the beach in Fiji. I woke up alone. Nuff said. She was right though. I needed a hook and it was clever. My input was to abbreviate it to @NQ30Love. Just cryptic enough to salvage some pride.

Jen grabbed my phone and took a pic of my empty flat. She posted my first story caption: 'All packed up and somewhere epic to go #BigAdventure, #TennisDream.' It was all linked up to my Facebook and on the net before I could chug my wine.

'Now, instead of writing *My Brilliant Career*, you can post it,' said Jen, totally chuffed with herself.

#SchoolsOut, #LinzCrisis

Half past six, a perfect autumn morning, lying in my king-sized bed at the Arcotel Nike Linz hotel on the dawn of my second day in my dream job. I mentally frame this shot. An ideal opening scene for the movie version of my brilliant career. They pan from me to the Danube River sparkling blue as the song suggests. The sky is a mixture of pinks, mauves and hints of the deepest blue coming to life. The streaked clouds appear to race towards something, yet move at a glacial pace. I sit up and stretch. Birds fly around my head singing. Hang on, isn't that Cinderella? I grab my phone to check emails before showering, when the unfamiliar ring of the in-room telephone disrupts. It is all the way on the other side of the massive bed. I can't reach it without dragging the doona, as I crawl across the breadth. The ring seems to become more insistent. 'Okay, hold your horses.'

'Katie Cook?' says an unfamiliar American female voice.

'Yes.' My posture snaps to attention. 'May I ask who's –'

'It's the woman who hired you, Katie. Perhaps the worst decision of my career.'

The birds are silent. The soundtrack screeches to a halt. This angry voice is not in my script. The river recedes from view as I identify the voice at the other end. Jane Townsend is the director of communications for the WTA (Women's Tennis Association). She hired me with one Skype phone call and several emails – we have never met. My mouth is now dry. 'Jane, I'm sorry. Is something wrong?'

'That's the understatement of the century. You obviously haven't checked your emails this morning.'

'I was just about to.'

My iPhone downloads what seems to be thousands of emails.

'I'll shortcut it for you. There was a shooting today in a Philadelphia high school. Ten students are dead.'

'Oh my God, that's terrible.' Small beads of sweat assemble on my forehead.

'The shooter upon entering the school was quoted as saying "School's Out".'

Coins started to drop at a million miles an hour. 'Fuck, the post… the Instagram post.'

'Fuck, indeed,' says Jane. 'We are the number one trend in the country. The team tells me your post was scheduled for 3p.m. eastern daylight time – about thirty minutes before the gunman entered the school.' She pauses. I can't speak. My tongue swells to fill my mouth. 'It started trending within minutes of the media covering the story. The digital team here in Florida had it removed within twenty minutes. Twenty minutes too late.'

'I never meant –'

'Don't even bother, Katie. I'm sure I don't have to paint you a picture of how the post was received. Read some of the emails, look online, the commentary is not exactly hard to find.'

My brain races, *say something smart, meaningful, thoughtful, for God's sake.* 'What can I do? Can I put out a statement?' *Really, Katie, that's the best you can manage?*

'That's already been done... As has the damage.'

Looking through the emails as we speak, for all the vitriol that is coming over the airwaves you would think the WTA was responsible for the murders. The most painful headline comes from the *Daily Mail*: 'WTA Dances on the Grave of Slain Students.' Could it get worse?

It's such a great picture. Twenty up-and-coming tennis players who had graduated from WTA University in Florida, all throwing their tennis caps in the air. 'School's Out' was the obvious caption.

'Katie, we are a 24/7 organisation. There's always someone awake to post digital, why did you schedule the post?'

I want to say 'Brenda suggested it' but I know how lame that would sound. 'I thought it was a simple story. Something happy... and didn't want to bother anybody.'

'Well, that's worked out perfectly, hasn't it? What's the point of a fucking manual if you don't read it.'

'What do you mean?'

'The digital media manual you were given on induction. You should read it – it's very prescriptive. In the meantime, don't say anything to anyone without clearing it through me. I don't have to repeat that, do I?'

'No.'

'I don't have any more time to waste on you. I need to get back to damage control.'

The phone goes dead – like my career.

I scramble to my feet and over to my bag. Manuals, manuals, where are all those fucking manuals they gave me? I find the umpires' manual, the court rules manual, on-site etiquette manual, expenses rules and regulations, and then the digital media guide.

Page one, paragraph one:

**

The WTA operates in a global 24/7 environment where anything can and does happen. That's why we have members of the team in place in every time zone, enabling us to respond to whatever, whenever. Use your colleagues to make sure we are always awake and never forget the cardinal rule – **NO SCHEDULING OF ANY SOCIAL MEDIA POSTS EVER.**

**

Fuck, fuck, fuck, fuck, fuck. I probably should have read this on the plane instead of that new Janet Evanovich novel. If Stephanie Plum can't pick between Ranger and Morelli after fifty books, there's no saving her.

Sitting on the floor of my hotel room scrolling through the newsfeed, occasionally glancing across at the in-room minibar. Somehow, because of me, a happy picture of tennis graduates is playing alongside images of body bags containing innocent teenagers.

The flight from Australia landed at 7a.m. yesterday morning. Straight to the tennis stadium – no shower, just a clothes change and teeth clean in the players' locker room, my suitcase standing in the corner. By 6p.m., sitting at my desk in the press room, the jet lag was begging my brain to give in. This was the job. This was what I signed up for. Adrenaline and caffeine, via my Coke Zero addiction, fuelled my brain.

With our work seemingly done for the day, the fantastic happy news story hit my desk in the form of a player photograph from our St Petersburg, Florida office. I captioned it and was about to post it to the WTA's Instagram account. I checked with my on-site manager. 'What do you think of "School's Out", as a caption?' She shrugged and went back to her laptop.

'I'm going to post it.'

'Wouldn't it be better to post it when school's actually coming out for the day in the US?' she offered.

My fog-filled brain attempted to calculate the Linz time difference. 'I think that would be about midnight here.'

'If you can't handle the hours, maybe this job's not for you.' *Wow, that's harsh. First day, just off a plane from Oz.*

'No, it's no problem, I'll do it. But wouldn't it be smart to get the US office to do it?'

'Sure, if you want other people to do your job for you.' *This conversation was going really well.*

I started programming an alarm in my phone.

'You could always schedule the post. You know how to do that, don't you?'

'Yes, of course I do. Great idea. Thanks, Brenda

#TheChocolateFactory

Flaccid. A word that strikes fear into the hearts of men. More than famine, war or pestilence. More than the words 'There's no more beer', 'Do you want to talk?' or 'Where is our relationship going?' Flaccid is how I made former Aussie tennis hero Peter Fallon feel, as he sat next to me in the Wimbledon President's Box.

'Do you come here often?' said Mr Fallon.

'No, I mean, never, this is my first time.'

'A virgin. You don't meet them often.' He nudged a little too hard. His grin illuminating teeth bleached to offset his leather tanned face. 'Would you like someone to show you around?'

'Are you serious? That would be amazing.'

'After the match, let me show you how it feels to be a player.' He put his hand on my thigh. Technically it was still my thigh, my upper thigh. I wished I was wearing my new trouser suit, instead of a flimsy sundress.

'I used to love watching you play, when I was a kid.'

I didn't mean to say it, not like that, anyway. It just came out. Not the best thing to say to a man in his late 40s who sees himself as virile and attractive while failing to notice deepening crow's feet and lines. An inevitable reminder of glory days playing tennis in the unforgiving sun.

As we watched the fuzzy yellow ball get smacked across the net, we sat in silence except for the ever so slight squeak of his ego deflating. I felt a little uncomfortable. Not as bad as feeling flaccid.

Around us, twelve thousand spectators had paid and queued to be seated on the centre court. Instead of billboards and banners, there were beds of flowers. Instead of rock music pumping between points, there were the titters of polite conversation and the clinking of Pimm's cups. I clutched my golden ticket into Willy Wimbledon's chocolate factory. While other kids had been conjuring images of chocolate rivers, I had envisioned heroes dressed in white, swinging racquets and playing long days of world's best tennis in a classic English summer.

If Wimbledon is the chocolate factory, the president's suite is the nerve centre. It faces the royal box, where the Duke and Duchess of Kent sit in all their royal glory. The box is where the dealmakers sit; tournament directors and their guests holding court, deciding who plays where and who gets what.

Unlike the chocolate room, however, nothing is gratis. The strawberries and cream cost ten pounds – that's twenty dollars – for three strawberries with a drizzle of cream. If it wasn't for Brexit the conversion would have been worse. The seats are a money-can't-buy experience. Less than fifty recipients at a time sit on the cushions provided.

The box was full and there was a continuous queue outside. They waited, and hoped for someone to vacate a seat. The seats were situated directly behind the court, at the perfect height to watch the action. Not to mention guaranteed TV exposure for the seated guests.

Two spots along was a British morning TV host. One down and one across was a VJ. Many other faces were hard to pinpoint, it was like looking at your kindergarten class picture. 'I know her, I know her…how do I know her?' The plethora of this season's Dior, Chanel, LV and Longchamp handbags were recognisable as I kicked my unbranded straw tote under the seat.

After a full session sitting in the box yesterday, too scared to move in case I ended up back in the queue, my Facebook was full of likes and comments. My cheeky selfies with an 'accidental' celebrity in the background had been the most popular. My new Instagram account @NQ30Love was also gaining some traction. Maybe Jen had been right? I had taken a selfie with Peter Fallon earlier today. How should I tag that? #FormerGlory.

My parents had spotted me on TV. Mum had emailed approval at my outfit of choice. I'd worn a pretty blue and white sundress, nice navy shoes, my oversized copies of Prada sunglasses, a wide-brimmed straw hat, and my signature MAC Redwood lipstick.

I still couldn't believe I was here. I didn't want to do anything as clichéd as pinch myself, but ouch! Exactly twelve months ago I had been sitting at home in my flat in Bondi watching Wimby on TV, agonising about what to do with my career, and it was only four weeks ago that I had left Sydney in search of a new life. Now I was sitting next to Mr Fallon, courtesy of my new job in New Haven. The seat was mine, time to get the handbag to match.

#HotWater, #LinzCrisis

A shower interrupted reading the hate emails and digital media manual. As the steaming water ran down my face, I considered drafting my resignation letter. A moment of silence for the great career that could have been – then it hit me, a moment's silence. I turned off the water and dripped my way to the bedroom, grabbing my phone. I fired off a message on WhatsApp to Jane. It seemed pretty strange communicating with my boss over this casual network. I didn't want to call her and had noticed a comment in the manual about this being a cost-effective mechanism to reach team members. 'I'm sorry to interrupt you, Jane, but I was wondering if a moment's silence on all WTA courts at the start of play today, to commemorate students lost around the world in gun violence, might be a form of atonement for my mistake.'

I dripped and waited, waited and dripped, and then the reply. 'We are currently working on an idea along similar lines. I will draft the press release and get back to the team with details about how to handle everything. Don't move without my say so.'

How dumb does she think I am? Pretty fucking dumb. I messaged back. 'Will await instructions.'

**

Dressed appropriately for the day ahead – in black. The black trousers, black shirt and sensible shoes mourned the senseless slaughter of innocents and the destruction of my career. I felt partially responsible for the death of these ten youngsters – social media agreed with me. The hate coming over the net was visceral. Sure, the timing of the post was a mistake, but it shouldn't have been. Celebrating people graduating from any class should not be misconstrued for anything more than that. Had we lost all perspective in the desperate search for blame?

I waited for a car in the hotel lobby, with no idea who knew that I was the one who posted the caption. Eyes bored into me from every direction. I imagined being on the run Jason-Bourne style – every person, seen or unseen, a potential assassin.

In the corner of the lobby was a large flat-screen TV. It was tuned to what must have been the equivalent of *Good Morning Linz*. It had all the hallmarks of breakfast TV, including the male and female hosting duo – complete with their perfectly complementary hair, skin and smiles. The couch contained guests dressed in their best suits, looking grave and knowledgeable. The subtitles were in German, but there were no prizes for guessing today's debate. Behind the coiffed analysts was the image of our players throwing their hats in the ring with the 'School's Out' tag in English below. This was the equivalent of a modern-day lynching run by 'social experts'. They debated back and forth, the female host getting heated on several occasions and putting her hand on the chest of her male counterpart, pushing him back in an attempt to make her point – I have no idea what that point was. Then the mood changed. The stakes escalated in a way that was difficult to understand without volume or language skills. A question was written on the screen behind them – an adjunct to my caption. The phrase clearly bothered the younger male guest. I grabbed my phone and took a picture of the screen: 'WTA Soziale Medien Fehler oder Absicht?' Someone would have to translate for me.

My new colleague Marine exited the lift and stood by me. 'Have you got a car?'

'Still waiting, they said it wouldn't be long.' Marine put her hand on my shoulder for a nanosecond and then withdrew it. She smiled at me. We met 23 hours ago. Today was her second day in the job as well. I had six months experience in various tennis jobs, she had none – she had ten years experience working in Formula One racing. She was average height and had shoulder length jet black ringlet curls with crystal blue eyes. She was French, living in London, and her accent reflected both locations.

'I suppose you know about the Instagram post?'

'I do.'

'Do you know it was my fault?'

'I know you scheduled the post. I would hardly call the incident your fault.'

I could have hugged her. Instead I put my hands on my face, attempting to push the tears that were welling in my eyes back into my head.

'Thank you.' I managed.

'You made a mistake. It will be okay.' Then she whispered to me. 'We did not shoot anyone.'

'Jane's pretty pissed at me. She has some plans in the works, but I'm not allowed to say anything.'

'I assume we will do a tribute on court.' *Was my idea that obvious?* I nodded.

'I doubt I'll have a job tomorrow.'

'Katie, don't let them push you out. Keep your head high and do your job. And for God's sake, read the manuals. They are very useful.'

'Brenda told me to schedule the post.'

'Yes, she is a bitch. But she can't hurt you if you're smart. Be smart.'

Marine was smart, she spoke several languages and seemed to calm everyone in her vicinity.

'Do you speak German?'

'Enough to get by – why?'

I grabbed my phone and showed her the image of the TV screen.

'Do you know what this means?'

Her face was similar to that of the young man on the TV couch. 'It asks a question. It asks if the post was a mistake or a deliberate stunt.'

'Fuck. Oh, fuck. How could anyone think we would be that callous?'

'It would be a new low – for any organisation. We should check Twitter for trending stories. Hopefully it's just a German thing. They are obsessed with schadenfreude.'

We both entered our own social networks looking for trending WTA stories. Within seconds, the worst result imaginable uploaded, #WTAStuntFail. It was everywhere – the number 1 trending story on Twitter. Closely followed by #WTAVsTheWorld and the slightly less highbrow #WTASucks.

'Do we contact Jane?'

'She will know,' said Marine.

The tournament desk official indicated that our car was ready. Marine and I rode the short trip to the tennis site in silence, both scrolling through the hate dripping out of our phones. My Google alerts were set to find anything related to professional tennis with keyword searches for WTA, ATP, Professional Tennis, Pilot Pen International and Nikolai Petrov. I should delete Petrov, he was not going to help me now.

#TheMusicMan, #PreCrisis

My soon-to-be New Haven boss, James, was like the music man walking through the Wimbledon players' restaurant, saying 'hello' to everyone. They all wanted to talk to him too. That's what happens when you own a tournament with a multi-million-dollar prize pool. This was the first time I had had access to the player areas. In Sydney, Rome and with the Lawn Tennis Association, it was economy-class access only. Now I was in first class.

As James' shadow, I stared at the famous faces that were coming in and out of view. It was like being invited to the Academy Awards, except they were all wearing branded tracksuits. The girls accessorised with diamonds the size of my fist, the men accessorised with girls wearing diamonds the size of my fist. My fake Prada sunglasses stayed on my head as James introduced me around. There were lots of other tournament directors, reporters and operational people. It was fascinating.

Federer, his wife and their two sets of twins hung out in the restaurant waiting for his next match. They looked like an internet meme. An advertising agency could not have created a more enticing family image. Perfection personified. Venus Williams sashayed past. She was at least seven inches taller than me. Taller than any guy I had dated. But she moved effortlessly. Her head high in the clouds, there was no chance of eye-contact.

Nobody was alone. They all had entourages. Most of them sat in silence on their phones, while their entourages did the same. Typical modern-day relationships, where online presence trumped physical realities. Despite the lack of interaction, it was still important to have people around you, even if you ignored them.

I was careful not to breach trust by taking photos in the players' restaurant, but a sly selfie in front of the entrance with the 'Players Only' sign was a must – @NQ30Love now had over 1,000 followers. My sister Lou posted #LivingTheDream with a huge smilie emoji on my Facebook page. Jen posted #ShowUsTheMensLockerroom with a wink.

**

On the last day James was in town, we were sitting in the players' restaurant when Peter Fallon was walked through the player lounge, flanked by his token diamond-crusted female. I stood. He stopped, raised his hand to acknowledge James, and attempted to walk on.

'Peter, come on, don't be shy. Come meet my new assistant, Katie.'

Peter looked around for a saviour, visibly shrank when he realised none would appear, swivelled on the spot and came over.

'Do you two know each other? All Aussies know each other, right?' said James.

'Yes,' I said, simultaneous with Peter's 'No'. Blushing, I added. 'I mean, of course I know of Peter. He's a legend.'

At James' behest, Peter shook my hand without making eye contact, patted James on the back and left.

'Well, that was nice, wasn't it, Katie?'

I nodded.

'I bet he was one of your childhood heroes.'

At least James understood the age relationship.

'Did you enjoy taking my seat in the president's box yesterday?'

'Yes sir. Oh my God, I sure did.'

'Well, I'm leaving tomorrow, but I know you'll probably be in London for a couple of weeks until they sort that visa out for you.'

'Yes, Mr Peterson.'

'I've got a suggestion on how you can pass some of that time. How about you take my pass and watch some tennis while you're here? Sound good to you?'

'Are you sure that's okay? It sounds fantastic to me, but I don't want to get you into any trouble.'

'Don't you worry about that, Katie. I've cleared it with the tournament. You can take my place in the president's box right up until the semifinals. After that, the seats have all been allocated.'

'Thank you.' *OMG, I could kiss you.*

'Don't worry about it, Katie. You'll pay me back in hard work during our event this summer.'

'Yes sir, I will, sir.'

#TeamMeeting, #LinzCrisis

At any tournament, the lead person on site from the WTA is the tour manager or supervisor. It is his or her role to liaise with the tournament on match schedules, player requirements and to help with any issues that other WTA staff or players may have. They cop all the shit from every direction. The three I've met have been women and very calm professionals with soothing personalities. My initial meeting with Birgit Akerman on the walk around yesterday gave me no reason to suspect she was an exception. Blonde (aren't all the Swedes?) and in her late 30s, she seemed competent and smiley. I wondered if she could handle the shit-storm I've created.

At 9a.m. the entire WTA team were in her tiny office. Sixteen of us. Six physios and massage therapists, three media staff, two player liaisons, one assistant supervisor, three WTA umpires and Birgit. Most of team had takeaway coffee cups in their hands. Caffeine might not be the ideal lubricant given the scenario. A hip flask on the other hand…

'Quiet please, everyone take a seat. I know it's crowded in here and we all have very busy days scheduled, but we need to make sure that the team is across what has happened overnight and the official message that has been scripted,' said Birgit.

'Can I just add,' said Brenda, interrupting, 'the media team has never made a mistake of this nature. We don't usually give new staff the opportunity to create so much drama.'

Brenda, along with the entire room, turned to face me.

'Thank you, Brenda,' said Birgit. 'Can we please focus on the issue and the solution.'

Birgit explained what had happened with the mistaken post. She outlined the timeline of events and read the press release that Jane had sent out a few hours ago, while we were all sleeping. She never took her eyes off me as she explained. 'We are looking at one minute of silence before the first match today. Our number one seed Ulli Fischer is going to make a very short statement beforehand. Then she and the two players from the first match – Lemonjian and Bartens – and all the officials will stand with their heads bowed for one minute. Video of this will be uploaded by the media team, it will be on TV and a press release explaining that the WTA is committed to supporting safe environments world-wide for our youth, will be distributed through our global network. Any questions?'

Thirteen hands went up. Marine, Birgit and I were the only ones with both hands firmly at our sides.

Jenny the physio wanted to know, 'What do we tell the players?'

Birgit responded. 'We tell the players the truth. It was a mistake due to computer scheduling. A horrible mistake.' Four hands dropped.

Margaret from player relations wondered if we should encourage players to make their own statements on social media.

Brenda responded to this. 'We think it's best for players to remain quiet, but if they want to say something. They should come to the media team and clear it with us first.' *Good luck with that happening.* Six more hands dropped.

Elke, an umpire, raised the elephant. 'The media are now saying it was a deliberate stunt. Won't this minute of silence be playing into their hands?' It was a damn good question – one that had been festering in my brain since Marine translated the *Good Morning Linz* bombshell.

'This has been discussed,' said Birgit. 'We have scripted Ulli's statement to focus on caring about youth globally, rather than the error. It is most important that we all stick to the facts. It was a mistake and we have proof. The post went out thirty minutes before the gunman entered the school. It could not have been deliberate.' *I remembered vacillating between 3p.m. and 3.30p.m. for scheduling the post.*

The team nodded unanimously, the remainder of hands dropped. Nobody wanted to work their arses off, day and night, for an organisation that would have perpetrated a stunt like the one we were being accused of.

**

We left the room in teams to walk towards our respective homes on site. The media room was a long walk down a faceless corridor towards impending doom.

#NewHavenTough, #PreCrisis

Even blindfolded, I would have known it was the USA. The unmistakable aroma of burnt Starbucks coffee and the salty yet somehow sweet smell of fried potatoes were omnipresent.

It was 9a.m., eight hours since leaving London. I had barely touched the plastic meal offered on the plane. My stomach rumbled. Despite the scaffolding decorating JFK, the food court was immediately visible. All the concession stands appeared to have an unfamiliar smiling cartoon mascot. I chose one with an image of a chicken in a red, white and blue waistcoat. The chicken was missing both wings and legs, and the caption 'We only sell breast meat' flashed below. I ordered a chicken breastfast burger, hash brown, plus a soft drink. The woman asked, 'Is that for here or to go?'

'I'd like to go, but my flight doesn't leave for two hours.'

She stared at me. 'That will be nine dollars and ninety-eight cents, please ma'am.'

I think I gave her ten dollars out of my stash of notes all the same size and colour.

'Thank you so much ma'am. Have a great day.'

After finishing about half the food, I threw out the rest. It was not worth the kilometres I would have to run to burn off the calories.

My next task was to find the gate for the twenty-seat plane that was to shuttle me to New Haven. The outdated flickering monitors took several minutes to display my flight and the required Gate 21B. After following signs which took me in two wrong directions, I found gates 19, 20, 21 and 22, but no 21B. The gates around me were all unstaffed, as the flights were not for several hours. The immediate area was deserted. Everywhere was grey – grey carpets, grey walls, grey desks and grey screens. After wandering around for forty minutes, it seemed 21B was akin to the mysterious Platform 9¾ in the Harry Potter novels. Maybe if I ran at a grey wall I would slip right through? But which wall? Tired and frustrated, I sat, put down my laptop bag, handbag, my favourite duty-free perfume – Estee Lauder's Beautiful – and a travel pillow.

Two suited men walked past me screaming at each other. I did not know what they were shouting about, but I overheard the words 'delay' and 'fuck' – many fucks. Then I saw a small laminated sign stuck to the rail of a grey metal staircase. The sign said 21B and had a black arrow pointing down the stairs. Taking a picture of the sign, I posted #HightechNYCSignage then picked up my bags, made my way down and the holy grail of gates appeared. Instead of witches and wizards, there were several businessmen, one of whom was extremely large or, as they say in the US, 'big and tall'. The large man was sweating, dabbing himself with an enormous handkerchief. The plane we were to travel on was visible through the window. It was tiny. He could have been scared of flying, or of not fitting into his allocated seat. Nearby, there were two guys who looked like they had stepped out of one of those frat-boy movies. Good looking in a perfectly unsexy way. Both were wearing Yale University sweaters and were talking loudly about football, or maybe it was basketball.

'Ryan, buddy, you're a disgrace to that sweater. Bulldogs are going all the way this fall or I'm going to…'

I went through my handbag: boarding card, passport, wallet – all there.

A few minutes later our flight was called. In the queue, a tall blonde lady whose teeth were more dangerous to face directly than a total eclipse of the sun, wished me a safe trip. My seat was across the aisle from the large sweating man. He smiled at me. His enormous cheeks spread to accommodate the width of his mouth. He had one very deep dimple on the right side of his face, which was previously hidden. He must have heard me speak to the flight attendant, as he leant forward and asked, 'You're not from around here, are you, sweetie?' He had one of those wonderful southern drawls that pulled me in immediately. I told him I was from Australia.

'Australia, my goodness, that's a long way from New Haven. Are you on a holiday?'

'No, I'm starting a new job. It'll be my first time in New Haven. What's it like?'

'Some good restaurants, but the centre of town is a little bit rough. I'm sure you won't be living there.'

Our flight resembled a boat ride on a windy Sydney Harbour. After we alighted, he shook my hand and said, 'Good luck with the new job, sweetie.' He lifted his bag off the carousel and walked out of the terminal. Right before exiting, he turned, smiled and tipped his hat.

Surrounding the baggage carousels was a sea of men wearing Adidas, Nike and Wilson. There must have been an invisible pact regarding player entourages as they all seemed to consist of an overweight coach balanced out by an underweight girlfriend. As I dragged my battered red suitcase onto my trolley, a guy, around my age, wearing a blue and white checkered shirt and khaki pants approached. He looked like he had walked out of a J.Crew catalogue and was holding up an iPad with my name on the screen. I walked over to him.

We introduced ourselves. His name was Joe and he said his instructions were to take me to the tournament hotel. We walked towards a huge SUV with Pilot Pen International Tennis Tournament signage all over it. In previous tournaments, like Rome, they had a simple script 'Foro Italico' on both front doors and, at Wimbledon, a discrete purple and green W logo on the driver's door. *It will be easy to find my new life in a country with such clear signage.*

Joe opened my door, waited for me to get into the car and closed it behind me. Then he walked around to the driver's side. I asked how long we would be in the car and he told me about forty minutes.

My butt sank into the black leather seat and my head leant against the window, wishing it could be opened. The heat outside made airconditioning compulsory. We drove past hundreds of square buildings with flat tops that looked like painted cardboard boxes. They resembled a movie set, likely to be torn down at any moment, and were called strip malls, as any character had been stripped from the design. The boxes had endless rows of enormous cars parked in front. The four-wheel drives appeared two storeys high due to the size of their wheels, and the 'pick-ups' resembled Aussie 'utes' on steroids.

'Does all of New Haven look like this?'

My question opened Pandora's Box. Joe took it as an invitation to talk and started playing twenty questions. He seemed nice enough, but my head felt heavy and my eyes wanted to close. Joe was studying for a masters in law and wanted to break into management or something. He seemed most interested in 'How the fuck a girl like you ended up on the other side of the world as a tournament director assistant?'

'Got any tips?' he glanced at me through the rear-view mirror.

Was his question really, 'How does a nice girl like you end up in a shithole like this?'

'I read a book – Do What You Want and the Money Will Follow.' He mumbled something about getting a copy. My head resumed its position against the window.

At the hotel check-in, the receptionist told me my room was paid for and handed me a letter. It was from my new boss telling me to make my way to the tournament site ASAP. Opposite me was a sign saying 'Pilot Pen, the world's largest ballpoint pen manufacturer.' It seemed like a good place to ask about getting to the tennis or, at the very least, to borrow a pen. I was told a minibus would be leaving for the tennis centre in twenty minutes. The lift ride to my room gave me time to decide on the day's outfit. The room was at least twice the size of those in Europe. Spinning around to get a quick view of a beige space with a king-sized bed overladen with pillows and a movie screen–sized TV. I dropped my bags, undid the padlock on my suitcase, grabbed my toilet bag and went into the bathroom. The bathroom seemed larger than the bedroom. Dominating was a spa bath with room for a family of four. It called to me. But, the bubbles would have to wait. With barely time to wash twelve hours of travel off my face, freshen my makeup, add my Redwood lipstick, squirt on deodorant and put on my chosen fuchsia skirt and navy polo, I caught the bus downstairs with the engine revving. Posting pics of the room would happen tonight.

#Doomsville, #LinzCrisis

I was thrilled to find myself in a press room sitting amongst these vibrant wordsmiths on tight deadlines, literally making the news we read. Except today social media was inventing the story as it went along and the journalists were desperately playing catch-up without straying too far into the abyss of 'fake news'.

Brenda had not spoken to or looked at me on the interminable walk to the press room. Marine's presence was a contributing factor. Brenda may have set me up, but anyone could see a Formula One seasoned pro like Marine was wide awake.

Brenda was itching to drop me in it. But she had instructions from Jane. No specifics on the breach of protocol re: scheduling posts, and no individuals mentioned. Jane knew that would drive the story even further. They needed to get rid of me quietly. A public hanging would only make them look worse. No doubt the WTA hierarchy in Florida considered scapegoating me. Social media's take on that would be: new girl, first day on the job, not enough training. The WTA would look like arseholes or bullies. They had to stand united as a team of people who cared about everybody – stupid staff members included.

A reporter from *Good Morning Linz* stuck his camera and microphone in Brenda's face. He asked her, 'WTA Soziale Medien Fehler oder Absicht?' Brenda said, 'It was a mistake. A poorly scheduled post, designed only to celebrate our tennis players' happiness at their graduations. The WTA post went out thirty minutes before the incident in Philadelphia, which proves it could only have been an error.'

The TV journalist indicated for the camera to be turned to his face. He spoke earnestly in German. I have no idea what he said, but Marine's jaw relaxed as he spoke. The Germans and Austrians do love their facts – a small mercy for us at this point.

The questions came thick and fast and in many languages. I could only field the English ones. The journalists seemed fascinated with the fact it was only my second day on the job.

'How does it feel to be in the middle of such a crisis on your second day?' *In the middle – I was the fucking cause.*

'I'm proud to be a member of the WTA team. This mistake was unfortunate, but the true tragedy is the loss of innocent lives due to the violence perpetrated by a lone gunman. We must not forget the real crisis.' This response was straight from the WTA's playbook. I was not going to stray one word out of line today – or ever again.

We attempted to steer the media towards the full day of fantastic matches scheduled on the courts. No chance of that. Serena Williams could lose to a Donald Trump today and nobody would give a shit. Luckily neither was playing.

**

It was about thirty minutes before the start of matches. We had yet to announce the minute of silence. Management believed it would appear more genuine if it hadn't been dissected in the media beforehand. The gold dress ring on my right hand slipped and slid along my sweaty finger. Off my finger and into the pencil case it went. No chance of my hands drying up any time soon.

#WhoIsWhoInTheZoo, #PreCrisis

On site at the Pilot Pen International, my photo accreditation and introductions began. First to Julie who told me, 'James hasn't been able to find the right assistant since Pam got pregnant. He wants someone who anticipates his needs, someone who doesn't wait for instructions.'

James was off site all day today, making it the perfect opportunity to get settled in. Julie introduced me around. The names and faces were starting to blur. I was going to lose track of this information and started to make notes on my phone:

**

Joe (J-Crew): Desperately trying to be smooth. But seems genuine.
Julie: Huge smile. I'm pretty sure she wants my job.
Jane: Tall, blonde, maybe 30s, big busted – nobody looks at her face. Works with accounts payable – seems friendly.
Mary: Older, brunette, rounded Teletubby style. Head of ticketing. Officious.

Paul: Very tall, 50s & greying – chuckles. Head of transport and a bit touchy-feely.
Mark: Accountant, I think. Just the facts jack!
Kay: Head of Ops. Very short, spiky-blonde hair, pleasant to me, but saw her rip into one of her staff – don't cross.

**

Within a couple of hours, there were six screens full like this.

**

Julie was not the only person to spill the beans on James. Mark told me James consumes a Starbucks grande vanilla latte every morning.

Paul told me, 'James is fanatical about being on time, but he's hopeless at making it happen.'

'He hates suck-ups,' said Kay, staring at me with unnerving intensity.

'He has a really good memory for names and numbers, but sometimes he forgets conversations you've had with him,' said Marissa.

**

Marissa: Useful. Not a suck-up.

**

It was after midnight before I finally made it back to the Omni Hotel and room 629. The faces, names and activities raced around in my head like rushes from a movie. I attempted to relax as I unpacked my suitcase, hung skirts, dresses and jackets, then folded my tops and underwear. My suitcase emptied and stored away, I tried to quiet my thoughts with meditation. My technique was learnt from a singing teacher in Sydney. I was not going to win Star Search, but got something out of the lessons. Breathe in one nostril and hold; breathe out the other nostril and repeat. My heart relaxed and my breathing deepened, but my thoughts kept interrupting. Sleep was going to be impossible without some serious tub action.

While the bath filled, I started to clean my teeth and wash my face. Behind me the sound of water rushing into the bath triggered an awareness of the stiffness in my body that had been forgotten about or ignored. The water was halfway up the tub when I added a bath bomb from my new favourite spa shop in Convent Garden – The Sanctuary. The bomb fizzled and spun through the water, tracing a circular pattern and spreading its mineral goodies. When the water was above the jets, I pushed the 'on' button and the spa jump-started into action. First, one foot into the water. It was just above a comfortable heat – perfect. When my foot had adjusted to the temperature, I put the other one in, waited for a few seconds as the water begged me to sink down. I relinquished the day and slid into the bubbles. Starting with my toes, my muscles and thoughts gave up the fight. My head was too heavy for my now softened neck and my eyelids refused to stay open. I somehow managed posting a modest bubble-bath selfie. A sound sleep was not far away.

At dawn the alarm forced me to lift my leaden head off the pillows. I was surrounded by a fortress in the king-sized bed, the pillows boxing me in on both sides. With less than an hour to get ready for my first morning briefing, I dragged my stiff body into the shower, washed my hair and shaved my legs. In just under thirty-five minutes I was downstairs, praising the tournament desk for the free bagels on offer. I grabbed one laden with peanut butter and boarded the minibus. I looked around and found a spare seat and noted almost all the occupants had their eyes closed. Fifteen more minutes of quiet bliss, until I checked my emails, Facebook and Instagram. My bubble-bath post had been a hit. It didn't make sense until I looked at the photo again. It wasn't quite as modest as remembered. No nipples, thank God, but there was some floating tittage. Two Facebook private messages. One from Jen: 'More bubbles required babe'. The other from Lou: 'Katie, you really need to be more careful. Don't let this stupid social stuff get in the way of your dream.' Crap, crap, crap. Lou was right, @NQ30Love was not intended to be a porn site. Thank God my parents were social-media illiterates.

The first day of the tournament and the site was alive. Dodging the delivery men with their trolleys full of towels, water bottles and tennis balls, I stopped at the Starbucks concession stand. Fifth in the queue, I waited with my eyes closed for James' latte. Both of my hands were full and my phone was under my arm as I joined the throng of staff being herded into the interview room. Most of them were carrying a variety of huge branded disposable coffee cups. I had met a million people yesterday, but in front of me was a gaggle of new ones. Searching for someone familiar to join, I recognised a woman's face. In fact, I recognised her bust – Jane. Still carrying the coffee, I tried to get her attention, but she was talking to another blonde woman and never looked in my direction.

We spilled into the interview room, which was large enough to seat about one hundred people classroom style. The chairs faced an elevated stage hosting a large desk draped in white cloth with Pilot Pen signage behind.

As if some invisible command had been signalled, people started moving chairs. Some dragging and stacking, others pulling chairs forward. In less than two minutes, a shape appeared. They were constructing a circle, a forty-person sharing circle. Great, less than twenty-four hours in the US of A and I was in therapy. God knows I loved watching Ellen as much as the next twenty-something woman, but I would never sign up to sit on her couch.

People took their unidentified yet somehow allocated seats. I made several attempts to claim one, but was warned off by stares and grunts from the correct owners. If this was a game of musical chairs, I was going to be the one left standing when the music stopped. There was no sign of James. As his assistant, I should sit next to him. Across from me, was an empty seat, which people seemed to be avoiding, 'Is this seat taken?'

'It's James's,' barked Kay. 'The executives sit next to him. You sit over there,' she said pointing way across the circle.

I nodded at her instruction and slunk away, mentally revising my notes:

**

Kay: Head of Ops. Big Bitch.

**

Not finding a seat, or even space for one, I walked to the back of the room, put down the coffee, picked up a chair and returned to the closed circle. 'Excuse me, can you please move, so I can fit my seat in?' With rolling eyes and collective mumbles, the circle gave way and I took my place.

Almost immediately the briefing began and people started taking turns to speak. To my relief they were not revealing their innermost feelings, instead, they were pitching how well their departments were doing. Ticket sales were up ten percent on last year, sponsorship was up fifteen percent. There must have been an invisible applause sign flashing somewhere.

Typing notes on James' daily schedule, it seemed that James needed to be live on the local CBS TV affiliate at 7.48a.m. and

6.27p.m. every day. Following that, he had a live radio broadcast from site at 8.32a.m. and 5.23p.m. Although nobody mentioned my name, it became apparent that the sponsor's party tent was open all day and night, and his assistant was required to greet the sponsors at the beginning of each session.

James arrived ten minutes late and took his guarded seat. I had no luck catching his eye during the meeting and there was no way to get the coffee to him, but I made damn sure to push my way in front of him as soon as we all stood up. He looked at me, I smiled and handed him the latte I had purchased. As I handed it to him I was aware of the time difference between purchase and delivery. It was still warm in my hand, but the temperature had dissipated during the meeting. Hardly ideal.

'Hello Katie, has the team been getting you up to speed?'

'Yes sir.'

'Good to hear, thank you for the coffee,' he said, taking a sip. 'Vanilla's my favourite, what a pity it's cold.' He put the coffee down on the chair beside him and started to walk out of the room. Halfway out, he turned, 'Hurry up Katie, TV won't wait.'

He did not look back, and I had to break into a jog to keep up with him.

**

James: Maybe not the sweet gentleman I met at Wimbledon.

An hour later, on my way to the party tent, J.Crew Joe stopped me.

'Hi Katie, how are you doing? I bought your book online, the one about the money following.'

I looked behind me, turned back and said, 'I'm already on Amazon looking for a replacement.'

'That's a damn shame. If it's any consolation, a group of us are going for a drink after work tonight, come along, and we can figure out a Plan B.'

Well past bedtime, Joe led six others and me into The Anchor bar around the corner from the hotel. During semester it was a regular Yale hang out, but tonight it was quiet and dark. We slid into a circular red leather booth with darkened mirrors and heavy mahogany wood panelling. I was welcomed into this strange mix of twenty-to-thirty-somethings from accounts, production, marketing and crew. They were a support group for those not-in-favour with the executive. I felt at home.

Two of the girls, Danielle and Emma, had been around tennis for years and filled me in on all the gossip. Like who was sleeping with whom, which players got around and who to avoid like the plague. I tried to hide my interest when they started talking about Nikolai Petrov. Neither of them had slept with him, but they told me about one of the girls who had.

Look, Katie, that's her,' said Danielle, pointing at one of the waitresses serving tables.

'Who?'

'The one we told you about, that slept with Petrov – Pam, your predecessor.'

'They told me Pam got pregnant.'

'God, they're still peddling that lie, are they?'

'She's very pretty and young.'

'Not as young as she was when they slept with her,' said Emma.

'They? What do you mean, "they"? I thought you said she slept with Petrov?'

'Yeah, she did, and then he passed her around to all his friends,' said Emma.

'That's so repulsive. Did she... I mean, was it rape?'

'No, she thought she was special. I bet she doesn't feel so special now,' said Danielle.

'Everybody knows. That's why she couldn't work for James any more,' said Emma.

**

The first time I saw Petrov in the flesh was four weeks ago in Rome when I was helping with his press conference. He was 6 feet 4 inches of perfectly toned tanned muscle, black hair and impossible green eyes – like a male Snow White or a trendy vampire; but even that doesn't do him justice. After the press conference, he walked past me, inches from my skin and every hair on my body prickled. The translator Antonio was sitting next to me and saw my reaction. He said; 'Careful Katie, that one has been everywhere... and I mean everywhere. It's like a rite of passage or something for the girls in tennis to sleep with him.'

'Oh my God, Antonio, that's disgusting.'

'Yep – Katie it *is* disgusting.'

'That's what I said.'

'I know that's what you *said*. Keep reminding yourself that.'

Back in Pilot Pen land, the gang had switched into alcohol-therapy mode. Telling stories of working the tournament, alternating with sculling shots. George told us, 'I had a call today from a woman who wanted to know who would be playing on Friday. I replied, "Whoever wins on Thursday".'

We all had to scull.

'I can beat that,' said Joe. 'I got asked who was going to be in the final.'

We sculled.

'I can beat you all,' said Phil. 'I got asked if I could tell Pam Shriver in the commentary booth to shut up, because her voice was annoying.'

**

Danielle & Emma: Great fun, unless they're stabbing you in the back.
George: Sweats profusely. Couldn't stop looking.
Phil: I have no idea what he does.

**

The sculling continued until we had run out of stories. Somehow Joe manoeuvered me into a corner and his alcohol-soaked breath was intoxicating. Over the last few days I had felt like a boat taking on water, bailing as fast as I could, but the water kept coming. Joe had responded to my distress call, and I grabbed hold of the life-line, pulling him close. His tongue invaded my too willing mouth. I responded with passion that felt more like aggression. We bashed into the panelled wall behind us with a force that caused our foreheads to collide. We broke apart. The rush of pain brought clarity. I did not want to sleep with a dinghy. 'Let's go back to the hotel,' I said.

We got into the lift at the Omni and I pushed the button for the sixth floor. Joe did not push number eight. At that moment, I realised through the alcohol haze that my words had sounded like an invitation.

'Aren't you on the eighth floor?' I pushed the button for his floor. Joe looked at me as if I had slapped his face. When the doors opened on six, I jumped out.

'Night, Joe, sleep well.'

Plan B was to do a good job.

#YouCantMakeMe, #LinzCrisis

'But you can't make me.' Was the first thing I heard exiting the toilet in the women's locker room. My perfect timing had landed me in the middle of the negotiation between tour supervisor Birgit and player Ulli Fischer. I stepped back out of view.

'Ulli, your agent has already agreed to you reading this statement, and we go on court in twenty minutes.'

'I don't care what he agreed. Nobody asked me.'

'If we had asked you, you would have told us to go to your agent.' *Lesson number one when working with players: 'Talk to my agent' is code for 'I don't want to do this'.*

'I can't do this. It is in English. I will say it if you let me do it in German.'

'We need it to be in English, so everyone can understand.'

'My English is bad.'

'Don't be silly. Your English is perfect.'

'What if I get something wrong? Everyone will hate me.'

'Nobody will hate you. This is a good thing you are doing.'

'Everybody hates the WTA. They will hate me too.'

There were no winners here. Birgit had to get her to do it and if I were Ulli I would want to be as far away from this clusterfuck as possible. Birgit pulled out the big guns.

'Don't you want to show that you care about these poor dead children?'

'That is very mean to me. You should not say that.'

'I'm sorry. But this is very important to women's tennis. You all want to be able to keep playing tennis, don't you?' Birgit was getting truly desperate. But sponsorships dropping out was a real possibility if we couldn't stem the hate.

'Show me what you want me to say. I'm not saying yes. Just show me.'

I sneaked a peak at Birgit and Ulli looking at the statement. *Fingers crossed it's short.* Ulli kept shaking her head as she read. 'What does "premier" mean?'

'It means important.'

'Can I just say "important"?'

'It's not exactly the same. You better say "premier". Why don't you practise reading it?'

**

'Today we are sad at the tragic loss of precious young lives at a Philadelphian high school in the USA. Young people should feel safe at school. They should be able to learn without fear everywhere in the world. The WTA represents a group of young women from nearly one hundred countries, proud to be able to participate in one of the world's premier sports. We are proud to represent a place where women can learn and grow and feel safe. We wish this for all young women and men. Can we please have a minute's silence for all the people in the world who are not as lucky as we are today?'

**

Holy shit. That's a big statement. No mention of gun violence, no mention of the mistake. It feels important, who knows how it will go down. I wouldn't want to be reading it.

'I don't want to read this. You can't make me.' Said Ulli.

**

Shit.

#IWantThatMan, #PreCrisis

The rising sun appeared through the crack in my curtains. Four hours sleep, ninety degrees and one hundred percent humidity, not the perfect combination for my first jog around New Haven. The numbers were not going to improve, and I needed to run. I needed the time on my own. I needed the struggle for breath. The time for ideas to germinate.

A quick study of the map the concierge gave me. Turn right on Church Street after exiting the Omni, past the town green, take a left on Elm, and back via Crown. 'It's a grid. You can't make a mistake,' he said. But, to my quote Dad, 'Your other right, Katie.'

Setting the FitBit to 'run' mode, I inhaled the thick stale air. Might as well get used to it. I had allotted myself a precious thirty minutes, and within seconds my body put up its familiar resistance. First a niggle in my left knee, then a twinge in my back and a shot of nerve pain on the side of my right ankle. Five minutes later, they were all gone.

Halfway through, my hair was stuck to my head and sweat stung my eyes. At this point, it would have been just my luck to run into Petrov. My BFF Jen says women shouldn't sweat, they should glow. She never sweated when we ran together. I would wring water out of my ponytail, while Jen looked the same at the end as at the start of the run.

Running past the Yale library, which looked a bit like Notre-Dame cathedral in Paris, I thought of Dad – he loved old buildings. Was he okay? He and Mum were so vague. 'We're fine, Katie.' Mum had no credibility after keeping that tumour secret from us, a few years ago. Thank God it was benign.

Shit, which way… York, Broadway or Park Street? The concierge told me to look out for a theatre. I saw a sign for Yale Repertory Theatre and was back on track.

Later that morning, James suggested I try to watch some tennis during the day, rare for people working in the game. My eye was on Petrov vs Dimitrov later that afternoon. Throughout the day, the monitors showed the matches progressing. When Petrov's match went to court, the sponsors had arrived in the party tent for the evening's session.

'Welcome Mr and Mrs Shaw, are you going to watch some tennis or take some refreshments first?'

Mr and Mrs Shaw decided on refreshments and chatted to me. Petrov was already up 6-0, 3-0 over Dimitrov. The match would be over soon, no point trying to watch today.

Minutes later there was a massive roar from the crowd. Then another and another. Anna from sponsorship came over and excused herself. She whispered in my ear, 'Petrov is imploding out there on court. He got a bad call and he's just spraying balls everywhere. Dimitrov is going to take the second set.'

The noise from the crowd kept rising, and all the sponsors were deserting the tent and taking their seats. Everyone wanted to watch the train wreck in action. We watched via the monitors. Trying not to show emotion, glancing at each other. For some inexplicable reason, I was willing Petrov to win. At the same time, he did not seem to care.

The crowd booed their disapproval. In less than forty minutes since he had lost the service game at 3-1, the match was over, with Dimitrov the victor 0-6, 6-3, 6-0.

James would be in his office, so I hurried in that direction. His bellows arrived before me. I did not dare to go in, but everybody around the office could hear what he was saying.

'What kind of a joke is that? People paid good money to see that idiot tank a match. I want him fined,' James said.

'We'll be looking into it, James. But let's not jump to any conclusions. He could have just had a bad day.' I recognised ATP supervisor Paul Sand's voice.

'A bad day, a bad day. My sponsors will be out for blood,' James was yelling louder. 'The players want to get paid, don't they? Let's see how happy they are if the money dries up.'

James blasted out of the office and slammed the door. Paul was left inside. Nobody looked up. James had always seemed a silent assassin. This bluster was an entirely new experience.

I made my way to the interview room and snuck into a corner. Glancing around the room at the journalists present, there were several familiar faces, including Tim Waters, the arsehole media manager I worked for in Sydney. Memories flooded back. 'Katie, you forgot the mic flag in the interview room', 'Katie, are you sure you have a degree in marketing?' 'Katie, only an imbecile would do it that way.' Fuck you Tim, I thought, but was distracted from further hateful thoughts by

Petrov's entrance. You didn't have to be a mind reader to establish Petrov was pissed off.

**

Q: 'Mr Petrov, do you think you played well today?'
A: 'No, I play like crap.'
Q: 'What do you think you have to do to improve?'
A: 'Not play like crap.'
Q: 'Yes, but more specifically?'
A: 'I have to hit the ball over the fucking net and between the lines. Is that specific enough for you?'

**

I followed the throng of journalists out of the room and felt a tap on my shoulder. It was Tim, the arsehole.

'Katie Cook, what are you doing in a dive like New Haven?'

Without acknowledging the slur, I told him about my new role.

'What brings you here?' I asked.

We made our way into the hallway as he explained he was researching a piece on the dominance of Russian tennis players. Focusing on their hunger, desire and the communist training methods. I nodded and smiled politely as he rambled on about the interviews he had secured. My ears pricked when he mentioned Petrov.

'His parents virtually sold him to agents at ten. I'm likening it to child slavery.'

Not wanting to seem over interested, I wished him luck with his research and explained that I needed to welcome some sponsors. He smiled and shook my hand. He put his hand on my back and said, 'If you ever want to come back and work the tournament in Sydney again, your job's there.'

I twisted back, looked him square in the face; he smiled. Nothing about his comment seemed sarcastic.

'Thanks Tim.'

The conundrum of people in this sport continued to baffle me. That week working for him was hell. He treated me like a clumsy idiot. Now he's complimenting me? Hopefully the truth of my competency was somewhere in the middle of those extremes.

**

Tim: Probably still a dickhead.

**

Back at the party tent, James made an appearance. He smiled and chatted with our sponsors. He did not acknowledge me. After fulfilling my duties in the tent, I went back to my desk and was buried in work for maybe an hour, when a clipped deep voice announced himself.

Nikolai Petrov wanted to pick up the loser's prize money. *Don't look, don't look, don't look*, I chanted to myself as he exchanged pleasantries with Julie.

'I want to speak to the tournament director to say goodbye.' *Had I mentioned to Julie that Nikolai was cute?*

'I'm sorry Nikolai. I don't know where James Petersham is,' said Julie as she looked towards me. 'Katie's his assistant, maybe she can help you?' *Yep, it seems I did.*

I looked up, and felt the rush of red from my chest to my face. He turned in my direction and looked at me. I fixated on trying to remember how to stand up. My movements were stilted and alien-like as I walked over to Nikolai, one foot in front of the other, kept breathing, kept smiling, and said, 'I'm sorry, but James Petersham is unavailable at the moment.'

The words came out, but each one took seconds longer than it should have. English was his second language, not mine, but you would not have known it. 'Okay, tell him thank you for a great tournament, Katie.'

In an attempt at regaining composure, I managed to stick my hand out. He grabbed and held it tight. His hand was twice the size of mine, and his grip was crushing my fingers. He was over a foot taller than me. My eyes level with his chest. His body cast a shadow over mine. There was a scent coming from him, a mix of designer body wash and arrogance that made me giddy. He dropped his head and shoulders to meet my gaze. His eyes were the clearest green. They were emerald – not hazel. Green like the Cartier panther with long thick black lashes framing the stones. Piercing, literally stunning. I was transfixed, staring, hypnotised – making a complete dick of myself. The memory of every man I had worshipped or kissed flashed through my mind and then melted away. He released my hand and strode out the door. As soon as he was out of view, the entire office laughed. The ground would not swallow me up. The only choice left for me was to join in.

*

Nikolai: TROUBLE.

*

#AMinuteSilence, #LinzCrisis

Ten a.m. and the sun was still climbing its ascent into the cloudless sky. Another perfect autumn day – but we were all inside, a zillion miles from perfection. Indoor stadiums, like casinos, give away nothing regarding the time of day. The echoes of thousands of feet climbing the wooden stadium seats rang throughout the building – on their way to an execution.

The punters had purchased tickets for a full day of tennis. Most of them would have heard of our media catastrophe via their ever-present smart phones, *Good Morning Linz*, and/or the car radio. A spell had been cast over our usual Monday morning matches. Yesterday was supposed to have been the preparation for the days of tennis ahead, that is, until I sent our world in an entirely new direction.

Great matches were planned for today. Aussie sensation Zoe Lemonjian was playing Swede Elke Bartens. Bartens is a top-twenty player and after Lemonjian's third-round showing at the Aussie Open this year, she is our next great hope. Yesterday, I had been hoping to watch some of the match.

Between my trip to the locker room and now – less than ten minutes – Ulli Fischer had agreed to represent the WTA on court. From the look on her face, "agreed" might not be the correct word. All the staff had lined up alongside the court. We were all expected to stand by her while she read the statement – a show of solidarity.

The emcee announced Lemonjian and Bartens onto the court. The crowd clapped. Both girls walked with their heads bowed, briefly looking up to wave and acknowledge the applause. They put their racquet bags down at their respective benches courtside – and did not unpack them. Normally, at this point, the umpire would conduct a coin toss with the players and they would start to warm up. The umpire, instead of sitting high on her perch, was standing with the rest of the staff.

The emcee continued, he announced that the WTA's number one seed Ulli Fischer would like to address the crowd. This breach of protocol caused the crowd to titter. Although they were whispering to one another, there were nearly 6,000 of them and their collective whisper reached a crescendo as Ulli walked to the centre of the court with her speech clutched in her dominant left hand.

Ulli was handed the microphone by the emcee. She held it too close to her mouth as she cleared her throat causing a piercing screech of feedback. All the WTA staff, myself included, walked to the side of the court to ensure visibility. Lemonjian and Bartens bowed their heads and stood next to their benches.

Ulli began. She read the statement exactly as written. She managed to look up occasionally, making eye contact with the crowd, who were transfixed. Probably seventy percent of them were filming the statement on their phones. Streaming live, perhaps?

Ulli's terror added an aura of genuineness to the delivery of the carefully chosen words. She trembled as she forced out the words and this increased in all the right places, punctuating 'tragic loss', 'safe' and 'lucky'. My eyes were blurred with tears before the end.

To ensure the crowd understood every word, German subtitles appeared on the giant suspended screens normally reserved for showing tennis replays.

The Austrian crowd stayed silent for the entire minute. A heritage of war and loss of life not removed from them. At the conclusion, the emcee managed to bring the crowd back to the tennis. The umpire and players conducted a solemn coin toss and began their warm-up. It was time to get back to business.

**

As my WTA colleagues exited the court, most of their eyes were red. Ten children had been slaughtered less than twelve hours ago. Neither my social faux pas nor any arse covering should eclipse that.

#PackingUp, #PreCrisis

On Monday morning, the New Haven tournament was over, the players and crowds had left, and the event façade was being unceremoniously ripped from Yale's Cullman-Heyman Tennis Center. Always the last to leave, staff checked out of the Omni hotel. James had organised for me to move to a furnished serviced apartment a few blocks away. He had paid for a month's rent to give me time to find something more permanent.

This generosity and the vote of confidence attached to it came as a welcome shock and a vital assist to my bank balance. Although I had not spent much money the previous week, the stint in London had eaten away most of my savings. My last account balance showed just under five hundred dollars, and my Pilot Pen payday was another week away. I had not asked my parents for money in ten years, but with only a month to find somewhere to live…pride swallowing looked inevitable.

'You'll need a big strong man to help you move,' said Joe. 'Do you have anybody's number?'

**

Despite the awkwardness, I was grateful for Joe's presence and accepted his offer.

**

We lugged my suitcase and some of the goodies given to me during the previous week, out of his beaten up old car. It had a faded blue paint job and was mammoth. The B52s would have said something about a whale. 'How much does a tank of gas cost?' I asked. Joe mumbled something about women not respecting classics.

House keys in my hand, Joe and I shared the weight of my bags as we walked up the stairs to 5F. 'These stairs will be good exercise, Katie. You won't have to go running.' *FitBit will love this place.*

We stopped at the third-floor landing, breathing heavily. There was some paint peeling, worn carpet, and the air had a hangover from the occupants' collective previous night's dinners. Continuing to the top, we put down the bags and I ceremoniously opened the door and said, 'Ta-da.'

Okay, this is okay. The furniture was second hand but functional, and the room was light enough. The musty air indicated it had been closed up for a while. I walked over to the window, which, after resisting my initial tugs, flew open. Hot air and an odd mix of the smells from the taco place, pizzeria and grocery store below rushed in.

'Maybe the airconditioning will cool things down and freshen up the place?' said Joe as he walked over to the dusty square box, which hung precariously out the living-room window.

Bursting into action, the airconditioner sounded like a 747 had parked in the apartment. An image of my light, airy flat in Bondi flashed into my head.

'Let's have a look around,' I shouted.

We walked straight through the living room. To one side was a small but adequate galley-style kitchen. 'I'm not much of a cook anyway.'

I walked into the light-blue tiled, plastic-tapped bathroom – no bath.

Joe called out from the bedroom, 'There's a TV in here. You'll be an insomniac watching all those late-night shows.' He was lying on my bed, his head against the backboard, remote control in one hand, grinning. *Not me, I plan on going out a lot. But who with? Yale's semester starts in a few weeks. I'll meet some masters students or a young professor or two. They couldn't all be like those rednecks from the airport.*

'Sorry Joe, what did you say?'

Joe patted the space next to him on my bed, indicating for me to join. I moved to the living room and called out for him to see how comfy the lounge was. After a few minutes he joined me. He sat close, very close.

I stood. 'Time to get back to the office.'

He dragged his feet the entire walk down the stairs and to the driveway.

'You owe me a drink when I see you in two weeks,' he said as he leant on his car.

I smiled. He stepped forward and leant down for a kiss. My head turned at the last second ensuring his lips hit my cheek. He groaned, I shrugged; he got in his car and sped off. Joe was smart, good looking and way too nice.

**

There was no chance to absorb my new surroundings as my day continued back in the office. We packed, lifted and re-arranged boxes, signage and equipment that had been relocated from the tennis site. The lifeblood of the event was sectioned away into storage. All that was left was a shell.

* *

Joe: Needs to find his inner bad boy.

* *

#BrendaBitch, #LinzCrisis

After the scripted silence, I needed a moment to compose myself. The match had started on court and the WTA staff had gone to their respective cubbyholes to fulfill their duties. Marine and Brenda were ahead of me, en route to the press room. I wanted, no, needed to wash my face before the photographers snapped an image of me that would make a perfect addition to the story.

The nearest public amenity was empty – I checked before having a quiet sob in a cubicle. I allocated myself five minutes before facing the press room.

Three minutes later, I exited the cubicle to find Brenda facing me. She was smiling – perhaps something new as it looked uncomfortable. 'I'm surprised to find you here. I thought you'd be packing your bags at the hotel,' she said.

'Why would I be doing that?'

'If I was you, I'd be so humiliated. You've caused so many people so much pain.'

'I guess that's where we are different. I made a mistake. I'll own that mistake, but I won't hang myself for it.'

'Someone will.'

'Well that's their prerogative I guess.' I moved to the wash basin. 'I'm not going to hand it to them on a platter. By the way, thanks for your part in it all.'

'You're very welcome.' She said, leaning oh so casually, against the wall. 'I just thought you'd be slammed for scheduling a post. Who knew I'd be this lucky.'

My fists curled up. If only, I'd been recording this on my phone.

'What the fuck is your problem? What have I done to you?'

'Nothing yet, but it's what you were going to do.'

'What was I going to do?'

'You were going to use us to find some rich man and float off into rich-people land. We don't need your type. We need people who are passionate about the game. People who are here to work.'

'Brenda, you're delusional. I love tennis. All I ever wanted to do is work in tennis.'

'People who look like you don't work for a living.' *What the fuck was she going on about. I've worked since I was eighteen. I've had like two sick days in ten years. Who the fuck is she to judge me like this?*

'How fucking dare you? You don't know me. You haven't even given me a chance. But you'll have to. I'll prove you wrong.'

'You won't get the chance.' She was no longer leaning, she was straight and tall, talking through a clenched jaw. 'They'll get rid of you for sure. Especially now everyone's talking about the post being deliberate. They will feed you to the wolves.'

'That's bullshit. The facts are on our side. God even knows where that stupid rumour came from.'

'Really? You have no idea who seeded that story?' Her grin reached Cheshire-cat proportions.

'Are you kidding me? Are you insane? They'll find out.'

'They won't. Give me some credit. It's not like I used my personal account. Maybe it came from @NQ30Love? Such a fucking lame handle.'

My knees buckled. 'You hacked my account. No way, you can't of. There's no way you could have done that.' She shrugged her shoulders, turned and left the bathroom. I scrambled for my phone and searched everywhere for @NQ30Love. I hadn't posted since landing in Linz. Please God she hadn't done this in my name.

Nothing. Nothing came up. Nothing since a few friends shared my post on The Blue Danube. Thank God. She was bluffing. Had she been bluffing about seeding the story? There was something about that grin when she told me. She was genuinely happy with herself for the shit-storm she'd created. Also, the rumour appeared to originate in Austria and she spoke fluent German. Maybe it was time to pack my bags?

#HomeFires, #PreCrisis

That night in my new apartment, with the local paper open at the flat-sharing ads, some circled, I resigned myself to the shower, which removed the dirt, but not the aches. Next was the consumption of greasy delivered pizza from downstairs. The shower should have followed the pizza, I thought, while channel surfing; time for an update from home. A quick dial on my iPhone brought the desired result.

'Hey sis, how are you?'

'Great, Katie, how's the tournament going?'

'Finished. What's your news, Lou, is everything okay?'

'More than okay, Dave asked me to marry him. I said yes.'

'Oh Lou, congratulations. That's fantastic news. He's wonderful. I know you'll be happy.'

'I'm very happy, Katie. I hope you are too.'

We talked diets, dresses and dates for the next hour. She sounded like a kid at Christmas, and I could not wait to stand next to her, in a dress she promised would not be too dreadful, next year. The family arguments had already started. Mum and Dad had booked the golf club for the reception. Lou was adamant she was going to get married somewhere cooler. She and Dave had hoped for a destination wedding, maybe even Hawaii. She asked me what I thought. 'No pineapple themes' was my advice – yellow was nobody's best colour. We laughed and reminisced about my plan to get married in Vegas by an Elvis impersonator.

'Is that still the plan, Katie?'

'I still love Elvis.'

This was not my wedding. It was not about me. She said she would make sure there was plenty of notice, so I could get a holiday from work. Lou sounded different – older, settled. Memories of watching her first day at school, of formals and graduation from nursing came into my head. My little sister getting married, not pregnant yet, but children would not be too far away.

White weddings filled my dreams. I watched faceless brides and grooms spin, dance and giggle. The music morphed into Viva Las Vegas, and my dreams turned neon. The dancing was heating up when Petrov's eyes met mine.

I sat up, drenched in sweat, in my unfamiliar bedroom.

Next morning, there was no food in my apartment. I planned to get a Coke Zero and breakfast at the convenience store two doors from my building. As I came out onto the landing, yellow tape forced me to turn left instead of right – on the ground was a chalk outline of a body. It looked like something out the TV show *Law & Order*. Navigating my way around the tape, I went into the grocery store, grabbed a couple of donuts, acknowledged to myself the extra pounding of kilometres they would require. Fruit and vegetable shopping was a must do.

At the register the attendant volunteered, 'There was a shootin' here last night. Some kid tried to rob the dry cleaners. He won't be doing that again.'

Five hundred dollars or not, apartment hunting moved up my to-do list.

#GodSaveMarine, #LinzCrisis

Entering the press room after Brenda – she had around a five-minute head start while I panicked looking for evidence of her planting on @NQ30Love – I wondered what or whom she had been torturing in the interim. Regardless, the place was running like a well-oiled machine. Marine was conversing with multiple journalists in at least four languages – simultaneously it seemed. She had print outs of the statement from the WTA and the place was a hive of activity. Something had shifted. The journalists all seemed satisfied. Satisfied that they were ahead of the story, instead of playing catch-up with hashtags. Marine had them eating out of her hands. Nobody commented that it was also *her* second day on the job.

Brenda had a look on her face. The smile had gone. She saw Marine for what she was – more of a threat to her job than I would ever be. Jane Townsend may be regretting hiring me, but she certainly wouldn't be with Marine.

Marine waved us over. 'I've put together a brief summary of the response on site to the statement. Please read it, Brenda.

I'm happy if you want it to come from you.' *Smart, smart, smart, why didn't I...?*

Brenda read the statement, with me over her shoulder. Marine had said the mood in the stadium during and after the silence was solemn. She then listed the key media on site and their reaction to the statement. Overall the media reaction was positive. They felt the statement showed a mature and considered response to the crisis. The discussion surrounding intent seemed to have quieted. We may just survive this after all.

'I think we should include what's being said online,' said Brenda.

'I considered that,' said Marine. 'But Jane and the team are no doubt on top of that. What they can't see is what's happening here.'

Brenda looked back at the screen, attempting to keep the expression on her face as neutral as possible – she was failing miserably.

'Do you want to send this or should I?' questioned Marine.

'I'll send it. Email it to me now,' barked Brenda.

'It is done,' said Marine, hitting send.

Brenda returned to her seat and her computer. I sat at my desk and sneaked a small smile at Marine; she winked back. Journalists were frantically posting stories, but what was the mood online?

An initial search found a bit of a mixed bag in terms of reaction. The haters were still out there, but a couple of positive hashtags were starting to trend. There was #WTACares, #UlliFischerRules and #WTASilenceSpeaksVolumes. But there was also #WTAStuntFailV2 – although it wasn't being shared as quickly.

At least fifty versions of Ulli's speech were on YouTube, in addition to the official one on the WTA channel. Over twenty million hits already – with about seventy percent thumbs up and only fifteen percent thumbs down. A pretty massive turn-around – maybe we could get on with the job of promoting tennis matches?

Looking at the scoreboard, Zoe Lemonjian had won the first set and was already a break up in the second. My concentration broken by the sound of Brenda's laptop slamming shut with such force it nearly jumped off the table. Marine and I looked at her.

'I have a meeting. Try not to fuck anything up while I'm gone.' She was looking at both of us. Then she practically jogged from the room.

'Brenda told me she seeded the story about our post being deliberate. Of course, she knows I can't prove it.' I said.

Marine turned her face towards me, she didn't look surprised by my bombshell. She pointed to an email from Jane. Brenda had sent Marine's email, not copying us, but Jane had responded to the three of us:

**

Hello Brenda,

Thank you for this well-crafted analysis of the situation on site. Please continue the good work and stay on message. I will update the team shortly on the global response.

Regards,
Jane

**

Marine then pointed to the version of her report that Brenda had sent; Jane had left it in the email chain. Almost unchanged from the original by Marine, except for the copious addition of the word 'I'. 'I spoke to each journalist individually…'

'It will be interesting to see what her next move is,' said Marine, mimicking the movement of a chess piece on top of her closed laptop. 'Nobody is in check yet.'

#WTACalls, #PreCrisis

On Wednesday morning, following an email from James, I waited outside the office for the limousine that had been ordered to take me to the US Open in New York. When it pulled up, instead of a stretched-out black car, it was a white minibus, with 'New Haven Limos' written in fancy script on the side. I clambered up the three stairs and nearly tripped in my high black pumps. The rest of the passengers, in their shorts and t-shirts, stared. I stared back, smoothed out my black and white linen sundress and placed the wide-brimmed black sunhat in my lap.

The airconditioning vent above me was broken; half the passengers, including me, sweltered. The other half shivered. After being jostled for well over an hour, a look out the 'limo' window revealed New York City. We were on the George Washington Bridge with Manhattan stretched before me. The Chrysler Building and the Empire State were discernible. The city was covered in a heat haze, making it appear ethereal. Like Brigadoon, the magical Scottish town that only appears every hundred years. Only this town never sleeps. I hummed 'New

York, New York' quietly to myself, before realising several of my bus mates were also humming with their gazes transfixed by the infamous view. The bus was full of NYC virgins. After a few minutes, we left the bridge and bypassed Manhattan on our way to the tennis. With the eye candy gone, I went back to feeling sweaty and rattled until the bus pulled up in front of Flushing Meadows. My dress and hat looked crumpled – to match my mood. The driver stopped at the main entrance, and we were ejected from the 'limo'. Reassembling myself, I looked up. In front of me stood a ten-metre high steel-globe sculpture. My fellow limo passengers joined the throngs of tourists pushing and shoving, all attempting a selfie in front of the sculpture. I took a quick snap for @NQ30Love. Was the globe's purpose to imply sport brings the world together? Like everything here, it was a huge statement.

A sign pointed to accreditation and I joined the queue of self-important people waiting for official passes. Guided through the process – sign please, smile for the camera, wait here – and, thirty minutes later with a photo on a lanyard around my neck, it was off to the player lounge to meet James.

Compared to my experience at Wimbledon, the player lounge was quiet. It was early and most of the players were either practising, or would not come to the site until later in the day. The people that were in the lounge were mainly agents, tournament directors and officials.

James was sitting in a group of about twenty men at the back of the room. Not the secret location I was expecting. Their intensity reminded me of a group of young boys in the playground trading football cards.

I walked over and they stood up. James half smiled and put his hand on my shoulder, 'Say hello to my assistant Katie.' I shook a few hands, sat down and gave James the documents he'd requested from the office. My job was to take minutes and email them to him tonight for approval. The meeting's purpose was to draft an official complaint to the ATP regarding male players' behaviour and attitude.

The meeting was conducted in a feigned whisper, which often rose to shouts. Fists slammed the coffee table for emphasis as attendees recounted situations, which 'must be included'.

The list of player infringements included Petrov's 'tanking', players pulling out of tournaments before they started, being unable to play the final, claiming illnesses nobody believed, refusals to visit sponsors or indifference when meeting them. Even one incident where Bulgarian champion Peter Malade put his hand firmly on the butt of the Berlin tournament sponsor's young wife. Even though some of the incidents seemed ludicrous to me, they were recounted with such vitriol that laughing was not the appropriate response.

My fingers cramped typing the drama into my phone. James looked at me, his face creased with worry and frustration, and said, 'Did you get all that?'

'Yes.'

'Don't talk to anyone about this.' His face softened slightly into an attempted smile. 'Good job, Katie. Take the afternoon off. I'll talk to you tomorrow.' He walked off with a determined gait, leaving me standing in the corner of the lounge. He said good job. That was new. Again showing I'm a shit judge of character.

Watching tennis was next on my agenda. Scanning the monitors, it was clear Petrov was not playing, but that Nadal would be first match on Arthur Ashe Stadium. En route to the stadium, Debbie Penfold from the WTA walked up to me. I had met Debbie at the tournaments in Rome and Eastbourne. The only thing stuck in my memory was she always wore purple. Today, even her nails were painted lilac. 'Katie Cook, isn't it? Katie, can I talk to you in confidence?'

She led me into a temporary office the WTA had set up in the lounge and closed the door. Why was a complete mystery. Had she heard about James' meeting – but that was about ATP players?

She indicated for me to sit down, and I was lowering myself into the seat when she said, 'Katie, some months ago you applied for a job as a communications manager with the WTA. Is that something you're still interested in?'

I stopped mid squat, 'Umm, I'm working for the New Haven event.'

'Yes, we know. We've heard very good things. My question still remains.'

'Are you offering me a job?'

'We may be – if you were interested. You would still have to interview via Skype with our VP of communications, but we want you to be part of the travelling tournament staff team, going to about twenty-five women's events a year.'

She indicated for me to sit and my butt lowered as I explained, 'I was very interested in working for the WTA. Do I have to decide right now?'

'We would need you to speak to our VP and, if she approves, everything would need to be confirmed within the week. If you decide to take the job, you start in Linz, Austria next month. Do you have any questions?'

'Plenty.'

She looked at me and waited. I asked about the salary and conditions. She went through them. The money was marginally better than working for James. When not at tournaments, I could base myself in the US or even Australia. It would be working full-throttle about thirty weeks a year. The rest of the time would be mine. 'Most jobs are like marathons, this is a series of sprints… You'll really need the down time,' she said, and gave me her number and email.

'What about training?'

'There are lots of manuals and you'll receive individual training in Linz from our senior comms team.'

'What have you heard about me?'

'Firstly, Katie, you're the only person who's ever written to every tournament director in the tennis world. A few people showed me the emails – you certainly know how to make an impression. Secondly, Tim Waters, who you worked with in Sydney, raved about you. I think it's the first time I've heard him say a nice word about anybody.'

I stumbled a little as I walked out of the room discombobulated. God only knows what the expression on my face indicated.

**

Debbie: A good salesperson.

**

On court at Arthur Ashe Stadium, Nadal defeated Aussie John Millman, but I could not describe one point of the match. It was hot and I put my hat on. My mind ran through what Debbie had said. I could be based in Australia, see my friends and family and live in my Bondi flat – no apartment hunting. I would be travelling to events all year, mostly women's events, but some would be men's and women's combined. There would be no office work, but I would be on planes and in airports endlessly.

I went to the bathroom. My face was red and blotchy. A splash of water, makeup and lipstick refreshed, was an improvement. I still felt dirty. I was cheating on James even considering the offer.

Transport was my next step. They would give me a lift to Grand Central station where a train would take me back to New Haven. Moving through the player lounge, parallel to James who was talking with the tournament director from Madrid, I dove behind a pillar out of view. As they walked past, James said, 'I can't keep this pace up much longer. Maybe next year, maybe the year after…'

They kept walking and I slumped in my hiding place. What did that mean? Would he sell the tournament? Was my job in New Haven secure? Why did I have to hear that?

Still processing information, I bumped into a tall young girl with a long dark ponytail. She was dressed in Adidas blue warm-up clothes and had a huge racquet bag next to her. She was looking down at her feet. 'I'm sorry, I wasn't looking,' I said.

'Okay,' she said and did not look up.

'I'm Katie Cook, and you are?'

'Anastasia,' long pause, 'Topova.'

'Are you a player?'

'I want to be.'

She was maybe six foot three, all legs and arms, and needed to grow into her body. Something struck me. It was the eyes, a green I felt like I'd seen before. She, like me, was waiting for a car to take her to the city. Anastasia was at the bottom of the list and had been there for over an hour. I offered to share my car, and she was polite but eager in her acceptance. The man at the desk said a car would be along soon.

Using tools from the Spanish Inquisition, I learned that Anastasia was fourteen, from Russia, playing in the juniors here, and new to the WTA circuit. Google told me, as she would not say, that she had been doing very well in the junior competition.

While we chatted and waited, the queue for cars grew. We were at the front, until a group of men barged ahead of us. A sleek black Mercedes pulled up and security rushed to open the passenger door. Petrov appeared and strode into the limousine. Just as the car door was closing, he turned and looked my way. He seemed to be confused for a second. The door shut and the car pulled away. Anastasia had her head down, and she was shuffling from foot to foot. 'The stars always get the cars first,' I said.

'Maybe they weren't always stars,' she said.

Early on in our ride, Anastasia was monosyllabic. I asked when she started playing tennis. She said, 'Six'. I asked what was her favourite shot. She said, 'Serve'. I persisted until stumbling on the right question, the one that unlocked her voice: 'How do you feel when you play?'

She had not drawn breath for nearly twenty-five minutes when the driver indicated we had reached Grand Central station. We got out and I wished Anastasia good luck. She threw her arms around me in a bear hug, squeezing the air out of me. 'Thank you for taking care of me,' she said, picking up her heavy racquet bag and skipping up Sixth Avenue.

**

Anastasia: I hope I get to see her play on the big stage one day soon.

**

#UlliSavesTheDayAgain, #LinzCrisis

Brenda, Marine and I were hard at work in the press room when Zoe Lemonjian won her match. A couple of journalists indicated they wanted to speak to her. They were not Aussie press and it was obvious they wanted to ask her about the crisis.

'You're Australian. You go and get her,' ordered Brenda.

I rose from my seat and walked down the corridor to the court. Zoe was signing autographs. I introduced myself and told her of the media request.

'Can I have twenty minutes? I really want to shower first.'

I told her okay, but suggested we meet a few minutes earlier to brief her on how to handle any difficult questions. She nodded and went off to the locker room.

Back in the press room there was a new drama. 'There's another rumour online,' said Marine. She spoke directly to me in a hush, although the journalists on site were already asking questions. Apparently, a new thread was being followed. It appears an insider had contacted *Die Presse*, a major Viennese newspaper, and implied that Ulli Fischer was forced by the

WTA to hold the minute's silence on court. The hashtags had already started. Most notably #WTASlaveDrivers. On top of it all, we were now child torturers.

Brenda wondered if the 'insider' was Ulli's coach. Marine and I nodded in mock agreement. The chess pieces were again on the move.

Summoned by Birgit to her office, we were met with our tour supervisor and a sobbing Ulli. Birgit was attempting to console her. 'I told you they would hate me,' she blubbered.

'Nobody hates you. But they think we forced you to speak.'

'You did force me.'

Birgit gave her a sympathetic smile and put her arm around Ulli's shoulder. 'You know that's not true. We did have to convince you. But you understood how important it was. You said you felt good after it.'

'I did?' She looked up at Birgit with swollen eyes.

'You did.'

'I did.'

I was not sure if we were making progress or if Birgit was capable of Jedi mind tricks. Ulli had stopped sobbing.

'The WTA think it would be better if you put something on your social-media pages, saying you were proud of the statement. We think it should be in German. In your own words.'

'My own words?'

'Yes, but we will help you if you like.'

This was most definitely a Jedi mind trick. We were all nodding. Birgit told us, without removing her hand from Ulli's shoulder, that we should make sure to brief all players before speaking to the media. We should be directing everyone, media and players, to Ulli's Facebook page. Birgit would let us know when Ulli's statement had gone live. We were then dismissed from her office.

I waited for Zoe in the locker room. It was getting close to her press time and I wanted to make sure she was on message and wasn't blind-sided by any comments. In the locker room, Zoe was sitting dressed in her warm-ups, freshly showered, glued to her phone. 'Getting congrats from home?'

'Nope. I'm reading the shit about Ulli's statement. There are a lot of bastards out there, hiding behind fake names and shit.'

'There are. Listen, Ulli's going to make a statement on her Facebook page. Saying she wasn't forced. I want to give you a heads-up on what are bound to be some of the questions the press will ask you. I doubt the focus will be your match.'

Several players came out of nooks and crannies. Some came from the showers wrapped in towels, some had been getting prepared for matches or practice. They all wanted to know how Ulli was.

'She's fine. A bit upset about what people are saying.'

'We thought she spoke very well,' said Maria Vario, an Italian up-and-comer. Others nodded.

'When her Facebook statement comes up, why don't you all share and support her,' I suggested. More nodding. For an individual sport, this was starting to look a lot more like a team to me.

Zoe and I walked towards the press room talking strategy. She was a bright young woman. Despite her lack of experience, she'd handled the media pressure at home in Oz well. She would do the WTA proud. As we walked past Birgit's office, I stuck my head in to let her know Zoe was going to press. Ulli was typing on the laptop. Birgit was standing over her. Jane's face was in the corner of the screen – she was Skyped in. Birgit waved me away. They were on a mission. Lucky Birgit's German was fluent.

Zoe spoke to fifty-six journalists from all over Europe in the cramped interview room. There were TV cameras lined up at the back at the room all pointed at her.

'I guess you're all here to talk about Aussie tennis,' she quipped. The journalists tittered. She broke the ice. Her intelligence did the rest.

'We're all very proud of Ulli. She spoke beautifully on behalf of us players. The tragic death of students in the US is sad for us all. People should feel safe going to school. I think the media should be talking about that. Nothing else.'

When asked if she believed Ulli spoke of her own free will, she responded, 'I haven't spoken to Ulli since the statement as I was playing on court. But Ulli's a strong woman. I can't imagine her being forced into anything.' *Good on you Zoe.*

When we came out of the interview room, Marine made an announcement. 'Ulli Fischer has made a personal comment on the rumours regarding her appearance on court this morning. That statement is on her Facebook page.' She confirmed she had emailed a link to all the journalists on site. They rushed to their desks and started tapping away. I nodded to Marine and escorted Zoe back to the locker room.

As we walked down the corridor, I navigated my iPhone to Ulli's Facebook page. The post consisted of the official video of Ulli's statement and a small paragraph in German. Neither of us could read it, but we could see it already had about two thousand loves and shocked emoji faces. The numbers were climbing by the second. Zoe and I Googled the translation. In a nutshell, Ulli had confirmed that she was happy and proud to have made the statement on court today on behalf of the players. She believed it was important for the players to speak their minds on this important issue. She did all of this of her own free will, but with the help and guidance of the WTA – who were there to support players.

We both thought Ulli had handled the situation well. Zoe said she was going to share the post on her Facebook and encourage other players to do the same. I walked between the locker room and the press room for the umpteenth time. My FitBit showed I had reached the required fifteen thousand steps for the day.

The media room was buzzing. Marine beckoned me over to her computer. 'Look what's happening. All the players are sharing Ulli's post and commenting.'

Every second, new players, both in Linz and around the world, were adding their two cents and it was all in support of Ulli and the WTA. We sat glued to the screen as more and more players joined in. Within an hour, it seemed like all the current and former No. 1's had retweeted, shared and supported the WTA. They reached tens of millions around the globe. Brenda stayed very quiet. We looked over at her laptop. The outpouring of player support was not visible on her screen, she was 'working on something important for tomorrow'.

'Check fucking mate,' I whispered to Marine.

We did a tiny low five under the desk.

#RunningAhead, #PreCrisis

Back in my apartment, I woke up with pillows on the floor, one sheet half off the bed, and the other twisted around my ankle. The alarm clock said it was time to get up.

It was hot and sticky. Regardless, running was a must. I had tried to ring Lou the night before, with no answer; next on the list was BFF Jen.

'What job's more likely to get you near the hot guys?' was her first question. I changed the topic to discuss her life in Sydney, and she happily obliged.

The past year ran through my mind. Fifteen months ago, I had been aimless and bored in Sydney. Since then, I had worked in Sydney, volunteered in Rome, worked for room and board in Nottingham and Eastbourne, landed an amazing job in New Haven, and now I was being offered the holy grail of PR jobs in tennis. Would accepting mean deserting James and becoming a pariah? A sweaty run was mandatory.

**

My body demanded full attention at the start. As usual, its complaints consumed the minutes until my breathing regulated, and my pace fell into a familiar rhythm. FitBit could measure my output and I could focus on the next big decision.

#SavedForNow, #LinzCrisis

Linz's hotel shower cubicle was getting another workout. This time, washing off the past twenty-four hours was going to be a hard ask. My head back, the water deluged over me. Lucky it wasn't one of those low-flow showerheads.

As I sat on my bed in a robe with wet hair, my laptop rang. I flung open the lid and there was a Skype call from Jane coming through.

'Nice outfit, Katie.'

'Sorry, I didn't have time to…'

'Don't worry,' she interrupted. 'I won't take up much of your time. I've been up for about thirty hours and could use some sleep myself.' It was late afternoon in the US and Jane had been online in crisis management mode since I fell asleep last night.

'Yeah, I understand more of what this job takes now.'

'Don't worry, this isn't the everyday.' *This wasn't the everyday. Did that mean, I would live to see another day?*

'Listen Katie, you really caused a hell of a mess. But you've shown you can think on your feet and follow instructions when required. A lot of people in and out of the WTA are baying for your blood and you're hanging by a thread here. We also know you haven't exactly had the best training environment. I wish that I had the chance to be on site with Marine and you for your first event, it just wasn't possible.'

'I think Marine's doing okay.'

'Yes, she's a very good hire.' I nodded and lowered my head.

'Katie, I believe in my initial decision to hire you. Don't let me down again.'

'You mean, I get to keep my job?' My voice echoing a kid who'd been told they could go to the fun fair, which was pretty much how I felt.

Jane smiled. 'You do. Remember, you only get one get-out-of-jail-free card. I won't be able to buy you another one.'

'You won't need to. I promise.'

'Sleep well, Katie.'

'You too, Jane.' With that she clicked off and I was sitting in the hotel room alone. The Blue Danube was black outside my window. Stars twinkled. There was peace on earth. For now…

#Muscovites, #PostCrisis

It is unfathomable to imagine anyone being more excited than me to be in the departure lounge at Linz airport. Having survived by the skin of my teeth, my destination was not a one-way ticket to Sydney, instead it was to Siberia – well, to be honest, 10,000 kilometres west. Moscow was my next stop. Not a punishment for an Instagram fuck-up, Moscow was a major combined event on the WTA and ATP Tours. I downloaded a Lonely Planet guide. With its colourful images of Red Square and a glorious, violent and passionate history to boot, the city was the inspiration for some of my favourite books, *War and Peace* and *Anna Karenina*. There is nothing like a good epic family drama or romance to keep you up all night – well, maybe something, but the books had far fewer repercussions.

The Cold War was over in theory, but I didn't feel that when landing at Moscow's Sheremetyevo international airport. A little online research about this city uncovered the fact that Russians do not see smiling at strangers as a welcoming gesture. They save smiles for friends. During the 2018 soccer World Cup, in addition to renovating this airport, they attempted to renovate the locals' attitudes – giving them smiling lessons. I tested their prowess. After three attempts smiling at passers-by resulted in disturbed responses akin to 'get the white coats ready boys', I concluded the lessons either hadn't worked or had worn off. My experiment was over.

At customs, the brown-suited attendant studied my letter from the consulate explaining the reason for my visit. He looked at the letter, then at me, back at the letter, then back at me. Did he want me to speak? Silence seemed my best option. He must have agreed, as he put copious stamps all over my letter and took up an entire page in my passport. Just before he waved me through, his face broke into a distorted grimace. I was unnerved and then realised he was attempting a smile. 'Welcome to Moscow,' he said.

I edged past him with my passport and luggage, waiting for the part in the thriller movies where twenty guards drag me to a lonely cell. When that didn't happen, I walked through the green 'nothing to declare' gates without incident.

The only non-Cyrillic sign in the airport contained the tournament logo and my name. I rushed to the man holding it, pointing at the sign and at my body. He nodded, snatched my bag from my grasp and wheeled it to the car. Rather than a tournament-branded luxury vehicle, we rode through the streets in a beat-up van. My seat in the back highlighted the shot suspension and gave me an insight into the conditions of the roads.

As we drove, I perused my guidebook. The sight outside my window bore no resemblance to the grand Moscow in the pictures. It was grey. With autumn well settled, the sky was icy and trees had lost their colour. The leaves on the ground, already dead, seemed to be the only contrast between a bleak sky and landscape. The welcome in the airport echoed the city's demeanour. The Muscovites are accused of burning this city to the ground to thwart the French. Their passion appeared to have burnt with it.

At the end of the first day's play in Moscow, we had finished our work in the press room and had to wait for the minibus to take all the staff to the hotel. Marine used the chance to Skype with her partner; I didn't know or care what Brenda was doing. This was my opportunity to anonymously hit balls against one of the back walls. Most empty stadiums are eerie, but Moscow was downright Gothic. The former Olympic venue was out of scale with its current purpose. If you've heard the expression 'you could land a plane in it', the Moscow arena was so enormous planes could take off. Instead of flimsy partition walls, twenty-metre high black curtains divided the courts. It felt like being inside a life-sized puppet theatre. Now the puppet theatre was dormant, except for the '70s classics that someone had started playing over the tannoy, a little too much soft rock for my taste – but my parents would have been in heaven.

My dad's a golfer. Not professional, but competitive. It is his life's obsession. When Lou and I were kids, he hit golf balls to us on the front lawn, and we tried to catch them. When Mum found out, she warned of the danger. He placated her and said he was only chipping the ball. He explained to me that the reason he practised and played was for that moment when the ball comes off the club cleanly. 'When the two are in unison, it's magic,' he said.

The sound of a tennis ball hit perfectly has become the backdrop to my life. It is authoritative, like the slam of a solid car door. A thunk noise that signifies the ball has hit the middle of the racquet, and the strings applaud to indicate their thanks.

When the ball hits my racquet it is more of an apology. If I get my racquet to the ball on time, it barely catches the edge of the strings. The result is a thrink sound, more like a short screech of tires on a slippery road.

Every time there was an unfamiliar noise, I stopped hitting. Some intense lessons back home in Sydney were on the agenda for when I am home for Christmas.

Accuracy, consistency, persistence. That's the key to everything – my job, my life, this game. My favourite quote is by Calvin Coolidge: 'Nothing in the world can take the place of persistence…persistence and determination alone are omnipotent.'

The rhythm of the music in the background informed my strokes. Lost in my thoughts, I was surprised by the squeak of a tennis shoe, and missed the ball as it rebounded off the wall.

'Hello Katie.'

'Umm, hello Nikolai.'

His smile was beautiful. He put out his hand for me to shake. A static electric shock caused me to pull my hand away and drop the ball in my other hand. As it rolled, Nikolai deftly stopped and scooped it onto his racquet in one move.

'Do you want to hit?'

'I, I can't. I hurt my arm.'

'What's wrong with it?'

'I can't stay. I have to get back to work. I mean the hotel.' I tried to pick up the tennis ball next to me with my racquet the way he did. It rolled out of my reach, but he stopped it.

'Okay, next time,' he said, and picked up the empty can of balls on the ground, put the two balls inside and handed it to me.

I thanked him, turned and started to walk towards the door.

'You're the only one who's nice to Nasty.'

I stopped walking and turned around. 'Nasty? Who's Nasty?'

'Anastasia Topova.'

His green eyes stared too long. I blinked and looked away.

'She's my niece,' he blurted.

He waited and stared. I held his gaze.

'Thank you for helping her.'

'You're welcome. She seemed a bit lost.'

'It's very hard when you start... for some players.'

'I'm sure it is. Don't worry about her.' I felt a need to reassure him.

He gave me a nod. Did he smile? Not the same broad grin he gave me earlier. It was more closed, more contained. It seemed appropriate to smile back before I turned away and walked off the court.

'Put ice on your arm, it helps.'

Each morning the sky was gloomy. When we left in the evening it was pitch black. Our minivan escorted us past colourless concrete blocks that could not contain any happiness. The only feeling Moscow inspired in me was cold. On advice from Marine, I purchased my first pair of gloves and a wool hat to pull down over my ears. Nobody could have explained the cold to me. It incomprehensible that your face could be cold enough to feel burnt. People kept saying that the weather was mild and that true winter had not hit yet. No wonder Napoleon and his men could not hack it.

This morning, my compatriots on the minibus were two American doubles players. They were laughing and chatting about the 'girls' at the party from last night. It didn't take much to guess they were talking about prostitutes. One said, 'My wife keeps asking to come with me to Moscow.'

'Fuck off, this place is a no-wife zone.'

'That's what I told her. Or something about it being cold and miserable.' They laughed like two naughty little boys. They were either being loud to embarrass me or were so arrogant my presence meant nothing.

**

In the press room, Brenda sat between Marine and me. We had been working in silence for over an hour when Marine leant back on her seat. I did the same, she winked, and my suppressed giggle came out as a bit of a snort. Brenda tilted her head away from her screen towards me. I smiled, a mock apology.

Anastasia raced into the room, caught a computer cord on one of her boat-sized feet and nearly toppled over. Brenda looked to the ceiling and said, 'You're not supposed to be in here, Anastasia. Go back to the players' lounge.'

Anastasia insisted she needed to speak to me.

Brenda said, 'Katie, we're not babysitters.'

I told Anastasia I'd meet her in a few minutes and, as she left the room, Brenda spoke to Marine and me, in a voice loud enough for Anastasia to hear, 'Don't waste your time on her, Katie, she's going nowhere.'

'Is that your professional coaching opinion?' I asked the stupid red-headed bitch. I mean who the fuck does that to a fourteen-year-old?

Brenda glared at me, I glared back. She went back to her work, and I to mine, for the ten minutes it took to finish my notes, then I made a deliberate squeaking noise, sliding my chair back across the old varnished hardwood floors, stood, closed my laptop and made my way to meet Anastasia.

**

The players' lounge was also big enough to contain one of the aforementioned aircraft carriers. At one end, players were eating and talking. In another section, they were playing '80s-themed video games and watching TV. The rest were pretty much all multi-screening with their phones, tablets and laptops – the brands depending on their sponsorship deals.

All players' lounges are reminiscent of high school. In particular, the wealthy prep schools you see in American movies. The cliques are ever present. The Spanish sit with the Spanish, the French with the French, the Russians with the Russians, and the stars sit with ever-growing posses. The higher you rise in the rankings, the bigger your posse. It starts with a coach and maybe a parent or two. Then comes the agent, personal trainer, personal physio and culminates with a slew of personal #WhatTheFuckDoYouDos?

Directly in front of me, solo players occupied cushy sofas and buried their heads in personal screens. Anastasia sat opposite, sprawled over one of the seats, playing with her fingernails. She looked up and saw me. All one hundred inches of her legs propelled her awkwardly into the air as she leapt off the seat, bounding towards me. Her energy ensured players turned to look at us. I cringed, wishing for an invisibility cloak. Anastasia dragged me to a corner, and started speaking in a loud whisper.

'Katie, I can't believe he tells you.'

'Who told me, what?'

'You know, Nikolai. He says, you know what he says.' Her eyes darted around the room. Players' short attention spans meant we were no longer interesting.

'Yes, he did. But I don't know why you want to keep it a secret.'

'But then I'm never a champion, I'm always,' she leant in closer and whispered, 'Nikolai Petrov's niece.'

'He cares about you,' I said.

Anastasia explained that she had only recently gotten to know Nikolai. He had been sent to Germany to train when he was ten. He had not seen the family again until he was eighteen. This sparked a memory of Tim Waters' comment about child slavery. Nikolai would have grown up without family Christmases, birthdays and hugs from his mother. I asked her if she had been taken from the family.

'The agents don't own me. Not like they did him or my Mum. I didn't need a contract, Nikolai makes sure I stay with my mother...' She looked down at her shoes and fidgeted with her fingernails. She had done this in the car to Grand Central station, and her cuticles had bled from it.

'Take care, Nasty. I have to get back to the press room.'

'Very funny you call me that. I like it.' She turned and started to walk back to the sofa, then stopped, turned back and called out, 'He likes you, too.'

My mouth open, I looked at her. Having achieved the desired affect, she smiled, giggled, picked up her racquet bag and skipped off towards the locker room.

Back on my silent stage that night, I hummed 'Viva Las Vegas' and drilled balls against the back wall. Today was a good day. Venus smiled at me. A few of the players recognised me, even though they did not remember my name.

With a solo rally going, counting my strokes gave me something to strive for. One. Two. Three. Four. Five. Six. Seven. 'Damn.'

'You need to shorten your backswing.' I turned around too fast, losing my balance, barely managing to save myself from falling over.

'From the other night, you improve.'

'You saw me hitting?'

'First I heard you. The sound was terrible, so I came to look.' His bluntness took me by surprise. *It wasn't that bad.*

'Whoever taught you to play should be shot.'

I put down my racquet and placed my hands on my hips. 'Yes, well, I'm just a bit rusty, and I was out here on my own, not bothering anybody.'

'Come here, your grip is wrong, let me show you.'

I turned and started to walk away.

'Come here.'

I stopped walking and turned around. 'Okay Nikolai,' I stared at him and set the challenge. 'What am I doing wrong?' He beckoned me closer. I walked towards him and stopped about an arm's length away. He grabbed the end of the racquet, hanging by my hip and used it to pull me towards him.

'Show me how you grip.'

Somehow I managed to get my hands in the position I was taught. He looked at my hands, shook his head and twisted my wrist counter-clockwise around the racquet handle. His warm hand was gentle, but firm. It met with no resistance.

'Good. Now you go down that end and we'll see what you can do.'

I jogged to the other end of the court and got into position. He hit the ball directly to me. I managed to connect and hit it over the net. In two huge steps he reached the ball, which was nowhere near him, and hit it gently back to me again. I missed. He said nothing, just took another ball out of his pocket and hit to me again. Randomly he offered advice.

'Turn earlier... Watch the ball... Turn with your shoulders.' We kept hitting, and the rallies extended. Tonight's musical backdrop was an Elvis fest. Who was that DJ? We had hit through all of Elvis' greatest hits, when Nikolai stopped and turned around. Marine had walked onto the court. She told me the last bus was leaving. The spell was broken.

I picked up the balls and ran to the edge of the court and grabbed my laptop bag and handbag. Looking at Nikolai I smiled and mouthed thanks. He nodded and said, 'Tomorrow, wear something better to run in.'

I repressed the urge to skip off the court.

The next night, despite a twelve-hour day, after work was finished I changed into yoga pants, t-shirt and tennis shoes and went to the court where Nikolai was waiting. The sound of ball-on-racquet perfection reached my ears before I saw him. He was hitting against the wall. He stopped and looked me up and down and said, 'Better.'

Was the direction of his gaze indicating the appropriateness of my outfit or my low-cut t-shirt? Hopefully it was a bit of both.

Without words we slipped into the rhythm of the night before. The more balls I got back, the more he directed them away from me, forcing me to run. Tonight his tips were more about my position on the court. 'Get back to the middle,' he repeated a few times.

At random intervals a man dressed in a black tracksuit peeped out from behind the dark curtains. He was broad, short-necked and looked like a hood from a New York gangster movie. Every time I caught his eye, he disappeared. More frustrating than a game of Where's Wally, it was throwing out my all-too-delicate rhythm.

'Ignore him,' Nikolai said.

'Who is he?'

There was no response from Nikolai. Probably some sort of minder.

Exhausted from running, I heard it. That magic sound, but this time, it came from my racquet. I stopped dead. Nikolai understood, and he smiled as he clapped one hand against his racquet.

'Let's get some water,' he suggested.

We were standing by the side of the net sipping from water bottles, playing cat and mouse with our eyes. We looked into each other's eyes; looked away, then back again. Marine came into view. She caught my attention and tilted her head towards the exit.

I wanted to ask why a champion like him was up so late, practising on a court with a nobody like me. Shouldn't he be in bed resting? Why were his minders hiding in shadows, rather than insisting on better preparation for competition? Instead I managed, 'Same time tomorrow?'

'As long as I win,' he said.

Tomorrow was a big match for him, his first semifinal all year. Even more reason that he should not have been here.

'Good luck.'

I looked down at my feet. He put his hand on my shoulder, and slid it down my back. He stopped at the base of my spine. Our eyes met. This time he was the first to look away. I jogged off the court to the sound of Nikolai pounding the ball in sync with Bon Jovi's 'I'll Sleep When I'm Dead'.

The indelible lesson from Linz was no mistake. Paranoid about every score and quote sent, I cleared every social post with the digital team. Marine and I had set up a buddy system, checking each other's work. We caught typos before the dreaded send button had been hit. Before our crosscheck, she had Venus losing instead of winning and I had written Sloane Stephens was from RUS instead of the USA.

While we worked, Petrov went on to play. The crowd's cheers reached a crescendo as the local player arrived.

I went to the locker room to pick up Stephens for her press conference.

'Congratulations, Sloane.'

'Thanks, Kate.'

Yesterday, she called me Marine. I must have done something right.

She took her place on stage; my role was to stand beside her and field questions from the media. 'My serve was strong today… I only want to focus on my game… tomorrow will definitely be a challenge.' Sloane's rehearsed answers soothed the journalists through the twenty minutes we were in the room.

When we emerged, the noise from the court was louder than it had been all day. I managed some chit-chat while glimpsing at the monitor. Petrov had won the first set.

Back in the press room, Brenda was on a mission. She had an argument with one of the player's agents about resistance to a public appearance that was supposed to happen tomorrow morning. 'Fucking agents. The deal was done. Why can't they follow their own motto and just do it?'

Another glance at the monitor showed Petrov was racing away with the second set.

'What are you looking at, Katie? It's only men's matches on court now.'

'Our match is next on centre court.'

She seemed satisfied and sat down at her desk, almost throwing the laptop screen up as she began to type an angry email. I was amazed her laptop held together.

An hour later, Nikolai had won. The last women's match went on court. Marine, who had tag teamed with me and taken Maria Sharapova and a media crew to Red Square, flopped down at her desk. 'Good result, eh?' she said.

'What result? Oh you mean Maria and the Square?' Brenda said, completely misunderstanding Marine's comment.

'Absolutely,' said Marine.

'At least something went fucking right today.'

Brenda continued her email. No doubt on its fifth draft.

That evening on the way to our court, I heard the solid thumping of the ball that made me think Nikolai had started without me. Except it wasn't the sound of a ball hitting a wall. There were two hitters. When I skipped onto the court, Anastasia was hitting with some dark-haired woman I couldn't quite make out due to the shadows. The rally was intense. The dark-haired woman was screaming in Russian, her strokes authoritative, punishing and forcing Anastasia around the court, until she caught sight of me.

Within seconds the woman stopped the rally and exited from the back of the court, leaving Anastasia alone. She turned, saw me and smiled.

'Hello Katie.'

'Who was that? I'm sorry, did I upset her?'

'That was my Mum. She hates the WTA.' *Wow, hates us. What's up her arse?*

'She hits well.'

'She was a champion. Well, she would have been.'

Anastasia dropped her head for a moment, then randomly took off and started to pick up the balls. I decided to help her. With the balls back in the basket, Anastasia gave me a hug and told me she had to go and find mystery Mum. Alone again, I went through the motions of a quasi-warm-up. Just my luck, Nikolai arrived when I was bent over stretching my hamstrings. Upright and red faced, I congratulated him on his win.

'Thanks. I have a good hitting partner this week.'

Our evening dance began. We got up to a fifteen-stroke rally before I miss-hit a ball off the court.

'Shit happens,' he said, and we continued.

When Marine arrived, he waved her away and said, 'Catch a car with me later.' Hesitating, I tried to read his expression, but he turned and went back onto the court, indicating for me to do the same. I wanted to stay and simultaneously hoped it would and wouldn't be more than a car ride. Marine left with a smirk. In the background, the music had mellowed. Van Morrison's 'Brown Eyed Girl' started up. Nikolai was humming along. He noticed me looking at him.

'Good song,' he said.

'Don't you have the final tomorrow?'

'I never go to bed before three,' he said. I got up the nerve and asked him why he behaved so differently from the other athletes.

'I go to bed when I want, I get up when I want, I practise when I want and nobody tells me what to do anymore,' he said, and hit a ball at full force across the net, whizzing by me.

It was only a couple of hours to daybreak when we stood at the site entrance, empty of tournament cars. Nikolai got on his mobile and started to speak in Russian to somebody.

'Da' was my total comprehension. A driver appeared. Seconds later, a black tournament limousine pulled up and Nikolai opened the door for me. I slid along the backseat, and he followed. I sat on the far edge of the seat. My hands were white from their strangle hold of the purse in my lap. His arm slid around the backrest just above my head. I tensed and sat forward, he removed his arm. I sat back again. He asked me what I thought of his city.

'Umm.' *Hopeless, depressing, sad and disappointing.* He stiffened in his seat, then leant forward and spoke in Russian to the driver. The car swerved, turned around and sped off in the wrong direction. When I asked where he was taking me, he looked out the window.

We sat in the car not speaking or touching. I looked out the opposite window, the same black night and concrete blocks looked back. After a few minutes the landscape started to change. Older buildings with grander architecture started to take over. The streets were lit by old style electric lamps that illuminated a European charm previously hidden.

The car stopped. My door opened. The driver pointed and I followed the direction of his arm through a pitch-black alley. Nikolai's shadow loomed behind me. Shivering from the rushing wind, a fur coat landed on my shoulders. I continued to walk whilst shrugging my arms into place and closing the coat around me. The alley opened into an enormous square. Red Square. Despite the time, the square was crowded with tourists taking photos. I turned and followed the aim of their phones. All at once I was Dorothy and had landed in Oz. The black, white and grey were replaced by technicolour. St Basil's Cathedral shone like no other building I had ever seen. I understood why armies had fought for this city, why painters and writers had attempted to bring it to life.

More than a princess castle, it was every colour of the rainbow, like Joseph's coat was supposed to be: 'It was red and yellow and green and…' The closest man could come to emulating the rainbow. My world was reflected through a kaleidoscope.

Here was the real Moscow. The surrounds were camouflage for the fire that had never burnt out.

I managed to take some photos with my phone that would have no hope of doing the scene justice. A pathetic attempt at a selfie with my head half in and half out, resulted in Nikolai taking the phone and procuring a much better shot. Then he jumped in and we had a selfie together. His long arms ensured the whole scene was captured.

'Don't post this,' he said. I nodded.

If it had been up to me, I would never have left the spot. The word 'Petrov' rang in the distance and then people started moving towards us. Somebody picked me up and in seconds we were back in the car, driving away.

'Thank you,' I said.

He smiled.

#WinnersAreGrinners, #PostCrisis

Nikolai and I were dancing to the pounding rhythm of Elvis' medleys. The music was louder, faster, more insistent, and our bodies mirrored its need. He scooped me up, one arm around my back, the other around my butt and carried me to a magical round bed in the middle of a forest. When he kissed me, my body exploded in agreement. I wrapped my legs around him and he pressed closer and closer to me. He pulled up my dress and deftly removed my underwear. I relished the movement of our bodies to the distant rhythm we followed.

The music morphed into a series of short beeps, which got louder and louder until he disappeared and I found myself alone, entangled in my pillow, wet from head to toe. I slammed the snooze button on the alarm clock. Ten more minutes to finish what he started.

Venus dropped her racquet and held her arms in the air. She danced around and then ran up to Maria Sharapova who waited at the net. They embraced. Venus managed a few words of rehearsed Russian in her speech. The crowd roared and clapped, eating out of her hand. As they came off court, Brenda ignored Marine and me, pushing past us to take Venus on a press tour, which included a photo shoot in the Kremlin Palace. She had been working on securing this location all week, and the uniqueness would ensure global press reach – kudos for her…damn it.

I asked Maria how much time she wanted before doing her press conference. Her voice had lost its usual authority. 'Can you give me forty minutes, please Katie?' I nodded and left her alone.

Marine and I sat next to each other to type up a summary of the match. We used the word gracious to describe Venus' speech, while we attempted to ignore the thunder that came from centre court as the men's final started. We kept working for about thirty minutes, then Brenda exploded into the room. Running late, she scooped up her poor laptop and shoved it into her bag. She turned, fired off a list of instructions and warned us not to stuff up.

'Bye Brenda,' we said in unison. She snorted, turned and walked out. I had yet to find the perfect way to punish her for Linz. Patience would supply that.

When we guessed she was out of earshot, the giggles we had been suppressing took on a life of their own. Every time we managed to stop, one of us would look at the other and we would start again. Journalists in the press room, trying to write up their stories, told us to 'shh'. I'm sure they said worse but, as it was in Russian, we did not understand or care.

Nadal took the first set while we were giggling. I felt a pang of guilt. Maybe if I had been concentrating, Nikolai would be winning?

Forty minutes later I went to collect Maria from the locker room. She was sitting by herself in a corner, texting on her phone. She saw me and stood up. We continued in silence to the interview room, she took her place and the questions commenced. With style and humility she admitted it was not her day and complimented Venus. I called for the last question and a Russian journalist asked, 'Do you think you can win again at this level?'

Maria stared at him. From my vantage point, I heard her breathing accelerate. I wanted to interject, tell the bastards to leave her alone. She's been through enough and still she fights her guts out every time she steps on the court. Then she said, 'Every time I step on a court, I believe that I'm going to win, no matter who I'm playing or what the odds say.'

It was like ripping off a bandaid – quick, painful and over. I wanted to squeeze her knee or put my arm around her, something to show solidarity. But I barely knew her.

Maria played with her phone on our walk back to the locker room. She nodded to me and went through the swinging doors. Marine, coming in the opposite direction, grabbed my arm. 'It's a second set tie-break.' Her eyes were blazing.

'That's good.' I told her I had to type up Maria's quotes.

'Okay, I'm going for a walk. Maybe I'll watch from the side. Are you sure you don't want to join me?'

I shook my head and sat down. I was here to do a job. My eyes focused on the laptop, on regurgitating Maria's words, as the noise continued to grow. When the screaming got unbearable, I sneaked a look at the monitor. It was match point in Nadal's favour. I saved my work and crossed my fingers. Nadal served a fault – the crowd noise peaked and then fell away to nothing. I held my breath as he served again. Nikolai hit a huge return and stepped forward, closed in on the net and won the point. The noise was deafening. I walked out of the room, towards the locker room. Instead of being empty, Anastasia was sitting in a corner, her eyes glued to one of the monitors. She had her legs grasped to her chest. She turned and looked at me. Her eyes indicated the seat beside her, and she turned back to the screen. Nikolai won the second set. We exhaled in unison.

The third set gave me motion sickness, with both players trading the lead. The crowd had boundless energy and no problem showing their partisanship. Anastasia and I held hands at each critical moment. She used her tennis player's grip to strangle my fingers into submission. If my hand was Nadal, he would have limped away defeated. But it was not and he played on.

Nikolai eventually managed to gain his own match point. A hush fell. Anastasia put her head on my shoulder. He served… an ace. The crowd erupted. 'Out,' screamed the line judge. Nadal had started to walk towards the net to concede defeat. Nikolai dropped his racquet and remained on the baseline. He indicated his desire to challenge the call. The crowd were booing and screaming. Many had risen to their feet.

'Mr Petrov has elected to challenge the call. The ball was called out.'

Both players were transfixed by the giant screen as it replayed the trajectory of the ball in slow motion. I stood, moving closer to the screen and blocking Nasty's view – except she was now alongside me. The ball landed, it caught a hair-width portion of the line.

'Correction, the ball was in,' said the umpire. 'Game, set, match, Petrov.'

If I thought my hand was sore, that was nothing compared to my ribs at the moment Anastasia grabbed me. She picked me up and carried me around the room, until I tapped out.

'I have to go and find Mummy,' she said and instead of her usual skip, she pirouetted out of the locker room. The most gangly, graceless and joyful pirouette of all time.

I relocated to the side of the court and felt a hand grab mine; it was Marine. We were not alone. Half the workers from the stadium were squished up against each other, trying to get a glimpse of the local hero.

Nikolai went to the podium for the presentation ceremony. President Vladimir Putin came onto the court to present the trophy. Flashes from over a hundred photographers lit up the stadium. My happiness was boosted by the realisation that with all the attention diverted to Petrov's win, despite my admiration for Venus, Brenda's PR stunt would bomb.

Nikolai spoke. After a few minutes, the screaming subsided and he switched to English, 'I dedicate today's win to my new hitting partner. Thank you.'

#YouGetWhatYouNeed, #PostCrisis

A strange little man, dressed in a cheap black suit, delivered our invitation. His too-tight pants strangled his goodies in such an eye-watering way that it was impossible not to look, yet hideous to do so. Marine and I immediately named him Gorgol, because we thought it was an unattractive Russian sounding name that fitted him better than the pants.

Gorgol walked into the press room and headed straight for our desk. We were emailing out results and finishing up our work. Nikolai's win had caused mania. His press conference was in such high demand that the tournament managers had to put speakers outside the main interview room in order for the overflow of journalists to hear his words of wisdom.

Gorgol was on a mission. With a non-existent grasp of the English language, he slammed a piece of paper onto our desk. We looked at the paper. It was the back of a printed Petrov bio, where a phone number had been scrawled. Gorgol managed to mime dialling a phone, pointing to the number and then to us.

Marine and I played along with his game of charades, initially making stupid guesses and giggling, due to the absurdity of the situation. 'Call this number if you want to live,' guessed Marine. She said this a little too loud and a few faces in the room looked at us with alarmed expressions. I suggested to her in a whisper that those jokes were only funny when the punch line was an unlikely outcome.

Eventually Gorgol's charades led us to understand that Petrov was having a celebration and we were invited. We should ring the number when we were ready and a car would take us to the party.

When the car arrived at our hotel it was past midnight. We were exhausted, excited and a little apprehensive. To our knowledge, nobody else from the WTA had been invited. We didn't know if anybody would speak English. Between us we had about five Russian words. At least Marine spoke virtually every other language.

I made Marine promise not to leave without me. We both needed to be on a flight to Paris at noon the next day and the clock was ticking. I was a bit nervous about over-rewarding Nikolai for his win.

Our driver was silent and foreboding. We sat in the back of the car, eyes wide and facing forward, covered in goose bumps. The car cruised on.

A few minutes later the car stopped and two men joined us. One sat in the front and another man in the back, which forced Marine and me to sit close – mainly because we wanted to leave significant distance between the others and us. The man in the back leant forward and chattered away in Russian to the man in the front. Marine whispered they might have been discussing 'where to dump our bodies'. This didn't help.

On our next stop, a leggy Russian blonde, who had to be a model, jumped in. She sprawled her long barely covered body on top of the man next to us. He kept running his hand between her thighs, not stopping at an appropriate spot. Marine and I were so disgusted we huddled and turned, staring out our window.

The next indignity occurred when the man in the front lit up a cigar. Marine and I coughed. We were ignored. Despite the freezing air, we opened our window and stuck our heads out. The rest of the passengers snickered.

The car stopped again. Surely this putrid clown car couldn't get any fuller. When all the doors opened it became apparent we'd arrived. Marine and I followed the others towards a Gothic building with an enormous door that looked like it belonged in a scene from Camelot. To our surprise the door opened inward, rather than dropping like a drawbridge. Inside, we were greeted by a similar number of black-clad bodyguards and leggy blondes.

One of the blondes seemed in charge. She had a clipboard and a list and was ticking people off as they came through. She spoke to us in Russian. We stared back helpless.

'What are your fucking names?'

'I'm Katie Cook and this is Marine Jardin,'

Without another word, she indicated we could go through. Marine and I linked our arms and entered, dumbstruck by the opulence that met us.

We could have walked into the palace at Versailles and been less in awe. The ceilings were ten metres high. Luminous gold carvings were so prevalent the room would have shone without lighting. Chandeliers grander than any movie I'd seen hung throughout the space. Burgundy drapes with gold cord sectioned off areas. The music was unfamiliar and loud. 'Dorothy I don't think we're in Kansas anymore.'

I felt my free arm grabbed and turned. It was Where's Wally from my nights on the court with Nikolai. 'You are Katie. Come,' he said.

Wally pulled one arm and Marine clung to the other as we made our way through the crowd. Behind one of the burgundy curtains sat an enormous black leather coach and a slew of single chairs. Crystal glasses were scattered around and ashtrays were overflowing. Nikolai was sitting in the middle of the couch with one supermodel blonde on each side – the girls were pouting and taking selfies. When he saw us, he stood up, indicated without words for the supermodels to disappear, and walked towards us smiling.

He stood directly in front of me, looked down, took my free hand and kissed it.

'Now the celebration can begin,' he said.

I bit my lip and felt certain parts of my body awaken. Marine kicked me. I remembered they'd never actually been introduced, so I did the honours. He took her free hand, kissed it and smiled.

Nikolai indicated for us to join him on the couch. I sat next to him and Marine took my other side. A waiter appeared with a tray full of champagne glasses, we took one each and within seconds of doing so, people came out of the shadows and everybody loudly yelled 'Nah zda-rovh-yeh.'

I felt his hand stretch around the back of my neck, and this time leant back into it. His touch caused a sensation much lower in my body. I moved closer to him. He reacted by putting the hand that was resting behind me, around my body and pulling me even closer. In this strange place where nothing was familiar, his touch and the warmth of his body enabled me to completely relax.

'Congratulations.'

He turned, tilted his head to meet mine and kissed me on the forehead. My brain managed to stop my hands from grabbing his face and kissing him. My body wanted to jump into his lap and do things that would have made the passengers in our earlier car blush. Lucky for me, my brain was still in charge – but for how long?

A line of worshippers took their turns to congratulate Nikolai. He shook their hands, talked to some and posed for the endless stream of photos. His face hosting a permanent grin, he drank and laughed at nothing in particular.

I sat in his arms, like an extra in a movie scene with no part to play. Marine had moved to a chair opposite and was speaking French to a young couple. She did not look my way.

Despite loving the feeling of being in his arms, after what could have been an hour or more, one of my legs fell asleep. I started moving it to get back the circulation and kicked Nikolai in the process. 'Sorry.'

He suggested we go for a walk and get some air. I agreed, but stumbled on my numb leg when standing up. Nikolai held me and we both laughed. He took my hand and led me through the crowd. As we made our way, I noticed Wally and another bodyguard were walking in front of us – the crowd parted like the Red Sea. Where Nikolai walked, phones flashed, people nodded, smiled, clapped, and many touched his arm or shoulder. Hoping for some of the stardust to rub onto them.

He led me outside into the cold air, a relief from the stuffiness and smoking inside. Wally and his friend had disappeared.

We faced each other and his arms circled my waist. I felt a mixture of safety from his touch and apprehension about how much he expected of me.

'You have a lot of friends.'

He must have found that amusing as the corners of his mouth twisted upwards into the beginning of a smile, then his eyes flickered and he leant down and kissed me on the mouth. Within a millisecond my mouth responded to his and opened. His tongue met mine, which sent shocks through my body. He pulled me against him with a force that limited my breath. I gave way to the pleasure as I felt him pushing us both towards the wall behind us. My back hit the bricks and he lifted me in the air so that our faces were level. I wrapped my legs around his hips and felt his stiff penis straining to escape. When my brain was waving the white flag for my body to proceed, a noise startled me. It sounded like a bottle being dropped on the cement. I stopped kissing him and pulled my face away. He tried to kiss me again, but I put my hands on his face and pushed him away.

'No.'

The spell had been broken. I'd remembered Wally and his friend. They were probably watching us.

'I'm sorry. I want to. I'm just not that kind of girl.'

His breath was rapid and I struggled with inhaling the intoxicating sexroma he was exuding. I wanted him bad, but not bad enough to fuck him in an alley with his bodyguards watching.

He continued to stare at me, without speaking. He was still holding me in the air, even after I had uncoiled my legs from his waist.

'Put me down, Nikolai.'

He released me, took two steps away from me and turned. Then he bowed his head and put his hands over his face and mumbled something. I wanted to make sure he understood why I stopped. 'I'm sorry…' My voiced faded.

He turned to look at me, his face was red, and his fists clenched by his side. Was he going to hit me? Instead he managed to regain control, release his hands and turn to the door we had exited through.

Nikolai pushed it open, strode through and did not look back. I followed his much larger footsteps. One second slower and the door would have hit me in the face. The path that appeared as Nikolai walked closed immediately after him. I was forced to duck and weave in an attempt to keep up. Shit, shit, shit. He obviously didn't care if I was behind him or back in the alley – he did not even turn once on the route back to the couches. By the time I reached the spot, only seconds behind him, he had a model attached to each arm. Maybe they were different from the ones sitting beside him when we arrived. They looked the same – factory models.

I scanned the area and found Marine. She saw me and smiled, then her expression turned into a question mark. I tilted my head and indicated for her to follow me, which she did. Marine linked her arm in mine and I pulled her back in the direction I'd come from.

'I need to talk to you.' She nodded and followed.

When we were back at the scene of the crime, I started to cry. Marine was so surprised she stepped back and then moved forward to comfort me. I was blubbering, 'he kissed… but then…hates me.'

Marine told me not to talk and to breathe slowly. Shaking from the shock of the previous hour and the cold, after a few minutes I was able to fill her in on what had happened.

'He's a creep, forget about him.'

'He's not. I don't think a woman has ever said no to him before.'

'Well, there's a first lesson for him… Let's get back to the hotel, we can get a little sleep before our flight.'

Her words made me realise how tired I was. Sleep in a comfy bed; nothing could be more enticing at that moment. I had never been to Paris. Marine had grown up there and promised to show me around.

Heading back into the party, we worked our way around to the front entrance. The rude blonde who'd granted us entry was still standing there, playing God with the line of people outside. Marine had taken control of our situation and went up to the blonde and said something to her. Without a change of expression, she moved forward to the road, waved her hand and a black limo arrived. The driver alighted and opened the door.

'Get in,' said the blonde. 'He will take you to the hotel.'

We got into the car and he closed the door. Startled by a knock at my window, I turned to see Nikolai's face was looking back at me. He waved his hand, directing me to lower the window.

'Are you flying to Paris?' he asked. I nodded.

'Travel safe,' he said, smiled, turned and left.

I looked at Marine as the driver pulled away. 'That was weird,' she said.

I managed another nod.

#GirlsAreHerosToo, #PostCrisis

Our airport pick-up was at 9a.m. Out of a possible six hours sleep, I managed two partial hours. The evening with Nikolai raced around my mind. A little like picking the petals of a flower – he likes me, he likes me not... Love seemed a bit far-fetched at this point. He was rejected and pissed off. Then he made the effort to say goodbye to me at the car. What happened after we left, I kept trying to guess. He probably went back to the party and celebrated with multiple models. If the rumours were true, he would have had sex with more than one of them before the night was through. I had made the right decision, but hated the thought of him with other women.

Standing under a scorching shower I recalled my true purpose. This job with the WTA was my shot at a unique career, a challenge and an exciting life. Nikolai was a dangerous distraction. Having already deserted James in New Haven, and after my mistake in Linz, it was time to step up. Not time to melt into the throng of girls who had slept with Petrov and become a footnote for gossip by the likes of Danielle and Emma.

Bags packed and a somewhat decent appearance managed, I entered the ancient lift and rested my head against the wooden panels. The jerky ride lulled me into a nanna nap. Like a toddler in a stroller on rough pavement, I drifted away for the six-storey descent. The doors opened and closed at my stop and we rose again. The loud entry of a couple of unknown travellers into my sleeping box broke the spell. On my second visit to the lobby, I exited. Marine was already in the queue to check out. Walking towards her, I noticed a woman leaning in the corner. She was tall – nearly six feet – and had long sleek black hair. She wore a tailored grey pantsuit and carried a Prada handbag. Our eyes met. Hers were bright emerald green. She was Nikolai's sister – Anastasia's mother. We'd never been introduced, and she was only a fleeting shadow running off the court the other night, but with those eyes she couldn't be anyone else.

Elena Topova walked towards me. She stood several inches inside my personal space dwarfing me. 'So, you're Katie.'

'Yes,' I said. 'You must be Nasty's mum.'

'Anastasia. Yes, I am. I believe you know my brother.' Elena's tone was clipped. She did not break eye contact and waited for me to reply.

'We've met. I'm sorry, I can't chat. I have to check out. I'm on my way to –'

'Paris. I know. I felt we should meet. My daughter likes you. A convenient way to her uncle, I think.'

My brain started to race. She thought I'd known Nikolai was Nasty's uncle and had been taking advantage.

'No, I mean, absolutely not. I met your daughter in New York. I'm sorry, but you have me wrong. And your brother behaved badly towards me last night. I'm really not interested in any of this.'

Elena laughed, catching me by surprise. Not a belly laugh or a raucous laugh; a deep muffled sound you'd expect to come from a serial killer. The hairs on the back of my arms stood up. There was a distinct temperature change in the room.

'My brother treats women like shit. Why should you be different.'

This was clearly a statement. I doubt she ever asked questions. Elena turned and exited the building; a large black limousine pulled up. A man, dressed to match, jumped out and opened the door for her. The car sped off. I managed to wheel my bag over to the desk and join Marine. Everyone had watched the encounter. Marine put her hand on my shoulder as I shakily handed over my room key and credit card. The receptionist processed check-out without a word.

'Maybe I should introduce her to Brenda,' I said.

Marine rolled her eyes.

**

Elena: Scary mother-fucker.

**

Minutes later we were in our own car speeding away. Leaving Moscow behind.

Marine and I navigated the awkward seat-choice moment at check-in. She wanted a window seat to sleep. Which sounded blissful. The young woman at check-in offered us window seats one row apart. We accepted and nodded to each other as we placed our bags in the overhead lockers and used our travel pillows to prop our heads against the cold window frames. I ripped open the plastic wrap from my hermetically sealed blanket, which smelt of dry cleaning fluid. Regardless,

I threw it over me and nodded off. The four-hour journey was slumber perfect with smooth air and a gentle landing at Charles de Gaulle in the early afternoon.

Despite a chill, the sun was shining. As we drove through the streets of Paris, I was transfixed by the scale and beauty of the buildings. In Sydney, our oldest colonial building is maybe two hundred years – here that's a modern addition. We drove along the River Seine past bridges that spanned millennia of love and dreams. Marine had asked the cab driver to take the scenic route. She knew this was my first trip to Paris and the WTA was paying. As we circled around the Arc de Triomphe and entered the Champs-Élysées, traffic slowed to a crawl allowing me to take it all in. The avenue was wide and people seemed cemented to their café seats. No doubt there would be queues for these prime positions, as there are for Wimbledon's Centre Court boxes. We have outdoor cafés in Sydney and they have umbrellas with French brands or slogans on them. But it is not the same. The global half-arsed facsimiles of Paris do not even come close to the real thing. For a start, the natives, not the tourists, are dressed to perfection. As we drove, I realised the need for a new scarf, something chic like the countless ones wrapped around these women. Not to forget the men, they looked clean. Clean enough to eat off!

Marine asked me what I was thinking and I replied it was nice.

'No, she said. 'This is your first trip to Paris. Nice is not a suitable adjective. I've seen the eloquent reviews of boring tennis matches you've written. This is Paris, you can do better than that.'

She was right. But there was no word that summed up how I felt. Finally, I settled on 'authentique'. She nodded and indicated for me to continue. Instead I stuck my head out the window and inhaled. Romantic was a cliché. But it was romantic, not man–woman romantic, human history romantic. In Australia, places like Bondi made me appreciate the majesty of nature and the insignificance of us all by comparison. Paris was the reverse. These testaments to human history instilled a sense of pride that we could create such beauty. It was where people were given permission to experiment, to dream. As the car approached the end of the Champs, an avenue of trees had taken over from the shops. I felt like a dog with her head stuck out the window and wanted to get out of the cab and walk. Walk and breathe.

Surrounded by momentous buildings that were five hundred plus years old, making Sydney's oldest structures look like pop-up shops, we reached the hotel. The Sofitel Paris Le Faubourg was a stunning boutique five-star hotel. Located in the prestigious Faubourg Saint-Honoré shopping quarter across the road from the US Embassy, this was expensive real estate. It was spitting distance from the Place de la Concorde and Marine told me I would be able to run through the Tuileries gardens and see the sights in the mornings.

With enough time to check in and dump our bags in the miniature baroque-styled rooms, we were whisked off in a van to the indoor arena, which was going to be our home for the week.

Indoor arenas are replicas of each other, with the exception of the cavernous Moscow site. Most are soulless and free of natural light. After a couple of fourteen-hour days inside, you had no idea of where you were or what day it was, the days and dates identified by the tennis results being churned out to the world hour by hour and day by day.

We arrived early evening and only had to set up, put out some information for the press and send out phone numbers to the media. Moscow champion Venus Williams had a press interview, managed by Brenda, while we were flying in. The rest would kick off the next day. Brenda left us to our own devices and Marine suggested we go to Montmartre for dinner. She told me it was very touristy, but the view over Paris was to die for. We knew it would be our only night leaving the arena before midnight so, although exhausted, we took a car and headed out.

It was dark and the earlier chill had won over the sun's warmth when we arrived at the base of the hill near Anvers metro station. Marine told the driver to stop and we would walk the rest of the way. We had both been indoors – in planes, automobiles and hermetically sealed cribs known as indoor tennis arenas – far too long. Fresh air was a must.

As we walked up the cobblestone streets and wound our way up the steep hill, I marvelled at the closed shops and cafés. Marine told me that in summer they would all be open and it would be light until nearly 11p.m. Tonight, at 8p.m., not many were open, but the age of the buildings and the streetlights made for a surreal walk. It wasn't misty, but it felt as if it should be. When we reached the top, Marine introduced me to the Basilique du Sacré-Coeur. A white marble church that looked over the city, perhaps placed here to watch all the heathens below. Marine explained that at the base of the hill was where Moulin Rouge and other famed bohemian haunts stood; the current crop of brothels and drug dens stand alongside. Pickpockets are everywhere, she warned. As if La Basilique wasn't glorious enough, when I spun around to take in the view she was looking at, I actually squealed. Paris was lying clichéd at my feet; sparkling away, the city of lights lived up to its name. The Eiffel Tower shone, and all around it beckoned us to come and play.

'Oh Marine, this is so…'

'Nice?'

'I couldn't have put it better myself.'

After five attempts, we had a somewhat decent selfie posted on @NQ30Love. All that had been up there in the past three weeks were this shot and a picture of me in Red Square. My followers were not exactly being engaged. Better to be safe than sorry, was my new motto. Marine posted on her Facebook. We were now firm friends, online and IRL.

Marine linked her arm in mine. 'Let's go and buy an overpriced crêpe.'

We wandered into Montmartre proper and saw where the artists set up their canvases to paint tourists by day. One large restaurant was open. Pretty fairy lights lit up the outside carousel-like structure, which was too cold to brave this evening. We went inside and were quickly served. As Marine spoke in French, the waiter gave her his full attention. I could have stripped naked and ran around the restaurant screaming and not raised one of his eyebrows. No doubt he was so sick of tourists that hearing his native tongue was like finding a diamond in a coalmine.

We ate our crêpes in exhausted silence. They were good. Touristy good and I was hungry. I asked Marine about her partner John. He was cockney and she French. How did they meet?

'I was in London for a three-week contract working an event. I met him at a party. He was tall, blonde and rugged. A real man's man, until I discovered his soft underbelly. We moved in together before my contract was up.'

'And you've been together ever since?'

She nodded, polishing off the last of her crêpe.

'Why aren't you married?'

'I don't know. Timing maybe. I think we will do it. Maybe when we are ready to have kids. It isn't really that important. Half of my friends are divorced already.' She had a point. Several of the girls I grew up with in Sydney were already knocking on their second marriage.

Marine told me that if we got an early night at the end of the week, she'd take me somewhere with less to look at, but better food. Sounded like an idea to me, although the odds of another early night were not high.

As we sat and ate, I thought about having Paris at my feet. The view had sparked something in my imagination. Paris was a photogenic city and many tennis player shoots had taken place around the Eiffel Tower, but was there something different we could do up here – from this height?

That night, my dreams were full of Russians, the mafia and Paris. Images floated randomly through my head, like movie rushes that seemed totally disconnected. Awake, I felt unsettled, trying to remember and make sense of my dreams. There was something not connecting and it was driving me crazy. A run seemed in order.

Turning left out of the hotel, I followed a mental map of my surroundings and shortly ended up in the majestic Place de la Concorde. The mammoth square opened up around me. In one direction was the Arc, in another, the Tuileries gardens and, in another, across the Seine and beyond. It was like an historical map of the city. Statues of long-gone kings and the history of Paris connected the dots in my head in rapid fire. Napoleon, I thought. He tried to invade Russia and now all the journalists are talking about the Russians at the tournament invading Paris. That's my photo shoot. The top-five Russian female players linking arms, cloaked in flags, up at Montmartre with Paris at their feet. The flags will fly in the breeze like superhero capes. I could barely breathe. It would be a perfect shot. But it had to happen today. The sky was crystal blue, the tournament had started and the press was hungry for something unique. I started to sprint back to the hotel. Marine's help was a must if this was going to this happen. At 7.15a.m. there was less than two hours to get this thing in gear.

Marine was in her room eating a croissant; she offered me one, but I couldn't eat, I was too keyed up. I spat out my idea and she stopped eating.

'Slow down, Katie. I love your enthusiasm and I love the idea of the superheroes, but the Russian angle worries me.' *No way... was she shitting on my idea?*

'But Napoleon and the Russians.'

'Sure, but that was some time ago, Katie, and this is not the first crop of Russian tennis players. Sharapova, Kournikova, Dementieva, Myskina, they've all made their mark in Paris. It doesn't feel unique enough.'

She was right. But I had something.

'Okay, so the shoot location is fantastic, the superheroes works. What about five up-and-coming stars from various countries?' I asked.

'I like it. It would appeal to a young audience. We'd need a social-media hook.'

'I've got it. We get them dressed up with their national flags as capes, tennis clothes and something else to make them look Marvel comic–type heroes, and tie it all together with a hashtag. Something like #GirlsCanBeHeroes. No wait, #GirlsAreHeroesToo.'

'That's perfect. You'll have to get Nadia Katarinkova on board.'

Nadia is the current Russian No. 1, having reached this year's US Open semifinal. She's the 'It Girl' of the moment.

'Plus it gives you a little of your Russian idea.'

'Mario's her agent, right?'

Marine nodded.

'Do we have a number for him?'

Marine opened her laptop, there had to be one in the database. Mario Panucci was an Italian agent who managed a few of the Russian players. One of them happened to be Nikolai. We were introduced at the celebration in Moscow two nights ago. I didn't know if he would remember me. Or what he would have thought of me draped over Nikolai, or whether they had laughed about me? I had to try.

Marine turned her laptop around and Mario's cell phone number was on the screen. I took a deep breath and dialled. It was still very early and agents tended to sleep in after long nights, but it was now or never. A groggy voice answered the phone.

'Is this Mario Panucci?'

'Si.'

'Mario, I'm sorry to wake you. This is Katie Cook from the WTA. I have this amazing idea for a photo shoot in Paris, which I know will get global coverage. I'd love Nadia to be the star.' I blurted all this out, hoping to get his attention fast so he didn't hang up on me.

It worked. 'What is the photo?' His voice had lost some of the grogginess.

I explained the superheroes theme and the hashtag. He kept asking questions and with each question his voice was clearing. He was waking up.

'Why can't it be a photo of Nadia by herself?' he asked.

I explained that we needed the impact of a Marvel comics Avengers–type image. He seemed to understand. I told him we needed to be at Montmartre by 10a.m.. He said he would call Nadia. The next step was to decide on four other players. Together Marine and I worked out our wish list.

**

Delphine Bisset – A French girl who'd had a few big wins. Strategic to include a local.
Loi Chen – The next touted Chinese sensation.
Ani Ho – A young Hawaiian-American who was making headlines after a big Wimbledon showing.
Arantxa Garcia – the Spanish up-and-comer who had stunned by reaching the semifinals at Roland Garros.

**

Marine helped me find their agents' numbers and one by one they agreed to call their players. Mario had texted back a 'Yes' from Nadia. Once she was secured for the photo, the others weren't going to let their players miss out.

After a lightning-fast shower and change, we were on our way to site. In the press room, I'd spoken to the Getty Images photographer, who was immediately on board. I organised several cars to pick up the players and get them to Montmartre. Then Brenda arrived.

'What the hell is this superhero photo shoot all about?'

'It was an idea I had. Nadia's on board and we shoot in about an hour.'

'No, you're not. I'm in charge here. Not you. Nothing happens without my approval.'

I was about to lose control when the head of the Paris tournament press team, Jacques, came up to us.

'Brenda, this is genius. The superhero photo shoot. I can't believe we didn't think of it before.'

'Yes, well, sometimes inspiration is a last-minute thing,' Brenda said. 'Katie is organising the photographer now.'

'Could we take a film crew?' I asked. 'To shoot behind-the-scenes footage.'

'No,' said Brenda.

'What a fabulous idea,' said Jacques. 'I'll organise the crew now. They can meet you at transportation.'

'One more thing,' I said. 'It would be great if we could extend this coverage beyond images. I'm sure we'll have the general public taking photos and sending them out pretty quick, so we need to secure our key publications something unique. Could you organise some of them to meet us on site and we'll give them mini interviews?'

'Absolutely. What about *Paris Match*? They've been writing a preview piece and they are so important to us.'

'We could give them an exclusive with Nadia in the car on the way back.' Fingers crossed this would be okay – I'd email Mario to confirm.

'Perfect. I'll get on all of it. Stay on your phone.' He raced out of the press room.

Brenda was shooting daggers at me, but she was stuck. Mike Spence, the Getty photographer, came by the desk. 'I'm all set and I have a portable fan in the van in case we need to give the capes a boost.'

'Shit – the flags! I'll make some calls and organise that now. See you at the top of the hill.'

I went to the press desk and asked for their help finding a shop that sells flags. It was now 9a.m. and I hoped some shops would be opening up. Everyone says that all Parisians are rude and unhelpful, but the two young women behind the desk were straight on it. They rang three shops before they found one that was open and he put aside the five flags for me. I would pick them up on my way to Montmartre. One of the girls came up with a brilliant idea to put the players in boots – high-heeled, thigh-high boots. It would look amazing with the tennis skirts and capes. She could organise it, if we could get the girls' shoe sizes. Marine was on it before I could blink.

It seemed that all the pieces were falling into place. I'd double-checked that transportation had cars booked for the camera crew, knew where to pick up each of the players and had a car for me. It was stretching their resources on the first day of the tournament, but Jacques' enthusiasm opened some car doors for us.

'One last thing,' said Marine. 'Contact Jane. You don't want her finding out from someone else.' She gestured with her head towards Brenda who was typing away at her desk. I nodded and shot off a WhatsApp message. It would be the middle of the night in NYC, but Jane never seemed to sleep:

**

Hi Jane,

Marine and I are working with the Paris press team on an image and story about up-and-coming players. It's a Marvel Comic superhero theme and we're shooting at Montmartre this morning. I'll send photos through as they happen.

Katie

In less than twenty-four hours, I was again in a car watching Paris through the looking glass. I tried to recognise more from my downloaded guidebook – my luggage couldn't handle any more books. We flew by the bridge where lovers chained padlocks to signify their commitment. What a perfect honeymoon moment. This would be the perfect honeymoon for Lou and Dave. It would probably be out of budget; maybe I would have enough frequent-flyer miles by then?

The driver double-parked outside the flag shop. As I entered, a bell attached to the door rang – a bit like an old-fashioned dinner bell. Immediately, I was assaulted by the sound of clocks ticking. Hundreds of clocks beat in unison. Maps, clocks and flags from around the world adorned the walls and ceiling. Like my mind, order was present in the apparent chaos, as rolled maps were stacked to the ceiling in every direction. Awed by my surroundings, I initially failed to notice the man standing beside me. Rather than an old librarian, this man was a god. He was a conundrum. From the neck up, he was dark skinned with a mass of black hair – a Rastafarian, almost Bob Marley. I couldn't help my awkward noticeable check out as my eyes scanned down. He had a rock-hard body, which was visible through the immaculate fit of his three-piece suit and tie. The suit looked tailor made. Probably English, maybe Saville Rowe. All I knew about this kind of get-up was through movies. Perhaps he was a spy, maybe active, maybe retired. This would be a perfect hideout. I bet this was no ordinary map shop. It was bound to contain treasure maps and codes. He had a secret stash of weapons, Indiana Jones–style, in a back room. I stared. He smiled. I continued to stare. He continued to smile.

I searched for the French words for 'show me the back room'. And he spoke. A dark deep heavily accented word I couldn't understand.

'Sorry? I mean… pardon?'

'Flags?' he said, smiling.

Of course he would say flags, it must be code for something.

Then he spoke again. 'Flags?'

'Tennis?' he asked.

This time my brain returned to the land of the living and I nodded. He went behind the counter and pulled out a large wrapped package.

'Cinq drapeaux.'

My French was appalling but I gathered that was 'five flags'. I wanted to see the flags. I didn't want to end up in French prison for carting a container of cocaine or something even more sinister. Also, I needed them for the Montmartre shoot. I pointed at my eyes and then the package. He understood and unwrapped a corner. It was enough for me to see they were flags and they were fabric. I could make out the top one was Russian. I only hoped the others were correct. As he handed the package to me, our skin touched. His hand was warm and contained a static charge equivalent to a small electric shock. Why did hot men keep doing this to me? He steadied me with his other hand. Maybe it was the musty carpet causing the charge, or maybe he was carrying heat? Either way, the ticking clocks reminded me of my mission. He charged 200 euros onto my WTA credit card. *Shit this shoot better work.*

Minutes later we were fighting the Paris traffic to Montmartre. I felt a bit of a dipshit for my spy fantasy in the store. Then again, he had only shown me a tiny corner of the package. I looked down at the brown wrapping and considered checking. After all, that's what a secret agent would do. But I wasn't a secret agent and we were late for the shoot. Photo shoot, not shoot out... I hope.

Driving through the tail end of rush hour, the French were changing lanes like the men change their mistresses – often. A few minutes from our destination, Mike from Getty called me. 'The girls are all here and I've found a spot – are you close?'

I told him we were coming up the hill and he audibly exhaled. Usually, his interaction with players was monosyllabic and it wouldn't be long before one of them had a diva attack, if it hadn't happened already.

I jumped out of the car with the flags and ran to the spot Mike had indicated. There they were. Five fabulous tennis players, dressed in their tennis skirts as instructed, with racquets. Mike had set up his tripod, Jacques and his crew had arrived and the makeup woman the tournament recommended was already working on the girls. I went up to her and indicated we wanted to look 'au naturel'. She seemed to understand. The film crew was recording the set up and the girls being made up – perfect. Mike said they'd interviewed him on the logistics of the shoot. All seemed to be going to plan. I unwrapped the flag package inches at a time. Mike watched me. He noted my sigh of relief and hint of disappointment as the five required flags unfolded – Russia, China, USA, France and Spain. I shook each one of them, just in case. 'Getting out the wrinkles.' He nodded and turned away. As I shook the final flag, Nadia came up to me and whispered in my ear.

'I don't want to do this shot with them.' She turned her head to indicate the other players. *Shit, here we go.* Nadia and I needed to go for a walk out of earshot.

'What's the problem, Nadia? Did Mario explain to you why the shot needed to be multiple players.'

'He said something about heroes. I think I can be a hero on my own.'

The expected diva tantrum was bubbling and I wanted to put a lid on it before the shoot was blown. If the other players got wind of Nadia's attitude, no doubt they would want to stop the shoot as well. Here were five individual competitors prepared to kill each other out on the court; this was no team. Each had their own ego, agent, family and individual set of pressures. I looked up at Nadia. She was sixteen, but she had six inches on me. Sometimes it's hard to remember their age because of their size. They are still teenagers with raging hormones and you have to deal with them accordingly. 'What's your favourite girl band Nadia?'

She hesitated and then smiled, 'I like Little Mix.' I thought about putting my fingers in my mouth as a sign of disgust, but continued with my plan.

'Okay, let's imagine you're in Little Mix. You're the star – like Perrie Edwards – but you need backup singers. That's what this shoot is.'

'So I will be in front?'

'Yes.'

'Okay, then I will do it.'

**

Nadia: Understands her value.

**

Bloody brilliant. Now I have to hope the others don't mind Nadia taking centre stage. It was always intended for her to be in front with two players flanking her either side. That's what I had discussed with Mike. It made the most sense and would give the superhero feel.

Nadia was the last to get made up. I had to step in twice as she kept instructing the woman to put more makeup on. Nadia needed to look like a hero not a hooker.

**

The crowd of onlookers had swelled – there's nothing like a film crew in a public place to attract attention. I made sure a few people knew the names of the players to start the social chat early. 'Don't you think they look a bit like heroes?' I said to one young woman. She nodded and posted.

Jacques had come through with the journalists. We had representatives from *L'Équipe, Pravda, Statista, Herald Sun, China Daily* and, of course, *Paris Match*. They were mingling with the players, talking to them about their heroes and keeping the atmosphere hyped up.

In the nick of time, a car pulled up and out came the young girl from the press office. She was lugging five huge boxes. Each of the players squealed in delight as she pulled out glossy, sleek and sexy boots. A red pair for Nadia, purple for Loi, blue for Delphine, gold for Ani and green for Arantxa. They struggled into the boots and tottered over to the shooting spot. The growing crowd, film crew, journalists, Mike and I were all grabbing shots as they went. Each of the players gave me their phones and told me to take photos.

We took the flags and tied them around their necks like capes and Mike and I instructed each one where to stand. Nadia initially stood way too far forward, which looked absurd, until I cajoled her into place. There were a couple of repositions based on height and hair colour and, after about ten minutes, they were in place. The natural breeze blowing meant we wouldn't need the fan, although the wind was temperamental and not always blowing in the correct direction.

Mike took hundreds of shots before feeling satisfied he got 'the shot'. He showed me through the viewer and there were a couple that were magic. He packed up and said he would race back to site, edit the photos and upload them to the Getty site within the hour. Then it was up to the rest of us to push the mainstream media and seed the social stories. Marine was raring to go and had already started the hashtag with the 'before' images I'd been sending her. *Paris Match*, the most popular weekly magazine in France, was going to hold the cover if we could get it to them fast enough, and if they got a good enough story from Nadia during the car ride. I had put in a call to the Russian press director, plus having *Pravda* on site would generate local interest. If the shots were as good as I thought they would be, we would get some fantastic coverage out of this.

I kissed and thanked the players, gave them back their phones and told them to post on their social sites with #GirlsAreHeroesToo. Their agents also had the hashtag details. I told them I would forward the official photos to them ASAP via WhatsApp and they could also add them to their sites. They all seemed most happy that they got to keep the boots.

**

On the drive back to site, I considered asking the driver to stop at the flag shop. Even if the Rastafarian librarian was an assassin, he would have been a smarter choice than Nikolai. Instead, I sat in the front seat while Nadia and Mark from *Paris Match* talked tennis. She was remarkably chatty and opened up about the pressures of the expectation that players would climb the rankings once a few good wins had been achieved. I was sure he had the makings of a cover story.

As we drove, I checked out the progress of the story on my phone. The players had started posting. Already there was a focus on the pictures taken from their phones. Images of the boots proliferated. The girls had used our hashtag, but #HeroesWearBoots and #SexyTennisBoots were already starting to make headway.

At noon, Marine, Brenda and I were looking over Mike's shoulder as he showed us the winning photo. It was better than the one in my head. The colours of the flags sparkled, the sky was perfect (with a bit of photoshopping) and Paris was clearly visible in the background.

'Fuck,' said Brenda. 'It's a great shot.'

I managed a thank you instead of a fuck you, and a genuine thanks to Marine for all her help. Jacques came up to us and he was talking a million miles an hour in French. Marine reminded him to switch languages.

'Everywhere, the photo is going to be everywhere. Even *USA Today* is interested.'

Jacques' team had edited the behind-the-scenes footage and it was on their website. They had also sent it to the local TV stations; receiving assurance producers would run a few seconds of footage on the nightly news.

Jacques told us *Paris Match* were very positive about what they had. Their usual lead time for a feature was four weeks, but they had been working on a tennis story and needed some images and words to help flesh it out. Jacques had pitched hard for our superhero photo to be used. All our fingers were crossed.

I messaged the players with the shot – their social pages were already being shared – boots and all. The hashtag was trending well and growing every minute. @NQ30Love had even scored a few behind-the-scenes photos. It was a great news story. Why not spread it? The WTA's digital team was seeding posts. Even those located in the US, where it was barely dawn. Marine and the team had gotten a jump on the boots trend and had used it to help push the story along. I sent another message to Jane:

**

Hi Jane,

The shoot went well and the #GirlsAreHeroesToo is currently trending. We had journalists from *Paris Match*, *L'Équipe*, *Pravda*, *Statista* and *Herald Sun* on site with us. I'm messaging you the official shot and a few behind-the-scenes taken, plus links to other sites already posting and sharing our images. Will keep you up to date as the story grows.

Katie

**

I hit send on my insurance policy and hoped we got some stunning coverage. Otherwise, I had shone a big bright light on another failure.

#StrikeAPose, #PostCrisis

Waking at 5a.m. after tossing, turning and dreaming about my superhero photo, I grabbed my phone. We had been the leading hashtag in the US, France and Russia for more than twelve hours. A couple of pesky political crises knocked us off the pedestal. Last night, the local TV stations had run the behind-the-scenes footage as promised. A strong result. But would other traditional media run the images? It was too early to find out.

In the meantime, to preserve my sanity, I needed to run. Unnerved by the dark sky and streetlights when I started, the rhythm of my gait and beauty of the city enveloped me. I steered clear of the parks for safety and ran the quiet streets alone, with the exception of cleaning vehicles and a few brave souls that had finished partying and were walking, shoes in hand. When I run, I think and plan. This morning I needed to decide how to manage failure, if it was to occur. I had done all I could to rally people together and make the shoot happen. The photo was perfect and the pitch was solid. The online media had played but the traditional media needed longer lead time and were at the mercy of ever-changing events that steal coverage. I had seen Brenda's photos of Venus in Red Square and had to admit they were amazing, even though Petrov's win rendered them invisible.

I started to run in darkness with a sparkling city that morphed into daybreak. The sun rose, casting its dusty-pink hue over the city of love. My first Paris sunrise was no disappointment. The sandstone monuments competed with the sky for my attention. I stopped, watched and listened. In mere minutes, as the city woke, the traffic intensified, garbage trucks started to roar and the pink turned to yellow, highlighting the pollution and dirt hosted over the centuries. The secret moment shared between a city and a young woman had passed. Fingers crossed it was time for this woman to kick some butt.

Back from my run covered in sweat and the newspapers were piled high in the lobby waiting for room delivery. *Paris Match* was right on top and staring back at me was the shot – front and centre, huge and in full colour, headlined: 'Heros conquèrants descendent sur Paris.' Even I could translate that. I asked the bellboy for a copy. After showing him my room key, he agreed. I pressed the button for the elevator, but decided to run the four flights to my room. I placed the magazine on my bed and stared at it. Marine would need to translate the article. The whole front page was dedicated to the shot, and a three-page spread inside included some of the behind-the-scenes photos. Even if the photo ran nowhere else, nearly half a million people bought *Paris Match* each week, this was a big win for the WTA and the players, not to mention me.

A little after 7.30, I rang Marine's room. She'd seen *Paris Match* and told me photos were in *Le Monde* and a slew of other papers as well. When we got on site, Jacques would no doubt have a coverage report.

In the past two hours, fifty new emails – mostly connected to the photo publication – had hit my inbox. Several congratulations, including a thanks from Nadia's agent Mario, and an email from Jane that I hovered over for a least a minute before opening:

**

Katie,

Thank you for your message regarding the superhero photo shoot you orchestrated yesterday. Appreciating you've only been with us a short time, I would like you to know that generally photos such of these would be organised by me and implemented by you. That way the WTA's strategic direction is always top-of-mind and we are unlikely to make poor decisions on how to manage our resources – namely the players. Please in future defer all ideas and decisions to me. On this occasion, it appears the photo is getting significant positive coverage, which is pleasing.

At the WTA we applaud creativity, but respect procedure. Please keep this in mind in the future.

Regards,

Jane

**

Was this a joke? Did I get slammed for creating a global photo success? I rang Marine and read the email to her. Marine was surprised, telling me that she had received a congratulatory email for being part of the successful shoot. Was

I being too sensitive? Maybe it was my fuck-up in Linz that made her think she needed to keep me on a short leash? All these questions were running around in my head when my mobile rang. It was Nadia.

'Katie, did you see my picture?'

'Yes Nadia, I did. It's on the cover of *Paris Match*.'

'I don't care of that. It's the cover of *Pravda*.'

'Really? That's amazing.'

'Everybody at home will see me as a hero. Katie, I love you.'

Silence. What could I say to her? She was a happy child.

'I'm very happy for you, Nadia. If you keep playing well, there will be many more photos of you in *Pravda*.'

'I will play good. I will win Wimbledon next year.'

The diva was happy. *Pravda* was Russia's largest newspaper, it had millions of readers and would no doubt help Nadia with sponsorship back home.

Two hours later, on site, Marine, Brenda and I were poring over Jacques' coverage report. The photo was everywhere. It was featured in France's *L'Équipe*, *Sport Bild* in Germany, *La Gazzetta dello Sport* in Italy, *The Guardian* in the UK and of course *Pravda* in Russia.

Television news broadcasters in France were still playing the footage Jacques' team had shot and Russian national television had requested, and was running, the grabs as well. I wanted to extend my happiness beyond these four walls:

**

Dear Jen,

It's been ages since I've emailed and I hope life's good in Sydney. I've been in three cities in three weeks (Linz, Moscow and now Paris) and have to keep checking the roads to see which direction cars are coming from to avoid being hit. I got to know Nikolai Petrov a little in Moscow. He's nice but a bit screwed up in the head. I thought something was going to happen between us. But now I think it's better it didn't. I was part of the most amazing photo shoot in Paris with players holding their flags. It's been shown everywhere in Europe and looks great. I'm not sure what my Yankee boss thinks though. She seems to think the idea should have been run by her first. I'm not sure if she wanted more credit, but overall it's an amazing boost for me.

Love Katie

**

Dear Katie,

Congrats on the photo. I saw it all over social media and shared your posts – everybody did. Check out my post. Your photo was in the paper in Sydney and on the TV news as well. Don't worry about your boss, she sounds jealous. As long as people know it was your idea it will be good for you. It sounds like Petrov is a jerk. Stay away, life's too short to waste on arseholes.

Love Jen

**

Jen's email concerned me. Since when had she recommended staying clear of any guy? Another bad break-up was the inevitable cause. I would try to call her in the next few days when things settled down a little in Paris. On the other hand, her post was brilliant. She had photoshopped herself into the image, sporting a Wonder Woman stance. I showed Marine. 'Why don't we grab some of this momentum and encourage other players and crew to pose like superheroes too?'

Marine's face lit up. 'Let's set up a hashtag #StrikeAHeroPose. We can run around and encourage the players to get involved and leverage their social networks.'

'Should we run it by Jane?'

'If we want to live!'

I messaged Jane. She loved it, but had some caveats. She reminded us of the Linz fiasco (as if we'd forget).

'No gun poses,' she said. 'We don't want to start that debate up again.'

Good save, Jane. Within minutes Jane had typed up a brief and sent it to the entire team. We were all encouraged to seed the story in our own social networks – staff, players, tournament staff, basically everybody, were to get involved. Follow the #StrikeAHeroPose with #WTAHeroes and 'Let's see if we can get this thing to go nuts', was Jane's sign-off. Marine and I were more than up for the challenge.

Quickly it was established that my friend Jen wasn't the only one who wanted to be Wonder Woman. There were lots of hands on hips and more than a few lassos of truth being tossed. The variety of poses was infinite, as were the number of heroes to copy. Black Widow, Storm, Elektra, Gamora, Spider-Woman (who knew), Supergirl, Bat-Woman… I needed to watch more movies.

The player lounge, locker room and practice courts were buzzing with players, coaches and entourages playing hero. Dozens of photos were uploading at a time. Marine and I were also recruiting the staff. Sick of being painted as villains, they were all happy to participate. Jacques and the girls in the press room all donned boots similar to those the players had worn – Jacques looked hysterical. Their photos were my favourites.

Marine and I managed one lucky save when we saw three Spanish players striking a *Charlie's Angels* pose. Not traditional superheroes, but they were women who kicked serious arse. They looked terrific – except that one of them was miming a gun. We got them to re-shoot – no pun intended – with a tennis racquet. We then got the digital team to help us make the photo look like a shadow vector. The image was amazing, the players were happy and we uploaded. It had ten thousand shares within hours.

The tournament office came up with the great idea of putting images of the players and staff on the big screen over the court between matches and at the change of ends. The crowds loved it. So much so, that they started doing poses in their seats. Before we knew it, the cameras were following the spectators kiss-cam style – everybody was doing it.

All day, the on-site media joined in. The photographers took photos of the spectators and the journalists interviewed them between matches. The atmosphere on site was electric.

Despite all of this, our regular jobs continued. Players had press conferences, previews and notes were written, and on-site events managed. Somehow it all got done. Brenda showed no interest in participating.

We weren't back at the hotel until 1a.m. I closed my eyes as we rode to the fourth floor. We blew each other kisses when I exited at my stop. Outside the room, I struggled to find the plastic swipe key. My eyes were heavy as I went through the same pockets of my bag over and over. I upturned my bag on the floor and, amongst the day's papers, found the key. Shoving the contents back in my bag, I stuffed the key into the slot and stumbled forward into my petite room. The bed looked like heaven and I face planted onto it.

Face down for several minutes, I convinced myself to strip and clean my teeth. Turning to the bathroom, I noticed a mammoth bunch of red roses standing in a gilt vase on the dresser. There must have been four-dozen of them. Finding the card, it read:

**

Congratulations on making the cover of Pravda. Glad you see some of us as heroes not villains.

Your hitting partner. N

**

Nikolai had sent them. How did he know it was me who organised the shoot? Had Mario told him? The roses were perfect and they smelt intoxicating. I had no way to respond to Nikolai and I wasn't sure what to say anyway. This photoshoot success was about doing my job well. That had to be my focus for now.

#TrustTheBuddha, #PostCrisis

@NQ30Love and my Facebook pages were bursting with new followers, likes, loves and shares. Jane had encouraged us to use our personal social media to promote the hero story and, this time, I had the foresight to check the digital manual. It read:

**

The WTA encourages you to use your personal social media sites to promote women's tennis. We encourage you to share, follow and friend players, tournament staff, media and fellow WTA staff. We ask that you understand that these pages are part of the public domain and although you naturally use them to communicate with your non-tennis friends, always consider what you post or share. Before you act, ask yourself 'How would this reflect upon the WTA?' Use your discretion, but if in doubt check with the digital team or Director.

**

Okay, so that was clear. My lack of posts from Linz and Moscow as I settled in was smart. Paris posts were on message, but now, another social dilemma. Nikolai Petrov had sent a friend request – via Facebook. It wasn't his fan page. It was his private page with no public posts for me to view. What was his game? If he wanted a fling, why would he invite me into his private online world? *Oh, fuck it, fortune favours the brave.* I hit accept. I could always block him later.

The rest of Paris went by in a blur of busy, except for worrying about Jen. Her Facebook page had been deleted. I left messages for her two mornings in a row and no response. Sunday – finals day – came around and there was an email waiting for me:

**

Hi Katie,

Sorry I missed your calls. Work's been busy and I haven't been home much. Don't worry about me. All is well. I broke up with Brad – don't know if you even met him. Anyway, my Facebook page was hacked so I had to shut it down. Contact me via email for now.

Love Jen

**

Her Facebook was hacked? The last thing posted was the Wonder Woman photo and then some strange comments from people I didn't know about her being superhuman. Now no Facebook? Very weird. So I checked her other accounts. It seemed her Instagram and Twitter sites were also gone.

**

Hi Jen,

Did they hack all your social media sites? Everything seems to be down. I'm really worried.

Love Katie

**

Hi Katie,

It wasn't really a hack, more some trolls and haters that were friends of Brad's. I'll tell you more when you're home in a few weeks. Hope you kill it til then.

Love Jen

I was going to have to unravel more of this at home. Jen didn't sound like Jen at all.

After the finals wrapped up, Brenda surprised Marine and me by suggesting we go out for a late dinner and drinks. She suggested a place within walking distance of our hotel where all the celebrities hung out – the Buddha-Bar. We were surprised by the invite, but curious. Marine had heard about it, but never visited. I was keen, but determined to stay sober. My last two trips to bars ended in making out with Joe in New Haven (Oh God, don't remind me) and Nikolai in Moscow (a fine mess). I wanted the superhero hashtags and photos to be my memory of Paris, not making a complete idiot of myself with Buddha and Brenda watching.

Not Quite 30-Love

* *

The entrance to the bar was imposing to say the least. A giant wooden door opened (we had the required reservation) and a grand gilt staircase delivered us into the bar proper. The space was enormous, with seating on two levels. Even if the door or the stairs had failed to awe us, we would have been rendered dumbstruck by the size of the Buddha who presided over it – about three storeys high. He was gold and shimmering and omnipresent throughout our dining and drinking experience.

We had read online reviews about the Asian-fusion food, cocktails and fab music. Paris was famous for its DJs and the Buddha-Bar was a renowned haunt of these night dwellers. The lighting was dark and moody, making it difficult to spot individual diners. Celebrities made themselves known or chose to disappear into the shadows. As we were led to our table, we noticed several tennis players. Marine spotted a couple of French film stars. And we all spotted George Clooney sitting in the corner with a group of friends. We considered hitting him up for a selfie; until we saw a young American woman approach him. She was conspicuous and he was uncomfortable. We walked on.

'For the best,' said Marine.

Our table was fantastic, thanks to a few strings pulled by Jacques as a thank you for our hard work and the photo's success. We could survey everything going on around us. The music was loud, loud enough to make it ideal for people watching, rather than conversation. We ordered drinks. I had a Cosmopolitan, Marine a soda water and Brenda ordered a drink called Heart of Darkness – perfect.

Brenda's drink must have been a doozy, because less than halfway through she started to talk. In fact, due to the noise, she started to shout.

'I've been such a bitch to you both.'

Marine and I looked at each other. I was sure the polite response was 'No you haven't'. But she had. She was also our boss on site, so a bit of delicacy was required.

'I'm sure you've been very stressed,' said Marine.

'No, well... yes. But, really, the truth is, I am a bitch.'

Shit, where do you go from that? 'Why do you think that is?' I asked.

Marine looked dumbstruck by my bluntness.

'The truth is I'm over this. I'm over training new pretty girls, who want to find a rich player to marry and live happily ever after.'

'Is that who you think we are?' Marine asked.

'Yes. Well... maybe. I've seen it too often.'

'How many WTA staff have married players?' I asked.

'None. Well, maybe one. An English girl from the LTA married a South African player.'

That was Helen, who I had met in Nottingham. Hard to believe she was the only one. I asked Brenda if it was so rare for staff to marry players, and why she thought we were after one.

'I suppose it's like winning the lottery. The success rate may be low, but the prize is worth it.'

Marine scoffed at this. 'I've worked with F1 drivers and tennis players. I don't see any of them making good partners. I'll take my man over those wankers any day.'

Brenda and I both laughed at Marine. The words sounded unnatural with her lilting French accent. Nothing missed her gaze. She was sharp, yet soft. Observant but not confrontational. I had experienced the manners of tennis players first hand and thought she was probably right.

'So are you sleeping with Petrov?' Brenda dropped the bomb.

We stopped drinking and stared at her. The waiter arrived at our table. Brenda waved him away. She was gauging my reaction. Trying to catch me in a lie.

'No,' I said. 'I can't believe you've asked me that.'

'Come on. I'm not blind.'

'He tried. I said no.'

'Wow, I bet that was a first for him. How did he react.'

'Not well.'

Marine put her hand up to indicate a halt in conversation. 'I'm hungry, let's order.'

She signalled to the waiter and we ordered food and more drinks. I selected the water. Brenda ordered another Heart of Darkness.

We continued drinking and eating without much more conversation. Brenda kept ordering drinks for herself. Marine and I watched as she showed signs of the alcohol building in her system. Reaching for her glass and not quite grabbing it, then spilling food on herself. After four drinks, she knocked over a water glass.

'I slept with a couple of players when I first started working in tennis.'

Now things were going to get interesting. 'Who?' I asked.

Marine kicked me under the table.

'I can't tell you or I'd have to kill you.' She cackled at this one.

'Okay, don't tell us,' said Marine.

'I'll give you a hint. She played on the women's tour.'

'She dumped me. The bitch. All she wanted was a green card. That's why I'm a bitch.'

I considered my response carefully. Marine leant over and put her hand on Brenda's shoulder. 'Don't let others' actions define you.'

Brenda looked at Marine and burst into tears. Marine moved her chair so she could comfort Brenda. As Brenda wept into Marine's arms, Marine looked at me and shrugged. I wanted to vomit. Now we all had to be nice to the bitch. I did not want to become Brenda's friend and confidante. But I did want her to lay off sabotaging us so we could get on with the job. I stood up walked around the table and knelt down at Brenda's side.

'I think it's probably time we went back to the hotel. A good sleep before your flight home tomorrow will help.'

Brenda looked up from Marine's chest and nodded. I called the waiter over and we settled the bill. Walking out of the bar, I looked back at Buddha.

'You've tamed the beast,' I mumbled.

I swear he shook his head.

#ParisSetsTheStage, #PostCrisis

I did not have to be in Singapore until Friday – four days from now. It was too time consuming and expensive to fly back to Oz; the WTA needed to put me up in a hotel and they didn't care where that was. Marine offered for me to stay at her place in London, but she had been away from home for three weeks and might want some alone time with her partner. Three days in Paris all expenses paid was a good deal. I would go to Singapore a day early and do some sightseeing and jet-lag recovery at the other end.

Even in one of the most exciting cities in the world, the constant challenges of the last few months had exhausted me. It was 2p.m. on my first day of freedom before I confronted the land of the living. I ordered some food from room service and sat down with my downloaded guidebook; I wished for a physical book to dog ear. On the other hand, the online version meant activating GPS and planning my time in Paris to perfection. It was Monday and two of my must-do places, the Musée d'Orsay and the Rodin Museum, were closed. They would be open tomorrow. The Louvre was closed tomorrow, but it would need several hours to explore, so I'd leave that until Wednesday. I was on the Wednesday night flight to Singapore, so that would be perfect. There were only a few daylight hours left today and my guidebook and Marine's suggestions left me with one obvious choice – shopping.

Galeries Lafayette was like Sydney's David Jones on steroids. I spent two hours combing through the racks of clothes, touching exquisite fabrics I doubted I would ever be able to afford. I had the unique pleasure of being ignored by some of the most beautiful and stylish shop assistants ever to grace the earth. In the end, I purchased two divine scarves for me, plus one each for Mum, Lou and Jen – all on sale. There was a little black dress that made my boobs pop and my waist shrink. It was considerably above my allocated spend for the trip, or even the year, but when I looked in the mirror – *hell, even I'd fuck me*. Given my recent options, masturbation was probably a good choice. I took a picture of me in the dress and my recent purchases and posted on @NQ30Love. Shopping bags and LBDs, I figured that encapsulated Paris – for now.

It was dark when I left the store. I had my shopping bags and comfortable shoes and the magnificence of Paris was starting to twinkle. I decided to walk. Around the corner was the Opéra Garnier. Sydney Opera House is a series of sails and sparkles on the harbour. The Palais Garnier opera house was hundreds of years old and stood proudly in a crowded square. She was a lady that didn't need to shout. I could feel the music emanating from her, even though it didn't appear that anything was playing tonight. My guidebook said she was commissioned by Napoleon and was the setting for the Phantom of the Opera. There is not a lake but a huge water tank underneath her, where fire fighters practise swimming. I imagined I'd swim pretty fast in a pitch-dark underground water tank.

I found a brasserie and ordered a half carafe of cheap red wine, uploaded a pic to @NQ30Love #JustACheekyRed and tapped away on my guidebook. The waiter offered me a menu and I chose from the *prix fix* selection. I was on expenses, but didn't want to draw attention to myself back at the office. While I ate and read, Paris strolled by. In the cool weather, the Parisians dressed up their coats with coloured scarves, hats and broaches. They did not allow winter to dull their sense of style. I wanted to be a writer. It was impossible not to imagine myself in a little Parisian garret painting or writing. My imagination glossed over my lack of talent.

It was 10p.m. before I staggered, a little tipsy from the second half carafe, back to my hotel. I ordered a wake-up call for 7a.m., as I planned to walk all day and wanted to start with a leisurely breakfast for the first time in months.

* *

Sleep came easily. The heady scent of wilting roses filled my head. Paris was mine to explore, I willed on the magical dreams.

As I was savouring the last bite of a perfect baguette in the charming breakfast room of my hotel, the concierge approached me. He confirmed I was Katie Cook before handing me a note:

* *

Meet me at La Galerie at the George V hotel at 3p.m. for tea. N

**

What the fuck? Nikolai and his obtuse notes – how goddamn arrogant. Today was my walking and museum day. I was not going to have it hijacked. I grabbed the concierge, but he didn't know how the message was delivered. I sent Nikolai a Facebook message:

**

Thanks for the invite to tea – very busy today, not sure if I can make it. K

**

Of course he'd know it was me as it was coming through my Facebook, but I wanted to match his arrogance.

Musée d'Orsay was open at 9.30. While waiting in the queue, I checked my Instagram feed. The LBD pic had been a popular one – a few tasty and inappropriate comments made me giggle. The most surprising reaction was that Nikolai had given it a love emoji. I couldn't decide if this made me feel happy or the creeps. I checked Facebook to see if he'd responded to my message – nothing.

After 30 minutes the Musée doors opened. The main gallery was built around an old train station and the infrastructure was still intact. The glass ceilings stretched beyond the clouds. Even the Buddha from the bar a couple of nights ago would have been dwarfed by this space. My lack of art savvy was embarrassing. There were a few prints on my walls in Bondi, but they were mainly selected for their colours. Matching cushions and art was about as complex as it got for me. Paintings by Picasso, Monet, Degas – he loved the ballerinas, I think he may also have had a foot fetish. Van Gogh's

Starry Night is something everybody's seen images of but, in the flesh, even with a queue of people taking their turn for a glimpse, I was in love. People sat and sketched, school children were on excursions, some people raced through, focusing on the masters, others lingered. As I wondered, I thought of taking art classes.

I walked along the Seine. Past the Notre-Dame and its legends, past cafés and monuments, along and across bridges, past artists selling their wares by the side of the river. I took photos of everything. Some a blatant attempt at being arty. I snapped images of interesting doors and partial street signs, all uploaded to @NQ30Love, each time checking my Facebook for messages. I walked for hours before arriving at the Rodin Museum.

I was standing in front of his sculpture *The Kiss* at 2.30p.m. A sculpture of two lovers entwined, engaged in a passionate kiss. The lovers are frozen in their passion and it's impossible not to ache with desire standing in front of them. That's when it hit me that I did want to see Nikolai. Torn between giving in to his presumptions and the danger of association and my desire to be near him, my decision was made when a couple struck by the sculpture decided to emulate the activity. Their kiss and the statue's passion had me checking Facebook for the millionth time. This time there was a '1' next to the message icon.

* *

If you're able to take a break from sightseeing, I'll be at tea at 3p.m. N

* *

I turned for the exit and hailed a taxi.

At 3.10p.m. I was in front of the George V Hotel. I wondered how long he would wait and decided to visit the lobby bathroom to touch up my makeup.

I saw him sitting at a window table with a cup of tea in front of him. He was dressed in a black suit. Checking myself for drool, I walked up, put my hand on his shoulder and said, 'Nikolai, what a surprise. I didn't know you were in Paris.'

He stood, towering over me, leant down and kissed me on the cheek. He indicated to the chair opposite him. He moved around and pulled it out for me. I shouldn't have been surprised because before that fateful night he had always been the perfect gentleman. He had picked up the tennis balls, carried my racquet and opened doors for me.

I sat down and the waiter was at our table within seconds.

'Are you hungry?' Nikolai asked.

I hadn't eaten since breakfast and, with all that walking, was famished. I nodded and the waiter handed me a menu. I looked down at the selection, which luckily contained both English and French, and read for a few minutes before looking up. I could feel Nikolai's attention on me while I read. I was not going to be rushed.

Due to the hour, they were serving afternoon tea, but I wanted a salad. I looked up and the waiter arrived. I asked in my mix of bad French and English if it were possible. The waiter shook his head. Nikolai interrupted in fluent French and, I can only assume, pleaded my case. The waiter seemed unmoved until he looked directly at Nikolai. After about a minute's silence staring at each other, the waiter nodded his head and left the table. I was getting a salad.

'I didn't know you spoke French.'

'Russian, German, French... and some English,' he said.

'I speak some English,' I said, and couldn't help smiling. He smiled back. The tension dropped. His smile made me feel like I was standing in front of *The Kiss* again. I had so many questions. Why was he so upset with me in Moscow? Did he know his sister had confronted me? And, most importantly, what did he want? Was it a conquest or did he feel what I felt? *Shit, I don't even understand what I feel.*

'Shouldn't you be training for the championships next week?'

'How could I do that without my favourite hitting partner?'

'Well, we could go back to the stadium after I finish my salad, if you like?'

He smiled again. A different smile. He did not want to go to the stadium and hit tennis balls. I felt a blush rising in my body, which was only partially saved by the waiter arriving with my salad. Both the waiter and Nikolai wished me 'bon appétit' and I started to eat. I attacked the salad with voracity. My mind, body and soul were unified in their desire for more. The last six months had been crazy, stimulating, frightening and inspiring all at once. I had been sleepwalking for years, now I was wide awake.

Eating my salad gave me time to think. I needed to know more about the man sitting in front of me. I knew his stats – height, weight, playing style, ranking and results. I knew he was sexy as hell. However, I also knew he had many women, but Google couldn't find a record of anyone special. On top of that he had a bat-shit scary sister and a beautiful niece. I couldn't get Tim Waters' comment in New Haven out of my mind. 'His parents virtually sold him to agents when he was ten years old.' I decided to probe. What did I have to lose? I wasn't going to get more deeply involved with a man who was the perfect gentleman one minute and a misogynist the next. I looked up from the romaine lettuce.

'Tell me about your childhood.'

Nikolai sat back on his chair and stared at me.

'Tell me about *your* childhood,' he returned.

'Okay, well, I have a mother, a father and a younger sister – two years younger. I grew up in Sydney near the water. My parents were always very encouraging, but not pushy enough. If I didn't want to do something, they always let me off the hook. That's why it took me so long to get off my arse and push myself to try something.'

I finished talking and gestured that it was his turn.

'I played tennis.'

'And…?'

He sat back, looked down, putting his chin on his hand in the pose of Rodin's *The Thinker*, then looked back at me. 'That's pretty much it.'

'Wow. Thanks for the insight, Nikolai. I feel like I could write your biography now.'

'Go for it. Yours would be the sixth already written.'

'Were you as forthcoming with your other biographers?'

'Less, much less.'

'Okay, let's start with something a bit less scary. Where did you grow up?'

'Russia, then Germany.'

'Where in Germany?'

'Near Stuttgart.'

'That's where they have the women's tournament – where they give away all the Porsches.'

'Close… that's Filderstadt.

'Do you have a Porsche?'

'I have five.'

'I bet they're all black.'

'Incorrect. One is red.'

I needed a different tack. Maybe a crowded restaurant wasn't the place to have any sort of genuine conversation with him.

'Do you feel like a walk in the park? It's a beautiful day.'

'It was a beautiful day. It's almost dark now.' He was right. The winter sun was setting. 'We can walk, but you will need a coat. It's cold.'

I told him that I only had my jacket, but I would be okay.

He waived the waiter over.

'Is the women's clothes shop downstairs still open?' The waiter shrugged and said he would check.

Minutes later, Nikolai had paid the bill and we were in the exclusive women's boutique on the ground floor, trying on cashmere coats. Despite my reservations that this was not a game, I played along as the coats were divine to touch and snuggle into. The assistant found the most magnificent soft camel-coloured coat and matching hat; she accessorised with a Hermès scarf and leather gloves. I giggled away as she tugged and prodded. She looked at Nikolai and he nodded. With a deft hand she removed the tags and was ringing them up before I had registered what was going on. 'Are you fucking crazy?' I whispered. 'I can't afford this and I'm certainly not letting you buy it.'

Nikolai ignored me and walked over to the counter, where the assistant had put them through on his credit card. He must have handed it to her when we walked in. Knowing it was in the vicinity of ten thousand euro, I had to stop him. I walked over to the counter as I attempted to extricate myself from the clothes. 'No,' I said. 'You're not doing this.'

'You wanted to go for a walk,' he said, as he entered his pin. He had bought the clothes. The assistant was now invisible. Nikolai leant over me and buttoned the coat back up. 'We walk,' he said, and offered me his arm.

#CashmereCanBeItchy, #PostCrisis

Arm in arm we strolled down the Champs – a cliché for sure, but a fabulous one. The temperature had dropped and I was torn between my love for the divine coat cocooning me and the guilt and frustration that came from Nikolai's dominance.

Soon we were beyond the shops and into the Jardin des Champs-Élysées. Despite the cold, many couples and tourists were also strolling the pathways. For a while we didn't speak. I wasn't cold; however, I couldn't help from snuggling into him a little. He wrapped a huge arm around me. Despite the crowded streets, I felt we were alone. No bodyguards jumping out from behind trees like a bad detective movie.

It became apparent that Nikolai was directing our walk. We appeared to be moving in the direction of my hotel. I asked him where we were going.

'Your hotel.'

'Why?'

'To drop you back safely.'

'No other motive?'

He smiled and continued walking. *I am not sleeping with him. I am not sleeping with him.*

When we arrived at the lobby, he leant down, kissed me on the cheek and wished me goodnight. I wasn't sure what to do. Ninety percent of me wanted to take him to my room. Thank God, ten percent knew that would be disastrous.

'Can I meet you for breakfast?' he asked. I nodded and he said he would meet me back in the lobby of my hotel at 8a.m. He left without looking back and I floated in the elevator to my floor.

**

I dreamt that I had brought him back to my room and we had made love all night. It was the first time I climaxed in my sleep – no assistance required. I did not wake until 7.45. *Shit, Nikolai will be in the lobby in fifteen minutes.*

I jumped under the shower, washing off my dream. There was no way to avoid washing my hair. At least my legs were shaved. At 7.55 I was drying my hair and cleaning my teeth simultaneously. These two tasks do not work well together, with toothpaste in my hair at best and electrocution at worst. At 8.05 I was dressed in chinos and a long-sleeved shirt, the scarf he had bought me last night and a tan leather jacket that, along with yesterday's black dress, had been another recent splurge. Some serious scrimping over the coming months was a necessity.

Applying lipstick and mascara in the elevator, the doors opened and I spotted him, sitting on a bench dressed casually in jeans, shirt and jacket. Out of tennis gear, he looked even more like a male model – airbrushed to perfection. He was beautiful, even more so because he was not surrounded by an entourage and seemed just a tiny bit vulnerable.

He stood up as I walked towards him. He kissed me on the cheek and touched my scarf smiling.

'It was too much, buying me all those clothes.'

'You helped me win Moscow. It's simply your share of the prize money.'

'Very sweet, but we both know I had nothing to do with you winning Moscow.'

'Do we?' he said. 'I think you underestimate your impact.'

He offered me his arm and I slipped into this now familiar position. As we strolled out into the street, he asked me if I was up for a little walk to a special breakfast place.

**

We walked past people rushing to work, women walking their dogs and tourists with their maps. After a few minutes we stopped at one of the many boulangeries. The aroma of fresh croissants, bread and pastries that filled every Parisian morning grew more enticing as we entered. Nikolai went up to the counter and used his perfect French to order everything. The women behind the counter fussed around filling white paper bags with his requests. He paid the bill, opened the knapsack he had slung over his shoulder and put the produce inside. I tried to sneak a peek, but he pulled the bag out of my vision with a playful smile. 'Later,' he said.

We walked a little further and came to a café.

'Do you want some coffee with breakfast?' I nodded.

We went inside and he ordered two café au laits to go and some bottled water.

We continued on until we reached the Tuileries gardens. When we had reached an open space with Luxembourg chairs and a view of the Louvre, he stopped and indicated I should sit on one of the chairs. He opened the knapsack. It was filled with the pastries, water, miniature jams and spreads, napkins and a picnic rug. In minutes he had set up a picnic breakfast for us. I moved from the chair to the rug and he managed to manoeuvre his huge body next to mine. We sipped coffee and tore bread and pastries together.

Although the gardens were busy with tourists and locals passing through, at this point in the morning, nobody was stopping.

'You wanted to know about my childhood?' I nodded.

'I don't remember much before I moved to Germany. I remember playing with my sister and I remember my parents fighting, mostly over money.' He told me that he, his sister and a few other kids had hit tennis balls, using a racquet with broken strings, against a brick wall at the end of his street. They would take turns to use the racquet. One day somebody saw him hitting and went to his parents. Before he knew it, he was packed up and sent to Germany to become a professional tennis player. He said that although his sister was better than him – she was also older – the agents showed no interest.

'I would hit tennis balls for six hours a day, sometimes more. The Germans love routine and rules. Exercise, eat, sleep, then do it again.' He told me it took him nearly two years to learn German and the other kids excluded him. He was bullied, although Nikolai didn't use that word, for years until he got so big they decided to leave him alone.

'Being rich is all about freedom for me. Freedom to practise when I want and tell people to fuck off that want to control me.'

'The mafia doesn't try to control you?' I couldn't help asking. Every time I had seen Nikolai, apart from the past two days, they surrounded him.

'If I win, they leave me to myself.'

'You better keep winning then.'

He smiled and ripped open a piece of baguette in fake defiance.

'We will have to practise a lot,' I said, and he leant over and kissed me on the cheek. That was it. The moment my feelings turned from lust into something more. This huge man was desperate for my approval and affection and I was going to give it to him. I took his head in my hands and kissed him on the lips. He kissed back hard. His tongue was in my mouth and mine in his. I climbed into his lap and things started to escalate. This time, *he* stopped. We were both panting and staring into each other's eyes, our faces only millimetres apart.

'Not here,' he said, and I nodded. The picnic was packed up in seconds as we took off in the direction of my hotel. We were in the lobby in only a few minutes, barely making it to my room with any clothes remaining. As I fumbled for my room key while he kissed me, one of the housekeepers came by. She giggled and I blushed. Nikolai took the key from my hand and opened the door. He slammed it behind us.

Nikolai's huge hands moved with a gentle, yet urgent determination as he helped me out of my clothes. I felt the need to reciprocate. His hands were calloused from his trade and felt rough on my skin. His bulging boxers were the last layer in a game of pass-the-parcel I could not wait to tear off. As I sprung the prize from its wrapper I could barely contain myself from singing 'Happy birthday to me'. We were both naked and looked at each other. No words passed between us. Every inch of him was hard, and I mean every inch. There was plenty to appreciate. My body shivered with a mixture of anticipation and mild concern. It had been a couple of years and perhaps starting smaller would have been wiser, but here he was, naked, perfect, and ready to go. The staring stopped and the groping resumed. He had me pinned on the bed and started to kiss my nipples. They agreed wholeheartedly, accepting his tongue's presence. It got hotter and hotter. So hot that

I thought I might combust before blast-off. Lucky for me, although Nikolai was in a hurry, he slowed himself down to give my body time to be ready. He fitted the condom so deftly. This was not his first time. He entered me slowly at first. My body dripped with anticipation. His size was still a factor and my muscles resisted. He persisted. Kissing my neck as he got deeper and deeper. He was inside me and I wanted him to stay forever. Once my body accepted all of him, we found the perfect rhythm. The explosion inside me shattered my distant memory of previous orgasms. He came while I was in a trance.

He tried to stay inside me as long as possible, neither one of us wanted to separate. The inevitable biological realities forced us apart and we clung, wrapped around each other, staring and panting for minutes or hours… time meant nothing.

We started to kiss, small repetitive meetings of our lips, followed by longer deeper connections. We made love twice more before even speaking. Nikolai's first words were 'I'm starving'. We laughed and I dialled room service – we ordered steak, fries, bread and wine or 'entrecôte', as the French call it. We realised that it was 2p.m., which threw me into a panic. My flight to Singapore was that night. I had to check out of the hotel at 6p.m. and I was not finished with Nikolai. He said that we had to take advantage of every minute and we made love again, before the room service arrived.

Nikolai hid in the bathroom while the waiter brought in the food. I had made myself somewhat decent and the waiter wheeled in an enormous trolley overflowing with our order. His eyes darted between the volume of food and me. I tipped him, he left and Nikolai returned.

We talked, laughed and ate voraciously. I hadn't really eaten much in the past 24 hours and the mixture of vigorous exercise and sensory overload had gone to my stomach. We fed each other pommes frites, licked the salt from each other's fingers and before long we were at it again. This time I was on top and he held my breasts in his hands as I rode him to mutual orgasm. My sexual confidence had gone from zero to hero over the past six hours and I was becoming more adventurous with each session.

At 5.30, I was throwing clothes in a bag while he watched. I needed a shower and he joined me, in every sense. Lifting me against the glass and fucking me into a frenzy, I was giddy and shaky as we left the room.

Nikolai wheeled my bag into the staircase.

'No lift, they have cameras.' *He wasn't worried about cameras last night.* He carried my bag and held my hand as we walked down the four flights of stairs. At the first floor, he stopped and grabbed my face with both hands. 'I will miss you,' he said and kissed me hard. I felt sorrow and ecstasy in mutual amounts.

'When will I see you again?' I asked.

He shrugged. We both knew I was going to Singapore and he would be at the ATP Finals at the O2 in London. After that both of us would go home for Christmas, he to Moscow and me to Sydney.

'I'll call you in Singapore,' he said, breaking away from me and picking up my bag. He left me in the lobby, disappearing with his knapsack as I checked out and was ushered into the car for the airport.

Maybe my Instagram name is coming true?

#SelfieHeaven, #PostCrisis

Nearly thirteen hours sitting bolt upright in economy is a joy that has to be felt not described. Most times I'm bored out of my brain, but this time I had pleasant dreams, very pleasant dreams, too pleasant dreams. I'm not sure if I talked in my sleep, but the couple next to me offered strange looks when I woke up. Nikolai was almost as good in my dream as he was IRL.

Upon landing, I checked into the Marina Bay Sands hotel. This was the championships with only eight singles players, eight doubles players and a host of living legends on the menu; everything was amped up to eleven. 'Names, names, names, sweetie, darling'. That was the theme of the week and of the Marina Bay Sands complex. Shaped like an alien machine from *War of the Worlds* with three tentacles leading to a sky-high complex, this was Instagram heaven. Given that, and that it was a day before my colleagues arrived, I prepared to sight see. Before setting out, I checked my email, always with my eyes half open and my body braced for shock post-Linz. Nothing to write home about appeared, so I decided to write home.

**

Dear Lou,

I think I may be in love. He feels the same, I hope. It's impossible of course and going to cause me a lot of problems with work. My stomach is in knots. I can't wait to be home and try to get some perspective. Hope all's well with you and the family.

Love Katie

**

It was hot and humid outside. Always. The consensus was to stay indoors. The airconditioning in the Sands kept the temperature perfect for shopping. Another soothing sensation was the river running through it. I kid you not, it was a river with gondolas. This was one way to save your feet when shopping, but I needed to walk after all those hours with cabin fever.

Designer shops were abundant. My budget was not. Window-shopping was the perfect solution. I stuck my nose on the glass at Dior, Chanel and Prada, before having a baguette at one of the Parisian-styled concessions. Paris this was not; it tasted good anyway. People around me were not window-shopping. Locals or tourists, who knows, they came out of the boutiques laden with branded bags. This was #CrazyRichAsians IRL. Fabulous!

@NQ30Love scored a couple of selfies outside designer boutique before I realised that the grammable shot was the infinity pool selfie from the rooftop. I went back to my room to don my swimming cossie.

**

A quick check of my emails showed Marine was arriving this evening and did I want dinner? I quickly replied yes and that I would meet her in the lobby in a couple of hours. Another from Lou:

**

Dear Katie,

Love shouldn't be that hard. Remember why you're out there – this job was something you really wanted. Don't blow on it some guy, unless you're very sure. We can't wait to see you at home. You can help with the wedding plans and get Mum off my back.

Love Lou

**

I hated Lou bursting my love bubble, but perhaps she was right? Being with Nikolai was inevitable trouble. I didn't want to end up like one of the many other girls seduced by his charms and thrown away. I wanted to believe this was different – but maybe all the others had too?

Sleeping with Nikolai had broken my two-year drought. My last dalliance was a Fiji disaster. I'd woken up alone on the beach. The experience was never far from my thoughts. I can barely conjure up his face in my mind, but the solo walk of shame from the beach back to the cabin where my five girlfriends, including Jen, were waking from their slumber was a sharp memory. At least then I had kava as an excuse. In Paris, I had been stone-cold sober. Had I abstained for two years only to choose a man that would cause me even more humiliation?

A lot to think about – maybe a swim would clear out the cobwebs and wake me up. Googling the images of said pool, a million selfies came up. I was going to add mine to the collection. That is, if I could work out how to get a good shot.

First world problems hit crisis point taking this selfie. Number one, how to frame the shot so it looks as though I'm alone in the pool – which I was not! Number two, how to float and keep my head above water, without getting the phone wet. Number three, how not to cut off my head and, also, not to include too much floating boob. People must be bringing specialist equipment in to make this happen.

Finding a lounge chair to drip onto and post my selfie was also arduous. Lots of competition for seats musical-chairs style. By the time I got back to my room and dried off, it was time to meet Marine for dinner. With over sixty restaurants in the complex, I'd messaged Marine to meet me at Din Tai Fung as I love their dumplings in Sydney. I managed to score us a table way at the back and Marine gave me the obligatory three kisses when she eventually found me. I had messaged her the directions to the table – what did we do before Google Maps?

After an hour of eating dumplings and talking she hit me with it. 'Something's different Katie. What happened to you this week?'

'Nothing.'

'Bullshit.'

'Nikolai sent me roses when we were in Paris.'

'And?'

'And what?'

'Roses are nice, but that wouldn't have you this distracted.'

'Okay, and he came to Paris to see me.'

'How much of you did he see?'

I blushed and looked down. Marine had her answer.

'You need to keep this quiet. For God's sake, don't let Brenda or Jane know.'

I knew she was right. Not that I was planning on telling anyone. This was the first time I would be meeting my boss Jane in person. I didn't need to give her any more ammunition.

'I really want this job,' I said.

'And you're going to be good at it. Don't throw it away on some player.'

Singapore needed to be about work. Then I would get home and have some breathing space. Nikolai had his championships to focus on and probably more women to screw. As much as I hated to admit it, he had gotten what he wanted. Chances were that was the last I would hear from him. At least there weren't witnesses.

#ChampionsEverywhere, #PostCrisis

The WTA championships were held at the OCBC Arena, built as part of the Singapore Indoor Stadium – all components of a mammoth sporting precinct very close to the city centre, only a couple of stops on the MRT (trains). Staff trained it – players cabbed it. The trains were so clean I'd probably have eaten off the floor if I had dropped something. The arena was immense, it was configured to hold three indoor courts and seat about 7,500 people for our event. It was a little tired inside, having been built in the late '80s, but outside it was imposing. It looked like a piece of concrete origami, but apparently the roof was supposed to give the appearance of a temple. People did come here to worship – worship athletes at their peak, giving their all.

The event was all glam and glitter with a bit of sweat thrown in. Players were constantly receiving gifts from sponsors – including an engraved Tiffany bracelet – as if they couldn't afford to buy them anyway.

Speaking of sweat, it was a constant in Singapore. The practice courts were at an indoor arena only one hundred metres away and the press room was again a short walk from the courts. It didn't matter, you couldn't walk the distance without being drenched in sweat. The only solution was golf carts – here, there and everywhere. I felt like a middle-aged grandmother in one, until I discovered that if you put your foot to the floor, going downhill, you could actually pick up a little speed.

Despite the fact that this event was the cream of the crop, we were still the meat in the sandwich, caught between two opposing forces pulling in different directions. Like forcing two magnets together, we cajoled, pleaded, begged and threatened, eventually reaching some sort of compromise. It was an age-old game in this sport where individuals were expected to act like team players.

I got to meet Jane in person, which was an eye-opener. She was immaculate – in poise, dress and voice. She was a doppelganger for the new Duchess Meghan Markle, right down to her runway-perfect shoes. If it wasn't for the expletive-ridden tirades she directed at me over the phone in Linz, I'd have thought her demenour matched as well. We had one brief sit-down with Marine and Brenda where we focused very heavily on process. Nobody's eyes met and no alluding to staff relations was on the agenda. I can't decide if she's weak or simply strategic.

**

Jane: Mentor or enemy? Too early to tell.

**

Another standout for the week was meeting all the legends. They mix and mingle with the current players in the same lounge and it's a great atmosphere. I got to meet Martina Navratilova, Chris Evert and Billie Jean King. I told BJK that I loved *Battle of the Sexes* – Emma Stone rocked those '70s glasses. That movie should be compulsory viewing for all aspirational female players. It made me want to take up regular playing, which reminded me of my hits with Nikolai.

During the week, I tried my best not to think about him too much. The sixteen-hour days and constant negotiating kept me preoccupied. I did take note of his results and he seemed to be playing well. On my second-last night in Singapore, he was in London playing the semifinals against German Alexander Zverev. We also had matches on court. Sharapova vs Williams and Kerber vs Stephens.

While I typed up statistics, quotes and notes on our matches, I watched the Petrov vs Zverev scores via the TV in our cubicle just off the press room. It was a heated battle, with Zverev prevailing. They shook hands at the net – it seemed friendly enough.

While presiding over a sponsor activity, I noticed my mobile was ringing – a UK number. I let it go to voicemail. It rang three more times in the space of ten minutes. When I finished the activity, I listened to the message on my voicemail. It was from Nikolai, the first I had heard from him since Paris.

'Katie, please call me. I need to talk to you.' He left his hotel phone number in London.

There was also a message to call him via WhatsApp and on Facebook messenger. I wasn't sure what to do. I was curious. I wanted to comfort him. There was no doubt from his voice that he was hurting. I also wanted to stick to my resolve to focus on my career. My decision was put on hold when Sharapova's match hit the middle of the third set. I had to be courtside ASAP.

An hour later back in the press room, my phone rang. It was past midnight; Jane had left for the evening and Marine was God knows where with some player. I answered the phone to Nikolai.

'Did you get my messages?'

'I did. I just arrived and haven't had a chance to call yet.' I whispered.

The WTA office appears private, but the walls don't go all the way to the ceiling. Sound travels to awaiting journalists' ears.

'Is that the truth or were you ignoring me?'

'Don't be paranoid. I saw some of your match. You played well.'

'I played like shit.'

'Okay, you played like shit.'

'That's not funny.'

'I wasn't trying to be funny.'

Our conversation continued in this vein until Nikolai broke.

'I miss you.'

My heart started to beat faster. *If I were another conquest, he wouldn't have said that – would he? I wanted to say 'I miss you too,' but I couldn't give him that much power.*

'It's a very difficult life, with all the travelling.'

'Will you come to Moscow?' I was silent. *How bizarre. Was he crazy? I wanted to see him, but Moscow? The only place I was going was home.*

'I have to go home to Sydney. My sister's getting married and I have to help her prepare.'

'Can I come to Sydney, then?' *What the fuck was going on? He wanted to come to Sydney to be with me. It was too surreal for words.*

'I could train for the Australian Open, acclimatise to the temperature.'

'You could *do* that?'

'I could get a trainer and my coach could come.'

'Are you for real?'

'Yes.'

'Okay, come to Sydney.'

'Can I stay with you?' *I had given my tenants notice in my Bondi flat and my mum was organising for my stuff to come out of storage. Having somewhere for him to stay wasn't the issue.*

'When would you come? For how long?'

'I should go home to Moscow for a week. Maybe I could come to Sydney then?' *Shit, that meant I would have to go home, set up my flat, see my family and explain to them that a Russian superstar was moving in with me.*

'I suppose you could stay with me.'

'Good. I will email you when I get home.' Then he hung up. No goodbye, no sweet nothings, simply a dial tone. I'd managed to get through the entire call without using any names, I'm sure anybody in the vicinity wouldn't have made head or tail of the conversation.

Scenarios ran through my head. Explaining Nikolai's appearance in my life to my family, my friends and, oh my God, the press. The chances of the Australian media not noticing Petrov practising in Sydney and tracing him back to me were slim at best. Damage control, or preferably a damage avoidance plan, was required.

#GDayMate, #PostCrisis

The best thing about the championships being in Singapore was the relative proximity to Oz. The moment I boarded the Qantas jet, the flight attendants' Aussie accents ignited a longing for home. Like Dorothy, I understood – there was no place like it. Unfortunately, clicking my heels wasn't going to help. I had to sit with my own thoughts in a cramped seat for eight hours.

Despite being treated like VIPs when we were on the tour, until you were a vice-president, economy class was the only option in the air. Compared to the plane cabin, the claustrophobic indoor tennis arenas seemed palatial. About six hours was my limit before the wriggles kicked in. Every way I moved, my butt hurt. Nobody's arse is designed to sit for more than a couple of hours – no matter how much padding you have.

As I sat watching the disproportionate image of our plane inching over the planet on my tiny seatback TV screen, my yet-to-be-cleared dinner pinned me in. The remnants of a plastic meal eaten with plastic implements, which I had finished thirty minutes earlier, made it impossible to twist, or reach my headphones or book. The flight attendant seemed to move at a snail's pace through the cabin collecting the trays. The smile she had painted on her face as we boarded had disintegrated into a grimace.

With my dinner removed, I joined the queue for the bathroom. There was always a race after being freed from the tray-chained seats. It only took a few minutes for my turn and, once in the tiny cubicle, after struggling with completing the essentials without touching any of the overused surfaces, I wondered how people even considered joining the mile-high club. You wouldn't shine a black light in here, unless you wanted nightmares.

Back in my seat, my headphones secured, I watched romantic comedies back to back. By the end I was confusing storylines from the first film with the last. Why do people always seem to fall in love with characters that are dying? It seemed to be an epidemic.

When I landed in Sydney, Mum, Dad and Lou were at the airport. Seeing their safe faces I struggled to hold back tears. My mother's hug lasted too long and my father's hand patted my back as if he was trying to burp me. Lou started to laugh. We broke apart and all joined in the laughter. Walking to the car, my mother held my hand, cutting off the circulation a little. My father wheeled my bag and Lou talked non-stop about what had happened in my absence.

It was a warm and sunny day at the end of November. My family, seated around the dining table eating Mum's famous chicken salad sandwiches, were all talking at once. Trying to take in all the stories, I could not help smiling. I was home.

I wanted to hear about Lou and Dave's wedding plans. Lou told me they thought this time next year would be best. They both wanted a spring wedding and wanted me to be there. They were scouting venues beyond the golf club, much to my parents' disgust. The destination wedding was proving too hard as they both wanted as many of their friends and family around as possible. The venue front-runner was the Watsons Bay barracks, which they had tentatively booked. It would be cocktails and canapés and dancing, rather than a formal sit-down affair. As Lou talked, my mother cringed. I'm pretty sure my father's main concern was the budget. He wanted to pay for the wedding.

They had held off on their engagement party because of my absence. I felt touched that my erratic movements were being factored into the equation of their most special days. That's when Lou informed me that the party was being held at my parents' place next Saturday night. 'You better get a dress,' she said. Shit, that was six days away. I had to get my flat into shape, move in and figure out the Nikolai thing. Luckily he wouldn't arrive until after the party.

That night I slept like the dead. No discernible dreams, no interruptions. I was staying in my childhood room for a couple of nights until my apartment was ready. Mum had converted the room into an office, but she had left a day bed. Although this space didn't look like my room, it still felt like it. The room used to be painted peach, now it was 'Antique White USA'. I always hated that peach. It was the result of a miscommunication between Mum and me that haunted my teenage years. Whenever I see the colour, I feel nauseous.

Buoyed by the absence of the pukey peach, I spent the next day at home, sleeping in, having brekkie with my parents and generally being fussed over. My mother needed grandchildren. All day she presented me with treats. She baked scones. They were crunchy on the outside and fluffy and warm on the inside. It wasn't all bad.

Cleaning day arrived. My tenants had moved out and Mum had organised for movers to bring my possessions out of storage tomorrow. Today was the day to make my apartment habitable. Absence makes the heart grow fond; accordingly, my mother and Lou had agreed to help me clean. We drove to Bondi with a car full of lotions, potions and paper towels – ready for anything.

We braced ourselves upon entering – but were pleasantly surprised. There was work to be done, but nothing that three women couldn't knock over. Lou had a kick-arse portable Bose speaker synced to her phone and we blasted familiar tunes though the apartment as we worked. Too much ABBA was included in the playlist and we shouted along attempting to carry the tunes. After we finished, it was such a beautiful sunny day, I asked if they wanted to grab some food and go for a walk. They both declined as the next job was preparing for the weekend's party. I said I would be home later to help. As my sister left, she whispered to me, 'Have you spoken to Jen?' I shook my head.

As soon as they were out the door, I phoned.

'I'm back.'

'No fucking way.'

'Yep, and in Bondi, no less. Can I meet you at Gusto in twenty minutes?'

'Why don't I come over to you?'

'Sorry darling, no food and, most importantly, no coffee.'

There was dead air for about thirty seconds.

'Um, okay, I'll see you at Gusto.'

She hugged me for over a minute. I hugged back. I asked if it was okay for her to be here on a workday; she swatted the comment away and hugged me again. Jen looked older. She had gotten some colour during the spring, but her skin looked sallow. Not wanting to get her on the defensive, I kept my observation to myself and we ordered coffee and muffins. 'Let's take the booty back to your place,' she said.

As we wandered the five-minute trip back to my apartment, Jen's head was down. It was a bright sunny day, so the hat and sunglasses made sense, but the hat was enormous and she seemed to be hiding from more than the sun.

We parked ourselves on the floor of my sunroom, given I was sans furniture until tomorrow. It was hard to believe that only six months ago we sat in this same empty space creating @NQ30Love. The hat and glasses came off, her shoulders dropped and she started picking at her muffin. The muffins didn't compare to pain au chocolat from a Paris boulangerie, but I didn't think that needed to be said. For a while we nattered about meaningless stuff. Who was dating whom etc. I told her about my jet lag, Singapore, work, my boss, but not Nikolai. She was on the non-disclosure train as well. How did this happen? We used to be able to tell each other everything. I decided to be more open in the hope she would too.

'Nikolai Petrov came to see me in Paris.'

'No shit – was it romantic?' Wow, Jen had changed. I had assumed her first question would be 'did you do it?'

'It was. I learned a lot about him. He surprised me, opening up the way he did.'

'Are you in love?'

'I don't know. He's been with a lot of women. I don't want to delude myself.'

'Katie, you're special. But be careful.'

'Me be careful? Coming from you, that is really weird. Are you okay?'

'It's nothing.'

'I don't believe you.'

She looked away. Then looked down at her lap. Almost instantaneously the floodgates opened. 'I thought he was the one.'

Through the tears, I learnt that Jen made a sex tape with a guy called Brad.

'I'd been working out really hard. You know, all that Pilates. I sort of thought it would be nice to have a record of my young hot self, for when I'm old.'

Shit. Couldn't she have just taken a bathroom selfie of herself in a bikini?

Unfortunately, Brad thought she looked hot as well. So hot, in fact, he thought others should see it. He posted it online.

'I tried to laugh it off. Acting really cool about it. It worked for Kim Kardashian. But guys started trolling me. Talking about my body and my moves. They made me sick. I shut down all my social sites the same day, but I still can't get some of the comments and images out of my head.'

Jen had to change her phone numbers and she couldn't step foot in Reveal nightclub or anywhere else without people staring. I told her it would blow over, but she moved in a small circle of people and this was going to follow her. Brad had been pressured to take it down, but I was sure it wouldn't be too hard to find the images online.

We decided that she and I would hang out in my flat for a few days. I had no inclination to go partying. We made a plan for her to help me cook dinner tomorrow night. Tonight was a family dinner, but Jen had been honorary family forever. I texted Mum, 'Is it okay to bring Jen tonight?' She responded in the affirmative.

That evening, when Jen and I arrived at the front door, Mum gave us both a hug. Clueless Dad kissed my cheek and greeted Jen with a 'How's tricks?' Jen, Lou and I squirmed. Lou gave Jen an extra squeezy hug.

Dave came over to help with the party preparation. Like my Dad, he wasn't very useful, but he kept us all entertained and laughing. Lou, Dave and Dad were planning short speeches at the engagement party and all three practised their sage words while Jen, Mum and I packed hostess gifts. Dave's speech was all fun. There was plenty of light-hearted teasing of his fiancée and not too much schmaltz. He didn't need it. Every time he looked at Lou, you could see how much he loved her. They finished each other's sentences, laughed at each other's jokes and were in sync. For me it was equal parts nauseating and heartwarming. For Jen, it all may have been nauseating.

Lou was conscious of Jen and tried to tone down the lovers' show. When Lou said she still felt butterflies every time she saw Dave, she made sure Jen was out of earshot. I understood the butterflies feeling, but couldn't imagine slotting Nikolai into this scene. In one week, he'd be in Oz – whether I was ready or not.

#MeCasaSuCasa, #NQLoveCrisis

After the storage truck dropped off my furniture and boxes, Mum, Lou and I reassembled my apartment. We arranged my furniture. I took a few pics and uploaded them, #ReassemblingMyLife. I had missed the light of Sydney. Somehow it was brighter and more uplifting than anywhere else I had travelled. I intended to spend time on the beach over my couple of weeks off and soak in the sun – with plenty of sunblock.

Jen joined us during her lunch break. She helped put away jars, pots, pans and utensils in the compact kitchen. The storage boxes were like little gifts. I kept being surprised as a cushion, picture or ornament appeared. My mother promised, as an early Christmas pressie, we could hit the shops for some new accessories. I had collected a few trinkets to put on bookshelves and the walls to remind me of the great places I'd been. A Statue of Liberty snow globe, a print from Rome and a miniature sculpture of *The Kiss* by Rodin.

By early afternoon the flat was a home again. The only thing missing was food. Mum offered me the car for a supermarket stock-up. She and Lou were also suddenly busy. I accepted this solo task. It would be a novelty to go grocery shopping after such a long time.

Two hours at Coles supermarket cured me of that novelty, but I had soap, toilet paper and food to show for the struggle. As I put my groceries away, a text pinged through to my phone. It was Nikolai. 'Can you talk?' It would have been morning in Moscow, so I sent him a 'yes' text.

Two minutes later the phone rang. 'I want to come to Sydney today.'

'Hello Nikolai, how are you?'

'I am wanting to come to Sydney.'

'I'm very well, thank you.' As stunned as I was by the statement, I was going to teach him to communicate like a human being. He could be such a gentleman, but he was shit on the phone.

He took the hint and exhaled down the phone. 'I'm pleased you are well. I would like to see that in person.'

'My sister is having her engagement party this Saturday.'

'Thank you, I would love to come.' *Shit. I was trying to use that as an excuse for getting him to delay his arrival.*

'The thing is, Nikolai, I haven't really told my family about you yet.'

'Tell them tonight and I will see you tomorrow. It takes more than one day for me to get there.' I was silent. Jen was coming to dinner tonight and I didn't want to tell the family on the phone. But as much as his behaviour infuriated me, I wanted to see him.

'Fine, see you tomorrow.'

'Do you have a car?'

'No.'

'Okay, I will get an Uber. What is your address?' I told him the address and asked him to message me his flight details. He hung up without any pleasantries. I planned to put him through phone etiquette role plays when he got to Sydney, unless we found something else to occupy us.

It was 5p.m. and Jen was coming over at 6.30. I texted her to say I might be a little late as I had to go and speak to my parents.

Without a car, it was off to the bus stop. Waiting for the 324 service to my parents' house, I lovingly recalled the second-hand Honda Civic I sold to finance my tennis expedition. Thirty minutes later, when I arrived, they were getting ready to go out and meet friends. I told them I had some news and asked them to sit down. They looked concerned.

'I'm not pregnant or sick or anything.'

They exhaled.

'I've met someone and he's coming to stay with me.'

My Dad squirmed in his seat. My Mum put her hand on his leg.

'Is he someone special, Katie?'

'Yes, Mum. I think so. He plays tennis.'

'Is he any good?' Trust my father to ask that.

'It's Nikolai Petrov.'

My mother sat back on her seat and my father managed a 'fuck'.

'Do you think Lou would mind if he came to the party?'

They looked at each other and then back at me. 'You'll have to ask her, but I can't see why not,' said Mum. I figured the news would sink in overnight and more questions would follow. I asked if they could drop me home on the way to dinner to avoid the bus.

In the car they attempted to make small talk and avoided asking questions. As we pulled up out the front my father turned around to face me. 'Be careful, Katie. He has a reputation.' I leant forward and kissed each of them. What could I say? My Dad was right.

Jen was waiting on the stoop and we went into the flat together.

'What's up?' she asked.

'Nikolai is coming to Sydney tomorrow.'

'Shit. That was quick.'

I filled her in while I poured us each a bucket-sized glass of wine.

'It must mean something that he's coming all the way here to see you.'

I nodded. Training in Sydney and acclimatising was not a bad idea, but I felt sure he wouldn't be doing it if I weren't here. I hoped that, anyway. We drank and talked, avoiding all mention of the tape. Tonight was not about regret. Tonight was about camaraderie. I told her about Paris and how I had felt seeing him walk out of the lobby. I told her about my resolve to focus on my work and how that was only ten days ago. I wondered if I had a touch of schizophrenia?

'Do you hear voices?' Jen laughed.

'Only my own, but it's so fucking indecisive.'

'Maybe you need more information to make a decision?'

We drank and made pasta. It felt surreal to cook. Something simple, made exactly how we wanted. After my weeks in Italy I had learnt one thing. Australians overcook pasta. I experimented by boiling for two minutes less than the packet indicated. It worked – *al dente.* Something concrete had come from my trip after all.

#HolyFuckHeIsHere, #NQLoveCrisis

Nikolai was due to arrive at 6p.m. He would take a couple more hours to clear customs and immigration and reach me. Although I doubted he would be flying economy, he would still be tired, hungry and in need of a shower. My shower was over the bath and not made for two like the shower in Paris. Nikolai was a tall man. I hoped he would fit.

I okayed Nikolai's attendance at the party with Lou and then preoccupied myself with shopping for an outfit. Lou told me she was wearing green silk. So green was out. I didn't want to wear black, because everyone would be. I found a divine sexy red number, but it had upstage the bride written all over it. At the giving-up point, I tried on a v-necked aubergine Sacha Drake dress that rocked. I paired it with new red pumps that sent my bank account into minus. Some fabulous earrings would be perfect if I could find them at the two-dollar shop. Perhaps Jen would have something I could borrow?

Back at the apartment I cleaned, rearranged and cleaned again. Then I fluffed, shifted and shuffled. I cleared out a small section of my built-in wardrobe for Nikolai's clothes. Sharing my closet felt very grown-up, as long as he didn't take up too much space.

Early evening my phone pinged. Nikolai was on his way in an Uber. I asked if he was hungry. He texted back 'always'. I wasn't sure if he meant for food, but started to cook anyway. I wanted to make something homely and settled on pre-cooked lasagna and salad. I managed to remove the lasagna from the give-away packaging before putting it in the oven. When the doorbell chimed, I had set the table, and two glasses of red wine were ready to go.

I checked my reflection. Hair good, makeup good, clothes good, nose clean and I opened the door. As I looked up at his face, I could not fathom how anybody could look so beautiful after a thirty-hour journey. He reached through the doorway and picked me up. He hugged me, carrying me into the room. Then he kissed me. That Rodin sculpture had nothing on this.

When my heart restarted, he grabbed his bags and dumped them in the living room. I asked if he wanted a tour. He laughed.

'This is it, right?'

'No, there's a kitchen, a bathroom and a bedroom.'

'Show me the bedroom.' I laughed and wagged my finger.

'Don't you want dinner? I made us lasagna.' He looked at me, then through the door leading to the bedroom, then at the kitchen.

'We can eat later.' With that, I was in his arms again. This time being carried like a bride over the threshold of my own bedroom. He threw me down on the bed and joined me. I was not shy. I had missed him. After Paris, I had done some research into the female orgasm. Apparently, it was not common to have ten in a row – only a slight exaggeration. I wondered if there was a Guinness Book of Records entry for it. Nikolai seemed intent on assisting me to become a contender.

We ate reheated lasagna and drank wine in my bed. He fed me and I him. It was like a bad movie, but it felt good.

It was no surprise that I did not get much sleep that night. Nikolai was jet lagged and his body had no idea of time or place. It did not affect his performance. It must have been around 9a.m. before we finally climbed out of bed. I suggested a walk on the beach to introduce him to Bondi. Nikolai wanted a shower first.

I showed him the shower. 'Do you want to join me?' he asked.

'Do you think we'll both fit?' He nodded.

I don't know how many times he hit his head, but he didn't seem to care. He hogged the water. I didn't care.

Dressed and with combed wet hair we strolled along Bondi Beach under the morning sun. 'Swimming is great recovery,' he said. I asked when he would start training and he told me his coach would arrive on Monday. They had located an Aussie fitness trainer and hitting partner to work with and would train at the City Community Tennis facility near Central station. It had upgraded courts like those at Olympic Park. Nikolai had done a deal with the owner and had organised to rent a car and drive each day. His coach would stay in a hotel nearby. He had it all sorted. No flies on him, as we Aussies say.

The true story was that Nikolai was a big name in tennis and people wanted to work with him. It looked good on their resumé. If you combine a big name and deep pockets, things are going to come together for you without a problem. Not to mention his agent Mario would have been orchestrating the lot. His results on the court did not come so easily. He was going to work hard to get what he wanted – a first Grand Slam title.

We stopped at a café for breakfast. All that exercise was fuel for the appetite. We ordered bacon and eggs and tucked in. The waitress did several double takes when looking at Nikolai. I wasn't sure if she recognised him or if it was that he was so goddamn gorgeous. Either way, she needed to get on with her job.

We ate, laughed and talked and people watched. Nikolai loved watching the crowd walk by. He said it was because it was normally the other way around.

Despite his years in Germany, there was no missing Nikolai's Russian accent. He fought hard to keep it. After only a month in the US, I had started to roll my r's and speak with a twang. That had all disappeared now. As soon as I boarded the Qantas flight, all my vowels flattened – the Aussie salute.

I have always liked the Russian accent. There is safety in their definite tone. Inhaling his voice, I was reminded that Bondi was a Russian enclave. Petrov was a big name in Russian tennis and they were more likely to recognise him than Aussies. This could cause us trouble. I broached it with him. 'It's only a matter of time. Let's enjoy ourselves until it happens.' He was fine with being recognised, resigned to it. On the other hand, for me, there were repercussions. I didn't think my bosses at the WTA would be too impressed by me being 'papped' with Petrov. Not to mention my great friend Brenda. I needed a strategy for this eventuality.

**

The next step in this journey was to introduce Nikolai to my family. It was Friday and the party was tomorrow. No time like the present.

#StarFuckers, #NQLoveCrisis

I had never seen anything like the performance Nikolai put on for my parents. My mother had invited us over for drinks – we all thought dinner might be too intense. Nikolai asked questions about what my father did, praised my mother's canapés and complimented the house. Dad showed Nikolai his golf swing and asked for tips. I explained that Nikolai played tennis and then he casually added that he also played golf from scratch. Dad started patting him on the back and suggesting a round of golf at the club. Mum wasn't much better, fawning all over him. It was cringe-worthy. I never imagined my parents as the types to be starstruck.

After an hour, Mum invited us to stay to dinner. I said we had reservations. Nikolai suggested we cancel our booking. Dinner with the parents, it was. Mum had prepared a fabulous meal for her and Dad, one that easily stretched to four servings. She wasn't much of a poker player, but she had played me tonight.

After the first course, my parents started to be themselves. Nikolai asked questions about my childhood and Dad was the first to mention my teenage crush on Russian player Marat Safin. They were on a roll and Nikolai loved it. There was nowhere to hide, so I joined in. The wine helped to disintegrate my embarrassment.

I managed to get us out the door before Mum pulled out the baby photos. Nikolai took my arm as we walked down the stairs to his rented black Mercedes. He opened the car door for me and took the driver's seat.

'Your family is very nice.'

'They were a bit embarrassing.'

'I was not embarrassed.'

'No, I meant embarrassing for me.'

'I could introduce you to Safin.' I could see a grin starting to spread across his face.

'No thanks, we've already met.' *In my teen dreams.*

This man was way too confident, smiling to himself as he drove. He'd only been here two days, yet he knew the way home with the minimum of assistance.

Despite my ego's bruising, that night was the first time I ever instigated sex. Nikolai wasn't difficult to convince. My few previous sexual partners had always taken the lead. It felt liberating to have somebody I wanted respond to my needs. Each time we made love, I was able to direct him towards what pleasured me the most. Before Nikolai, I had enjoyed sex, but was also frightened of it. The fear of releasing myself to someone else, without judgment, had been ever-present. I had only had one orgasm. With my first partner Jake. Since then, I had pulled back from the brink, terrified of losing control. I faked my orgasms rather than giving into them. Now my orgasms felt like rolling off the edge of a cliff into space. My body shuddered and my mind fizzled; then, like a short circuit, for a few seconds there was nothing. Perfect nothingness.

After, I was lying in his arms, happy, comfortable, wanted and alive. I tried to look into his mind to see what he felt. That door was closed. Not wanting him to exit the building, I refrained from the 'Where do you see this relationship going?' and similarly desperate questions. Instead I was trying to gain something by osmosis. He was here, wasn't he? He met my parents and was coming to my sister's engagement party. That had to mean something?

Next morning, I presented him with another challenge.

'I have to meet my friend Jen for breakfast. She's letting me borrow earrings to wear tonight.' He didn't respond.

'You're welcome to join us.' No response.

I got up and showered alone. I was wrapped in a towel cleaning my teeth when he came into the bathroom. I could see in the mirror that he was naked. He walked up behind me and kissed me on the head before getting in the shower. I went into the bedroom to give him some privacy. I was dressed and getting ready to leave when he came out and said, 'Wait five minutes and I will come with you.' I nodded and went into the living room. Did he want to meet my friend or did he want breakfast? I didn't care. He wanted to be part of my life and that had to be good. I texted Jen 'save three seats for breakfast'. She'd better be cool. I didn't want everyone to behave like star fuckers around him.

We walked hand in hand to Gusto. At the cross streets, Nikolai lent down to kiss me. I started to walk on red. Nikolai pulled me back.

Jen proved herself worthy of our lifetime friendship, showing no more interest in Nikolai than she would if he was an accountant from the North Shore. He seemed impressed by this. He asked questions about her and her life in Sydney. We ate muffins and drank coffee. Nikolai said that Australian coffee is almost as good as Italian. He told us both that he had only played the Sydney tournament twice, but had always felt at home here. I wasn't sure if this was a bit of spin or the truth. I did not feel the same way about Moscow.

Jen pulled out the earrings I wanted to borrow. They were perfect, and we discussed how they had the right amount of bling and the red would set off the purple hues in my dress to perfection. Nikolai stared into space.

After about an hour, Nikolai said he had to go. It came as news to me that he was meeting with his new trainer at the tennis courts and would be back that afternoon. I had given him the spare key to my apartment, which he had attached to the rental-car key ring. I had planned to take him on a tour of the city and some of my favourite spots. Of course, I hadn't told him this and put on my best 'have a good time' face. He kissed me on the lips, Jen on the cheek and strode off towards the car. Jen burst out laughing when he was out of sight.

'Katie, you should see your face. Like a kid who's had their Christmas present taken away.'

'Was it that obvious?'

'You want me to say no, don't you?'

'Yes.'

'Okay, no.'

'Shit.' Jen laughed again.

We ordered another coffee. It was Saturday and Jen didn't have to go to work. Knowing me too well, she asked what I had planned for Nikolai today. I told her and she admitted no interest in going with me on a tourist tour. Instead, we settled on hitting the shops.

We decided on a fantasy shopping tour. The one where you go into all the shops you can't afford, try things on and pretend you're going to buy. Then change your mind, leaving broken-hearted sales people. For this to be effective, you have to dress up to the nines. Thirty minutes later, we had both dressed in our best clothes and heels and were on a bus to the city. We had a plan of attack, David Jones couture level, Dolce and Gabbana, Versace, Gary Castles shoes and a trip down Castlereagh Street popping in and out of the diamond stores.

I tried on a Hervé Léger bandage dress. I couldn't breath and there was no possibility of sitting down, but we decided I looked amazing. It would be three thousand dollars well spent, if I had it.

After two hours of teasing shop assistants and no bags to show for it, we decided to try on engagement rings and tiaras. As we rounded the corner into Castlereagh Street, Jen spotted him. Nikolai was walking down the street towards us. Instinctively we ducked into a shop and watched from a window.

'Didn't he say he was going to the courts?' I asked Jen.

'Maybe he said the city?'

'No, he was meeting his trainer at the courts. I thought it was odd that he was wearing jeans.'

'He looks hot in jeans.'

'He looks hot in everything. But he wouldn't work out in jeans.'

'Katie, it's probably nothing. Let's go and say hi.'

'No,' I said, through gritted teeth. 'We leave it.' We watched him jump in a cab and disappear out of sight before exiting the store. I didn't feel like playing anymore.

'I'm hungry. Are you hungry?' I asked, not waiting for a response. Minutes later I was demolishing a McDonald's hamburger and fries. Jen picked at some of my fries.

'Are you sure you want to eat that?' she asked.

'Yes,' I answered, with my mouth full. Jen looked away while I stuffed my face.

The bus back to Bondi seemed longer than the trip in. I fidgeted with my Opal card until Jen removed it. When we alighted, Jen gave me a hug. 'Don't forget tonight's about your sister.' She left me with my selfishness. I had been an absent family member for the best part of a year. In the five days I had been back, my sister had helped me get my flat in order and accepted my revelation about Nikolai without judgment. On the other hand, I had gone shopping and shacked up with my new boyfriend. My thoughts about tonight's event had centred on what I was going to wear and managing Nikolai.

It was time to be the proud big sister and do my best to ensure Lou and Dave had a brilliant engagement party.

#TheGlitteryTruth, #NQLoveCrisis

Back at my apartment I found Nikolai sitting on the couch reading a book. Even with my new resolve to focus on my sister, I couldn't help but niggle him.

'Good session with your trainer?' He grunted something and came over to kiss me. I did my best to reciprocate.

'Is something wrong?'

'No, I'm just focused on my sister. We have to leave in an hour. I want to be there when the guests start arriving.' He nodded. I went to the bathroom to shower. He read my body language and did not follow.

I showered, washed my hair and tried to focus on getting ready. Nikolai's city trip kept popping into my brain. I pushed the thought away. Like a mosquito buzzing around my head, it kept returning.

When I was ready, I checked myself in the mirror. More than passable. Then I turned and saw Nikolai. He had on a grey designer suit, with an open white shirt and glossy black shoes. I wasn't going to be the one upstaging the bride.

'Where did you get the suit?'

'I brought it with me. You told me about the party on the phone.'

So I did. I was hoping this was his excuse for being in the city, although buying a suit would hardly be a secret.

We caught a cab to my parents. Nikolai directed the driver. This pissed me off. Which Nikolai either didn't notice or chose to ignore. When the cab driver pulled up, other guests had already arrived. I didn't wait for Nikolai to open my door; I was supposed to be greeting guests. He stopped me from going up the stairs, holding my arm.

'We're late.' I managed.

'I'm sorry, but before you go in, I wanted to give you this.' He pulled a box out of his inside jacket pocket. It had Cerrone printed on it.

'Open it,' he said.

I took the box, undid the ribbon and opened it. Inside were a pair of diamond drop earrings. They must have been three carats each. I stroked the diamonds. They were smooth and brilliant. The street-lights illuminated them and the colours refracted around the box. Blue, green, red and purple – total bling overload.

'I thought you might want to wear them.' I managed a nod. I wanted to wear them. Once on, I would never take them off. I wanted to be buried in them. I fumbled taking off my borrowed earrings, replacing them with the sparklers.

'Thank you,' I mumbled.

'You're welcome.'

'When did you get them?' I couldn't help myself.

'Today in the city. I didn't meet with my trainer. I wanted it to be a surprise.' I threw my arms around him. Not for the diamonds, for the truth. I needed truth from him more than a million carats of diamonds. Not that I mentioned hiding in the street watching him. We walked up the stairs arm in arm, my head resting on his shoulder.

The decorations were beautiful. Mum and Lou had strung fairy lights all around the front of the house and the garden. Torches lit the way to the party site under a marquee. Extended family, life-long friends and Lou and Dave's current posse were in attendance. I introduced Nikolai as my friend staying from Russia. He patted me on the butt and whispered, 'I prefer it when you call me Nicky.' I only call him Nicky when we're umm, you know, having sex. It's much easier to moan 'Yes, yes, *yes*, Nicky! More, more, *more*, Nicky!' When screamed at the crucial moment – 'Nickyyyyyyyyy'.

The highlight of the night was the speeches. Dad spoke beautifully about Lou as a child. He resurrected sections of her twenty-first speech, which played well a second time. He also made a big deal out of welcoming Dave into the family. He talked about the sport they watched together. I hadn't been aware of how much time the two spent hanging out.

Dave continued on with the speech I had heard him rehearse earlier in the week. He was charming, loving and funny. The biggest surprise was Lou's speech. She had definitely been holding out on us all during rehearsal. Lou talked about what she had learnt about love from our parents. She talked about the importance of friendship and trust. When we were all reaching for the tissues, she finished with a poem she had written for Dave. The poem was called 'Beloved Friend'. David is a Hebrew name which means beloved or friend and the poem talked about how Dave was both to her. Passion and friendship – the perfect package.

I had no idea my sister wrote poems. It seemed a lot happened in the world of my friends and family that I was oblivious to.

We drank champagne and chatted to all the familiar faces. A few people noticed my earrings. I felt a little conspicuous and thought about saying they were fake to play it down, but Nikolai was always around.

My Aunt Sarah was the first to broach the Nikolai subject. 'My you're a strapping young man,' she said, as I tried to burrow under the floor. I introduced them. Nikolai was his polite self; Aunt Sarah took him by the arm and proceeded to monopolise him, using the dessert bar as an excuse. She wanted to know everything. How had we met, his family, his job – I had neglected to mention the tennis thing – and what he thought of our little country. He deflected most and kept looking to me. I smiled back and kept talking to a group of Lou's friends I hadn't seen in ages. Aunt Sarah was a force to be reckoned with. I was a coward and figured he could fend for himself. Dave performed the extraction. Fearless as ever, he moved in with another friend who he hooked onto Aunt Sarah and manoeuvred Nikolai away.

As the night progressed, I kept expecting somebody to recognise Nikolai, but out of context nobody seemed to twig. I managed to remove us from as many photo ops as possible. The more that were uploaded, the more likely somebody, maybe even Facebook, would tag him and the jig would be up. To cover my tracks, I posted a couple of pics of my sister, parents and the happy couple on my social pages.

A few people took to the makeshift dance floor. Nikolai asked me to dance, but I was tired and wanted to watch my sister and Dave dance. We sat quietly sipping our drinks. I was thinking about trust and friendship when my mind started to wander. When Jen and I spotted Nikolai it had been at least three hours since he left us at Bondi. Also he had left in the car and we saw him get into a cab. The earrings wouldn't have taken three hours to purchase. What else had he being doing? So I asked, 'Nikolai, I love my earrings. Where did you get them?'

'In the city.'

'Oh yeah, you said that. Did you do anything else while you were there?'

'No. Why? Do you want more jewellery?'

'No, of course not, I thought you might have had some business or something.'

'Nyet.' When he answered in Russian, it was always the end of the conversation.

Back at my flat we made love. I kept the earrings on.

#SurfsUp, #NQLoveCrisis

A sunny Sunday morning was the ideal time to surf. I roused Nikolai into his board shorts and we walked the short distance from my flat to the beach. The water was crystal clear and just cold enough to provide relief from the heat that was already building up. We spread our towels out between the flags and ran into the water. That's when I found out that the perfect man next to me was not good at everything. I dove under wave after wave. Clearing the froth and skimming the sand until I was out far enough to feel free. I looked behind me and Nikolai was not much deeper than his ankles. He didn't seem interested in venturing any further. I waved to him and he waved back. I indicated for him to join me, but he stayed rooted to the spot. Surely he could swim?

I decided not to make a big deal out of it and kept body-surfing until all the cobwebs were blown out of my head. When I came in, Nikolai was lying on his towel.

'That was so refreshing. Don't you like to swim?'

'It is not my thing.'

'Do you want to learn?'

'Nyet.'

I looked up and two boys were staring at us. They must have been about thirteen and they were in boardies about three feet from our towels. They kept looking at us, then back at each other, mustering up courage. Finally, they asked, 'Are you Nikolai Petrov?'

'Yes.'

'Oh my God. We are like your biggest fans. We are number one and two on the tennis team at school.'

'Congratulations.'

'How can we get bigger serves? We want to serve at two hundred kilometres per hour like you.'

'Work on your leg drive.'

'Wow. Amazing. The leg drive, that's the secret?'

'Yes.'

One ran off, leaving the other standing and staring. A minute later the first one was back with a crumpled piece of paper and a pen. They didn't even have to ask, Nikolai got up and signed it. They hounded him into a selfie – he had to bend down as he was at least a head taller than them. Then they were off, patting each other on the back as they jogged back to their families.

The two seemed harmless enough until I realised they had highlighted the presence of someone interesting on the beach. Soon a crowd was gathering, staring and whispering. Nikolai and I knew it was time to go. As we left the beach, several teenagers trailed Nikolai getting autographs. I'm not even sure they all knew who was signing their various scraps of paper. Attempts at selfies and photobombs were comical. At one point I was almost tripped up by a young girl diving in front of me.

Back at my place, we decided to have breakfast inside.

'Is the leg drive really the secret?' I asked.

'There is no secret. But the drive is important for speed.'

'Good to know, I'll work on mine.'

'Practice starts tomorrow. We can work on your serve then.'

How cute, he thought I was going to practise with him.

'Actually, I think I'll spend some time with Jen.'

'You have to come. You are my udachu.'

'Your what?'

'My udachu. You're my charm for luck.'

How sweet. He thought I was lucky. I smiled at him, but he didn't smile back. His eyebrows were raised and his brow creased.

'You must come to practice.'

'Okay, if it's that important, I'll come.'

His face relaxed and he went back to eating breakfast. I wasn't sure whether I should be flattered or concerned. Tennis players were superstitious beings. Bouncing the ball the same number of times before they served, not stepping on the lines, wearing the same clothes and other various nutty behaviours. I wanted to be more than part of a ritual.

After breakfast I asked Nikolai if he minded me catching up with Jen and some friends today – since I would be practising tomorrow. I told him he was welcome to join, but he said he would be happy relaxing at home. It made sense for him to want some quiet time. It had been pretty crazy since he landed four days ago.

I met Jen at her share house in Bondi. She was dressed for the beach. We sat in the living area chatting.

'Nikolai wants me to practise with him. He says I'm good luck.'

'That's sweet.'

'It is, isn't it?'

'Of course.'

She was right. Silly me. I told her about the party and Lou's speech.

'I didn't even know she wrote poems.'

'You don't know a lot.'

I asked Jen how she was handling things. Did she have anyone else to talk to? We were interrupted by the arrival of her flatmate Mike. As he walked through the room, he said, 'Hi Jen, seen any good movies lately?' With that he gave us an exaggerated wink and walked into his room. Jen blushed and put her head in her hands. She shared the house with two guys and another girl. They had all seen her online performance and felt it was their duty to mercilessly comment on various aspects of it. She was living in hell.

'You have to move.'

She shook her head. Her name was on the lease and there was another six months to run. She would have to convince all three flatmates to move and get new ones. Probability zero. At this point, going to work each day was her only escape. Nobody there knew about her new-found fame – or at least they hadn't mentioned it – making it her last refuge.

'Come and stay on my couch for a few days. At least you'll get a break from these shitheads.'

'I'm sure Nikolai would love that.'

'He'd understand.'

'Don't tell him about the... you know.'

I would definitely not tell him. Nikolai would judge her. I knew it. If I hadn't known Jen, I would have judged her too. I didn't say that; I didn't need to. Jen knew me.

We packed her a bag to cover the next few days and walked back to my apartment. We heard talking as I opened the door. Nikolai was on the phone speaking in Russian. When he saw us, he hung up. I told him about Jen staying. He shrugged his shoulders and went into the bedroom.

'He's thrilled,' I said to Jen. We both laughed and I called out to Nikolai to let him know we were off to the beach. He grunted something unintelligible back.

Jen and I spent the rest of the day between the beach and the promenade. We massacred the diet gods with ice cream and burgers. We talked about old times, particularly those when we worked together at the real estate agent that was still Jen's sanctuary. It's funny. I was sure I hated that job, but when I look back, we did seem to have a lot of fun.

It was late afternoon when Jen showed me the photos. It seemed Nikolai's beach trip this morning was already lighting up social media. We had been 'papped'. Lucky for me, my face was obscured by a beach hat, sunglasses and the angle of the shots – even Mum would struggle to ID me. The other good news was that I looked pretty hot, with just the right amount of side boob – tasteful not trashy – and walking on the sand made my tummy, legs and butt look tight. Now people knew Nikolai was in Sydney, I needed to wear lots of hats and maintain a photo-wide distance from my man.

#TheArtofPractise, #NQLoveCrisis

That evening we took turns showering off the salt and sand and got dressed up for a night out. Nikolai agreed to come to dinner with us. We went to the local sushi train and gobbled up salmon and tuna. Nikolai ate in silence, while we giggled and people watched. I wanted Jen to feel safe and have a night free from thinking about that damn movie. The next stop was the Hotel Bondi.

The hotel is a sand-coloured castle on the beachfront. It's a favourite haunt of travellers and has recently undergone an expensive makeover. Formally seedy, now it looks like butter wouldn't melt in its mouth.

We started in the main bar. I was drinking vodka, lime and sodas and Jen was on the G&Ts. Nikolai stuck to beer. Every now and then he would look at his watch, stretch and yawn. After around four drinks, Jen and I thought it was time to try our vocal chords at karaoke. We had heard the frightening sounds emanating from the nightclub next door and decided the punters needed rescuing.

We dragged Nikolai, one on each bulging bicep, into the room. It was clear he wasn't going to sing. We grabbed the song sheet and found about twenty we wanted to sing, putting our name on the list for a couple of solos and a duet to start.

Waiting for our turn, we practised the dance moves for our duet. This was going to be a polished performance. Before our turn, two very drunk tone-deaf women butchered 'Dancing Queen' and a Japanese tourist channelled Elvis Presley. Then we were up – 'I Will Survive' was our chosen tune.

We belted out the iconic copyrighted first line without fear. We hit every note and nailed the moves. At the end of the performance the whole crowd erupted in applause. We bowed and blew kisses before exiting the stage.

'What did you think of that?' I said to Nikolai.

His pout had become a smile. More than a smile, he was giggling. I was trying to ascertain if he was giggling with us, or at us. I had seen him laugh but not giggle. Watching a huge Russian man giggle was a disconcerting sight. He would stop, trying to hold his breath and then his mouth would break into a smile and the giggling would restart. He even snorted, which was very unbecoming. I couldn't get a word out of him. I was about to start shouting at him, when I heard my name. My solo – 'It's Raining Men' – was upon us.

I strutted towards the stage with my head held high. *Fuck Nikolai, he wouldn't know talent if it hit him in the face.* I tossed my hair and started to belt. No rehearsed moves required. I had this one. I looked out into the crowd and saw Nikolai and Jen dancing, clapping and singing along. My belt got louder and my moves smoother. At the crescendo I threw my arms in the air and looked to the heavens – well... the ceiling. I bowed and my hair covered my face. The crowd howled their appreciation.

Nikolai and Jen hugged me – the returning victor. Another round of drinks was in order, or maybe even two.

The alarm went off. I was unable to lift my head off the pillow. Jen ran through the bedroom into the bathroom, slamming the door behind her. It was interesting to note that she threw up louder than she sang. And she sang pretty loud.

Three hungover humans took their respective turns in my bathroom. Nobody was in the mood to share. I wanted a greasy breakfast and suggested McDonald's. Jen threw up again at the suggestion and Nikolai walked into the kitchen for coffee. Not a great preparation for his first practice session in Sydney.

Early morning at City Community Tennis and it was already sweltering. Nikolai had hired a driver who went off-road and took us through the park to the gate in the fence of the scorching hard courts that were to be our punishment. Surrounded by a park, dog run and Olympic-sized swimming pool, and backing onto Sydney's major train hub, the early morning did not mean quiet. Already the adjacent basketball courts were in action, personal trainers were conducting boot camps and at least twenty dogs were getting their morning play. We were booked onto court 3 and had been given a code to get through the gate via a very officious looking keypad. Nikolai checked his phone for the code. He appeared to be struggling with focus – not a great sign.

Inside the court, there was not a lot of excess space. Two trendy metal stools were the only furniture. The boys dropped their bags next to the stools and I sat on one, put my hands in my head and prayed for death to come and take me. Soon the most soothing sound in the world began, the thumping of tennis balls being hit with raw unadulterated power. Two young guys were also hitting a couple of courts along. Their balls would make a variety of noises as they hit racquet strings – thring, thonk, but never the thumping that was heard from our court.

My job as udachu was not as glamorous as it sounded. Apparently, it consisted of being a combination ball-girl cheerleader. Neither of which suited a hangover on a hot day. After a few polite introductions to his German coach, Stephan Ditz, and Aussie trainer, Matt James, the boys got straight into practice. Nikolai said nothing of his state and his body moved effortlessly across the court. Smoothly he manipulated the balls and added force when required. I ran around picking up the strays.

Drenched in sweat with my hair stuck to my head under my hat, it was not a glamour-queen moment. Every few minutes I would feel the vomit rise up my throat and I tried to force it back down. Nobody seemed to notice. In fact, I was invisible. Until I threw up at the back of the court. I had tried to open the gate that led off the court into the grass – but it wouldn't bloody open. So my vomit hit grass, fence and the court. The tennis stopped and three men walked up behind me and watched me continue to hurl the contents of my stomach. When I finished, they clapped. Not the way my audience had last night. It was a slow clap.

'Can I have some water please?'

Nikolai handed me his water bottle and said, 'You better clean that up. They will have a bucket in the pro shop.'

Humiliated, I went to the pro shop and walked straight into the bathroom. Rinsing out my mouth and hair, I looked at the woman in the mirror. Her face was red and green at the same time. I sat on the cool bathroom floor for a few minutes before getting up, washing my face again and making my way to the teenager behind the counter. I told him something had spilt on the court and I needed a mop and bucket. He produced one without comment and I returned to the court.

While I mopped and cleaned up the mess, the aroma of which nearly enabled me to produce a fresh offering, the men played tennis. I had returned to being invisible. I took the mop and bucket back to the pro shop and returned to the court in time for the finish of practice.

Nikolai was talking to his trainer as his coach Stephan came over to me and put his hand on my back. 'Sip some water,' he said, and then returned to the boys.

'Same time tomorrow and we will work more on footwork drills,' said Matt. And that was it.

Nikolai and I walked to the car.

'I could use a shower,' he said.

I looked at him in disbelief. '*You* could use a shower. I'm covered in fucking vomit.'

This time he belly laughed so hard he couldn't walk any more. His laugh repertoire was expanding at my expense.

#Discovery, #NQLoveCrisis

Later that day Nikolai's management posted a picture of him training. My sickly green face was almost discernible in the background. Not enough for Facebook to tag me, but somebody who knew me would be able to make the ID.

'I can't believe you posted that. You know we're meant to be a secret.'

'I didn't post it. Anyway, there were lots of photos taken today by the crowd.'

Crowd – I hadn't noticed a crowd. Oh God, I hope there were no vomit shots.

A quick search revealed more shots, but I was mostly unidentified woman in background, wearing a baseball cap in one, with my head between my knees in another.

'I can't come to practice with you. I can't take the risk of being named.'

'This is so stupid, Katie. You can't hide from the cameras forever.' *Forever. Did he mean forEVER as in happily ever after? Or as in, I've been waiting for the train forever? Katie, get a grip and get back to the point.*

'The WTA can't find out from social media that we're together.'

'So email somebody.'

'I'm not ready.'

'Well, you have to come to practice.' I went to the bedroom and he stayed in the lounge room. I could hear him on the phone speaking in Russian.

The next day training took place on the Northern Beaches – forty minutes and all the way across Sydney to reach another beach. This time we were in the backyard of a Russian oligarch. A billionaire with a perfect Plexicushion tennis court.

I can't tell you his name, nobody introduced us. He was at least fifty years old and the same number of pounds overweight. As self-appointed ball boy, he wheezed from a probable cigar habit and he handed the balls to Nikolai on bended knee. Once we butted heads over the same ball. I read his face and handed him the ball. I guess that kind of determination was how he made billions. He was the best ball man from then on.

#Udachu, #NQLoveCrisis

December proved to be a month of groundhog days. We got up, went for a run on the beach, I took a swim and then Nikolai did sand sprints with his trainer. We showered, changed and drove north for three hours of tennis training. With his prize ball girl in tow (the oligarch and I had reached a silent truce), Nikolai worked on his serve, footwork and fitness. His determination was relentless. Sometimes I swear his coach would feed him the same shot three hundred times before they moved on.

It was hot. The temperature wavered between the early to late thirties most days. For four interminable days it soared past all sanity into the forties. The routine did not change. There was no let up on practice due to the heat. In fact, I swear he ran faster.

I followed him and the crew to Palm Beach one day for sand dune sprints. I managed to get halfway up one dune. It was like running the wrong way up an escalator, if the escalator was moving at 60 kilometres per hour. Nikolai sprinted for two hours. He stopped to vomit, twice. Then kept going. Next time they went, I was approved to stay home.

Nikolai had created palm cards with motivational messages. He took them everywhere and read them in bed each night and morning. They were laminated to stop them being damaged in the bath. Early in the month, I tried to cajole him into a little bedtime exercise while the palm cards were present. He got up, left the bedroom and remained reading in the bathroom, with the cards, for an hour. That was the last time I interrupted. The cards were written in German. I don't know what they said, except, he started and ended each session with one card, which didn't need translating. It said, 'Australian Open Champion.'

Our sex life was barely alive during these punishing weeks. From walking like a cowgirl in the first week of Nikolai's arrival to self-appreciation after the training started. The odd jolt of electricity flowed, but it was nowhere near satisfying the appetite he had awakened.

He never complained about being sore or tired. He had massages every day to aid recovery and our shared shower sessions had turned into solo hot baths with Epsom salts.

Nikolai ate often and his menus were detailed. In addition to ball-girl duties, his muse needed to shop for and prepare food. He never outright asked me to, but one day he handed me a list acceptable foods provided by his trainer. The list was merciless, giving no wiggle room of what or when to eat. 'I thought you ate what you wanted, practised when you wanted and went to bed when you wanted,' I said, recollecting these words delivered late before the finals in Moscow.

'This is what I want,' he said. The conversation was over.

Before his morning run, he had nuts and fresh juice. After the morning run he ate an egg-white omelette with spinach and tomatoes on rye bread. Snacks of nuts and power bars permeated the day. Lunch was a complex salad with a variety of leaves, proteins and homemade dressing. Dinner was protein and salad – steak, salmon etc. I ate the same. Alcohol was not on the list.

Dinnertime was strictly 7p.m. – to aid digestion before rest. I called Nikolai from his bath three times before I entered and suggested he might like his meal served in the bath. 'Yes, that would be good. Please bring it on a tray,' he said going back to the cards. In the kitchen I wondered how my joke had backfired. Nikolai was a deft hand at sarcasm, but on this occasion – not so much.

My routine now included dinner served in the bath. While he ate, I pondered what to call this new sensation. Breakfast and lunch combined into brunch. I had heard of lunch and dinner becoming linner. By that logic dinner in the bath could be binner or perhaps dath. After much thought, I settled on calling it fucking stupid.

Ever since I turned sixteen, December had been my month for parties. Drinking and eating to excess was assumed and I regularly piled on at least two kilograms. I weighed myself and I was three kilograms lighter now than when I started working on the tour. My clothes were gaping. I was particularly concerned about my deflating chest. Why is it we never lose weight from our trouble spots? Nikolai didn't comment but he would probably fund implants if I asked.

During this month of hard labour, food was not the only thing on a strict schedule. Sleep was timetabled, along with fucking. One night, we were sitting on the bed as he played with my hair, his huge calloused hands impossibly gentle. I had a question to ask. I knew it would be sensitive, and given it was looking like an opportunity for sex, which I never wanted to miss, I was in two minds about risking the change of mood. I looked down at the bed.

'I want to ask you something very personal,' I said.

'You want to do anal?'

'No, not *that* personal.' He was smirking at me, his eyes shone, pleased with the offense.

'Did your parents sell you? I mean to the agents. Did they get money for sending you to Germany?'

He stood up and backed away from the bed. 'No! Are you crazy? My parents didn't sell me. What type of people do you think they are?'

'People are talking about how many of the Russians were farmed off to other countries.'

'They gave me a once in a lifetime opportunity.'

'Oh, come on. Spare me the glossy brochure. You were a child.'

'That's the trouble with you. You don't understand hard work or sacrifice.'

'I work very hard.' He looked at me with what could only be described as a mix of disgust and pity coupled with more than a pinch of irritation.

'Please, talk to me about hard work when you've run a million miles or hit ten million tennis balls.'

He started to leave the room. I tried to give him my cute sorry look, but he wasn't interested in meeting my gaze.

'Nikolai, come on. Let's talk about something else.'

'No. I think I will go for a walk, perhaps I will run into some parents who want to sell me their children.' The front door closed purposely behind him.

I paced the apartment for what seemed like hours. I watched TV, surfed endless meaningless bullshit, until I gave up and crawled into bed. At some point in my slumber he joined me. Instead of curling up behind me the chasm between us could have been as wide as the distance from Moscow to Leipzig. Mental note, no more talk about childhoods.

On Christmas Eve, Nikolai's practice schedule remained unchanged. Wanting to acknowledge Christmas, I bought his trainer and coach a bottle of Australian shiraz and presented them at the end of the session. They each kissed me on both cheeks as Nikolai packed up his kit bag. Nikolai said nothing of my gifts, he was too busy tweeting a picture of himself and his billionaire ball boy. Payback for all the free court time. I had to jog to catch up to him as he walked to the car.

Back at Bondi, he disappeared into the bathroom for a soak. I had been invited to three different parties that night and had yet to navigate Nikolai's preference for the evening. After thirty minutes of hearing him empty and refill the tub, alternating between hot and cold water, I cleared my throat and made my best attempt to be nonchalant. 'Nikolai, will you be long?' No response. 'Nikolai, I've been invited to some parties tonight. Do you want to go out?' I paused and waited three whole minutes, no response. This time, I invaded the bathroom. I noticed he was meditating on the cards. He heard me enter the room and looked up.

'What do you want?' he asked. *A shower in my own fucking bathroom.*

'Sorry to bother you sir, but it's Christmas Eve and I was hoping to partake in some celebratory festivities.'

'What?'

'I want to go and celebrate Christmas, Scrooge.'

'I'll talk to you when I'm finished my bath.' He went back to looking at the cards. I considered pulling the plug; instead, I left, slamming the door behind me.

Sitting on the bed, I contemplated my next move. Dress up and go out, just leave him, was the overriding thought. If I hadn't needed a shower, I would have. Instead, I went to my wardrobe to select a dress to wear. I found a red sparkly shift dress that I hadn't worn since I was twenty-one. With my flatter chest and reduced weight, it would fit to perfection. Teamed with sky-high heels and my diamond-drop earrings, courtesy of bathing beauty, I would sparkle like a Christmas tree.

What seemed like three years later he emerged from the bathroom with a towel wrapped around his magnificent torso. I pushed past, with my outfit in tow and took command of the steamy room. Neither of us spoke.

In less than twenty minutes I looked pretty fine, if I do say so myself. I exited the bathroom and Nikolai was sitting on the bed in the suit he wore to my sister's engagement party. He was immaculate.

'Nice earrings,' he said.

'These old things,' I responded.

'I'm ready for the parties. I want to be home by midnight. I have to train tomorrow.'

'You're training on Christmas day?'

'We're training on Christmas day.'

'No we're not. I have to help my mother with the lunch.'

'We will compromise. You can help your mother after the first hour of training.'

I felt the anger rising from my tummy to my face. My fists both clenched by my sides. I wasn't deluded enough to think I could take him, but I figured if I launched at him all guns blazing I might just... who was I kidding, I would only hurt myself.

I left the bedroom, slamming the door behind me, picked up my purse and left the apartment, slamming that door too. Slamming doors had become my primary form of communication. I walked into the street and stood outside the building fuming. My next step was not clear. I knew I wanted out. That was it.

Nikolai followed me into the street with his keys.

'So you will miss practice tomorrow.'

'Damn fucking straight I will.'

He put his arm around my shoulders and I shrugged him off.

'I have the car keys, where is the first party?'

We left party number one after my friend Petra sat on Nikolai's lap and proceeded to announce – loud enough for all to hear – that she had had a Brazilian wax that morning.

Party two was over after my friend/acquaintance Geoff challenged Nikolai to an arm wrestle. 'Come on big fella, don't be scared.' I swear Nikolai was holding his breath to stop himself from clobbering the idiot.

Party three was just right. People were inebriated yet mellow. They didn't know or care who Nikolai was. I drank, we laughed, danced and talked, staying until the early hours.

Nikolai had made nice with all my friends and played Prince Charming. My lust returned and he responded. We made love with pre-training enthusiasm and my fabulous orgasm was the best Christmas gift I could imagine. That is, until, lying in bed post-coital, Nikolai pulled out a box from his bedside table. It was another box from Cerrone. Long and rectangular in shape, it was not a box for a ring.

'Merry Christmas,' he said as he handed it to me. It took me all of three seconds to discover the princess-cut diamond tennis bracelet inside. I gasped.

'You have worked hard, you deserve it,' he said.

There were no words. I kissed and hugged him and then put my new bracelet on. I had a present for him. I reached down to the bottom drawer of my bedside table and got it. Jen had helped me. Together we had wrangled a friend who had some recording gear and I recorded three songs, 'I Will Survive' and 'It's Raining Men' from our karaoke sessions, and Adele's version of 'Make You Feel My Love'. I had uploaded them to an iPod and engraved a love heart and 'udachu' on the back. Leaning over the bed with the iPod in hand, my bracelet sparkled. It had to be worth thousands. My singing effort would be a pathetic response to this. I put it on the ground and pushed it under the bed. I turned back to Nikolai who had started to read his palm cards. He was gone.

#ChristmasCheer, #NQLoveCrisis

When I woke up a few hours later, Nikolai was absent. No note, no details nothing. The man was a machine. How did he manage to train today?

It was nine o'clock and Lou was picking me up in thirty minutes. Family tradition dictated that Mum, Lou and I prepared and cooked the turkey, stuffing, potatoes and sides. I showered, dressed and wrote a note to Nikolai saying that lunch was at 3p.m. Then waited outside for Lou.

Lou was tanned and smiling when she picked me up in her ageing silver Holden Barina. She and Dave had just returned from two weeks in Tahiti on a practice honeymoon. She didn't turn off the engine because it was warm and may not have started again. We embraced and I insisted she tell me about her holiday, 'the PG version please'. Lou talked fast and furiously about their trip. I gathered the first few days were not PG as they didn't feature much in the story. Every sentence contained Dave's name. 'Dave said this…' They managed to snorkel, scuba and surf. Dave loved to surf and I learned that some of the best breaks in the world happened off the Tahiti reefs. They sang and danced each night and made friends with couples from the US, the UK and one couple from Melbourne.

At our parents' home, preparation began in earnest. I was on potato peeling duty and worked my way through six kilos. A bit of overkill, but Mum always ensured nobody left her house hungry.

Dave arrived a few hours later and watched the cricket replays with Dad. After some time he came into the kitchen to join us. 'What's all this giggling? Aren't you women supposed to be working?' he said, putting his arms around Lou and kissing her. Lou showed us the necklace Dave had bought her for Christmas. It was a seahorse and she showed us the three tiny diamonds dotted in its tail. I showed them my new tennis bracelet. 'Nice,' said Dave, and he went back to Dad.

Lou's face was scarlet, she gripped my arm, her nails digging into my skin and dragged me from the kitchen. 'You're a stupid, selfish bitch, Katie.' I stepped back and looked at my little sister. This was no joke.

'My beautiful man saved months for this necklace,' she said, holding onto her chain. 'How long do you think your tennis hero saved for that?' She pointed to my bracelet. 'How could you rub it in his face?' Lou's expression was violent. I've never seen her stare with such intensity. She stood behind a chair with her hands white from the ferocity of her grip.

'I'm sorry. I wasn't thinking.'

'No, you don't think, do you. You're living in a very fake world. Don't forget the real people.'

I felt tears welling in my eyes. I had been a monster to Dave. I wanted to take the bracelet off, but the damage was done. My mother entered the room. She took Lou back into the kitchen and allocated her the brandy butter for the pudding. Lou pounded the butter into submission.

I returned to the kitchen and continued on with my peeling. Mum said nothing for a while and then put on some Christmas carols. Gradually, we joined her in singing as we worked. Lou's voice maintained a decided edge.

At 3p.m., lunch was ready to be served, but there was no Nikolai. I checked my phone, nothing. 'He's probably just running a little late.'

Mum seemed happy to wait. We all had a glass of champagne and toasted another family Christmas. At 3.30p.m., still no word.

At 3.45p.m. Mum disappeared into the kitchen and returned with chips and crackers. Dad and Dave attacked them. I suggested we start, Mum wanted to wait, but the turkey had been out of the oven wrapped in towels for nearly two hours. If it wasn't carved soon, it would dry out. The clock struck four and Mum, Lou and I brought all the food to the dining table. Dad carved the turkey. It was his job each year and he was terrible at it. His slices were too thick and there seemed to be no logic to where he started and finished. My mother rolled her eyes, but stayed silent. Dave offered to carve the ham and we all thought that was a great idea. Dad looked up from his job and pouted. Dave said that if he carved too, we would get to eat sooner. Dad nodded and went back to destroying the turkey.

We sat at the dining table with our coloured crepe paper crowns on our heads. The temperature outside was in the early thirties and, combined with the oven being on full blast for six hours, it meant we were also roasting. As the carving continued, our hats stuck to our heads and little beads of coloured sweat dripped down our faces. My crown/face were yellow.

It wasn't quite 4.30p.m. when the first bite of Christmas dinner passed our lips. The turkey despite its odd-shaped slices was delicious. We were all silent and chewing when Nikolai arrived. He entered the dining room with flowers and champagne. My mother stood and he handed them to her, kissing her on both cheeks and profusely apologising to all for his delay. Practice had gone long. My father stood and shook his hand. Dave slapped him on the back. Nikolai kissed Lou and wished her a Merry Christmas. I stayed seated. He came over, kissed me and whispered sorry in my ear. I did not respond. Mum handed Nikolai a plate and Dad offered him a drink. 'Just water, sir,' he responded.

Nikolai inserted himself into the conversation as if he had been here all along. He was surprised we were eating hot foot on such a steamy day. 'I thought Australians ate cold seafood at Christmas?'

'Only the sane ones,' said Lou.

We all had second helpings and were sitting with our bulging bellies when Mum asked for my help in the kitchen. She loved the theatre of setting the pudding alight. As she warmed the brandy she said, 'Don't be too angry, Katie. Tennis is his life.' I nodded, but said nothing.

Everyone clapped as Mum lit the pudding. A few seconds of drama each year was sufficient for my family. I now encountered drama on a daily basis.

When it was not possible to consume any more food, the clean-up began. Dave was the first in the kitchen and set himself up at the kitchen sink. Lou gave him an apron and he began scrubbing. We all took turns scraping plates, loading the dishwasher and wiping up. Nikolai turned out to be a deft hand with the dishcloth. As a team, the work was done 'quick-smart' as my Dad said.

With lunch complete, it was time to sit around the Christmas tree and distribute the presents. I had written 'love Katie and Nikolai' on my family gifts.

Lou and Dave's gifts all came from Tahiti. I got a grass skirt and Nikolai a lei. They gave Mum and Dad some hula music. We put the music on, I tied the skirt over my dress and Lou showed Mum and me how to hula.

Mum and Dad gave Nikolai an Australian art book. He was mesmerised by it. He thanked my parents twenty times before we left.

After the kissing and hugging was complete, Nikolai and I walked down the stairs to the car. He said, 'I haven't had a Christmas present since I moved to Germany.'

I stopped walking and looked at him. 'You were ten!'

'Nine. That was our last family Christmas.'

I felt sick at the thought of any child growing up without Christmas. I couldn't bear to ask about birthdays. Without celebrations what does a child have to look forward to?

When we got back to Bondi, I suggested a walk along the beach. I felt heavy from all the food and a soft breeze was blowing. The day had been warm, and with the oven on from early morning, relief from the heat was welcome.

As we walked, we talked. I dared to broach the taboo subject and asked about his childhood Christmases before he left home. He talked of Christmas Eve traditions of hiding presents, candles and music. He remembered the smells, sounds, the songs they sang, even the minutest detail. When I asked about Christmas in Germany, he shut down.

I had been very angry with him at lunch. Now the revelations about his family had softened me. I still couldn't help asking. 'Why were you late?'

'I told you. Practice went long.'

'Six hours long?'

'Yes.'

'That's insane.'

'I'm here to win, Katie. Not play.'

'I thought you were here for me.'

'You can't be that naive.'

A slap in the face would have hurt less. Did he really say that I was not the reason he was here? I knew he had to prepare for the Open, but I genuinely believed the reason he came to Australia was to be with me. I pulled my hand from his and started to walk in the opposite direction. He turned and walked after me. His stride was bigger than mine and he caught up in a couple of steps.

'Katie, be serious. Love –'

He stopped himself, and started again. 'I care about you, but I'm at the top of my game. My career is my priority now.'

'I understand.' But I didn't. *What about my career? Where's my priority?*

That night I tossed and turned. I had worked hard to make my dream of a new life a reality. Perhaps I needed a set of palm cards? Mine would read: 'Don't sabotage yourself', 'Keep your eye on the prize', 'A man is not a plan'. It seemed I needed constant reminding of the purpose of this journey.

I was showered and dressed before Nikolai woke. On my laptop, I emailed my colleagues Christmas wishes and tried to get the jump on my work. I needed to come up with some solid ideas for publicity before I left for the Brisbane event tomorrow. I had been regularly responding to the tournament requests, but I had not shown much initiative. Nikolai's

Facebook featured a selfie of him wearing a paper Christmas hat wishing his fans a Merry Christmas from Down Under. He was alone in the pic.

When he came into my living room dressed for practice, I told him breakfast was ready in the kitchen. I was not dressed in my ball-girl gear.

He asked if I was coming. 'Not today. I have some work to do before I leave for Queensland in the morning.' He ate breakfast, kissed me goodbye and left. He knew where he had to be and so did I.

My nightie had slipped under the bed. It hadn't been worn much this past summer. When I went to grab it, I noticed Nikolai's Christmas iPod. I considered giving it to him, but it would be a meaningless gesture now. Then there was that word 'love'. I had not said it to him yet, but the songs implied it. I left my gift under the bed.

**

That night we made love with an unspoken awareness that our lives were about to change. Although his training schedule had been gruelling, at least there was a sense of normalcy around our time together in Bondi. Things were about to escalate and external pressures were imminent. Most nights after we made love we cuddled for a short while and then rolled away from each other to sleep. This night I lay in his arms til dawn.

#BrisVegas, #NQLoveCrisis

I left Nikolai in charge of my apartment and caught a taxi to the domestic terminal. The Brisbane flight was just over an hour and I had given myself a further hour to get to the airport and check in. Big mistake. The terminal was clogged with families on their way to beach holidays. Parents with strollers, Christmas toys, luggage, and even flotation devices were crammed into ramshackle queues jockeying for the desk. I was alone in a sea of chaos and unsure how to navigate the terrain. Due to my frequent flyer status, I had access to the business-class lines, but these had been given over to the airport invaders. I considered fainting, but thought the strollers might just run over me.

Something happens to a person wielding a stroller. It becomes a weapon. They drive the thing at you rather than around you and those goddamn wheels hurt when they bash into you or squash your toes. The noise was at fever pitch. Kids screamed, laughed, cried and made some noises I did not recognise. I decided to have my tubes tied at the very next opportunity.

With determination and stealth, I managed to work my way to the front of a queue and check in. The next hurdle was security. I had my laptop and was well rehearsed in the art of the security scan. On most occasions, I travelled with fellow business people who knew the drill and had their laptops, shoes, belts and jackets on and off with military precision. Today, parents fought with non-obliging collapsible strollers, baby bags and kids insisting on taking their dolls, transformers etc. through the scanner. It was a complete clusterfuck.

The flight itself was just as bad. I had my favourite aisle seat. Unfortunately, next to me was a mother, babe in arms, and a young son. Across the aisle was the rest of their family. For one hour and twenty minutes, they talked through me and passed toys, food, drinks, and even the baby, back and forth. The baby cried, the children shrieked and the parents attempted to maintain their sanity – all with me playing piggy in the middle. A couple of times the flight attendants shot me a glance of camaraderie. They too were in hell, attempting to get toddlers, frazzled parents and the rest of the menagerie to comply with aviation laws – no small task.

I have never been so happy to get off a plane. Including the times when turbulence rocked me to the core. I lay back in the tournament car for the thirty-minute drive to the Queensland Tennis Centre, unable to do more than grunt replies to the very nice driver.

The Brisbane tournament takes 'fan friendly' to the max. With the Gold Coast and theme parks up the road to compete with, the purpose-built tennis stadium has to amp up the fun to pull the holiday crowds.

Players arrive around Christmas to prepare for the event. They need time to get over jet lag and acclimatise to the heat before competing. Many of them spend Christmas Day practising on the hot courts or sitting on the long-haul flight Down Under. I'm told Santa sometimes makes an appearance on the Qantas flight – whoopee do!

From a PR point of view, my job was all about getting kids through the gates. The major event held every year on day one is the aptly named Kids' Day. Entry is free for kids and there are activities on all day to entertain them.

Arriving on site the day before the event, I confirmed that Aussie hero and Queenslander Samantha Stosur would be the major female drawcard. I also secured Nadia Katarinkova as she was the top-seeded female. The men had Rafael Nadal, Nick Kyrgios and Lleyton Hewitt. There were mixed doubles planned, with the players mic'd up to bring the fans closer to their stars. Mario had committed to a contract for Nadia to promote the event and she was shitting herself about wearing the microphone. She was the only player in the group who hadn't done this sort of thing before. She didn't think anyone would understand her accent. I told her it was all about hamming it up for the crowd. She told me she was a vegetarian. I had to watch those Aussie expressions!

The next morning I arrived on site at 8a.m. to be greeted by Peppa Pig, Dora the Explorer and the Teenage Mutant Ninja Turtles. I couldn't help myself and photo bombed the turtles and the tournament director, Paul Clancey. He had two little girls and was trying to make Daddy look cool. I uploaded a shot of me and Raphael the turtle to @NQ30Love with the caption – 'oops wrong Rafael'. I'd been pretty absent from Instagram and Facebook, given the clandestine nature of the past month with Nikolai and Jen. Time to make some noise.

The gates were due to open at 10a.m. The main fan event on centre court was scheduled for 11a.m., after which the real matches would commence. Courts were set up for kids to play on, there were serving speed guns, jumping castles in the shape of tennis courts were inflating, it was all happening. Already the temperature had hit thirty degrees and the fountains and mega mist fans blowing cool air and water were probably going to be the most popular spots on site. I headed indoors to the aircon. The players' change room was eerily quiet for a first day. A lot of matches were scheduled – it seemed they were already hitting on the practice courts. Nadia came in and put her bags down on the bench in front of her allocated locker. Methodically, she unpacked her bag, picked up her racquet and started to re-tape the grip.

'Hey Nadia, how's it going?'

'I don't want to do this clinic today.'

'I know, but you're going to, right?'

'I think I might fall over in the shower.'

'And pull out of the tournament two weeks before the Aussie Open?'

'No, I can ice my foot and be better by tomorrow.'

'Do you think the tournament will accept that?'

'Who cares, what can they do?'

'Someone could plant a story on social media about you hating the fans.'

'You would do that to me?'

'I wouldn't.'

'Okay, so maybe I'm going to play. But I can't wear the microphone. They will all laugh at me.'

'That's the idea. You're all supposed to be funny.'

'I'm not funny.'

I couldn't argue. Maybe a bit of coaching on crowd pleasing wouldn't go astray. I got out my phone and starting searching for fun tennis antics and showing stuff to her. Bahrami was the pinnacle – he served with five balls in his hands, hit crazy trick shots. Then I showed her players who pretended to have a white cane when they missed a ball – basic clown gags that the crowd loved. She watched transfixed, taking it all in as if I was showing her a new way to hit her forehand. She nodded.

'Okay, so I can do more of the tricks and less of the talking?'

'Yep.'

'Let's do this,' she said, while catching me unaware in a high five. My hand tingled, but the desired result was achieved. Nadia had her groove back.

While we were talking and looking at my phone, the locker room had started to fill up. The showers were busy and players were on the move. Matches would be underway on all courts in less than thirty minutes.

The gates had admitted thousands of screaming kids with their parents in tow. Many were already in the stadium with their giant tennis balls and autograph pens at the ready, the show was about to begin.

I waited with Nadia, Sam Stosur and my counterparts from the ATP. They were all seasoned pros at this and raring to go. I held Nadia's sweaty hand and gave it a little pump. Standing on my tiptoes I reached her ear and whispered, 'You've got this.' She gave the least convincing nod I have ever seen.

Each player was announced onto court by the emcee, Craig Willis. The crowd screamed and the players acknowledged them. Starting with the warm-up, the antics began. Nadal was pretending to tamper with the balls, Sam waved to the crowd, Nick was playing mock basketball and Nadia looked completely lost. Those few minutes must have seemed excruciating to her.

She was partnered up with Nadal and he saved her, including her in his joke by headbutting the ball to her volleyball-style for her to continue the game. Her natural hand–eye coordination took over and she soccer-kicked the ball over the net. The crowd went wild and she never looked back. A new comedian was born.

**

After thirty minutes, they exited the court beaming. Signing tennis balls and programs that dangled from the court, the players high fived each other and joked with the fans. Nadal gave Nadia a friendly slap on the back as he left.

'Did you see that, Katie? Rafael Nadal joked with me. I can't believe it. This is the best day of my life. He's my hero.'

'After today, you'll be a hero to some of those kids out there too.' She looked at me with the same intensity she had when we watched the videos on my phone.

'Thank you,' she said and walked off towards the locker room.

My job was done – well, not really. I still had match notes to write, a ton of player interviews to follow, and about a million autograph sessions and kids' zone visits to organise.

At 9p.m. on New Year's Eve the press room was abuzz with the news that Kids' Day had broken all attendance records. I was messaging with colleagues around the world when, during a routine online search for coverage of the day, press director Cindy Laws found the image that would snatch defeat from

the jaws of victory. She gasped from her office and shrieked my name. I rushed to the room, she pointed at her laptop screen. A picture of a seventeen-year-old girl stared back at me. A young woman whose star was on the rise, who had today met her hero, whose hair was wet and limp and whose body was naked, completely exposed. She was looking down. Nadia Katarinkova's naked body was on the internet for all to see.

'It's everywhere,' said Cindy. 'What do we do?'

I immediately called the WTA tour supervisor, Sally Fletcher, and told her to come to the press room urgently: 'Bring the tournament director with you, this is not a drill.' Then I messaged Jane Townsend in the US – we would need all hands on deck for this one.

Cindy and I searched for the image – we wanted to know how far it had spread and to see if we could locate the origin. The rabbit hole was deep and wide. By the time Sally and tournament director Paul Clancey had arrived the hole was a chasm. We showed them the image. Sally looked green. Paul immediately looked away.

'It's taken in the locker room here,' I said. 'You can tell by the surrounds.'

Paul called for the head of his security to join us.

'It's bigger than that, I'm afraid,' said Jane from the speakerphone. 'Nadia's underage. This is a criminal matter.'

It would have been criminal anyway as it was a breach of privacy laws, but Nadia being underage put this in a whole new ball park.

An image of Nadia's beaming face as she came off court this morning filled my brain. 'What about Nadia?' I managed. 'We need to warn her.' Checking her social sites, we could see that trolls had already tweeted her. We didn't know if Nadia had seen anything yet – she had not responded.

Sally thought that the massage therapist, Sue, had a good rapport with Nadia. She suggested sending Sue back to the hotel to talk to her.

'And to talk to her parents. Somebody needs to talk to her parents. It probably should come from high up in the WTA.'

Sally was off and racing. The massage therapist was in a tournament car in less than ten minutes speeding back to the hotel. Sally was tasked with the job of ringing Nadia's agent Mario – also Nikolai's agent. He would know who needed to be told on Nadia's side.

Paul had mobilised his security team. He had also put a call into the Queensland police who told him this was AFP (Australian Federal Police) jurisdiction and gave him the number for child pornography. Paul disappeared into the men's room. Probably to vomit.

Cindy and I doctored the image of Nadia with modesty panels. If we had to show more people we wanted to retain as much of Nadia's dignity as possible. When I first saw the image, my feelings were all about how to minimise the damage, then I wanted to cry, now I wanted to kill. How could someone do this? Sure, she was tall and beautiful. She was successful and making money, but she was also a child. Heaven help the monster that did this.

The AFP was amazing, especially considering it was New Year's Eve. They were online with their forensic specialists searching for the origin picture and trawling through known sites, removing the image where they could and signposting to those sharing that this was an illegal image and all in possession would be prosecuted. The sharing slowed down and we could see the image disappearing. Thank God Facebook and Instagram didn't allow nudity – this was bad enough.

I wanted to speak to Nadia and see how she was, but I knew she had people with her. Mario was on a flight from Sydney to Brisbane and apparently had the world on the phone. He had spoken to her parents, and the WTA's CEO Brian Hull had also spoken to them. He had said that the WTA and Tennis Australia would not rest until every image had been taken down and the persecutors put to justice. They were also working on a joint statement to the media.

Cindy and I were given another role by the AFP. We were asked to speak to a few key high-powered journalists to get them to help us remove images. We had people from Nine, News Limited and Pedestrian. TV put the word out – share this image and you are distributing child pornography. Images started to disappear. The AFP also found the initial tweet and got that removed.

Before midnight, substantial progress had been made. Still, this wasn't going to be a happy new year in the tennis world. One of our own had been violated. We weren't going to stand for it. Sexual exploitation was certainly not new and social media's input via #MeToo showed solidarity with the victims. For the tennis world, we all felt violated with Nadia – although none of us were naked on the internet.

Mario and the AFP had simultaneous breakthroughs – Mario through his Russian network, and the AFP via their underground contacts. Mario found that the notorious shonky Russian news site – cheesily named Babushka – published the origin photo. I remembered this website from our Moscow trip. Journalists were not allowed on site at that tournament and the press director told me never to put players in touch with Babushka's representatives. The AFP had found out that the news site had purchased the picture and paid money into an Australian bank account. Since the AFP had no jurisdiction in Russia, they couldn't do anything about the photo, but they could chase the money.

Mario, on the other hand, had mobilised all the Russian power he could find. The origin picture was removed and the rest of the sites started to drop like flies.

While all this was going on, Nikolai messaged me. He knew about the image; Mario had told him. He said the Russians would shut Babushka down. I didn't know or care how. I could tell that Nikolai was incensed – imagine if this happened to Nasty, or any other young girl. My skin crawled at the thought of it. Then I remembered Jen. She may not have been underage, but she had been violated, and her life had been turned upside down. There really needed to be more effective ways to prosecute these monsters.

The WTA, Tennis Australia and Nadia Katarinkova released an official joint statement the following morning. It read:

**

The tennis world was last night saddened by the exploitation of minor Nadia Katarinkova. An image of her taken in the private locker rooms at the Brisbane International was a violation of trust and Australian law. The person or persons responsible for taking the image will be found and prosecuted. The image has been removed and anyone caught sharing or distributing this image will also be prosecuted. We take this violation extremely seriously. Our players' safety is paramount and we will not rest until Nadia Katarinkova's exploiters have been brought to justice. Any questions regarding this incident can be directed to WTA communications staff or Nadia's management. Nadia will not be responding directly.

**

In the shortest amount of time, we had mobilised resources and had achieved the best possible result. Still, at least a quarter of a million people had seen Nadia's naked body, maybe more; it was hard to judge. Jen was still walking around hiding under scarves and hats and her video was probably seen by less than one thousand people.

About halfway through New Year's Day, Sally and I met with a French player, Sabine Beaujardin. Sabine, like all the players, was pissed about what had happened to Nadia. But Sabine had some information. 'There was a player in the locker room yesterday, I have never seen her before. I thought she was acting weird. She had her phone up like she was looking at a video or something, but she kept hanging around.'

We asked what she looked like. 'Blonde, I don't know, nothing special. Like a player. Oh, and she had old Nike gear on. Maybe from like two seasons ago.'

Security had a list and photos of all the players with access to the locker room; they sat Sabine down with the images. She picked the stranger without hesitation. She was a sixteen-year-old Aussie wild card from Western Australia, Josie Farway. Yesterday she had lost her first-round doubles match, she would probably be already booking her flight home, so speed was important. We didn't know if she was the culprit, but it seemed a good place to start looking. The AFP was notified to see if the banking transfers might link up.

**

Josie cracked like an egg. Four days ago she had been approached by 'some foreign guys' and offered money in return for photos. They had given her a number to call. Five thousand dollars for nude photos of any Top 20 players. Ten thousand if that player was Russian. Josie had ignored them, until after her match loss. Her mother had rung and said they weren't going to fund her expensive tennis hobby any more. She had to come home and go back to school. Then Nadia walked out of the shower and was standing in front of Josie stark naked. Ten thousand could keep me playing tennis, she had thought. Tennis Australia handed her over to the AFP.

* *

Behind closed doors, Tennis Australia, the ITF and the WTA discussed Josie's tennis-playing future. Nadia was not on site on New Year's Day. She was not due to play until tomorrow, but she would normally want to practise. Today was not normal.

* *

Matches happened, players won and lost, fans cheered, and press conferences rolled on. The media wanted to ask every player, male or female, about Nadia's situation. My ATP colleague Stephen and I briefed them all. They unanimously condemned the photos, but would not address any questions beyond that. Nobody wanted to harp on about the incident and nobody wanted to speculate about how Nadia was feeling.

Nadia's first match was scheduled for Wednesday. Mario had assured us of her intention to play. 'She needs to get straight back on the horse,' he said.

I spoke at length to Jane Townsend about how to handle her post-match press conference. She suggested I speak to key media before the match and ask for their support. Our statement said that Nadia would not speak on the issue, but I was sure the tabloids would push her.

'She shouldn't be forced to face the press post-match. I know it's compulsory. But this is such a different situation,' I said.

Jane replied that players were often facing the press after difficult personal incidents. I said I would not make Nadia go if she didn't want to. 'I'm prepared to resign over this.'

'Katie, you're being overdramatic. If you feel that it is not in Nadia's best interest to face to the press after her match, and she expressly doesn't want to go, call me and we will discuss it. We will make a value judgment at the time.'

I was happy with that outcome. Nadia and I had some wiggle room if she needed it. Tomorrow couldn't come soon enough. I wanted her to play, win, do media and then get on with the rest of her career.

Tomorrow did come – too soon for some. Minutes before her match I saw Nadia in the locker room. She was sitting by herself with her headphones on – standard practice. Her legs were jigging up and down, her eyes on her feet. I wanted to go and hug her, but instead I went and hung out with the trainers. All the other players were in with the trainers as well – it was crowded in there.

Sally came into the locker room and touched Nadia on the shoulder. She jumped in response, looked up and saw Sally, and took off her headphones. 'It's time,' said Sally. Nadia rose and followed her out of the locker room. Together they walked down the corridor towards the entrance to the Pat Rafter Arena where her opponent, a young South African qualifier, was waiting. Then they waited for the signal and entered the court to thunderous applause. The applause seemed to be following Nadia. All the online commentary was currently about tougher penalties for people who post unauthorised photos and videos. You didn't have to be famous to be a victim of this modern crime.

Nadia went to her seat and unpacked her racquets. She selected one, and met her opponent and the umpire. Nadia won the coin toss and elected to serve. The five-minute warm-up began.

Nadia whiffed her forehand into the bottom of the net and couldn't get the ball in play. The crowd started to scream out her name. 'Come on, Nadia', 'We love you Nadia'. She shook her head and muttered to herself. She repetitively looked up at Mario in her player box. He signalled the thumbs up. Three minutes in they started to warm up the serves. Nadia's ball toss was all over the place. Her arm was shaking. Several times she stopped, closed her eyes and took deep breaths.

Despite the collective energy of the stadium and back-of-house willing her forward, Nadia ran to her seat, grabbed her bags, screamed 'I'm sorry' and ran off the court.

Once she was off the court, Sally followed her at a run into the locker room. I followed as well. Maybe the less people the better, but I kept coming. Sally and I found Nadia in a heap on the training-room floor. One of the trainers, Nicole, lifted her up and we took her into one of the massage rooms. Sue, Nicole, Sally and I were with Nadia. She was seated on the massage table bawling. Sally and Sue had their arms around her. Nicole had her hand and I knelt on the floor in front of her.

'They were all looking at me,' she sobbed. 'They all saw the picture.' There was no point in a comforting lie.

'Who gives a fuck what they did or didn't see. You're an amazing tennis player. That's all anyone should worry about,' I said. Sally looked at me. Her look signalled disbelief in my commentary and my language.

'I give a fuck,' Nadia said. 'It's my body and nobody should be looking at it.' This lovely young girl, who previously had shown no modesty in the locker room, prancing around proud of her fabulous fit figure, was broken.

'They will forget. These things get forgotten about quickly,' said Nicole.

'But the WTA will not forget. We will punish everyone concerned,' said Sally.

'I want that Josie girl dead,' said Nadia.

'She did a very stupid thing. But she was manipulated and desperate. Don't forget she is only sixteen,' said Sue, who always saw the best in everybody.

'She's only six months younger than me and I would never do that to anybody,' said Nadia.

Children exploiting children with adults pulling the strings.

Nadia's phone rang – it was her mother. Mario had rung to update her. As we left the room she sobbed down the phone in Russian. My eyes welled thinking of how helpless Nadia's mother would be feeling – half a world away.

I rang Jane. It was 5a.m. in NYC – she answered. 'We can't make her do press.' I stammered down the phone. Jane caught up at a million miles an hour, seeing the online coverage of Nadia running off the court before I could finish my sentence.

'No, we can't. I'll work on a statement from the WTA and email it to you in a few minutes. We will need you to address the press ASAP. I want to stop speculation quick-smart.' That summarised Jane to a tee – quick and smart.

**

Within fifteen minutes a message came through to my phone. Jane had a brief statement for me to release to the press. She suggested I read it to the press directly and be ready for questions – she had included some suggested answers. She had also cleared the statement with Mario and thought it was important for me to show Nadia the statement to make sure she was happy with it.

**

I knocked on the massage room door. Nadia opened. She had finished her phone conversation. Her face was blotchy red and she had dolloped tears sitting in her eyes. The kind you see on little kids when they've fallen over. I asked her to sit down and I read her the statement.

**

The WTA have excused Nadia Katarinkova from press conferences for the duration of the Brisbane International. Under these extraordinary circumstances and whilst an investigation is ongoing, all communication will continue to be via the tournament, WTA and Nadia's management. Please respect Nadia and her family's privacy during this difficult time.

**

'Are you okay with this?' She nodded. I gave her a hug, left her alone and went to face the press.

I could say the press understood, but that would be a lie. They wanted more. They wanted her to condemn the tournament's security, Josie and the Russian media. They wanted her to rail against the internet. Mostly they wanted her to fuel their story about player salaries. When tennis started to join other sports and have scandals about players gambling and match fixing, everyone wanted to blame the salary structure. The ABC had made an investigative TV program focused on how lower-ranked players could barely make a living, and how this incentivised gambling and other insidious opportunities (e.g. nude player pics). They had offered the argument that if all the players could afford to play on the tours then these bad decisions would be minimised. What they had failed to discuss was the concept of 'elite'. Everyone wants to watch elite people doing superior things – playing the piano, kicking a soccer ball, playing tennis. If anyone can make a living doing it – how is that elite?

Nadia had no interest in helping journalists write stories, and shame outweighed her anger. I took the media's questions and responded according to the guidelines given – which was to say very little. I hoped in vain that this lack of oxygen would move the story on. Instead, she was now a player in the #MeToo movement. Was this relevant? Her exploiter was an underage female. Then again, her true exploiters were faceless men, half a world away. Perhaps, in this case, as both Nadia and Josie had been victims, this was more a case of #SheToo.

* *

Nadia's management withdrew her from the Sydney tournament. A decision about the Australian Open was not yet made – at least not publicly. I didn't see her leave. She was gone by the time I left the press room.

Despite my better judgment, I sent Nadia a message via WhatsApp. 'If you ever need to talk or anything. Call me anytime. Take care, Katie.' I didn't expect or receive a response.

The rest of the week went by in a blur. Players, autographs and media conferences. A nice surprise was the comeback of local champion Samantha Stosur. Against all odds and despite constant media scrutiny that she wouldn't, she won the event.

It was a good news story that deflected the commentary back to matches. The world was somehow trying to balance out its yin against its yang. I felt happy for Sam. She was nice and she deserved a local win.

I had a strange dream. In my dream the media had discovered Nikolai and I were lovers and our naked bodies appeared everywhere. Naturally, as it was a dream, my body was half-human half-centipede. My bottom half was the centipede.

**

The ITF, WTA and Tennis Australia released a statement. Josie Farway received the first ever lifetime ban for a female playing competitive tennis. The inside talk was that she was never going to make it anyway. The AFP had frozen Josie's bank account and criminal charges were pending.

#HomeTownBlues, #NQLoveCrisis

Having missed the last flight out of Brisbane due to the long running final, I needed to be on the 6a.m. to Sydney and head straight on site to Homebush. Twelve months to the day from when I worked my first event, I wheeled my suitcase into the press room, checking in with the girl who had replaced me as Tim's assistant. As a WTA representative, I controlled the access to the players, even if that control was only an illusion, and I was the one to milk for valuable information. Last year I had been a shitkicker, now I could kick the shit – only a small amount of shit, but shit nonetheless.

Tim Waters sat in his makeshift office. The tournament had built him a cubicle to validate his position as press director. Tim granted audiences in his office to the journalists with enough clout to gain his attention. He needed the WTA, therefore access to the modular temple was permitted.

For this event I was working with a new employee, our only current male communications manager, Ricardo. Ricardo was about five years younger than me, a computer whiz kid and extremely attractive, in a dark-skinned, muscular, perfect kind of way. He shook my hand and looked me in the eye when introducing himself. Originally from Italy, having worked in soccer there, he had relocated to the London office and this was his first event. I asked Ricardo if he knew of many tennis players – the detail in his answer identified him as a lifetime fan.

Our first order of business was to find a couple of players for the kids' clinic tomorrow morning. We went to the tournament office to get an understanding of who might not be playing the following day as they were our best chances of securing a 'Yes.' Armed with a list of potentials, I gave Ricardo a copy of the media guide, so he could recognise players. He thanked me and kept it closed by his side as we entered the player area.

The Olympic tennis site was a concrete jungle with lots of space for players, staff and spectators. There was an upstairs players' lounge and restaurant with televisions and score monitors and a balcony overlooking Court 1. Players spent most of their time here when waiting for, or having just completed, a match. Downstairs were the locker rooms, physiotherapists' rooms, tournament officials and the gym.

Ricardo could not go inside the female player locker room or physio rooms for obvious reasons. Given so many players hide or hang out here, I couldn't help but think he would be at a disadvantage. Time would tell.

I scouted both rooms and found a young Aussie wild card, Jenny Fogerty. She was getting a massage and I had her trapped on the table while I convinced her of the merit of an 8a.m. kids' clinic. She was locked in with a commitment to ride in a car with Ricardo from the hotel tomorrow morning before she could offer the omnipresent excuse 'practice'.

Ricardo was standing at the base of the stairs the players used to reach the restaurant. It was the perfect place to catch them coming and going, heading them off at the pass. He had tried to approach two of the players on our list and they had dismissed him with lame excuses.

'How far is too far to push them?' he asked.

'When they fall off a cliff, you still have a couple more inches,' I answered and he laughed.

I suggested we work as a team and stick at his perfect location. After twenty minutes of watching people go up and down, my eyes started to glaze over. As I stared at nothing, I felt two enormous hands encircle my waist from behind. The hands lifted me in the air and moved me six inches to the left. Nikolai then walked up the stairs through the space now vacated.

'Excuse me,' he said as he passed. Ricardo turned to me with his pupils almost fully dilated.

'That was Petrov. Did you see him? Petrov just touched you. I'm so jealous.' Ricardo's façade of professionalism had evaporated. His Italian accent, which seemed moderate before, was thick and musical. Also, not that I gave a shit, he had just outed himself.

'Yep, I saw him.' Ricardo was gone. Not physically, but he was phaffing about saying 'Oh my God' over and over. I waited the ten minutes it took for him to regain his composure and suggested we look at the practice-court schedule. He nodded and followed. At the desk we identified two potential victims for our clinic. I led Ricardo to the courts and waited until Nathalie Preacher, who was talking to her coach, was free. She listened to my request while towelling off and nodded her head. I introduced Ricardo and told her that he would meet her in the lobby in the morning. Finally we went to the transport desk and booked cars to pick them all up. I also organised a car to pick me up from my house. Not thinking it prudent to hitch a ride with Nikolai.

Back in the press room, we emailed out contact information and printed out player biographies. Ricardo was a natural with all our systems. I responded to an email from Marine, who would be in Melbourne in four days. I could not wait to see her.

The tournament's main draw started tomorrow. At 6p.m., I suggested that Ricardo and I take the opportunity of an early night. 'We won't get another one,' I reminded him, as I packed up my laptop and printer.

I felt a little lame, not offering to show him around my city as so many others had done for me. I had commitments at home. At least I hoped so.

Ricardo caught the shuttle back to the hotel and I, a car back to Bondi.

**

Ricardo: Knows more about tennis than me. Might also like Nikolai better than me.

**

I dragged my tired body and suitcase up the four stairs to my apartment. As I located my front door key, there was an aroma coming from inside. The homey smell of garlic and onions frying. Entering, it was impossible not to notice the state of my living room. It was immaculate. The floor was shining, the cushions were plumped and there was a gigantic bunch of red roses in a vase on my coffee table. Turning towards my dining room, the table was set for two with more red roses taking centre stage.

'I hope you're hungry,' Nikolai called out from the kitchen. I left my bag where it stood and followed his voice. My stove had two pots and a frypan all filled with pasta, vegies and chicken. Nikolai was dressed in warm-up gear and my red chili apron. He smiled at me and I threw my arms around him, nearly getting scorched by the pan in his hand. He told me to unpack and freshen up while he finished cooking.

I dumped clothes into the laundry basket and my wardrobe and jumped under the shower. No shower is ever as good as the one at home, no matter how glamorous or high pressured. With my sweats on and wet hair I went to find Nikolai. He was serving up dinner and kissed me on the forehead. 'You look beautiful,' he said. He must have missed me. I couldn't remember being brave enough to face him with wet hair, no makeup and scummy trackies before. Although he had seen me hungover and vomiting. Everything's relative.

Dinner was a delicious mix of healthy and a little bit naughty. Nikolai had thrown in some cream for good measure and we shared a loaf of garlic bread. I ate two pieces and Nikolai ate six. I figured he had burnt a few more calories than me today. Nikolai was struck with verbal diarrhoea as he regaled me with his week. I heard detail of practice bookings and sessions, his trainer's torture, agents and press requests. He was no longer under cover and everyone wanted a piece of him. I asked if anyone had worked out where he was staying. He replied 'not yet'. Before I could stand up, Nikolai cleared the table and returned with dessert, fruit and ice-cream. That's when the true miracle happened. 'How was your week?' he asked. I fainted.

Okay, I didn't actually faint, but I was speechless as he chowed down on his strawberries. 'I, um, well. You've never asked me that before.'

'I'm asking now.' I was not able to argue with that logic. He already knew about Nadia of course, so we talked again about how sad that was. Nadia's age and vulnerability made me think of his niece.

'I couldn't see Nasty on any of the playing lists for Australia?'

'No, she didn't get into the tournaments. Maybe next year?'

'You love her, don't you?'

'Of course.'

'Who is her father? She never talks about him.' *I don't know why this question came into my head now. I'd often wondered about it. He just seemed so conspicuously absent.*

'I don't know.' *WTF, how could he not know?* I nearly choked on a strawberry.

'Elena keeps him a secret. I don't think it was happy. She had to stop her tennis.' My splutters subsided; my curiosity was piqued.

'Does Nasty know him?'

'I don't think so.' Dumbstruck, I fumbled for my next question.

'Has he…does he… is he involved at all?'

'He gave Elena money to pay for Nasty's tennis.'

'I thought you did that. Nasty told me you paid out her contract.'

'That's what Elena wants her to think. I would have, but Elena has plenty of money. I don't pay for anything.'

'Don't you think that's strange?'

'Elena's strange. She always has been.' I thought of all the conversations Lou and I have had over the years. She'd given me shit and I'd hurled it right back. I couldn't imagine keeping anything serious from her. I couldn't imagine keeping anything minor from her. How could Nikolai be so flippant about Nasty's father.

With the conversation lull feeling more than a bit awkward, I directed chat back to my week. I told him about the successful Kids' Day and how nice it was to have Sam Stosur finish as champion. I ended by telling him about our new recruit Ricardo.

'He's into you as well,' I said.

'I'm taken,' Nikolai said, without looking up from his fruit. My tummy flipped. Nikolai looked up, noticed my eyes were dewy and went back to his fruit.

* *

Maybe it was talking about my work, maybe it was simply absence/abstinence, but dessert led to a move into the bedroom. And what a move it was. His moves, my moves, our moves. Lots of moves!

* *

A good meal, three orgasms and my own bed were the perfect recipe for sleep. At dawn, I woke ready to take on the world. Nikolai went to training early to avoid the crowds on site and I went for a run and a swim. By the time the car picked me up at 7.30a.m., I was ready for anything.

Ricardo, Jenny and Nathalie beat me to Kids' Day by two minutes. Over forty kids aged between five and seven were happily screaming, while parents stood around the court taking photos paparazzi style. Ricardo had managed to get the players to the court on time and with racquets in hand. Not too bad for a rookie. The next step was to show him how to integrate the players into the games. There were two coaches already getting the kids moving and a microphone sitting idly by the side of the court. I took Ricardo, Jenny and Nathalie over to the coaches and introduced them. Jenny and Nathalie were instructed to take one side of the court and feed balls to the kids, who had made their best attempts at queues. I had written some notes for myself in the car and I took the microphone and introduced the players and their history to the crowd.

Thirty minutes later the players were taking group photos – with sponsor signage shoved into the background by yours truly – and signing autographs. We thanked them for their time and they thanked us. Players always whine about doing clinics, yet they always leave with smiles on their faces.

The rest of the day was panic stations. Getting players to press, autograph sessions, live interviews on the big stage and an on-site broadcast by 2GB radio station. Last year there were three experienced WTA people staffing this tournament, this year it was a rookie and me. Having said that, Ricardo was a quick study. He was learning how to corral the players and recognise the bullshit from a legitimate excuse. He was also innovative in getting around not being able to enter the locker room. I noticed him talking to player coaches and getting room attendants to be his eyes. I could learn from him.

Late in the day, I received an email from Marine:

**

Hi Katie,

Sorry to do this, but we need a player to do a live *Talk Tennis* appearance in Melbourne on Friday. Nadia was scheduled to do it, but that's not going to happen. Can you hunt someone else down?

Cheers,

Marine

**

My response was simple:

**

Hi Marine,

Anything for you babe.

Katie

**

Naturally, the reality was not so simple. A player would have to have lost here by Thursday. As my psychic skills could not predict who was going to win and lose, this was more about scouting options.

I went to the player restaurant to see who was around. I spotted Mario sitting at a table with guess who – Nikolai. Mario would definitely know about us. I wanted to walk by, avoid the awkward pretense, but I had to ask about Nadia. The tennis media, blogs and social sites had been alive with the story in Brisbane; now, out of sight meant out of the picture. A million other global scandals had lit up the newsfeeds. But I knew a young girl was still suffering. Walking up to the table, Nikolai spotted me and his brow creased in confusion. I tilted my head towards Mario, in a pathetic attempt at signalling the reason for my approach.

'Hi Mario. Hi everyone.' I looked at each of the people at the table in succession, giving equal time with my glance and nod. Nikolai's coach Stephan smiled at me. I put my hand on Mario's shoulder and knelt down next to him. 'How is Nadia? We are all pulling for her.' He nodded and thanked me but didn't give an answer. I guess that was to be expected. I smiled at each of them in return and apologised for interrupting their meals.

I couldn't see anyone with enough clout for *Talk Tennis*. Sam Stosur wasn't playing Sydney; I shot off an email to

Marine to try her agent. I also said I'd keep looking/watching here.

I joined Ricardo who was sitting at a distant table. He had already gone to the buffet and I put down my walkie-talkie and notebook and got myself some dinner.

※ ※

Arriving home so late it was already tomorrow, I dumped my bags and went into the bedroom. Nikolai was asleep. I cleaned up and climbed into bed. He rolled over and we spooned.

#Charades, #NQLoveCrisis

Next morning, Nikolai and I went for separate jogs to avoid being seen together. The subterfuge was exciting. Looking both directions as I exited the building, it felt like the start of a spy movie. Back after our synchronised separate re-entries, we ate breakfast. His first match of the season was to be tonight. There was a women's match prior and he would likely be on about 9 or 10p.m. I kissed him goodbye, wished him luck and caught my ride to the site.

Today was much like yesterday, way too busy for two staff, but we managed. Late in the afternoon, I received two texts in succession. The first was from Nikolai:

**

'I know you're busy. But please let me see my udachu tonight.'

**

I responded with a smiley emoji.

The next was from Jen: 'Can you get me two tickets for tonight? John's a Petrov fan and I'd love to bring him.' I said 'yes' and organised for them to be at the entrance for her to pick up. I remembered John from the real estate office. He had worked there when I did. He was that rare combination in a man – attractive and shy. Jen had never paid him attention before.

When Nikolai's match went on court, I was in press with Simona Halep, who had just won her match. I wanted to be there for him and could have passed the job on to Ricardo, but my resolve to prioritise my career was fixed. Plus, I hadn't seen Simona since Singapore and it was important to develop relationships with the top players. It took only twenty minutes for me to complete my duties with Simona and we shared a couple of stories about Christmas, in the snow and sun, respectively.

When I had the chance to look at the score, I saw Nikolai was down 2-5 in the first set. My tummy dropped. All that work over the past six weeks. Nerves must be getting to him. I excused myself from the press room and went courtside. With my badge, I was able to access the tunnel that led to the player entrance to the court. I was right on the edge of the court when he saw me. My timing couldn't have been better, Nikolai was serving to stay in the first set and had bounced the ball about twenty times when he lost control of it. He looked up to see me. From my vantage point I could see his entire body relax. He won that game to love.

It only took forty-five minutes for Nikolai to finish the match. He won 7-5, 6-1. No doubt he would be asked in his press conference how the match turned around. I avoided the scene, as I knew I would not be able to hide my feelings this time.

When I reached the press room, Ricardo was in a flutter. 'You missed Petrov. He was amazing tonight.' I nodded and smiled. I told Ricardo I had a friend in the stadium and was going to try and catch up with her.

Jen texted me that John really wanted to meet Petrov, could I help? I wanted to, but couldn't fathom how to do it without blowing my cover. I used my badge to get Jen and John into the player area. We were standing near the stairs when fate intervened and one of the officials called me over to ask a question. Nikolai came out of the locker room, saw Jen and walked up to her, giving her a hug and a kiss. She introduced him to John. They did the photo and autograph thing before Nikolai exited the site. I saw it all from the corner of my eye and when I returned they were both buzzing. I kissed them goodbye and went back to work.

It was after midnight when I got home. I gave Nikolai the best blow job of his life. No teeth, lots of suction and I even swallowed. He kissed me and we made love. Later in his arms, I thanked him for being so good to Jen. 'She hasn't had a very good time with men lately.'

'Because of the sex video?' he said. *How could he have known that? I never told him. Oh my God, I hope he hasn't seen it.* My mouth was slightly open and my face screwed up. 'You two talk very loud,' said Nikolai in response to my face.

Nikolai had the next day off, but I did not. He planned to spend it practising and getting a massage and physio. I spent the day running around like a 'blue-arsed fly' begging people to do things they didn't want to do. Some days on the tour were like games of hide-and-seek. Unfortunately for me, I was the seeker. In order to fill an exhaustive list of player activities, including autograph sessions, radio shows, live stage appearances and sponsor clinics, I had to beg, cajole, and often threaten, to reach my quota. Ricardo was helpful and a good hire. He didn't shirk from confrontation and he was innovative in finding solutions. Today and tomorrow were the worst days for us, and then it settled down, with players being allowed to focus on their matches.

Thank God Nikolai's next two matches were wins. He was growing in confidence with each outing. Although I couldn't attend the matches in full, I managed to peek my head out on court at the beginning and that seemed to be enough to satisfy Nikolai's superstitions.

My workload became more manageable as the days progressed. In addition to player and press activities for Sydney, I was helping Marine line up players for the big one – the Australian Open. As players lost, they hotfooted it down to Melbourne to start practising there. Although Sydney and Melbourne were the same court surface, players said there was a difference. Sydney played faster according to some; others thought Melbourne did. Regardless, they were out of Sydney quick. The Grand Slam, with its prize-money pool and kudos was their lure, not our beautiful city.

I had a rare decent window for lunch. Ricardo was working on his notes, leaving me to wander up to the player restaurant alone. I looked around for some WTA staff or friendly players to sit with and found Nikolai's coach Stephan sitting by himself. 'Can I join you?' I asked. He nodded. I came back with a tray of pasta and salad and sat down. For a while, we ate, smiled at each other and stayed silent.

'He plays better when you are watching,' said Stephan.

'Thanks, I don't know why,' I responded.

'It makes the tennis not so serious,' he said. We sat, ate and allowed both the food and the thoughts to digest. I realised that I knew nothing more than that Stephan was German and he had a friendly smile – so I asked. Stephan opened up his wallet and showed me a picture of a woman with three teenage boys. He told me their names, their hobbies and aspirations. One was at university in Munich studying to be a doctor, one was finishing school and the youngest was captain of his soccer team. Stephan's clipped German accent morphed into proud papa as he spoke.

'How many weeks are you away from home?' I asked

'Twenty-one,' he answered, looking down. I didn't know how to respond. That meant he was away over five months a year. He was missing the soccer season, school and university exams and all the day-to-day that make a family. He put his utensils together, indicating he had finished, stood up, thanked me for sharing a meal and left.

* *

Stephan: Needs to keep this job to support his family.

* *

The semifinal was a night match. It was slow in the press room and Ricardo wanted to watch. I said I would go with him and we could watch from the side of the court. Petrov was playing fellow hard-hitting top-ten player, Dominic Thiem from Austria.

The match was a three-set struggle with Nikolai prevailing 7-5 in the third set. He had looked over at Ricardo and I about fifty times during the match. I clenched my fists so tightly that my nails had dug into my palm, leaving tiny half-moon indentations. After the match, Ricardo and I walked through the tunnel back to the press room. I was whistling and chatting about nothing, when he asked, 'What's the deal with you and Petrov?'

Shit, fuck, shit. 'What do you mean "deal"?'

'Come on, Katie. Something is obviously going on between the two of you. He looked at you more than the ball.'

I giggled. 'I'm sure he wasn't looking at me. Maybe he was looking at you? You're pretty hot.'

Ricardo stopped walking, tilted his head, raised his eyebrows and put a ceremonious hand on his hip. 'I wish,' he said. I shrugged my shoulders and kept walking. After a short pause he followed and dropped the conversation.

**

The next night-match was Simona Halep vs Sacha Johnston. Sacha was a wild card Australian player who had won two matches and gotten a walkover into the semifinals. This would be by far the biggest match and biggest payday of her career. Ricardo and I watched the forty-six minute–match from the press room. At 6-0, 5-1 we jogged down to the court to run the interviews and make sure not to lose Sacha. Ricardo agreed to follow Sacha.

After Simona had done her interviews, I joined Ricardo stationed outside the women's locker room. 'She's not in there,' he said, looking horrified, as if he'd lost his wallet, not a sixteen-year-old tennis player.

After a quick chat with the locker room attendants, I managed to pry out of them that Sacha had gone to drug testing. This week, the official drug testing was on and every player after they lost had to pee into a cup. We went to the medical office and waited outside for her to finish. The press room called on the walkie-talkies wanting to know Sacha's ETA.

'She's at transport right now,' I said. 'We'll talk to her in a minute and get back to you.' Ricardo looked at me quizzically. 'Transport is code for drug testing. Doesn't look too good to talk about drug testing on an open channel,' I explained. He nodded.

Minutes later Sacha joined us. She looked addled. 'This is unbelievable. Every time I'm tested, I can't pee. This time, I've drunk too much water and they say the test is diluted. I have to wait until I can go again.' Forty-five minutes and one hard-fought pee later, we took Sacha to the three journalists who remained interested enough at midnight. The whole process took way longer than her match.

That night, back at my apartment, Nikolai was waiting for me, arms outstretched with a bag of laundry he had forgotten to give to his coach. 'I need it for the morning.' The bag contained his sweat-soaked match clothes. I screwed up my face at the stink and the thought of washing in the middle of the night.

'Don't you have, like, fifteen of these outfits?' I asked.

'This one is the one to win in,' he said. Discussion over, I trod downstairs to the communal laundry. I remember when two of my building mates dragged in the old school bench to become a folding table. Tonight it was perfect for a nanna nap. I could have slept on a bed of nails.

Mum and Dad wanted to come to the final to cheer Nikolai on. I told to them that nobody knew about our relationship and it was important for it to stay that way. They didn't understand, but agreed to respect my privacy. That's what they said to me. Behind my back, Mum rang Nikolai to wish him good luck and he invited them to the match to sit in his players' box. Now I had to pretend I didn't know my own parents. Pity I was the spitting image of my mother.

**

The women's doubles final was on first. Our singles final had been the night before. I had to manage the doubles ceremony, photos and media commitments. By the time I appeared courtside to join Ricardo, Petrov had lost the first set. He was cursing and throwing his racquet. I snuck a peek at my parents in his box. They were looking around and squirming in their seats.

Nikolai saw me, I smiled, which Ricardo saw too. I had hoped my smile would settle him. It had the reverse affect. 'Where the fuck have you been?' Nikolai screamed. Not knowing what to do, I looked around and behind me, fooling no one. Nikolai turned to the back of the court and started taking deep breaths. The umpire called time. Nikolai did not move. The umpire issued a time-violation warning. The next step was a point penalty. Slowly, Nikolai turned around, nodded to the ball boy indicating he wanted a ball and moved to the baseline line. He served. The ball moved through the air at 260 kilometres per hour and landed on the line. It was an ace that was only a few kilometres short of the world record. He served four more scorching balls to win that game. The final was decided.

The crowd seemed unsure of how to react. The display of tennis power was awesome. On the other hand, the first-set explosions were unsportsmanlike to say the least. The crowd only managed a polite clap as the players shook hands. The ceremony went ahead and in Nikolai's speech he thanked the supporters in his box. My parents looked at their laps.

I took my time walking to the press room. When I entered, heads turned. I'm sure it wasn't my paranoia. Ricardo informed me that in his press conference, Petrov had apologised for his behaviour. Another first for him.

Tim Waters called me into his lair. 'Katie, what's the deal with you and Petrov?'

'Petrov?'

'Okay, you're going to play it like that.'

'Play what?'

'Pity. I thought you were smarter than that,' he said waving me out of the room.

My parents went straight home after the match.

That night I returned to the flat first. I paced and packed for Melbourne. I practised telling him to 'go fuck himself' and other sparkling repartee until I heard a key in the lock. Nikolai's face was red, his eyes were dewy and his shoulders slumped. He dropped his bags, walked over to me and hugged me. Before I knew what was happening he was sobbing on my shoulder. After a few minutes, I navigated us over to the sofa and sat with his head in my lap. I stroked his hair while he cried. No words were spoken.

#GrandSlamin, #LoveCrisis

I woke alone. Walking around the apartment, all trace of Nikolai was gone. On the coffee table was a simple note: 'See you in Melbourne.'

Feeling groggy, I moved to the kitchen for instant coffee, which was disgusting, and poured some cereal. Eating and drinking helped a little. My watch showed I had about an hour before my airport car arrived. Packing was mostly complete. Making the bed, I noticed a text from my parents, 'Katie call us as soon as possible'. It didn't take a genius to figure out why. I showered, dressed and finished packing and set my laptop up to download emails. Then I braved my parents.

My mother answered. 'Katie, are you okay?'

'Yes Mum, I'm fine.'

'Is he there with you?'

'No, he's gone to Melbourne.'

'Good. Katie, normal people don't behave like that.'

'I know Mum.'

'Katie.' It was my father. 'Katie, has he hit you?'

'What? Dad, oh my God. No, never.'

'The way he yelled at you. That's a violent person. I don't want you having any more to do with him. Understand?' I'd never heard my father sound this definitive.

'Yes Dad, I do, but you're overreacting.'

'Katie.' It was my mother again and it sounded like she was crying. 'We've always supported you with everything. But he scares us. Please be careful.' I promised them both I'd be careful and told them how sorry he was. My parents were the most welcoming people in the world. They had made Nikolai feel like part of the family. His behaviour had shaken them.

The next bombshell hit as I read through my downloaded emails. My boss Jane had written.

**

Katie,

I have been informed of a rumour regarding yourself and Nikolai Petrov. Please come to see me as soon as you arrive in Melbourne.

Jane

**

Shit, shit, fuck, fuck, shit, fuck, shit. How did she find out? Did Ricardo tell her? That little bastard, I'm going to kill him. Who am I kidding? Everybody saw him yell at me. It could have been anybody. It could have been everybody. What am I going to do? What am I going to say to her? I'm going to lie. I'm going to deny everything. Play dumb. That's worked so far. Except for the fact that nobody's believed me. Will she sack me? I would. I would sack me. If I lie and she finds out – and she will find out, she will definitely sack me. I have to talk to Nikolai. I can't tell her without discussing it with him.

I dialled his phone and it went straight to voicemail. I left a message, doing my best to cover the shake in my voice. 'Call me as soon as you can, please.' I Facebook messaged him the same thing. Then I distracted myself with getting ready to leave. Every minute I checked my phone. I checked it was on, I checked I hadn't accidentally flicked it onto silent. I checked I had reception. Nothing.

The car came and I loaded two weeks' worth of luggage and ten years of emotional baggage. We rode in silence to the domestic terminal. No call. I checked in. No call. Went through security. No call. Wandered the terminal shops looking at gossip magazines, which, luckily at this point, did not contain my name. No call. Boarded. No call. I didn't turn off my useless phone until the plane was taxiing down the runway.

One hour and twenty minutes. That is the length of the Sydney to Melbourne flight. It felt like ten days. They showed the news and weather forecast on tiny screens throughout the cabin. I could not tell you if there had been a terrorist attack or tornadoes were forecast. I looked at my phone, even though it was off, maybe fifty times. When we landed and started to move towards the gate, the attendants told us we could turn on our phones. The two minutes it took for the phone to switch on and find service were interminable. I stared at the phone, hoping, praying, willing a message. Nothing. I dialled the voicemail: 'You have no new messages.' Bastard.

In the terminal, I walked and dialled Nikolai. This time he answered. 'What do you want, Katie? I'm at practice.'

'Sorry to bother you, but my whole fucking life is in the toilet.'

'What?'

'My boss, she knows.'

'Knows what?'

'About us, you fuckwit. She wants to meet with me. What do I say?'

'Tell her it is not her business.'

'But it is her business and she's going to sack me.'

'Then you can work for me.'

'That's just stupid and you're not helping. I'm going to tell her. Admit it, I mean. If I lie, it will be worse.'

'Yes, do not lie.'

'So, you're okay if I tell her.'

'It doesn't affect me.' I hated hearing it, but he was right. I hung up and went to pick up my case.

I watched as hundreds of bags tipped onto the conveyor belt and went round and round the carousel. *What's the worst that can happen? She sacks me. I come back to Sydney unemployed, broke and globally disgraced. I drink myself into a stupor and begin a life of crime. Shit. I'd be hopeless in prison. I can't even do boxercise. I would be someone's bitch on the first day.*

Breathe, Katie, breathe. First step is to figure out how not to be Jane's bitch. Prison can wait. I walked to the tournament desk to pick up my lift to the hotel. 'Car for Ms Katie Cook, WTA.' God, I love these perks. Being dropped at the airport, picked up at the other end. No money changes hand. They all have my name and treat me like I'm important. If I don't work this out, I'll be back in Bondi, hiding out with Jen. At least I haven't made a sex tape. I was pretty sure Nikolai hadn't either.

I sat in the car and planned the confrontation. I needed to be on the front foot. Should I just come out and tell her, or wait for her to say what she's heard? I'll wait. Be polite, listen, and intelligently explain it's a relationship between two consenting adults and it won't affect my work. Bullshit it won't. Marine. I needed to talk to Marine.

I checked into the hotel. My room wasn't ready. So I left my bags and went to a quiet spot to ring Marine. She answered.

'Hurry on site, Katie, it's crazy here. I need you.'

I asked her to move to a quiet spot to talk. She seemed frazzled and irritated. 'I don't have time, Katie, what is it?'

'I'm having an affair with Nikolai Petrov and I think Jane knows. I need your help.'

'Fuck.' It was the first time I had heard her swear. 'You idiot.' She left the press room and found a private spot. We talked strategy for twenty minutes. Marine said Jane was on site in meetings. She thought I should come to site as soon as possible, text Jane and confront her. No messing around. Nausea overwhelmed me, but I agreed. I was in a car and at the press room in less than fifteen minutes. I texted Jane and within seconds came a response: 'Meet me at the WTA office.' I showed Marine. She put her arm around my shoulders and said, 'I'm on your side. Good luck.'

It was a long walk through the white corridors to the WTA office. Past the practice desk, player restaurant, gym and locker rooms. When I arrived, Jane had cleared the room and was sitting behind a desk. She indicated for me to take a seat. Her face was unreadable. She would make a great poker player. My face couldn't even win Go Fish. With fifty deep breaths under my belt, I took a seat and started to speak. 'Jane, I –' She put up her hand to stop me talking. She wasn't going to let me control this meeting.

'Katie, I'd like to speak to you about a rumour. A rumour about Nikolai Petrov and yourself.'

'Yes, Jane. If the rumours are about us having a relationship – they are true.' I'd done it. I had taken back control.

'I see. I have to admit I was expecting you to deny it.'

'That would be dishonest and I am not dishonest.'

Jane's expression changed. Her face softened, was even sympathetic.

'Well, you are both adults. I have to warn you, though, everybody's talking and it's not favourable.'

'I can imagine. I didn't want this to happen. He pursued me and I –' She put up her hand to stop me talking again.

'I don't want the details. Katie, you were on a knife-edge in this job after the Instagram post. You've done some good work since and you handled the difficult Nadia situation with maturity and restraint, but you still have a lot to learn and starting an affair with a player is not exactly the most strategic career move.'

I nodded. She spoke the truth.

'What I also want to say to you, woman to woman, is that he has nothing to lose if this goes wrong. The same isn't true for you.'

I nodded again. She stood up, walked from behind the desk and indicated for me to leave the room. Her words sank in as I walked back to the press room.

'What did she say?' asked Marine.

'She didn't sack me.'

'Tell me every word.' I did.

I managed to get through the rest of the day due to the volume of pre-tournament appearances and player activities planned. I dragged players to four autograph sessions in the kids' zone, six pre-tournament press conferences and at least twenty television appearances. I was working at my first Grand Slam event and the scale was bigger than I could have imagined. One hundred and twenty-eight women and one hundred and twenty-eight men were in the competition. The world's sports media had descended. The television compound was the size of two football fields and the outside broadcast trucks lined up for a kilometre.

I caught a few of the media looking at me and wondered how far the rumour had spread. Despite countless online searches, I had yet to find anything on the internet. When Brenda greeted me with, 'I hear you've proved me right and fucked Petrov.'

'Excuse me?'

'You heard me,' she said and walked away. I looked at Marine who shrugged her shoulders.

That afternoon, when the prep was finally finished, Jane came to brief us for the next day. Brenda had worked plenty of Grand Slams, but both Marine and I were virgins, so to speak. The meeting was about the strategy of tackling the workload and assigning roles. Brenda had to bring up the rumour. 'How are we supposed to deal with the Katie thing?'

'You're not,' said Jane. 'Your job is to maximise WTA player exposure.' Brenda opened her mouth to continue and Jane put up her hand to stop. This seemed to be her move and it worked well – even if it was patronising and insulting. Brenda shut up, but shot me a glare that a toddler could interpret.

Our next stop was the hotel where the annual players' meeting was being held. I had been warned that these things often turn hostile, the players using it as an opportunity to rant against the WTA – usually about prize money and more opportunities to play for the lower-ranked players. We were all expecting it to get rough considering the media stories surrounding the fiasco in Brisbane.

We got in a car with Jane. She told us that Nadia's management had announced her withdrawal from the Australian Open. Nadia had met with the AFP, WTA and Tennis Australia before flying home. She didn't want to press charges against Josie. None of us could believe it until Jane explained that pressing charges would mean coming back to Australia and talking about the violation in court. As they were both minors, it would probably be a closed court, but Nadia knew it meant far more speculation and discussion about something she needed to go away. She had consented to and written a statement about damages, and Tennis Australia still wanted to press charges. This wasn't going to be solved quickly or easily – a lot of new laws were being tested.

The players' meeting was hostile as expected, but not for the reasons we assumed. The players were up in arms about what had happened to Nadia. They didn't touch on prize money as a cause, instead focusing on security. One suggested a ban on phones in the locker room. They all agreed, and then added the caveat 'not my phone'. It was an impossibly circular argument. Players needed their phones. They wanted to be able to call people, send messages, and while away boring hours playing on the phones, but they didn't want the bad people having them – whoever they were. Players were scared. Nobody wanted to wake up to being an unexpected porn star. There was to be no resolution today. Technology had opened up Pandora's Box and it wasn't closing any time soon.

I left the meeting and had to pick up my room key from reception. They gave me a note and I opened it in the lift on the way to my room. It was from Nikolai.

**

Katie, if the secret is out, you should stay in my room. 2315. N

**

Fuck, what do I do now? Go full throttle with this relationship and own it or slink away? A shower might help.

Showered and dressed, I sat on the hotel bed and dialled 2315. His coach answered and passed the phone to Nikolai.

'I have a huge two weeks ahead of me,' I said.

'I'm trying to win my first Grand Slam,' he replied.

'Is it just you in the room, or are we sharing with Stephan and Matt?'

'Katie, I don't have time for this bullshit. Come to my room or don't. You're a big girl. Make your choice.'

He was right. I had come clean about our relationship. People already hated me. I might as well embrace my decision. I had barely opened my bag. It would take less than two minutes to pack.

#ImAWAG, #LoveCrisis

It was the start of the Australian Open and the sun was barely peeking over the horizon. Today, I would be part of a comms team overseeing sixty-four women's and men's matches. At a normal event, twenty matches would be a huge day. This was going to be manic. Despite my trepidation at the daunting task ahead, I felt happy. Nikolai was asleep beside me. He had not moved since rolling off me six hours ago. His first match was this evening on centre court.

I checked my social pages and noticed Nikolai's relationship status had been changed – on both his public and private pages. Instead of single it now read: 'In a relationship.' It didn't say with whom. I went to my Facebook and did the same thing. It was the first time my relationship status had not been single.

Careful not to disturb Sleeping Beauty, I slid out of bed and into the bathroom. I showered, dressed and left the room, leaving a note for him:

**

'Good luck tonight. Your udachu.'

Marine was waiting for me at breakfast. We knew the chances of stopping for lunch or even dinner were slim, so we carb loaded for the day. She ate croissants and pastries; I consumed eggs, bacon and toast. Brenda sat opposite us with one of the physical trainers. She turned her head when we arrived and again when we exited. It was going to be a very long day.

To top it off, my phone rang and I could see it was Mum calling. I couldn't deal with that now, I sent the call to voicemail. I would call back later.

Within a few hours, I found out that Nikolai was not the only one who was stressed out at a Grand Slam. The officials, media and players were totally different beasts – and I do mean beasts. The calmest journalist was frantic. Media staff were under constant barrage. Players post-match were strung tight enough to pop. I don't know whether it was the money or the prestige that escalated the stakes, perhaps a combination or even the collective energy. By 7p.m., when the night session started, I had run a marathon. Literally, not figuratively. It was 72 steps from the ground floor to the media desk and interview room. If we didn't grab the players at the locker rooms on the ground floor of the four-storey Player Pod, they could be anywhere, including, the top two floors - both restaurants. My job may not be rocket science, but my FitBit had me at forty thousand steps and awarded me an astronaut badge on day one. My feet ached and my stomach growled. Bacon and eggs for breakfast had not lasted me twelve hours. I drank at least six cans of Coke Zero, taken from the players' locker room. 'At least' because, like a breadcrumb trail, I abandoned half-drunk cans throughout the site.

When the women's singles match between Venus William and Belinda Bencic started on Rod Laver Arena, Marine and I took our walkie-talkies and hotfooted our way to the player restaurant for food. En route, I peeked in the gym. Nikolai was warming up with his team. His match was next. I told Marine I'd meet her in the first floor player restaurant and strode into the gym. Other players on treadmills and stretching mats watched me walk up to my man, kiss him and wish him luck. Nikolai slapped me on the butt as I left – I giggled.

We ate fast while Bencic defeated Venus. I was courtside for her victory speech and Marine was in the locker room with Venus. We made the press rounds while Nikolai's match started. Belinda caught me sneaking a look at the score monitors as we left the press conference. She smiled.

It seemed my kiss had stood him in good stead. When my work was done for the evening, he was already up a set and a break and was steamrolling his opponent. The stadium court was huge, seating fifteen thousand tennis fans. Not a place to steal a glance. I made my way through the tunnel to the arena's exit. Emcee Craig Willis was standing there. He was a legend in the sport; and my friend since my first Sydney tournament. We joked around as the match progressed – in N's favour. Craig had been around the sport for years, he was as observant as he was jovial and had figured out the reason for my appearance.

'Going to work for the ATP now, Katie?' he said, giving me a friendly nudge.

'Ha-ha.'

'If you walk through that door and slide alongside the photographers, he'll see you.' I smiled and followed the directions.

At the change of ends, Nikolai spotted me and grinned. His face lit up as if he had been given a huge present, which made me crumble. I really loved this man. I couldn't help myself. I blew him a kiss. That clinched it. The match was over in a nanosecond.

We walked arm in arm back to the locker room. He dropped his racquet bag at the entrance and drew me in for a passionate kiss. I responded as if there weren't fifty people in the vicinity and walked on a cloud back to the press room.

Gossip beat me back. Marine and Brenda were packing up. Brenda did not speak to me. Marine seemed distant. On the bus, she said, 'A bit of discretion might be wise, Katie.'

I nodded. She was on my side. I knew that. But I felt free and happy. I would do my job to the best of my ability and he would win Grand Slams. We would travel the world together, support each other and be happy. This was our time. Nikolai and I were going to live happily ever after.

The days that followed strengthened my resolve. All day, I ran after players and managed activities. It was busy, yet fulfilling. Nikolai seemed unbeatable on court and his passion grew with each match. In week two, immediately after his quarter-final win over Marin Cilic, while he was drenched in sweat, I fulfilled another fantasy. We snuck into the indoor practice courts and fucked like wild animals behind a row of partitions. I screamed an octave or two above my normal range as I came. When we emerged from our hiding spot there was a kids' clinic on the court not twenty metres away. I think they learnt more than was intended from the session. Even Nikolai blushed as we exited.

Nasty had not made the cut-off for the Australian Open, leaving me the closest thing to family Nikolai had Down Under. My parents had left two more messages. One each. My mother sounded wounded and my father annoyed. I phoned home when I knew they would both be at work to leave a message, making sure to sound bright and breezy. 'It's crazy busy, but all is well.' And some similar bullshit. It wouldn't fool them, but perhaps it would placate them for a few days. I knew my father wanted me to break away. I convinced myself it was better for us all if I stayed silent.

On one of the many late-night sessions in the press room, Brenda had left and Marine and I remained. When men's matches start the night session, it's not unheard of for the women to have to wait until after midnight to play. Despite our workload, by then we were bored to tears and ended up playing stupid games. Marine's porn name was Foxy Latrobe and mine, Mugsy Village. I think she would get more film credits.

'Why him?' asked Marine.

'What do you mean?

'What do you see in him, that you are prepared to go through all this trouble?

'He's special.'

'How?'

'You think he's tough, but he's just a little boy.'

'Katie, all men are little boys.'

'It's different.'

She nodded gently, smiled and went back to her laptop.

Grand Slam semifinals are serious occasions. Only four women and four men remain out of two hundred and fifty-six. The prize money and points skyrocket from here on in. Reaching this stage is often a career high for the few players who get there. It gives them lifetime access to that Slam as part of the Last 8 Club (membership is automatic after a player reaches the quarterfinals). The WTA had a surprise semifinalist in an unseeded German girl named Mathilda Addleman. At eighteen, she was neither young nor old by tennis standards. Her best result at a previous Grand Slam had been second round at Roland Garros, making this a considerable leap in fortune. I walked Mathilda from the TV studios, to the media garden, crossing acres of cables, lights, and back alleys. I offered the golf cart, but she preferred to walk. Her English was word perfect, her grasp of the situation less so. Together with her coach, trainer and representatives from the German Tennis Federation, they felt focusing on her match was the priority. Results are important. Nobody is interested in a loser. But as a PR person, I know personality makes careers. Despite my coaching, Mathilda stared blankly into the camera and answered questions without embellishment, thereby boring the pants off the commentators, producers, journalists and fans. After today's appearances, she would have to make a sex tape to get that much media attention again.

Mathilda lost her big match. She was still young and time would tell what lay ahead for her.

Conversely, Grand Slam semifinals were not new to Nikolai. This was his third. Out of the three appearances, he had won one, falling in the final of the US Open to Roger Federer.

The media loved Petrov. He was untamed, unapologetic, unpredictable and not unattractive. It had been two years since Nikolai had made it this far in a Slam. Requests for interviews kept my counterparts at the ATP running. In every press conference and interview since Sydney, Nikolai had been asked about his inspiration. He had smiled and said something glib. 'You inspire me', 'I have a dream', 'Inspiration is everywhere' and, his most tongue in cheek, 'I have found God'. The God comment had not resonated well with the politically correct players who referenced the Lord in their speeches. Nikolai relished their angst.

Today, he was in the mood to spice things up even more, deciding to announce on US Television's NBC breakfast show that he had a good luck charm. I was in the player restaurant queuing for food when I heard my name whispered a thousand times. Like Voldemort calling for Harry Potter, my name echoed across the room. I felt eyes on me. Hundreds of eyes. I looked up from the food to confirm my suspicions. Everyone was staring. Abandoning my tray, I exited as quickly as I could, faking a walkie-talkie call-out. Eyes followed me. They followed me down the corridor, down three flights of stairs, across the compound and up three more flights of stairs to the press room and to the WTA press desk where Marine joined in.

Nikolai had told the world that I was his udachu and his lover. And yes, he had used both those words.

Minutes later the spell had broken and the media descended on our desk. They wanted to interview me. Drawn into the unknown universe, no longer the facilitator, I was the object. I managed 'no comment', which drew laughter. I was trapped in our cubicle. Flashes burnt my eyes and disorientated me. I saw Jane and Brenda staring and judging, just beyond the cameras. Marine whispered in my ear 'You have to say something.' My media training kicked in and I put up my hand to silence the cacophony.

'It seems like you have taken the bait Mr Petrov has dangled in front of you,' I said.

'Was he lying? Is it true?'

'I don't believe in charms or luck. I'm sure Mr Petrov doesn't need them to win tennis matches.' This drew laughter from my friends and acquaintances in the media core. Nobody cared if I was lucky. They wanted to know one thing.

'Are you sleeping with Nikolai Petrov?'

Okay, here goes nothing. 'As a lady, I will not answer that question.' The flashes went ballistic. I had given them what they wanted, enough to write their confirmations. The announcement of Roger Federer coming to his press conference dispersed the crowd. However, I was not safe. Jane and Brenda approached. Jane asked me to take a walk with her. Brenda grinned.

We walked in silence through the halls. Players, officials, hangers-on and media watched me walk. Jane noticed without comment. When we reached the office of the WTA, the sea of faces and bodies parted, leaving us alone. Jane did not offer me a seat. 'Did you know he was going to do that?'

'No.'

She looked at me, dissecting my face to extract the truth.

'You are a very stupid young woman.'

Anger rose through my body. *How dare she?* This situation was far from ideal, but personal insults were not going to help. I held my tongue, searching for the correct response. She was angry, I was angry. I channelled words I could not say to her, hoping they would be received through some transference that would not get me sacked. *Fuck you, bitch. This is my life, stay the fuck out of it.*

After an eternity, I managed, 'Jane, I am not happy with the situation. But I have to deal with it. The WTA can choose to support me or not.'

She said nothing, glared for several minutes and then walked out of the room. I guess that's a 'not.'

#Everywhere, #LoveCrisis

The traditional media coverage started with the nightly news, but the internet was already rife with commentary. Both my Facebook and Instagram accounts were hit hard, @NQ30Love, a particular favourite. Online commentary was more judgmental. The accusation that I slept my way into my job was a thread that kept recurring. The hashtags ranged from #WTASlut to #WhosAFuckingWAGNow. Nikolai's management had updated his status to say 'In a relationship with Katie Cook' and had linked to my page. I confirmed the status. My newsfeed went ballistic.

My parents called my phone in turns. I couldn't answer. Then Lou called. I pushed the green button.

'Katie, are you okay?'

'I don't know, Lou. I don't even know if I still have my job.'

'What are you going to do?'

'When I know, I'll tell you.'

'We love you and we're here for you.'

'I know. Handle Mum and Dad for me please. I can't deal with them at the moment. Tell them I'm safe.'

'Are you?'

'Yes.' *I was ninety-eight percent sure this was true.*

'Okay, I'll handle them.'

* *

And an email hit my inbox that I had to read.

* *

Dear Katie,

It has come to my attention that you and Nikolai Petrov are seeing each other. Although it is none of my business, this man caused considerable trouble for one of my previous assistants. Please be very careful.

Warm regards,

James

* *

Maybe this is why he was so angry when Nikolai lost that match in New Haven.

* *

That night, Nikolai discovered that I did not find his media revelations amusing. As I raged about his thoughtlessness, he took a shower. When I howled about my career, he stretched. At 11p.m., he put both his arms on my shoulders, looked me in the eyes and said, 'Did she actually fire you?'

'Well, not exactly.'

'Check your contract. They can't fire you for something that doesn't breach that. I'm going to bed. Tomorrow is a big day.'

He went to bed and turned off his bedside light. In minutes he was snoring and I was on my laptop reading through the contract. It was four pages long, with confidentiality clauses, non-compete clauses, obligations and morality checks. Not a skerrick about fraternising with players or staff. The only part that concerned me, referred to unauthorised media quotes. I had spoken to the media yesterday, but it wasn't in relation to the WTA or any of our players. Maybe I was safe?

I dreamt Jane had me handcuffed in a hidden basement room below the centre court. I could hear the crowds and Craig Willis announcing Nikolai on court. She told me I would remain there as punishment for my sins. I struggled against the cuffs, calling for help. Nobody came. Until Nikolai woke me, 'What the fuck are you dreaming about?' I told him. He shook his head and rolled back to sleep. Lucky him.

**

Next morning, we had room service for breakfast. Nikolai had a car pick him up at 8a.m.; I decided to join him rather than face the crowded bus. Pointless, as about a million people appeared to watch me get into his car at the hotel and out of it at the tennis site.

As I entered the press room a couple of select media thought it would be funny to refer to me as Mrs Petrov. I brushed off their comments with confidence and laughed along with their ribbing. Technically my name would have been Mrs Petrova as the feminine in Russian adds an 'a' at the end of the surname. Of course, I kept that to myself.

Marine and Brenda were already at the desk. I felt a wave of nausea crawl up my throat. I knew Brenda hated me. I thought Marine was on my side, but it was a big ask to be my friend now. She had only been with the WTA a few months and it seemed everyone was gunning for me. I didn't know if I would have had the stomach to stay friends with someone this unpopular.

'Hi Katie, we're just going through the schedule,' said Marine in a voice you would use if you wanted to include a small child that had entered the room.

Like a portrait in a horror film where the eyes move, but the face remains fixed, Brenda's dark eyes followed me as I made my way around the counter. The hairs on my arms stood up involuntarily. Marine patted the seat next to her and I sat on it. She took control of the meeting. I listened and nodded, but said nothing. Brenda remained silent until the end.

'If that's it, I'm going to the WTA office where I can be with friends,' said Brenda. Marine smiled in acknowledgement. As Brenda exited, Marine rubbed my back, soothing away the churning in my stomach. Marine was a miracle. She asked nothing of me, simply to share the workload.

We sat preparing notes and statistics. Today was men's semifinal day, leaving doubles matches and finals preview interviews for the women's side of the draw. Under normal circumstances it would have been a day to catch up. Today was not normal. As Nikolai took the court with his opponent Novak Djokovic, Jane entered the press room. She came behind the counter into our sacristy. Addressing Marine, she said, 'And you're supporting Katie, I suppose?' Marine nodded.

'Not unexpected.' She sat down and indicated for me to pass over my laptop. 'I want to check your finals preview.' I nodded and passed it over.

She read, nodded and edited the occasional word or phrase, I couldn't tell, but her input was sparing. 'Good,' she said, as she passed my laptop back.

'And yours,' she said, indicating to Marine, who followed suit. She read and did not touch a thing. 'Good,' she said, returning Marine's laptop.

Jane pulled her own laptop out of her briefcase. The three of us continued to work. To the outside world, all would have seemed normal. I felt sure I could hear the ticking of a bomb. I knew Nikolai's match had started. Jane would see any glance I made to the monitor; I kept my head down. After about forty minutes of passive torture, Jane addressed me.

'Katie, when this rumour first circulated, your honesty impressed me. I tried to shield you from the disapproval, but I can't do that anymore. I'm sure you've checked your contract – I can't fire you and I don't want to. But some people are going to do their best to make your life hell. Do you understand me?' I nodded.

'Well then, good luck.' She snapped her laptop shut, placed it in her bag and left us. We both exhaled.

'He won the first set 6-4,' Marine said.

It took me a few seconds to register what she meant. Nikolai was going to have to do this one without me. There was no way I was going to get caught sneaking onto the court. I was public enemy number one and would be an idiot to give them more fuel.

'We need to find a secret way to get you courtside.'

'Why are you being so nice to me?' I asked. Marine's brow furrowed and her eyes narrowed as she considered my question.

'You're my friend,' she said. 'Isn't that what friends do in Australia?'

I nearly knocked her over as I grabbed her in a bear hug. She stifled a giggle due to lack of oxygen. I didn't let go until she started coughing. I knew at that moment that if this whole world imploded and I ended up broke, unemployed and maligned, meeting Marine would have made the entire journey worth it. She was the real deal.

We never made our way to the court. Nikolai was in control. He defeated Djokovic 6-4, 7-5, 6-3. The media room was buzzing. They had all expected Djokovic's talent to prevail. Djokovic had been in white-hot form for the past week and a half, not losing a set on his way to the semis. Having won the Australian Open singles title more times than any other man, Djokovic's style suited the fast playing courts. Today, Petrov was the winner. In his on-court interview, Jim Courier tried to ask about luck. Nikolai shut him down. 'Today was not about luck.' At least *he* was having a good day.

At the end of play, Jane and Brenda turned up for our pre-finals session. Meetings between Russia and the US during the Cold War crisis were likely to have been more convivial. The mood was clear, I was a necessary evil that needed to be managed.

Jane allocated us roles for the next day. Brenda was to manage the singles final winner – on-court speech and ceremony, press appearances etc. Marine would manage the runner up. I would answer questions at the desk and deal with the doubles finals.

Marine indicated she had ideas for a new twist on the iconic Yarra river winner-with-trophy shot. Brenda attempted to shut her down. Jane told Brenda to listen to Marine before leaving us to work it out. Without Jane, I watched from my designated place in Siberia as Brenda took the reins. Marine's input was not incorporated. When I attempted to stick up for her, Brenda did not respond. My voice would not be heard from the wasteland.

Not Quite 30-Love

Back at the hotel, the elevator ride to level twenty-three was fraught with danger. Players, coaches, WTA and ATP staff piled in and took turns to stare at me. I huddled at the back, attempting to block out their loud whispers. When my stop arrived, I pushed past the throngs and exited. Bereft of energy, I shuffled down the hallway. About ten metres away, the cacophony coming from our room reached my ears. Shouting, music and wafts of smoke emanated. Resting my head on the door, I pondered my options. Marine had gone out to dinner with some of the trainers; I was not invited. I could go to the gym, but my gear was in the room. A swim – they would sell me a suit at the spa – a swim would be perfect. It was late and the pool would be blissfully empty. Before I could reposition myself, the door opened and I fell into the arms of an unknown man. He replaced me in the upright position and slapped my arse hard. Then walked out of the room. The decision made for me, I took three deep breaths and entered.

Inside the lush living space were at least twenty people. I recognised his trainer, coach and agent, the rest were a mystery. I could not extract a single English word from the din. Cigars were lit, alcohol was flowing and the singing had started. Russian ditties that required deep voices, stomping of feet and slapping of hands to punctuate the meaning. Through the haze I spotted Nikolai. He was sitting on the lounge with a bottle of beer in one hand and a cigar in the other. The final was thirty-six hours away.

I tried to slip unnoticed into the bedroom and put my bag away, but Mario spotted me. As if stuck in a greeting loop, he kissed each of my cheeks four times and dragged me to the couch. Nikolai pulled me into his lap, blowing smoke in my face as he kissed me hard on the mouth. I coughed and winced. Nobody cared. 'How was your day?' Nikolai asked.

'Totally fucked. And yours?'

He burst out laughing and slapped me on the back. Returning to Russian he conversed with his posse. I tried to stand; he pulled me back into his lap. Someone thrust a shot glass into my hand, the liquid was clear. Vodka, I assumed, downing it. The throng cheered and another glass appeared in my hand. Shots continued to flow. The celebrations got louder and more unintelligible with each round.

My senses were awash with confusion. The vodka had heightened awareness, but dulled comprehension. Russian, Spanish and German flowed with the booze. The words buzzed around my ears like flies, ever present yet without value. In my confusion I wandered out of the living room. Unfamiliar arms circled my waist and directed me towards the bathroom. A loud noise distracted my companion and I slipped into the bathroom alone, locking the door behind me. As I slid down the door frame and rested my head against it, the door handle turned. The handle turned over and over, the door shook, but the lock held. The mirror showed a woman with disappearing pupils and ruddy complexion. I made it to the toilet and vomited. Visions of past dingy nightclubs flooded my brain. I had journeyed around the world, met celebrities, forged a new career, fallen in love, and yet here I was in a hotel bathroom, drunk, disgusting and superfluous. I slid into the crevice between the toilet and the wall, resting my body on the cold tiles, and drifted into oblivion.

Minutes evaporated, or hours passed. I was in no position to judge. There was a banging sound that brought me back to consciousness. It came from the door. A voice became audible, then meaningful. It was my name, Katie, being said over and over. My body resisted movement; my vocal chords would not vibrate. I sat motionless, even when the door exploded open and Nikolai slammed into the wall. He grabbed and shook me. I met his gaze, but could offer no more. He carried me over his shoulder into the bedroom, placing me on the bed. I was watching a movie, where I was the star. The lines had been written and I was unable to affect them.

A man came, he listened to my heart, took my pulse and left. I slept again.

My head ached, my throat was dry and my limbs were heavy. With little cooperation from my body, I managed to reach the bathroom and put my head under the tap. Drawing the lifeblood into my body, I swallowed mouthful after mouthful. Gurgling and spitting, my body screamed for more fluid to be pumped faster and faster into my system. My need overwhelmed my capacity and the water started to come back up. Nikolai held my hair and supported my body. He kissed my head and murmured words I could not understand. When my body finished convulsing, he carried me back to the bed. Looking up at him, his eyes were red rimmed and his face was drawn and pale.

'You were drugged,' he said. I nodded.

I put my head on his shoulder and it felt cold – ice cold. It was not my imagination. Nikolai had three ice packs strapped from his shoulder to his elbow. His left arm, his serving arm. I blacked out before I could question him.

**

It was 10a.m., I was late for work. The first Grand Slam of the year, my first Grand Slam. Women's singles finals day; even with my diminished role, this was not the time for failure. Nikolai helped me to dress and look presentable. He got me a car and put me in it. I arrived on site and mumbled something about food poisoning. No one was interested, there was too much to be done.

Marine and Brenda watched the match from centre court. I watched from a monitor in the press room. My eyes ached from focus and my body strained against the need to stay vertical. Every thirty minutes, Nikolai rang my phone to check on me. He was practising, stretching and being treated. Tomorrow was the biggest day of his career. I had no idea how he managed to pull up after all the alcohol and smoking until he explained that he dumped drinks and held cigars for show. Everyone thought him an iron man; instead he was a master of illusion. I learnt this too late to help me.

Serena Williams was a hero that day. Her win lit up the tennis world and consumed the media. Margaret Court's Grand Slam record eclipsed. Marine and Brenda did the heavy lifting. I managed a small on-court ceremony and a press conference for the mixed-doubles champions with a limited crew of barely interested journalists whose bosses similarly didn't trust them with the main story of the day.

I was invisible on what should have been the biggest day of my career; I limped into the training room. I needed electrolytes and the physios had them. Laura, who I had dined with at least ten times over the past six months, informed me she had run out. I could see a box in her kit bag. Cathy's reaction was the same. I turned to leave and collapsed on the floor. When I came to, I was on a treatment table. The doctor was with the physios and he had been examining me.

'We need a urine sample,' he said handing me a small jar. Three sets of condemning eyes and silent mouths told me their story. This was a doping test; they thought I was on drugs.

'You'll find rohypnol or GBH or something like that,' I said, taking the jar. 'Someone tried to rape me last night. I've already seen a doctor.'

The faces morphed from accusatory to horrified. Laura took my hand. 'Was it Petrov?' she asked.

I shook my head. 'He saved me. Please, I just need some water or something, and sleep.' The doctor agreed that fluids and rest were the only treatment. My body had to process and expel the drug. I left the training room with Laura's box of electrolyte supplements.

**

Before boarding the bus back to the hotel, I checked my email. Brenda had sent images of Serena on the Yarra. She had thanked Marine for her help and input. Another email from Jane:

**

Hi Team,

Congratulations to Brenda and Marine for a successful Champion photo shoot, which will no doubt generate global coverage. The pair will manage tomorrow's Championship Press Tour, visiting TV morning shows, *Sunrise* and *The Today Show* and various variety/sports programs. Katie Cook will manage the Women's Doubles Final.

Regards,

Jane

PS: A special thank you for Katie managing to come to work after being drugged and humiliated last night in her hotel room. Oops, I guess that bit was left out.

The artic winds of Siberia continued to blow. They blew me back to my hotel room, where Nikolai was waiting. He had ordered room service. We drank water and ate bland pasta with little conversational accompaniment. I showed him Jane's email. He shrugged his shoulders (the left one still nursing an ice-pack). What was there to say? He asked me if I would watch the final.

'How can I? If I come to the players' box, everyone will see me. I'm on a knife edge already.'

'I've thought of that,' he said handing me an envelope. 'I got you a seat in the middle of the stadium. Nobody knows where but me.'

I would be his secret supporter, hidden in the stands away from prying eyes. I explained that I would need to get the doubles press done before taking my seat. He understood. With all the shit hitting the fan, he wanted me, and I wanted to be there for him. Tonight there was no sex. Athletic abstinence, he was saving everything for the match tomorrow. We held each other and slept soundly through the night.

#TheFinalCountdown, #LoveCrisis

We took time showering, dressing and eating breakfast in the privacy of our suite. Savouring the last moments together before the craziness descended. Win or lose, I would be here for him tonight, but I was aware the result would affect the type of evening we shared. At the entrance to Wimbledon's Centre Court, there is a famous quote from Rudyard Kipling: 'If you can meet with Triumph and Disaster and treat those two imposters just the same...' Neither of us seemed capable of this level of self-actualisation yet.

Hsieh Su-wei and Peng Shuai were charming and ecstatic after they won the women's doubles. They wanted to stretch and shower before the press conference, but upon seeing my face, agreed to come straight from court. I tried to assure them that the media would be more attentive before the men's singles final had started, but I guess like everyone else they had heard the rumours. Class acts through and through, they smiled and revelled in their win. I took a photo of them and the winners' trophy with Peng's camera and they were on their way.

All that stood between Section D Row E seat 27 and me was a teenage boy and a thin rope. The match had started and the public were not allowed to enter until the second change of ends – three games into the match. I leant against a concrete wall and closed my eyes. Anton Mikhailov had beaten Aussie Steve Wize in the other semi, removing all local hope. The crowd had no favourite in the all-Russian final between Petrov and Mikhailov. The crowds' appreciation rose as the balls made my favourite 'thunk' sound as they were pummelled into submission. Every point stretched to breaking. Each game reached multiple deuces and, by the time the rope dropped, the match was on serve, 2-1 to Petrov.

Wearing a straw hat, sunglasses and a red shirt that Nikolai had seen me pack, I took my seat. Looking straight ahead, I waited for him to look up from his seat. He did. Fifteen thousand fans packed the Rod Laver Arena to capacity. Despite them, our eyes met, both sets of shoulders dropped and we exhaled in unison. Petrov got to his feet and I could swear strutted John Travolta style, ready to receive.

The atmosphere at a five-set final is similar to a sexual encounter. The crowd wants to go hard in the first set; then they settle in, enjoying the rhythm, the ebbs and flows until the match nears conclusion – anywhere from the end of the third, to the fifth set. The problem happens when a comeback is made. The crowd has climaxed and needs to rest before a second coming.

The first set was full of exploration. Petrov went up 4-2 with a break, Mikhailov drew even at 4-4, they traded serves to reach a 6-6. The crowd braced itself to see who would draw first blood. To my immediate left and right were Mikhailov supporters. I sat motionless, fists clenched hard enough that my nails had again left semi-circular indents in my sweaty palms – if I was not careful, they would become permanent. I smiled. Smiled in case Nikolai looked up at me and needed reassurance. My face ached from the static forced grin that would hopefully fool my lover. In truth, I was shitting myself.

Petrov collected the first set and followed with an early service break in the second. Mikhailov was on the ropes. He looked at his box, swore at them, smashed a racquet – drawing a warning from the umpire – and regrouped. Before I had a chance to feel comfortable, Anton had taken the second set. Ninety minutes in and we were even.

Nikolai wandered in the desert through the third set. He clawed through each service game, holding on by his fingernails until 4-4 when Mikhailov broke him. As he slumped on his bench at the change of ends, I leant forward in my seat willing him to look up for support. A towel covered his face until the umpire called time. There was no strut in his stride and, as he crouched ready to receive, he stole a glance. It was all I needed to pump my fist and shout, 'Come on!'. Mikhailov served down the T and ran in, Nikolai returned at his feet, the volley popped up and Nikolai put it away. He had broken back.

The set was ours. However, a two-sets to one lead was not going to defeat Mikhailov. The fourth set was tortuous. Nikolai's serve was erratic. His arm was bothering him. He did not call for the trainer. He did not want his opponent to see weakness. Mikhailov took that set in another tie-break. Four hours into the match and we were even again. The crowd members around me had gone in and out of the stadium, visiting the toilet, the food outlets and beer stands. I had not moved. My butt ached, I was desperate for the toilet and my hands were shaking from the adrenalin.

For the fifth set, the punters were in their seats. Many drunk, all pumped to see which Russian would claim victory. Both players had taken a shirt change and toilet break. I considered leaving, but knew I would face queues of people who would not be missed if they didn't make it back in time. I sat in my seat, praying for victory – a quick victory and a dry seat at the end.

An hour later, at 5-5 in the fifth set, I was unsure whether my body was shaking from nerves or near bladder explosion. Every muscle was working overtime to control my emotions and bladder. Neither player had relinquished speed, power or accuracy and the quality of the fifth set was eerily high. The Australian Open now had a tie-break in the final set – but the match could still stretch beyond my bladder's limits.

At 6-5, I knew I had to leave. Nikolai looked up at me for support, I pumped my fist. He squatted to receive and I snuck out of the stadium. With no queues – who would leave at this point – I was back as they hit 6-6. Time for the tie-break. The new format for the final set required a player to win ten points, with a two-point advantage. I snuck under the rope to get back in. I did not make it back to my seat in time and was sitting on the ground in middle of the aisle. It was 0-1, Mikhailov had a mini-break. I saw Nikolai's face looking at my empty seat, he was staring as a child stares out the front window as their parents drive away. He had to know I was here. I stood and yelled at the top of my lungs 'Go Petrov.' He recognised my voice, followed the sound and saw me standing. The crowd turned and stared at the crazy woman interrupting play. The umpire called for quiet. Nikolai hit a winning return.

He broke and then held both serves. Mikhailov served an ace, switched ends, then Nikolai hit a scorching return, 5-2. Next, it was Nikolai's turn to hit an ace. They traded service holds until the score was, 9-4. Nikolai had five championship points. Mikhailov held both his serves, 9-6. Nikolai missed his third chance at the title on a double fault. His arm was shaking so much both balls hit the bottom of the net. On his next serve he hit another fault. The second serve's toss was too far in front. He let it drop. The crowd screamed and sighed in equal volumes. The tension was proving too much for many who had put their hands over their faces, horror-movie style. I had not blinked in nearly three minutes, way past the record achieved with my sister Lou in third grade. The second serve was short, but it was in. Anton chipped the return and charged the net, which Nikolai anticipated also moving forward. Mikhailov hit the ball directly at Nikolai and he reflexed it back. Mikhailov's racquet touched the ball as it wizzed by. The title was ours.

Nikolai fell to his feet at the net. Anton stood and waited for him to rise. They shook hands and embraced. They both took turns to shake the umpire's hand and Nikolai returned to the court and started blowing kisses at his box, the crowd and at my empty seat.

The assembling of the ceremony went into gear. Officials entered the stadium, TV cameras encroached on the court, red carpet was rolled out and my counterparts at the ATP were on court talking to Anton and Nikolai. The speeches began. Tennis Australia, sponsors and legends spoke; it was all a blur until Anton came to take the runner-up's trophy. He congratulated Nikolai and winked as he said, 'I want some of what he's having.' The crowd laughed. And then it was Nikolai's turn. His speech started as all championships speeches do, with thanks to the tournament, sponsors, ball kids and, of course, his opponent. He thanked his team for their hard work and support. Then he stopped, turned to my seat, which I now filled, and said 'ya lyublyu tyebya'. The only Russian, other than 'da' and 'nyet', I understood – 'I love you.'

Tears flooded down my cheeks. Oversized blobs of water ran down my neck Members of the public surrounding me understood who he was talking to. TV cameras were attempting to get a shot of the woman deep in the crowd that Petrov had declared his heart to. With the ceremony over and the cameras closing in, I made for the exit. People were patting me on the back, congratulating me. I needed to get out. I needed to be with Nikolai.

Despite the fifteen thousand people exiting the stadium with me, I managed to exit Rod Laver Arena, run down the back entrance into the player area, past the practice desk, down the corridor to where the players left the arena. He was there. His bag was on the floor and the ATP rep was next to him with the trophy. I ran into his arms sobbing. He held me and kissed my head. 'Congratulations,' I managed. Then I returned the favour. 'Ya lyublyu tyebya.' My pronunciation made him laugh. I had probably just said 'I'm a baby's bottom' or something. Neither of us cared.

We walked to the locker room. He kissed me and left. Stephan, Matt and Mario each gave me a high five as they followed him. Stephan stopped and kissed me on the cheek. 'Thank you,' he whispered in my ear, and continued through the door.

Peter from the ATP filled me in on Nikolai's schedule. He had press, photo shoots and TV appearances. I suggested the Russian flag as a cape. Peter winked at me. 'I think that's already been done, Katie.' Touché!

I texted Nikolai and told him I would see him back at the hotel when his press was done. As I walked down the corridor a text came through:

**

'Get dressed to party.'

**

#NotAFairytale, #LoveCrisis

Last night I was Cinderella at the ball. I looked at the floor beside the bed for glass slippers. No luck. I looked beside me in the bed and a six foot four Prince Charming lay snoring away. Very lucky. Even his snoring was sexy. Deep, gruff and manly, like a bear warning potential interlopers.

I remembered bits and pieces. I remembered his press conference and the tweet where he had accused the WTA of torturing me for our falling in love. Our Facebook feeds filled in some gaps, showing images of us embracing after his win, the Crown Casino high rollers room and various other dark clubs. I remembered Nikolai introducing me to people as his girlfriend, and I remembered making love. It was as I imagined I would feel if my numbers came up in the lottery. Complete bliss mixed with the satisfaction that I had beaten them all. I may not have played on Rod Laver Arena, but I had the WTA's attention. No longer the girl who was sleeping around with a player, I was the partner of a powerful athlete who was now vocally in my corner.

While Nikolai slept off the celebrations, I read the online coverage. He was portrayed as a victorious Russian general.

They discussed his talent and capacity to join the greats. If only he could sustain this level of play. I was described as the source of his power. Love had given him strength, commitment and will. The WTA were the villains, blocking true love's path. It was all a very Gothic fairytale. Who was I to correct them?

My emails told a different story. The head honcho of the WTA, Brian Hull, wanted to speak to me about breach of contract. Nikolai's tweet had brought negative publicity, which was strictly outlined as a no-no. Cinderella's dress was returning to rags. Soon she would be relegated to scrubbing out the hearth…that is, if she had a job at all. Still, Cinderella would go out with a bang. A sumptuous room-service breakfast was on the way and a hot shower would precede its arrival.

The smell of bacon brought Prince Charming to life. Cinderella served him breakfast in bed. They fed each other. First some bacon, then a kiss, a little toast, another kiss, some scrambled egg, more kissing. Then Cinderella dove under the covers and gave Prince Charming a blow job that would rattle any castle. Cinderella was becoming quite the expert at BJs.

**

When Prince Charming's blood had returned to his head, I told him of the email.

**

'Do you want me to get him taken out?' he said. I was ninety-nine percent sure he was joking. 'Katie, this is the biggest day of my career. Hell, my life. You're killing the moment.'

He had a point. It was my career on the line, but that seemed to be a daily occurrence. Nikolai would forever be a Grand Slam champion. It was something to revel in – for at least twenty-four hours. I smiled and got on top of him, a little more celebrating couldn't hurt.

**

After our breathing returned to normal, Nikolai let out a huge sigh. 'The only thing that would have made yesterday better was if Elena and Anastasia were here.'

I laughed and said, 'I think Anastasia may have been a little young for last night's party.'

'Family is everything, Katie.' Did he think I didn't know that? I needed to call my parents.

The bedside clock drew my attention. It was 11a.m. and I had instructions to be at the WTA office at noon. Nikolai suggested taking Mario with me. 'He can make sure they don't screw you over.'

'That will just antagonise them. I want to make peace.'

'Okay, but call if they're fucking with you, we will all come down.'

I loved this protective side of him. He had shown it with Nasty and Elena, but it felt nice to be included in his bubble. I dressed conservatively and decided to wear flats and walk to the site. It would only take about fifteen minutes and it would clear my head.

After exiting the hotel, I turned left and headed toward the arena. The sun screamed through the ozone-free atmosphere as I walked down Batman Avenue. The time alone had woken me up and given me some space to think about what I was going to say, but I was starting to sweat and regretted the decision to walk. I wanted them to know that, from my perspective, I didn't see them as the enemy, and that we all needed to take a step back and look at the facts. I was in a relationship with a player who had a high profile. I hadn't killed anyone and I hadn't neglected my duties. Surely, there could be an amicable solution?

I had just enough time to freshen up in the bathroom. I used the hand dryer to evaporate the sweat and zhoozhed up my hair. I entered the WTA office, *I should have brought Mario*. The firing squad awaited like a bad episode of *Law and Order*. Jane was standing with the head of operations, Peter, and CEO Brian was seated. Brian indicated for me to sit.

'Katie, no doubt you are aware of the press coverage surrounding your relationship with Nikolai Petrov.' I nodded.

'We are concerned that the WTA is being portrayed as your enemy.' I nodded again.

'It would be an understatement to say that we are concerned at the way the situation has progressed. It is our role to promote this sport, not get embroiled in personal relationships.'

I couldn't contain myself. 'I don't see the WTA as the enemy. I love my job and just want this to go away.'

Jane interrupted, 'It's affecting your work, Katie.'

'I don't believe that's true. Except that, because of it, you're punishing me.'

In what way?' she asked.

'Giving me the doubles final. While Marine and Brenda handled the high-profile work.'

'You have enough profile at the moment. And you did not even manage to keep that out of the work I did give you.'

'Excuse me?'

'The women's doubles final. You made them go to press early, so you could get to Petrov's match.'

'That is NOT true.'

'Katie, you practically dragged them from the locker room.'

'I can't believe this shit. I took them to press fast because once the men's final had started the media would all be watching the match and wouldn't be interested. You know I'm right. They wouldn't have got any coverage. Instead they had a nice interview and some small but thoughtful stories came out of it.'

'The Chinese media would have waited.'

'You're right, they would have, but the girls got local stories and Associate Press covered them. They wouldn't have if the men's final had started.'

'Perhaps that's true.'

'Did they complain about me?'

'No.'

Brian interrupted. 'Katie, we are not interested in your relationship. We just want the WTA to get on with what we do best – showing people what a great sport this is.'

'I want the same thing.'

'Then let's work out how we can make that happen together,' he said.

In my mind, Brian had declared himself good cop. Had they really acquiesced this easily? Or was it a trap? That's when the reality of the situation dawned on me. They had their hands tied. If they got rid of me, the press would tear them to pieces. It was in their best interest for me to be a happy camper. I really did have them in check.

'Do you think you could ask Mr Petrov to abstain from criticising the WTA?'

'I'm sure I could work with him on that.'

'Do you think shutting down your social media for a time might be prudent?' I agreed.

Jane decided it was her turn to enter the conversation.

'Katie, Marine may have started with us at the same time as you, but she's been working in Formula One for years. I think you could be a very good operator, but you still have a lot to learn.'

I felt my defences come up, but she looked sincere and her tone wasn't condescending. Marine did have years on me in the sports communications game, and Brenda obviously did too. I looked at Jane, Brian and their silent partner Peter. Humble pie seemed in order.

'I want to learn and I'm hungry to learn. I don't want my relationship to get in the way of that, Nikolai knows that as well.' I told them that this was a new situation for me and I was navigating the pitfalls, rather poorly.

They agreed that the scenario was new all round, and it was time to get on with promoting women's tennis.

As I walked back to the hotel, the sun had mellowed behind a bank of clouds. My temperament cooled to match. Some of these people would not be invited to my birthday party, but we did have one thing in common, the love of this game called tennis.

When I got back, the suite was back in party mode. I saw Nikolai through the throng and he signalled to me, thumbs up or thumbs down. I signalled back thumbs up. He smiled and went back to his posse. It was an oversimplification, but it did the job. Not wanting to be the party pooper, I dumped my stuff in the bedroom and joined the celebrations. I had a night flight to Tokyo and some packing to do before leaving for the airport. That was five hours away and merrymaking would fill the time.

#ChillingOut, #LoveCrisis

The Americans named flights that travel through the night, red-eyes. It doesn't take a brain surgeon to work out why. My red eyes had minor relief in the form of a clean-up and a squirt of trusty Visine before I changed and went on site for the Pan Pacific Open in Tokyo. The fierce heat of Melbourne was behind me. Tokyo had snow on the ground. Time to get out my cashmere coat and fur hat. A new city, temperature and crew were upon me.

I did a double take when I found Jane sitting at the WTA desk in the press room. She looked up and smiled. I had no capacity to hide my dumbstruck expression, which made her laugh.

'I'm your comms colleague this week, Katie. I thought some one-on-one training might be in order.'

I sat down next to her and unpacked my laptop, printer and other kit. This was either going to be unbelievably helpful or excruciating. *It couldn't be any worse than hanging out with Brenda. Or could it?*

Our first lesson was on targeting. 'Who do you think our audience is, Katie?'

'Tennis fans.'

She looked at me without speaking for about two minutes. Understanding she wanted me to elaborate, answers circled in my brain. But were they the right answers? I wondered whether it was worse to be silent or say something stupid.

'That's a bit of an oversimplification, don't you think?' Jane said.

Her look implied she was newly unsure whether I had the intelligence to master this role. She pulled up a spreadsheet on her laptop. We spent the next forty minutes dissecting TV ratings profiles, ticket sales, demographics, social media engagement and spectator feedback. The information was mind-blowing. We were able to see patterns and trends. Our target audience was ageing. Great, because they had money to spend; the downside was, there was negligible room for growth. We needed to recruit and focus on a younger following and we were competing with team and extreme sports, which were more fan friendly. The information put a whole new light on the job, we had to focus on media that targeted youth and we had to tailor our approach to them. I felt invigorated. This is why Marine and I were hired – to generate youth appeal.

Between player interviews, delivering press requests and writing notes, Jane spent the week tutoring me. She coached me on how to brief players better for interviews and how to give feedback so they could improve. I assumed the players would resist our input, but most were thrilled to learn something new. Not only the young ones. The seasoned professionals like Maria Sharapova and Venus Williams all listened to advice from Jane and me on how to maximise the exposure that you want and minimise the scary stuff. Turns out I did have a lot to learn, and if top players could listen, so could I.

It was all in the delivery. Jane had a knack for giving advice disguised as a compliment, 'It's amazing how the media respond to you, when you look up/smile/tell a joke...'. Who doesn't like a compliment?

She reminded me that information flows in two directions. The media were also a fount of knowledge – milk them, befriend them, they are half the equation. She explained that I needed to earn their respect. Then she delivered the warning, like the side effects of any drug. 'Remember Katie, no matter what anyone says, nothing is truly "off the record".'

On our third night, we took some key members of the press out for a meal. She told me to keep my head down and listen. Journos were human beings too and they could relax and reveal information that might be useful. Also, if they saw you as a colleague, then they might help you when the chips were down. This only happened if you were fair to them.

'Give them exclusives and be up-front. Everyone's trying to do a job. If we make theirs easier, they will reciprocate.'

Jane received an interesting tidbit from an American writer the next day. An Italian journalist was on the hunt for a controversial story about equal prize money. Before each press conference we briefed the players on how to handle the questions. The WTA was united on this front. We brought equal TV ratings, equal 'bums on seats' and often more media coverage than the men's tour. Equal prize money should be a topic for the history books. The players' response was unified and word perfect.

Rather than spending her days locked in front of a computer screen typing up notes, Jane worked the media room. She talked, offered help and made herself available. Watching Brenda, I had gotten into the habit of keeping the media at a distance. When I thought about it, Marine seemed to go and talk to them too. I needed to work these media rooms; otherwise I was always going to be branded as that girl from the WTA dating Petrov.

I missed Nikolai. He stayed in Melbourne for two days after I left for Tokyo. We talked late at night for hours on the phone. I talked; he listened. Actually, I'm not even sure he listened, there were a few long awkward silences when he could have been asleep. At least he didn't hang up. After leaving Melbourne, he flew home triumphant to Moscow.

After five days in Tokyo, Jane and I weren't exactly buddies, but a relatively early finish on Friday night was an opportunity to exit the stadium and see some of the famed night-life. We regrouped in the hotel lobby around 11p.m. with two of the trainers and a couple of supervisors. The vote was unanimous for karaoke. We piled into a taxi and made our way to Roppongi, where the nightclub scene took off.

The twinkling lights of Roppongi made New York look lacklustre. This place had serious sparkle. With the signs all in Japanese characters, a mythical aura hovered over us. The night was overcast, icy and drizzling. It reminded me of a scene from the movie *Blade Runner*. I half expected women with synthetic snakes to be sitting in windows and Harrison Ford or, more importantly, Ryan Gosling, to wander by looking shady.

To navigate the hieroglyphics we used a business card given to us by the media room manager with the name of a karaoke club. When we found a match to the characters on our card, we entered. The English name below was cause for concern – 'The Sexy Room'.

'We won't be able to use receipts from here on our expenses,' said Pam the supervisor. We all giggled imagining the accountant in Florida querying whether our expense allowance included visiting brothels.

The hostess, whose English was negligible, led us to a living room–sized space with speakers, a large TV screen and a phone. She pointed at the phone and shut the door. The room was sealed like a safe. We looked around at each other nervously. Were we about to be kidnapped by the Yakuza or similar mafia gang? Samantha, a physio from Ohio, spotted something next to the stereo. It was a catalogue of music and booze. Via the picture book, we recognised types of alcohol and album covers. It seemed you used the phone for booze, and entered numbers jukebox style into the stereo for music. There was a small box of four microphones – sharing was the imperative.

Nobody had the courage to start. The lights were bright and it's much more comfortable to make a fool of oneself in the dark. Alcohol was required. We managed to order drinks over the phone. Our order was complicated as they were unable to see the wild explanatory hand gestures we used to elicit understanding. Nonetheless, roughly what we ordered arrived. It took two drinks each for someone to load up music – a soft start with ABBA's 'Mamma Mia'.

An hour later, the trainers were standing on the sofas screaming heavy metal hits interspersed with show tunes. In the middle of 'I'll Sleep When I'm Dead', the music stopped. A chorus of screamed 'no's' rang out. Hands flailing over the phone, we managed to ascertain that you paid for the room by the hour. A subsequent hour was booked.

The trainers linked arms when they sang. This act of camaraderie did not help them stay on pitch as they belted into their shared mic. The supervisors and Jane had formed an open circle with two mics. I had the fourth. I felt like I was dancing solo at a nightclub. Nobody specifically excluded me. They sang around me, not with me. Four vodka, lime and sodas intensified the feeling of isolation until Rachel, a younger trainer from Italy who had been knocking back the gins, dropped the bombshell.

'What's it like to sleep with Petrov? He's so hot!'

Silence fell as the backing track thumped on solo. My face went red as all eyes attempted to extract an answer.

'A lady never tells,' I said. A chorus of disappointed 'oh's' rang out. My brain pondered through the alcohol haze and decided to add, 'but it ain't half bad'. I looked over at Jane, who was fighting to suppress a smile.

A few songs later, my arms were linked with the trainers and supervisors. I had even chosen a song, 'Total Eclipse of the Heart', as that was compulsory for all karaoke sessions. Perhaps it was I, not them, who had been holding out. I thought they were a pack of bitches out to get me. Maybe I was the bitch?

At 3a.m., someone suggested the party was over. Jane and I had just finished a flawless rendition of, at least to our ears, 'My Way'. Frank Sinatra eat your heart out. It pained us all to leave our musical box, but time was up.

I slept soundly and woke a little the worse for wear. A large bottle of water doused with two tablets from my travelling Berocca and a couple of Advils, a squirt from my near-empty Visine bottle, coupled with a scorching shower, and I was ready to go on site for the semis.

Jane looked fresh and professional standing in the lobby. Like her doppelgänger, Meghan Markle, ready to tour the colonies. She was waiting for a car to take her to the airport. I was to manage the last two days solo. She shook my hand and said, 'Remember Katie, it is amazing how well people respond to you when you act yourself.'

A few minutes later, sitting next to a snoozing Rachel, I realised that I had not thought about Nikolai all morning – a new record.

On the seventh day He rested; but, for the Tokyo crew, it was finals day. The second of February was also my twenty-ninth birthday. On the edge of a new decade, I momentarily contemplated what it would mean next year. This year, I was still in my twenties, the decade for exploration. Emails from my parents, Lou, Jen and Marine were read in the privacy of my room. My parents were clued in enough not to mention anything controversial, just wishing me a happy day.

The finals started later than normal matches, giving me a little Tokyo strolling time. My budget blown from the past year of excess, it was to be a voyeuristic experience. Busy locals rushed by me, kitted out in perfect outerwear. My cashmere was not a standout in this city that trades brands for personal space. Tokyo is probably the only city in the world where people queue outside Louis Vuitton.

Tokyo is disturbingly clean. Despite the lack of space and the number of inhabitants, people are eerily polite. The only place they push is getting on and off the overcrowded trains. I had heard about the pushers. Railway employees paid to shove passengers onto trains to ensure not an inch of carriage is empty. I watched them in action. If they tried this in Australia it would come to blows.

Back at the hotel, I changed into work gear. A rare knock at the door sparked my curiosity. A young Japanese porter in full uniform bowed. He bent down and picked up an enormous bouquet of red roses, already in a crystal vase. He handed it to me, bowing again. Then he bent down and picked up another red box. I put the flowers down and he handed me the box. After a total of five bows he exited and I closed the door behind him, eager to unwrap my bounty.

The card attached to the roses wished me happy birthday, 'Love N'. That word again. I put the vase by the TV so I could see it from my bed. Buoyed by his card, I unwrapped the red box. Not jewellery this time – my first designer handbag. A perfect quilted black Chanel clutch with a black and gold strap; it was the ultimate in elegance and class. I slung it over my shoulder and stole some time looking into the mirror. Perfection.

I snuck a look at my watch and realised it was the middle of the night in Russia, too late and too early for a call. Due to my promise to the WTA, my Facebook was shut down. I emailed him:

* *

Flowers and bag are stunning. You warm my heart. Love K.

The finals went without a hitch, I had drinks with the journos and a solid night's sleep. Next day, on my way to the airport, I gave away my beautiful roses to the ladies on the tournament transport desk. They were way too perfect to be left to die alone in an empty room.

#HotHotHot, #LoveCrisis

Three weeks of working and travelling were both exhausting and exhilarating. Armed with knowledge and enthusiasm, I had met, schmoozed and bonded with journalists, advised players and picked up on cues better than before.

Nikolai's generosity had fuelled my loneliness; I missed him and we were on the eve of a reunion in California's Indian Wells.

Marine was to work with me and we had not seen each other since Melbourne. Indian Wells is located in a desert town near Palm Springs and a short drive from LA, you can see why America is a country of affluence. In the middle of nowhere, artificial oases with golf courses greener than Kermit dominate the landscape. Five-star resorts are more common than Starbucks and public transport is replaced by black stretch limos.

One such limo met me at the airport. I was shaken and stirred from the flight as the plane almost clipped the mountains surrounding the runway on descent. I looked around for a tournament-branded staff member. An older bald man with khaki shorts and high-topped sneakers carried a sign with my name. 'Ma'am, follow me,' he said, wheeling my bag to the car park. I was escorted to a limo longer than a semi-trailer with no tournament signs.

'Um, I'm sorry, but are you with the BNP Paribas Open?'

'Yes ma'am, and you're with the Petrov party.'

'I'm Katie Cook, from the WTA.'

'And you're Mr Petrov's partner, correct? He organised the car for you.'

I nodded. What else could I say? Inside, there was enough seating for a press conference. Fully equipped with a bar and a TV, I considered loading up on the vodka, before remembering I had to go straight to work. For the last three weeks I had started to fit in with the WTA crew. Now I had my sunglasses on and head down. As I exited the limo, I waved the porter away and wheeled my own bag to reception. While waiting in the queue, a man in an immaculate black suit approached me.

'Ma'am, I'm John Taylor, the hotel's executive concierge, you don't need to wait in line. We've been expecting you.'

I looked around to see if I was on candid camera. I cautiously followed him to a desk in the lobby with a conspicuous gold VIP sign. I attempted to whisper.

'My name is Katie Cook, I'm with the WTA. I think you must have mistaken me for someone else.'

'No, Ms Cook, we know exactly who you are. Mr Petrov's suite is ready. He told us that you would check in today. We understand he arrives tomorrow morning.'

I signed the form he placed in front of me. He didn't even want a credit card imprint.

'Ma'am, may I take your bag? I will personally escort you to the suite.'

'Could you just direct me?'

He shook his head and grabbed my bag and we were off. I kept my head down as we approached the lift bank. Standing there was one of the supervisors, Lisa.

'Hi Lisa, just putting my bag in the room and I'll be off to site.'

She smiled and nodded and got in the lift with us. She pressed the button for the twelfth floor and my helpful concierge inserted a key into a slot on the lift and pressed the button marked VIP. Lisa looked at me; I shrugged and smiled, playing dumb seemed best. As she exited, I said, 'See you in a few'. She didn't respond.

The suite made our rooms in the Grand Hyatt Melbourne seem low-brow. My helper took me through each room, explaining the various insane inclusions. There was a sauna, a spa on the balcony, and three fridges loaded with champagne and caviar.

The bedroom was porn star heaven. An enormous circular bed stood like a stage. It had a ceiling mirror for our viewing pleasure. My helper pressed a button and the bed spun and vibrated. I shuddered. 'Will that be all, ma'am?' Nodding was all I could manage. He didn't wait for a tip and slipped out quietly. I checked out the other bedroom, which although opulent had a normal king bed and no mirrors above. I put my clothes in this room's closet.

Within twenty minutes, I was at the front of the hotel to meet the site bus when someone's hands slipped over my eyes. It was Marine. We hugged and kissed each other's cheeks so many times we lost count. 'It really should only be two kisses,' said Marine smiling.

We sat next to each other on the bus like kids off to school. We stopped short of holding hands, but we did giggle and update each other on all our news.

'I owe you an apology,' I said.

'For what?' asked Marine.

'I've learnt a lot about this job since I last saw you. Enough to know you're much better at this than I imagined.'

She waved her hand as if to say, nonsense. I wasn't prepared to let this go.

'No, don't dismiss me. I know I've been arrogant, but I want to learn. Will you teach me?'

She looked at me, tilting her head, sizing up my sincerity, then nodded.

That day on site was magical. Marine and I worked the press room. Talking to journalists, making notes on their wish lists, spending time with key writers. We discussed finding ways to appeal to a younger crowd. Indian Wells was a hard location. It was full of retirees craving the sun after years living in cold climates on the US East Coast or in Canada. We weren't going to appeal to fifteen-year-old boys with golf course photos. Miami was the next tournament; we decided that we needed to come up with something impactful to do there. Scouring the press and internet for clues, nothing had jumped out at us, until I found an advertisement for a skateboarding competition at Westwind Lakes. Skater guru Tony Hawk was hosting the event but, more importantly, cool current skateboarding stars Americans Nyjah Huston and Paul Rodriguez were going to be putting on an exhibition. The whole thing was to raise money for disenfranchised youth so we thought the idea had legs. We needed to find a player who would give skating a go – minus the insurance risk.

This is where Marine's expertise kicked in. She talked to our ATP colleague Jack, who thought a combo shoot would be great. Both teams were going to clear it with the hierarchy before approaching the skate event organisers and we were all going to slide it in with player conversations until we found our stars.

We got on with our work preparing information for this event, with a spring in our step knowing a great idea was unfolding for Miami.

That evening, Marine came and viewed my suite. She brought her camera and took photos. We helped ourselves to the minibar and ordered room service. Our hamburgers were served on silver platters with heavy silver cutlery. We ate with our fingers, initially seated at opposite ends of the dining room table – which was set for twelve guests. After pretending to scream at each other due to the distance, we moved next to each other and finished our meal.

I asked Marine to keep me company. She could sleep in the spinning bed. She declined. I showered in my room's en suite. There were six showerheads each pummelling me from a different angle. I pressed and pulled at levers and could not work out how to shut them off. It was all or nothing – like my life. In the end, I got onto my hands and knees and crawled out of the shower to avoid the jets. Soaking wet, I managed to flick the master switch and the whirlpool subsided. Nikolai was bound to ask me about the bruises I could feel developing.

Curled up in a corner at the very edge of the bed, I braved an internet search. My phone revealed that Nikolai and I were thankfully no longer flavour of the month. I set the alarm on my phone and succumbed to sleep.

**

The next day, I left for site before Nikolai hit town. Mid-morning he sent a text saying he was practising on site. I texted back saying I was busy but couldn't wait to see him that night back at the hotel.

The practice schedule showed Nikolai had a hit on an outside court at 1p.m. Despite telling Nikolai I'd see him tonight, I could see his court was out of view of prying eyes. A quick reunion kiss, nothing X-rated, seemed reasonable. My best-laid plans turned to crap when a paparazzi jumped out of the bushes and snapped us mid-kiss.

'See you tonight,' I said, as I stopped briefly to also kiss coach Stephan before slinking away from the court. Nikolai grinned and got back to his practice.

In the press room, I told Marine what had happened. She rolled her eyes. Sometimes I hated my poor judgment. An idiot could see I needed to be more careful. *How much of an idiot was I?*

Our private reunion was far more athletic. Three weeks without sex made Katie a VERY hungry girl and it turned Nikolai into an animal. I sweated more than in a double spin class. All activities were confined to the king bed. There was no way I was doing it with a mirror over my head, much to Nikolai's disappointment.

We spent our cuddle time catching up. Nikolai's tennis was at its peak. He had won the tournament in Paris and was ready to kill the competition in Indian Wells. I told him how much I had learnt and that I had to be more discrete with the press about our relationship. He groaned.

'I thought we were past that,' he said.

'We are. I don't want us to be a secret. Just not in their faces, so I can get on with my job.'

'Whatever,' he said, getting up and making his way to the shower. Couldn't he understand that I needed his support? I was so pissed, I didn't warn him about the jets.

* *

Twenty minutes later, he returned from the bathroom, his hair wet and a towel around his waist. 'Great shower,' he said. I rolled onto my side and he curled alongside me. He felt warm and his body was rock hard It seems I was capable of being pissed off and blissed out at the same time.

#IntoTheFire, #NoLoveCrisis

Nikolai left early to hit on centre court before the matches were underway. We didn't talk about work before he left, and I sat quietly eating my room-service brekkie at the runway-length dining table.

On site, Marine and I made a call to Jane. She loved our idea for the skating hook up in Miami, and also approved working with the ATP.

'It's all about finding the right players,' she said.

We were already on the hunt. That afternoon, when the training room was at peak capacity, Marine and I sat talking and chatting with the players. Marine dropped a comment about how hot skater dudes were. We threw around a few names, including Rodriguez, and they bit like frenzied piranhas.

Before we knew it, about six players were crowded around trainer Rachel's laptop ogling professional skateboarders. Marine and I joined in. I have to say, some of the guys were hot, even by Petrov standards. Not as big, but very cute. We had found our target.

One of the players, Elena Komenchova had a brother who was an Olympic snowboarder. He skated in the off-season. Elena had hung out at skate parks with him since she was a kid and shadowed a few moves for us on the locker room floor.

By late afternoon, three players, including Elena, had agreed to try their luck at the comp in Miami. The next step was to get the skaters' organisers to agree. We enlisted the press manager, Marcus in Miami, to feel them out.

I did not see Nikolai all day. But I did run into Stephan, or rather he ran into me. He seemed very concerned and asked me to meet with him. Despite looking out for him, our paths didn't cross again that day.

At midnight when I returned to our room, Nikolai was already asleep. Exhausted and scared of the shower, I ran a bath and soaked. Warm and softened, I cuddled into Nikolai's sleeping body and drifted off.

Next morning Nikolai decided we both needed an energy boost. He woke me with kisses that escalated too quickly for my body. One orgasm for him, zero for Katie. Lucky for me he was prepared for round two, which updated the tally to two-one. Far more acceptable.

**

On site, Nikolai appeared to have understood my message. Whether he agreed or not, he stayed away. I peeked out at his first-round match as he dismantled a young qualifier. He got the job done in around forty minutes. He was too quick for the fans today as well.

Stephan found me as I was dropping a player back to the locker room. He grabbed my arm a little too enthusiastically.

'Sorry, but I think you need to learn something,' he said.

I nodded and we walked to the tables and chairs reserved for players wanting to soak up the sun while eating their lunch. Stephan took us to the furthest table.

'Have you met Nikolai's sister?'

'Unfortunately, yes,' I said.

'She is not a fan of yours,' he offered. I told him that was mutual.

'Watch out Katie, she is very angry with you.'

'Why?'

'I don't know. I heard her screaming down the phone to Nikolai. I have some Russian, not enough. Your name, Anastasia's name and slukh or slut. I'm not quite sure, but Nikolai was listening, he was shaking his head and his face was red.'

I was surprised to hear they talked. In all the time we had spent together, I had never seen him take a call from her. I thanked Stephan for his advice and as he walked away I asked, 'How are the boys doing'?

He smiled and nodded his head to indicate all was okay at home. He was very sweet to be concerned, but really what could Elena do all the way from Russia?

Indian Wells and Miami were the big guns of American tournaments. Taking almost a month of the circuit, these back-to-back ATP/WTA combined events were huge business. America was a significant market for us. Unfortunately, it was saturated with sport, and tennis was pretty low on the totem pole. Both events coincided with 'March Madness', the American college basketball tournament. We had our work cut out, competing with them.

Despite the challenge, Marine and I were determined to start hitting the younger market. Not just with the skater idea, but here in Indian Wells. For years the event had put together a fashion show for the crowd. The female players dressed up in designer gear and the local news did a short piece. We wanted to amp up the volume and contacted a couple of hip young designers from LA – only a two-hour drive away. The tournament agreed to send a car to pick up the designers and the gear.

The players were fighting over the clothes – a little risqué and a lot hipster. Tournaments often forgot how young our players were. They dressed them in ball gowns and suits. Most of them were between sixteen and eighteen with their teenage years spent on a tennis court. They craved normal – normal with a platinum credit card.

Coverage went national. The event organisers bought most of the designer gear and gave it to the players. As a thank you, Marine and I were each given a dress. Mine was a short black shift with some seriously well-placed cutouts. A couple of millimetres either way and I would have been in a new profession.

Four more days passed. Nikolai had won three matches and was into the quarterfinals. All was well with the world – well, my world. Nikolai had a big match against Nick Kyrgios. Nick rebounded after losing the Aussie Open and was playing great tennis. He was on a mission.

That morning at the hotel, I kissed Nikolai and wished him a good match. He seemed distracted, more than pre-match jitters. I couldn't fathom his mood and went off to work. He was to be on the centre court at 2p.m. for the featured TV match.

I sneaked a peek at the score at 2.30p.m. Six all in the first set – pretty tight. I silently made the sign of the cross and went about my work. Two press conferences and an autograph session later, I noticed crowds huddled around the media room monitors. There were lots of oohs and aahhs and some pretty serious debates going on. Marine sidelined me. 'Nikolai's in trouble out there.'

'Is he losing?'

'Not just the match, his mind.'

I took a step closer. Nikolai was screaming at the umpire; his racquets lay broken in a pile at the base of the chair.

'You're a fucking disgrace, all of you,' he shouted.

I winced. The tournament referee had been called. Due to the wonders of modern technology and on-court microphones, we heard it all. Nikolai even stooped to the c-word, which resulted in instant disqualification. The media had cottoned on to the fact that I was watching, and cameras started to click. My face red from anger and embarrassment, I exited the room. Gutted and disgusted, I made my way to the players' exit. Nikolai was standing there smashing a chair with his one remaining racquet. Coach Stephan, the referee and several bystanders had backed off. Stephan waved his hand at me, indicating for me to leave.

'What the fuck are you doing?' I shrieked.

He stopped smashing and looked up.

'You're making a fucking idiot of yourself. Stop behaving like a five-year-old and get your shit together.'

Krygios walked passed us both into the locker room.

Then Nikolai retaliated, 'I don't know who the fuck you think you are. Nobody talks to me like that.'

'Well I do.'

Nikolai came towards me. Too fast. He put his arms around my throat. He did not squeeze. He stared into my eyes. I felt terror spread through my whole body. Terror that grounded me to the spot – he wouldn't have let me move if I wanted to. He spoke, he did not scream. His words came slow and clear.

'Do not fuck with my family. You are nobody.'

He released his hands from my neck and took three steps backwards without losing my gaze – making sure his words sank in. Then he turned and went into the locker room. He was gone. I was pretty sure I had peed in my pants.

Nikolai skipped his press conference, earning him a hefty fine. On top of the fine for being disqualified, it was going to be an expensive day. I was pleased he missed coming to the press room. I wasn't sure how to handle seeing him. Making friends with journalists over the past few weeks helped me. They seemed less inclined to pump me for information, until I heard the comment from the *USA Today* journalist: 'What a way to celebrate your birthday.'

I looked over at Marine sitting at our desk. She looked back.

'What did he mean?'

'Didn't you know it's Nikolai's birthday?'

I couldn't even shake my head. Marine looked at me for about a minute and then went back to her work. A few minutes later she managed, 'They had a cake for him. It was going to be delivered on court if he won and in the players' lounge if he lost. I'm pretty sure that won't see the light of day.'

I sat down at the desk next to her and stared at the ceiling, blinking away tears. It was his birthday and I'd forgotten.

Later that night, I went back to our suite. As I put the key in the door, I trembled. Would he still be violent? Would he have gone rock star and smashed up the room? Marine had suggested I stay with her in her room, but I knew I had to face the music.

'Call me, no matter how late,' she said.

I need not have worried as the suite was empty. Any sign of Nikolai had been removed. Nothing of mine had been touched and nothing was broken. That's when I knew this was more than a fight. I called his phone – no answer. I left a voice message to call and I texted as well. I sat in the dining room waiting for my phone to ring or ping. Nothing.

I felt a strange mix of fury and sadness. His behaviour was infantile and his violence towards me unforgivable, but what was the trigger? Had me forgetting his birthday sent him over the edge? What had possessed me to interfere? I should have read the situation better, given him some distance. But what did he mean about his family? Had Elena really gotten to him?

Fuck him – I did not need this stress. I retreated to the bedroom and curled my body into the smallest ball possible in that enormous space. *Surely, he'll calm down?*

I woke to a rustling sound coming from the entranceway. There was a note from the hotel, slipped under the door:

**

Dear Ms Cook,

Due to the departure of Mr N Petrov, this suite is no longer complimentary. The hotel requires you to vacate by 8a.m. or you will incur the full charge of the room, which is $10,000 per day.

Regards,
Peter Hemsbody
General Manager

**

I was in the lobby with my bags in eight minutes. My WTA-booked room had been reallocated. The hotel was full. They expected to have another room tomorrow. I rang Marine and went to her room. She ordered breakfast, but I couldn't eat. I could, however, cry. Bucketloads.

#DownAndOut, #NoLoveCrisis

No amount of Visine was going to wash this away. My eyes resembled a vampire, without the strength of purpose. I felt my entire reason for being was stripped away. Little Katie Cook had fucked up her life. In two minutes of frustration, I had sent Nikolai packing and he, in turn, had evicted me.

Marine watched me cry for an hour or so, and then she pushed me into the shower. More water came out of my eyes than the nozzle. I cried so hard I started to hiccup. Not sweet little noises – the full on hiccup combined with burps. Considering I had not eaten in about sixteen hours, the burps were quite an effort.

Marine suggested calling him again. 'If he doesn't answer, leave a calm message.'

I drank water from the back lip of a glass with my head upside down; that always cured the hiccups. It was Mum's sure-fire solution. This morning, I had to try the remedy three times. Eventually, the noisy intrusions succumbed. Hyperventilating followed the hiccups. Marine grabbed a paper bag. I put my head between my legs and my breathing settled. Still keyed up, I tried meditation, which was a joke. At the best of times I couldn't focus my mind for more than a few seconds.

I cleared my throat and practised speaking. 'Hi Nikolai, it's Katie. Hi Nikolai...' My voice sounded strained. I practised again – better. I dialled the number, which did not ring. Instead it went straight to a message. Not Nikolai's message. A recorded Russian female voice and I had no idea what she was saying. She repeated a single sentence several times before she translated: 'This number is no longer in service.' She repeated the message in Russian and English several times before it sank in. He had disconnected the phone.

First he banished me from our room, now from his life. Since I had deleted my social media accounts, the phone was the only way I had to reach him and it was gone. He really meant what he had said – I was nobody.

Tears drenched my lashes as they barrelled down my cheeks. Marine was at a loss. She hugged me, patted me, consoled me and finally asked, 'Is there someone at home you could talk to?'

'No,' I said, imagining explaining to my family.

They would be thrilled he was out of my life. Especially if they knew he had threatened to strangle me. I thought of Jen and how she managed to go to work each day, feeling their eyes on her, worrying if they had seen her naked – or worse. She would understand. I could call her. It would be mid-afternoon and she would be at work. I rang her.

I managed less than 'Hi Jen' before the tears restarted. She didn't need me to explain, Nikolai's exploits were all over the internet.

'Fuck him,' she said. 'Fuck them all, Katie. You have worked too hard to throw away your work. He's the one who acted like an arsehole on court. It's all over the internet, the footage. I'm surprised your parents haven't called.'

She talked at me and I nodded into the phone. Marine patted my back and handed me tissues.

'But I love him,' I managed.

'I know Katie. I'm just not sure he loves you.'

There it was, the final nail, bullet, or spear. The truth's aim is sharper than any weapon. I was an unemployed muse. In a matter of hours, he had deleted me from his life. That could not be love. Katie Cook needed to get her shit together. Jen was still talking as I rose to my feet. I was shaky, but upright.

'I have to get ready for work now, Jen.'

'Atta girl,' she said, and I hung up. I turned to Marine, took a deep breath, put on my best fake smile and went into the bathroom. Time to put on my show face.

We didn't talk much on the short car ride to site. There wasn't a lot left to say. I took many deep breaths and straightened my spine into ballerina perfect posture as I entered the press room. Eyes followed me as I took my seat at the WTA desk. The press clippings were already distributed. I flicked through them: 'Petrov Tantrum Taunts Fans', 'Monstrous Lack of Sportsmanship', 'Russian Spits the Dummy' and 'Birthday Badass'. And these were generous compared to what was being said online. It seemed nothing else of consequence happened in the world yesterday. Even John McEnroe had written a comment piece – the irony did not escape me. Last but not least was a meme on BuzzFeed: an image of me repeatedly shaking my head whilst watching Petrov explode on the TV monitor, my barely opened mouth dubbed with a recording of 'I'm not with stupid'. I remembered the moment the shot was taken. Every muscle in my body cramped in the attempt to hide my feelings.

I opened my email, which was not an improvement. Jane had sent me an email telling me to keep my head down and get on with the job. Lou had sent me one saying, 'Are you okay?' I clicked reply, entered only one word – 'Yes'. It was a statement of future intent. Then a ping from my phone; it seemed that Nikolai Petrov's Facebook had updated. His relationship status changed to single. A quick trip to the bathroom was required.

When I returned, Marine showed me some good news – the Miami tournament had secured us a meet and greet with Tony Hawk, Paul and Nyjah at the skate comp opening. We had to confirm the players.

Brad Sorentine from the *Wall Street Journal* cautiously approached our desk. Jane had introduced us in Tokyo and we had had several useful conversations since. He looked apprehensive.

'Katie, it's my job, I have to ask… How is Petrov?'

I shrugged my shoulders. He looked irritated.

'You really don't know.' Sarcasm dripped from him.

'No,' I said. He stared me in the face for more than a minute before his expression morphed from irritation to pity.

Marine and I made our way to the locker room to check in with our volunteer skaters: Elena, Giulia and Sandra. Giulia was on the treatment table.

'Elena's pulled out, she said it's dangerous. She talked us all out of it.' *Fuck, how did this happen, she seemed so keen?*

The trainer told us Elena was in the massage room. I made my way over to talk to her. Elena was lying face up on the table, with the therapist working on her legs. She saw me and turned her head.

'Hi Elena, I need to talk to you.' Elena motioned to the therapist who came up to her. She whispered something.

'Elena would like you to leave,' said Sue, the trainer.

What the fuck is happening here? I moved in an attempt to see her face; she shifted position. I tried again and the same thing happened. She was determined to avoid looking at me. Sue gave me a shrug and mouthed 'Sorry'. Something was up. Usually Elena and I played cards or backgammon while she received treatment. She was the last person to want privacy. I left, what else could I do?

On my way to find Marine, I saw three Russians playing cards. I sat down to chat. Before I could open my mouth, they got up and walked away without a sound, leaving their cards on the bench. One of them had a royal flush.

Marine came up to me.

'I think I've entered the Twilight Zone. Nobody's talking to me,' I said.

'Nobody? Or nobody Russian?' she asked.

'I, I don't know. I suppose I should check.'

We walked through the locker room and I stopped to talk to players. Everyone acknowledged me except the Russians, who universally turned their backs. When Marine spoke to the Russians, they addressed her. The target was on my back, or should I say face? Marine told me to go back to the press room. She was going to conduct an interrogation.

The only thing worse than hanging in the locker room and being ignored was sitting in the press room. Our desk was designed to make us accessible to the press, which made sense under normal circumstances. Today was not normal. Instead I was a freak on display to be gawked at and whispered about. I had never realised how loud people whispered until today. Sometimes all I could hear was 'mumble mumble Katie mumble mumble'. Sometimes I could hear the lot. Although everyone seemed to think Petrov had behaved like a 'dick' or worse, none of that translated into sympathy for me. I was, it seemed, to be tarred with the same brush.

When Marine sat down next to me, the expression on her face did not mask her concern.

'I want the good news,' I said.

'Okay, you're not dead.' I smiled. She was right.

'And the bad?'

'They've banned you.'

'Who?'

'The Russians.'

'All of them?'

She nodded. 'Men, women, coaches, maybe even staff. They will not look at you, talk to you, work with you.'

'What am I going to do?'

'You're screwed, unless we find a way to negotiate a truce. Maybe if you can get hold of Nikolai and ask him to lift the ban.'

I shook my head. I couldn't talk to him. I had no way to contact him.

Jesus Christ, he had put a ban on me. In less than eighteen hours, a whole country had been mobilised against me. When they had defended Nadia, I had seen their strength of conviction. No wonder the Russians were so successful in battle. And I had thought the WTA had given me the cold shoulder a few months back. This was at another level. I was about to find out what it felt like for blood to freeze.

'You need to organise the Miami skate appearance without me. If I drop out, maybe the players will come back.'

Marine nodded. She knew I was falling on my sword, but the game is bigger than its participants. She would go back and talk to the players later today.

In five days I was going to be in Miami. Nikolai would be there. If I could just talk to him, I knew I could sort it out. Even if we were finished, we meant something to each other. He had to lift this idiotic ban.

#SkaterGirl, #NoLoveCrisis

Marine managed to get the skater event back on track. Another bonus for me was that the semifinals in Indian Wells were Russian free, making it possible for me to do my job. Players from other nations weren't overly warm to me, but I could function.

The WTA had mobilised to my defence. I had received support from Jane (who had, remarkably, abstained from saying 'I told you so') and others, including the trainers and physios. They had tried to talk to the Russian players, without effect. The ban was absolute.

Petrov had arrived in Miami to a media shit-storm. To protect himself, he was armed with three supermodels. The newly single star was seen everywhere with the blondes draped over him. His social pages, CNN, ESPN Sports, NBC, CBC – all called them his harem. There was even a new meme: two photos side by side, one of Nikolai and me embracing after his Aus Open win, the other of him with the three aforementioned supermodels. They were captioned 'Before' and 'After'. I needed to get to Miami and confront him.

Not Quite 30-Love

Arriving in town, I had a sense of foreboding, mixed with an extremely small touch of hope. Getting in front of Nikolai was going to be near impossible with the amazons in tow, particularly if his posse closed ranks, but there were chinks in the armour – Stephan for one. I had met a lot of the team and learnt some Russian. I had to try. If the ban stayed in place, I couldn't do my job and I would have to resign. The WTA couldn't be expected to carry me. I had not been very loyal to them in the past, but I would do the right thing if I couldn't rectify this situation.

I dropped my bags off at the Miami Hilton, an ageing skyscraper in an industrial part of town. This area wasn't the reason tourists thronged to Miami. Although there were no customs checkpoints and the currency remained green, Miami had all the benefits of a holiday to South America without the extra travel. Cuban music permeated, the beaches were alive with dancing and the buildings were a pastel-coloured dreamscape.

The driver took us to the site. We exited downtown across an enormous bridge with seemed to span into the forever. Either side of us was green water dotted with jet skis, skiffs and luxury yachts. I had heard a lot about South Beach nightlife going off. I was keen for a cocktail or two, given the last few days.

We reached the site in about forty minutes. It was a familiar mix of concrete, plastic seats and people. Not nearly as attractive as the drive over, this part of town was more functional than beautiful. Before long, I was seated between Brenda and Marine at our press room desk. Déjà vu anyone?

The press team introduced themselves. Marco, the team manager, had been working with Marine and I on the skater shoot, which was to go ahead in a few hours. He apologised for not coming to see us earlier. Apparently he had been held up with an important press release. 'Bad news,' he said.

'Nikolai Petrov has pulled out,' he said.

It was all I could do to remain upright. Marine managed to ask the reason.

'He hurt his wrist at practice last night and has already left Miami. Probably exacerbated from smashing all those racquets in Indian Wells,' said Marco. 'There wasn't even a medical certificate. I hope the ATP fine him a million dollars – what a joke.'

It took him a minute to do the math. He looked at me and then down at his shoes. The penny dropped. He mumbled 'Sorry'. His words hit the floor with my career. No Nikolai meant I was persona non grata. Marine engaged an embarrassed Marco in conversation, attempting to cover for my dumbstruck expression and inability to contribute.

When he left, Marine told me to 'hold it together'. She had to set-up for the shoot in Coconut Grove. Brenda was taking my place. She seemed smug, but silent to my face – a small mercy.

**

Once Marine and Brenda departed, I continued my work in the press room. I sat at the laptop, pumping out stats and notes with the passion of a dot matrix printer. The meaningless numbers and words flew across the screen and I collated them into useable material. At least I could interpret this data and make it useful to thousands of people.

Reporters visited the desk and retrieved information. They asked questions, always avoiding eye contact. Nobody knew what to do with me. These men and women who had joked, worked, eaten and drunk with me, had lost connection. I tried to imagine being in their position. What would I say to this girl who had paraded herself around as Petrov's girlfriend and suffered such a public break-up? At least, for now, they weren't aware of the ban.

One piece of good news hit our desks – Nadia Katarinkova was in town. Her time away must have seemed like years to her.

* *

When Marine and Brenda returned from the skater shoot, I managed a smile. Elena had achieved air. Meaning she had all four wheels off the ground at the same time. TV, photographers, bloggers and a thousand cheering skaters had witnessed it. Paul Rodriguez had given her a kiss and video of the not-so-secret moment had gone viral.

'What about his niece?' asked Brenda.

'Sorry, what about who?

'Aren't you friends with that Anastasia girl? Couldn't you contact her?'

Brenda was a fucking genius. I had a number for Anastasia. She may even be in Miami. I hadn't seen her for a few months. She had sent me emails and we had instant messaged a few times – not for a few weeks, but at this point, anything was worth a try.

I took my mobile into the women's toilets, checked under every empty stall for feet, then dialled. My palms sweated and my hands shook. 'Come on Nasty, I need you, baby, answer the phone.' I willed her to answer as a gambler blows on dice. After four rings it went to voicemail. Her Russian message ended in a beep and I gave it my best shot: 'Nasty, it's Katie and I need your help. Nikolai and I had a fight. I'm sure you know. I'm very sad about it. He won't talk to me. None of the Russians will. Please call me. I never wanted to hurt anybody.'

I wondered why it always seemed that my most momentous emotional outpourings were in bathrooms. Crying, vomiting, pontificating or making important calls – the sanatorium effect of the cool white tiles seemed to be the catalyst for fervent self-exploration.

It was done. She would hear my message and decide. She was a strong girl, like her mother, but family was a big deal and her uncle a hero. My odds weren't good.

I went back to the desk. Marine and Brenda were waiting for an answer.

'Voicemail,' I said. They sighed and we went back to work.

Hours passed and my phone sat motionless. Every twenty minutes or so, I checked to ensure it wasn't on silent or without signal. No such luck.

We caught a bus with the players back to the hotel. As I walked past players to find a seat, the Russians continued their pact, acknowledging Marine and Brenda and turning their backs on me. I took my place, leant into the window frame, closed my eyes and pretended to sleep.

The next day passed the same way. Journalists, Russians and everybody important avoided me. I sleepwalked through my limited opportunities to contribute, glancing repetitively at my phone until Marine put it in a drawer.

At 2p.m. Nadia was due to take the court. The entire press-room contingent were in their courtside seats. She took the court – step 1. She completed the warm-up – step 2. She started the match – step 3. Her arm was shaking so hard she lost her service game to love. Then she was down 0-5. We were about to return to our desks when a member of the crowd shouted

'Nadia you're a champion'. She smiled and served deep and hard, winning the point and the game. She lost the first set 1-6, but won the next two 6-4, 7-5. The relief spread all over her face as she shook her opponent's hand across the net.

Brenda and Marco explained to the press that she would only answer questions about this match. As much as I desperately wanted to hold her hand, Nadia was Russian, so Marine managed her press conference. She came sweating, straight from the court, with only a jacket to cover her match clothes. She would not shower or change on site.

The media behaved – at least to her face. The inevitable re-posting of the naked image (with modesty strips to prevent lawsuits) to go along with Nadia's match quotes seeped into some of the more seedy tabloid sites. Most tried very hard to stay away from it, the threat of Nadia's minor status ever-present.

Behind closed doors it was revealed that no charges were to be laid against Josie Farway. Meetings between the WTA, Tennis Australia, Mario and the AFP had led to an agreement. Josie's tennis career was over and the ten thousand dollars would go towards a new scholarship for underprivileged tennis players. The scholarship would be in Nadia's name and Tennis Australia would administer it. They would also support the scholarship to the tune of ten thousand every year. There was to be no public announcement of this deal. The scholarship would be announced at next year's Australian Open and would appear to be the result of Nadia's generosity. Who could argue that it wasn't? Certainly not Josie.

That evening, despite the offer to join staff at South Beach, I did a Gloria Swanson and had room service. I did manage to consume a lovely bottle of red wine and two small vodkas from the minibar before passing out on the bed. Some time in the blackened future the vibrations from the phone on my chest awoke me. Nasty had sent a text.

**

'Stay away from me.'

**

Stunned and reacting without thought, I rang her phone. It rang out, unanswered.

Her words ran round and round in my head as my body and brain fought with each other over the need to sleep. Eventually, my body took the upper hand and as I slept, I dreamt of my lover. I dreamt we were lying in bed in Bondi, eating pizza, kissing and making love. Far from Miami, Indian Wells, Tokyo and wherever else this world had taken me. Bondi was our place. We were at peace there. He had told me he loved me three times. First, he had said 'love' and corrected himself. Second, he had whispered it to me when he thought I was asleep. And, finally, he had announced it to the world when he won the Australian Open. He did not say these words lightly. Despite the models, or perhaps because of them, I knew Nikolai was in pain too.

When I woke up, the dream remained vivid. It was telling me something I couldn't quite grasp. I wanted to believe that Nikolai had not put the ban on me. He didn't want to talk to or see me, that much was obvious, but I was sure he did not instigate the ban.

I stood in the shower, cleaned my teeth and dressed, all with the images from my dreams playing their disconnected pattern in my head. Seemingly senseless flashes, sentimental pictures of our time there, all centred around Bondi... It hit me – he's in Bondi. Nikolai had gone to Bondi. I was sure of it.

The only person I could trust with the knowledge was Jen. She would be even-handed if she found him, unlike my family who might throttle him. I rang her. It was evening and she was at a noisy bar. She stepped out to hear me. I told her of my suspicions, the ban and my worry.

She said 'Fuck him,' several times before I told her that I needed him to get the ban lifted. Then she agreed to go and check. Jen had a key to my flat. I'd given it to her in case she needed a place to escape. Nikolai still had his own key.

'Tread carefully,' I said.

#TheEagleHasLanded, #NoLoveCrisis

Throughout the day I sent Jen several texts. The messages were cryptic: 'Has the eagle landed?' 'Is there a toad in the hole?' Despite my thinly veiled desperate attempts, there was no response from Jen.

The agony of waiting was not new to me. I had waited for my career to start, waited for someone to love and waited for Nikolai during our work-enforced separations. I had been proactive and also patient, despite it never being one of my virtues. Somehow my life kept landing in the hands of others and it was giving me the shits.

Marine, Brenda and I managed the player interview and activity load. They handled the Russians – I never realised how many of them were around, had they been breeding? After a sleepless night with Jen still MIA, I got on with it as best I could until finally an email arrived:

**

Hi Katie,

Sorry not to have been in touch sooner. Had a crazy night. I'll call you tomorrow.

Jen

**

That was it. I searched for the hidden coded message. *What the fuck, was he there or not?* I sent her a three-letter email:

**

Jen, WTF?????

**

I checked my phone every few seconds throughout the day. Emails poured in. None were from Jen.

At 3a.m. my phone buzzed me awake. It was Jen.

'Hi Katie, did I wake you?'

'Of course you fucking woke me, it's 3a.m. Have you found him?'

'Yes.'

'Thank God. Did you talk to him?'

'Yes.'

'Could you give me a bit more?'

'No.'

I screamed down the phone. What was going on?

'Nikolai's in a heap of pain right now Katie.'

'He's in pain? Fuck him. I can't do my job.'

'Not everything is about you, Katie.' *Wow my best friend since I was fifteen had sold me out for a cute guy.*

'If you sleep with him, I'll kill you.'

'Katie, I can't believe you just said that. If you think Nikolai or I would do that, you've...oh, fuck off, Katie.' *She hung up. She just hung up on me. I can't fucking believe this. I'm going to get on a plane and go back to Sydney and kill both of them. Who the fuck does she think she is? Consoling my boyfriend and his pathetic problems. I'm trying to do a job here – doesn't anyone care about me?*

I threw my phone on the floor. The carpet muffled the sound of it hitting the ground. I threw it several more times before a voice from deep inside my soul crawled out and calmly said, 'You are not a rock star'. I stopped mid-slam, placed the phone down on the nightstand, threw myself on the bed and cried. I may not be a fucking rock star, but I sure as hell could be Marcia Brady if I wanted to.

Hours later, wide awake, I went to the minibar and skulled the gin and scotch – straight. After I finished coughing, I threw three pillows on the floor and jumped on them. I marched around the room stomping as hard as I could. Then I picked up my phone and starting typing:

**

Jen,

Friends support friends. I'm dying out here. Don't be a complete bitch. I supported you when you needed a friend. Do the right thing by me or find a new friend.

Katie

**

I hit send before I could change my mind. Then I changed my mind. *Shit, it was a bit harsh.* It took less than two minutes for a response to come through:

**

Katie,

I am your friend. I will always be your friend, regardless of you behaving like a complete child. Everything is not what it seems.

Jen

**

Well, this was a fine fucking mess I had gotten myself into. With a country against me, my family estranged, my best friend a deserter and my job on the line, I sat on the bed with clenched teeth and put a pox on all of them.

Sleepless, I calculated that Marcia Brady would have been about twelve when she threw TV tantrums; I showered and then opened a new bottle of Visine. I should buy shares in that company.

Marine and Brenda had gone to site early for a charity player event – two Russians had volunteered to help, which made me redundant. I sat at the back of the bus and leant against the window alone and waited for departure. I felt someone sit on the seat next to me. Nervous to see who had chosen to sit next to the pariah I looked up. Zoe Lemonjian, the young Aussie player I met in Linz, had taken the spot.

'What's up, Katie?'

'Really, you mean you don't know?'

'Yep, I know. Just wanted to hear it from you.'

'Shithouse. Thanks for asking.' She nodded and smiled and slapped her hand on my thigh.

'You do know you only have yourself to blame, right?'

I was pretty sure telling a player to fuck off would be pushing it too far, so I gave her my fakest possible smile.

'Oh, you don't know. Let me give you some advice, Aussie to Aussie, what you do with it is up to you,' she said.

'Please do,' I said, dripping with sarcasm.

And she did. First of all, she reminded me that I had been on the tour less than a year – even less time than her – which was true, although it felt like a lifetime. Secondly, I was not a former player, therefore had not experienced what it was to be one. I rolled my eyes.

'Most people think we're just a bunch of rich kids running around hitting a ball. You know that's not true. For most of us, this is all we know and a lot of people are riding on our success. If *you* fail, you go back to Sydney, lick your wounds, and then get another job. For us, it's different. Everything's at stake.'

I considered playing the world's tiniest violin for her.

She continued. 'You've been on a stadium court after a big match. Think about the focus of attention, imagine having all those people staring at you, willing you to victory or defeat – can you?'

I suppose I sort of could. When I had walked on court in front of ten or even fifteen thousand people, there is a sense of foreboding. The stands bear down on you, hands reach out, voices clash. A couple of times, I felt nauseous.

'Imagine having a bad day in front of that. Failing everyone that publicly.'

'I can.'

'No you can't. Today, after one of the matches, especially if a seed loses, go and put yourself down there and try to imagine it. Then you'll have some idea of how Petrov felt.'

'Oh, don't tell me you think he was right?'

'No, he behaved like an arse. Most of us have, including me. When I was a junior, I really lost it a few times. Luckily I had parents who pulled me into line.'

That would be a first.

'I manage the pressure better now, but I'm only getting started on my career. I'm not sure how I'll handle a Grand Slam final.'

'So what am I supposed to do?'

'Just understand us a bit better. If you want to work with us, you have to get us.'

She sat back, put on her headphones and listened to her beats. I looked out the window as we crossed the bridge. The sunlight refracted off the prisms in the diamonds on my wrist. I recalled Nikolai surprising me at Lou's engagement party. I should have left him alone in Indian Wells and given him time to calm down. I was embarrassed his actions would reflect on me. My bracelet continued to sparkle. I wore it every day. I wanted the hero, but not the villain. I stared into the tiny hearts inside each diamond. The bus motored along the highway. Zoe enjoyed her tunes, players slept, talked and fiddled with their racquets, strings and grips, nervous about the day ahead.

The players hadn't rejected me because he told them to; it was because I had no empathy for or understanding of their lives. I wanted them to appreciate the importance of public image and the media, without acknowledging the pressure and strain on their self-belief that was a part of their everyday lives.

I chastised Nikolai for being boring with his practice. He dared to be working towards a dream, which inconvenienced me. I was furious when he was late to Christmas lunch, because of practice. He had financially supported his family all his life and not celebrated Christmas since he was ten years old. When he won, I bathed in his glory, stayed in the suites, ate, drank and made merry at his expense. He stood up for me against the WTA, misguided as we both were, even offering me his lawyer. He had showered me with gifts and I forgot his birthday. I was a parasite that abandoned her host at the first sign of injury.

Katie Cook was a petulant child who expected everyone to fix her problems, The WTA, Jane, Marine, Brenda, my parents, Lou, Nikolai, Jen and now Zoe Lemonjian had all tried to help me. Had I listened? As we pulled into the carpark, I tapped Zoe on the shoulder. She took off her headphones.

'Thanks,' I said. She nodded and went back to her beats.

As we exited the bus, she said, 'Oh, it could also have something to do with that rumour you started.' She winked at me and walked away.

#IGetIt, #NoLoveCrisis

The queue to enter stretched around the block. Excited ticket holders laughed and chatted as they waited to spend a day in the sun watching their heroes fight it out on court. Many of them were dressed in tennis gear and carrying racquet bags, such was their devotion. They looked silly, but happy.

The event machinery was in full swing, with acrobats on stilts, people dressed as life-sized tennis balls and humans mimicking statues ready to entertain the crowd. Food was being delivered to concession stands and pop music blared through the loudspeakers. It was showtime.

I made my way to the press room, and watched the thirty or so media people turn their heads. The uncomfortable feeling in my stomach was magnified by a factor of one hundred when I imagined that instead of thirty it was thousands. As soon as I passed, they went back to their stories, conversations or whatever else they were engaged in. I was not interesting enough to hold their attention for more than a few seconds – let alone a three-hour tennis match.

Marine was at the desk. 'How did the clinic go?' I asked.

'Fine,' she said. 'Nothing to report,' she added with a smile.

'Marine, I've not thanked you for supporting me through all this.'

'Don't mention it.'

She wanted me to shut up and get on with work. I couldn't blame her, but I still needed her help. 'Zoe Lemonjian said something about me starting a rumour. Do you know anything about that?'

Marine looked at her screen.

'Katie, I can't do any more of your drama today. I don't know about a rumour. Please, can we just work.' She saw my reaction.

'Let's go to the locker room,' she suggested. I followed – what did the locker room have to do with anything?

**

A couple of minutes later we sat in the change room and watched the animals in their native habitat – not a flattering description, yet an honest one. Their environment reeked of a hideous concoction. A mix of Deep Heat, upset stomachs and fear. I had gotten used to the smell, immune to it. Now I inhaled the stench. These girls were sick with the agony and ecstasy of impending battle. Their bodies strained by the impossibility of perfection. Yet they continued. Continued to train, play, fight, win and lose. Some of their journeys would end in heartbreak, others in glory. And we would watch and prey upon them to celebrate their victories and relive their defeats. They lay on the treatment tables, being pulled, pushed, rubbed and taped up for their next encounter. Their young bodies stretched beyond reasonable limits over and over.

It was my turn to feel sick.

'They're so young,' I managed.

'Yes,' she said.

'How do they handle all this pressure?'

'The champions do, others don't.'

We lived in an alternate universe where children bore the weight of the world by chasing after a ball. No matter how fast they ran or how hard they hit, more was required. They were challenged by adults to answer for their failures. They continued to sprint, jump, twist and fall until their bodies could take no more – this was called retirement.

I had had moments, when Nikolai was talking about his family or the tennis camps in Germany, when I had understood how hard it had been for him. But I had not applied this universally. Not understood the extent to which families relied on this sport for survival. There are exceptions – families who supported their children's dream of tennis stardom, parents whose lives existed beyond the courts. In these cases, the pressure was self-perpetuated.

**

Later that day Nadia lost her match. She sat quietly, fully clothed, in the locker room. I wanted to speak to her to tell her she should be proud of herself, but I knew she needed more time to absorb the loss. Instead, I wrote her a note and slipped it in her racquet bag when she was talking to another player: 'Nadia, I know you can't and probably don't want to speak to me, but I want you to know you should be extremely proud of yourself for how you've done in Miami.'

That evening, Marine and I rode back to the hotel. Tonight, despite it all, I knew I would sleep. I longed for the soft bed and escape from reality.

My phone, which had been on silent in the press conferences, showed a missed call. It was from Jen.

'Katie, sorry I've missed you. I saw Nikolai. He won't explain why he snapped. He just keeps talking about betrayal. He is sorry he scared you. He seems ashamed. He wants to move on, I think, but he doesn't know how.'

I rang Jen's phone. It went to voicemail. I, too, left a message.

'Jen, it's been a huge day here and I'm going to bed, please tell Nikolai I don't want to cause him any trouble. I think we would both be better if we moved on. He can stay at my place as long as he likes.'

My alarm woke me for the first time in weeks. I showered, dressed and checked my email:

**

Hi Katie,

Nikolai left Sydney today. I gave him your message and he gave me his key to your flat. He was truly humiliated by his behaviour in Indian Wells and, as you know, I understand humiliation.

Sounds like you've been soul searching too. Not much fun is it.

Take care and I'll see you on your next Sydney stopover.

Love Jen

**

It may be a lot longer than a stopover next time.
I put my phone in my bag and went downstairs.

#Treadmill, #NoLoveCrisis

Three weeks passed with little to show for them. I continued the daily battle to earn my keep. The Russians still ignored me, yet luckily the WTA maintained their support.

The men's and women's tours separated after Miami and would not collide again until Rome. Petrov had returned to the tour. He had played two events and lost first round in each. He had finally tweeted an apology for his behavior. The media collectively declared his career was finished.

Despite my lack of popularity, I spent more time in the locker room. I owed it to the players. The trainers were generous, including me in conversations. The players watched me. I used the time with the girls to build up a mental dossier on their off-court personalities. I wasn't writing it down, I was aiming for a deeper understanding of their lives. Perhaps others could learn from their journey.

Marine was at home and Brenda was my work companion.

'Fun being dumped, isn't it?' she said, on our first morning together.

'So far, it's been a riot,' I replied.

'You can't trust a Russian,' she said. Was she still living in the '80s? I didn't know or care anymore what her problem was.

My runs each morning were a lifesaver, focused on the beauty that surrounded me. Week one was Amelia Island, a beach resort in Florida. The beach was long and straight, nothing like Bondi's semicircle. As I ran, the sand stretched to infinity. I marked the distance by familiar beach houses that rose out of the dunes. Mostly uninhabited during April, the houses hibernated until their families returned during the summer months. Twenty minutes equalled the navy-blue Cape Cod cottage. Forty minutes, the cream Hamptons-style mansion.

The following week I journeyed to Charleston, South Carolina. One of the last states to stop flying the Confederate flag. Not being born in the US, the flag held no meaning for me, but the fierceness with which the African-Americans spoke made their positions clear. It was a beautiful historical city; the downtown area resembled a movie set, except the homes were hundreds of years old. The Williams sisters used to refuse to play here. Again, our hotel was on a beach, this time the dunes were deep and the boardwalks narrow. The wind howled through the bracken and I returned from each run with sand in my teeth, up my nose and caked in my hair.

My punishment was to take on a new hue as I travelled home. From Charleston to Atlanta through LA to Sydney, over thirty hours lay ahead. Thirty hours sitting upright in economy thinking about how to reconcile with my family.

The time passed much as it would at a gym when you're told to sprint on the treadmill for a minute. How can sixty seconds last so long? Sixty seconds times sixty minutes times thirty hours equals 108,000 seconds. First I remembered my childhood. How my parents had put up with my crazy Safin crush, then my boredom at work, wild plans for tennis, bringing Petrov home, then the unravelling. For nearly thirty years they had supported my triumphs and disasters and I repaid them by cutting them out of my life. Like a game of snakes and ladders, my determination had gotten me far, but my pig-headedness had pulled me backwards. I had a lot of ladders to climb up.

When the plane landed, I gathered my bags and cleared customs. There was no one to meet me. I had not told them I was coming. It was the first time I had ever arrived home and not had family waiting for me. The airport was strangely unfamiliar without Dad to wheel my bags and Mum's arm linked through mine as we walked to the car. I had to locate the taxi rank and trudged with my bags to the queue. My bag was light compared to the weight of my emotions.

It was 10a.m. when I reached my flat. The rooms were just as I had left them. Except for the aroma of Nikolai. I could smell his presence in my bed linen and the towels, the musky masculine smell that I adored and hoped would not dissipate for several days. There was no note, and Jen had his key. He was gone.

I showered and unpacked. There was no food, so I walked to the corner grocery store and bought the basics.

Back at the flat, I curled under the bedcovers and drank in Nikolai's scent as I drifted into a druggy sleep. I dreamt that I was home watching Wimbledon and the past year was imagined. When I woke that evening with tears on my cheeks and a wet pillow, I knew, despite it all, I wanted to be part of the tennis world. How would it turn out for me?

I braved my first call to Jen. In less than an hour later, she was at my door with pizza. We ate, drank and talked. I didn't ask her about Nikolai and she offered nothing.

'It's been a year to learn from,' I said.

'Tell me about it,' said Jen. 'I've learnt not to make sex tapes.'

'Or, at the very least, to keep your face off camera,' I offered.

'No shit, Sherlock.' We fell about in hysterical giggles. We imagined ourselves two fifteen-year-old girls, yet to be tainted with bad decisions. Instead of two women in their very late twenties, who had fucked up big time.

Sick of thinking about my life, I pried into the details of Jen's life. It seemed that she had been seeing John on and off since their date at the tennis. It was very casual. He was a gentleman and understood her need to go slow. They had not even slept together yet.

'We've kissed,' she said. 'But I can't help but check everywhere for cameras when I'm at his place.' This caused a new round of giggles.

Jen left and I returned to slumber. When I woke, I was still short on courage, so I went for a run and a swim. Revived, I dialled my parents' number.

'Hi Mum, it's Katie.'

'Katie? Are you okay?'

'Yes, I'm fine.' I heard her call my father to pick up the other phone.

'Katie, where are you?' Dad asked.

'I'm in Sydney. I got in late last night,' a little white lie to save their feelings. 'I know I've been a shitty daughter lately.'

'That's an understatement Katie. Two texts in two months – if it wasn't for the social media scandals and news reports we wouldn't know you were alive,' said Mum, my father grunted in agreement.

'That's fair. Can we discuss this in person? Will you come to my place for lunch?' I asked.

'Are you still with him?' My father asked.

'No.'

'We will see you at 12.30,' he said and hung up.

Miraculously, Mum said nothing before she too hung up.

I prepared lunch for at least six people. There was chicken salad, pesto pasta salad, green salad, bread and some store-bought orange and poppyseed cake for dessert. It had better be nice, as I was going to have lots of leftovers.

My mother entered the apartment, paused and looked at me, and then she gave me a hug. She let go before me. My father nodded as he walked through the door. We took our seats at my dining table. I poured water and drank a full glass as my throat had completely dried up.

'You tried to warn me, but I didn't want to hear. I'm sorry.' I blurted out. I was fighting tears, but wanted to have an adult conversation.

'We raised you better than this,' my father said.

Mum grabbed his arm and interjected. 'We taught you to respect yourself. That man does not respect you.'

'I know you think that and I understand why you do. He hasn't had the support I've had from family, and look at the bad decisions I made. It doesn't matter anyway, we're done. I'm just working on saving my career.'

Mum reached across the table and touched my hand.

'I want to be part of this family. I'll try not to be so far up my own arse from now on.'

'Being part of this family is not optional,' said Mum.

'But you're an adult now, show us all some respect and start acting like one,' said Dad.

We ate lunch, quiet at first.

'I've always wanted to see Miami. Is it cool like in *Miami Vice?*' asked Mum.

'It kind of is. Lots of pastel buildings, but I didn't see any cops dressed in linen.'

Conversation continued around my travels. I told them about karaoke in Tokyo as we finished our meal and they helped me fill the tupperware.

'I need to call Lou and Dave,' I said. They agreed.

'Family dinner tomorrow night,' said Mum, as they left.

**

I called Lou.

'Do you still have a job?' she asked. I told her it was hanging by a thread, but I had a good grip. I explained about the Russian ban and the media attention.

'You've been pretty stupid, but I guess you don't need me to say that.'

'I don't. Although I would if I were you.'

'Do whatever you have to. Just keep that job,' Lou said. 'A bit of no bullshit hard work probably wouldn't go astray,' she offered.

Mum, Dad, Lou and Dave saw me off at the airport for the long haul back to Italy. Jen sent me an email:

**

Katie,

Good luck with life on tour. Last time I sent you off with an emergency condom. I see now that was a bad move. Keep it in your pants!

Love Jen

⁎ ⁎

I reacted straight away:

⁎ ⁎

Jen,

Keep yours off camera!

Love Katie

#Roma, #NoLoveCrisis

The circle completed itself as I stepped into the press room in Rome. Press director Beatrix was in her office. Fifteen months ago, I received my first offer of work from her when she answered my email. She smiled and stood as I entered.

'Katie, we meet again.' We kissed on both cheeks. 'It seems you have had an eventful year.' She smirked, winked at me and indicated in the direction of the WTA desks.

'I believe this is where you will sit this year.'

I went over to the desk and wrapped my arms around the brunette entrenched on the phone. Marine, my friend, was already hard at it. She turned and acknowledged me, all without missing a beat. I sat, unpacked, set up my laptop and hooked onto the wi-fi. No rest for the wicked.

The men's finals were on and the media were geared up to watch. They had little interest in the women's matches, which were due to start tomorrow. Petrov had bowed out in another first round and had left Italy days before. All hopes of signing a truce would need to be postponed at least one more week.

After lunch, I visited the locker room to grab Simona Halep for a kids' clinic. As I walked in, a group of Russian players were playing a game that was evidently hysterically funny. That is, until I appeared and instantly all mirth evaporated. As soon as I had passed, the laughter resumed.

Later that afternoon, with the men's final and the associated media complete, I ran into Antonio, the translator whom I had worked with so closely last year. He asked me to join him in the press restaurant for an espresso. With my work done for the day, I agreed.

'Katie, I hear you ignored all my sage advice last year.'

'I did.'

'And how did that work out for you?'

I laughed. What else was there to do?

'It seems to me you both got the better of one another. I saw him earlier in the week. He does not appear well,' he said.

'That's what I hear. He's a good person, Antonio. We're just better apart.'

'It may be true for you. It doesn't appear to be for him.'

'It will be. Time's a funny thing.'

'You seem older.'

'Twelve months on the tour is equivalent to five years in the real world.'

We continued to download the past year's activities. It seems he had completed a PhD in applied physics since I saw him last.

Rome had lost none of its charm. Each morning on my run, I would pass ancient temples and buildings. It seemed no matter which direction I ran, I always circled the Trevi Fountain – not by accident. I had thrown a coin into the water last year and here I was, the legend proved a reality.

The days blurred and the mood around me softened. The press had lost interest in my story. I was happily yesterday's news. The Russians continued with the ban and I continued to work around it, with the help of the team, which this week included Ricardo. He was on local soil and slipped between languages effortlessly. Thankfully, he made an effort not to mention Petrov.

My old friend Nadia Katarinkova had reached the semifinal against fellow Russian Maria Sharapova. After my morning run, I came back to the hotel sweaty, tired and in need of a shower. Nadia was sitting in the hallway a few doors down from my room with her headphones on. No doubt getting some space from her roommates. As I walked past, she looked up and, before she had time to look away, I said, 'Good luck today'. She nodded and, I could swear, managed the tiniest of smiles. We went on with our mornings.

It was a small victory. Each day my confidence grew infinitesimally. Like losing weight. Nobody notices anything for a month, then your pants fall off. The key for me was to keep my pants on.

Nadia lost a tight match against Maria, yet this week was a victory for her. It signalled a return to form and confirmed her return to the top of the game.

**

Maria was in Grand Slam championship form and her confidence secured a win in the final. Being Russian, her victory tour was allocated to Marine. I had suggested sticking her in the Trevi Fountain with her blonde hair cascading down her shoulders, *La Dolce Vita* style. Nobody knew the idea came from me, therefore they thought it was fantastic. The photo was old-style glamour – sexy and alluring, yet modest. It went viral and Marine made sure the WTA knew the idea's source. Jane emailed me:

**

Hi Katie,

I know you're having a difficult time right now, but I'm pleased that you're still coming up with the goods. Marine told me about the origin of the Trevi Fountain shot – well done. Hang in there. The Russians will find something else to worry about soon.

Jane

A couple of the Italian players thought Marine and I needed to see their city's nightlife. Silvi and Frances took us clubbing until 4a.m.. Marine barely drank and I was on my best behaviour, which meant we danced around our handbags whilst divine Italian men attempted to pick us up. The male talent was amazing. Not only were their features stronger than the marble sculptures around the city, they also loved women. They wanted to talk to you, compliment you, pamper you and, it goes without saying, fuck you. We drew the line just past the complimenting – to be safe.

**

At the end of the night, Silvi, a little the worse for wear with the grappa, took me to one side. 'Is it true that Anastasia Topova's pregnant?'

'What?'

'That she can't play because she's pregnant.'

'Holy shit. Nasty's pregnant?'

'I don't know. That's the rumour. I thought you started it.'

OMG. My brain was exploding with simultaneous questions and answers. Was Nasty pregnant? How could anybody think I would start a rumour like that? I knew her mother wanted to get rid of me but surely she wouldn't do this, it was so hurtful to Nasty.

I grabbed Marine and filled her in. She talked to Silvi. Somebody had to deny the rumour and it wouldn't ring true from me.

Somehow I had to find out if Nasty was okay. I couldn't bear to think of her in pain. I hated that she thought I could be so cruel. I wouldn't betray her like that. Betrayal… that's what Nikolai meant! I had to fix this. But where could I start?

**

Round and round and round my thoughts went as I sat on top of the covers in my assigned hotel room. In a few hours I would be in Paris for the French Open. Everyone would be there. Marine and I had checked the qualifying draw. Anastasia was due to play so she couldn't be pregnant. Unless, at fourteen, she had already taken care of it. I did the maths, her Mummy dearest was probably only sixteen when she had Anastasia. Was it possible that history was repeating itself?

#CityOfLostLove, #NoLoveCrisis

Paris, the city of lights, romance and broken dreams was raring to go. The French Open, known as Roland Garros, was a massive event that mobilised the city and had locals queuing. May in Paris was temperate. One day would be gloriously sunny, the next you'd be shivering in a cardigan. Parisians embraced the town before the last flourishes of spring morphed into the tourist-infested summer, when locals deserted the town for the coast and countryside.

This was my second Grand Slam event working for the WTA. I understood the pressure, the volume of work and the stakes, now I simply had to do it all in French. The Parisians were a unique breed, full of paradoxes. They were proud and a little loud – like the Americans they abhorred. Their city's life-blood was tourism, yet they despised the visiting hordes. They appreciated beauty like the Italians; they also loved their food. However, unlike the Italians they preferred intricate presentation and sensible portions. In fact, presentation was paramount in all things – dress, gardens, buildings and homes. Despite this, they seemed happy to leave their boulevards littered with dog shit, which it was customary to step in and then swear aloud. Their history was littered with stories of beauty and greed shattered by revolution. Every day they lived with this conundrum. A little schizophrenia went a long way.

It was less than six months since I had experienced the cliché of falling in love here, now I had to mop up the mess I had created. I wanted to speak to Anastasia to find the truth. I needed to get to Nikolai before the day of his first match. I wanted him to know I didn't betray him and to help him past his losing streak. That would be good closure for us both.

I put my tentacles out to try to find where he was staying, with no luck. It didn't help that the Russians weren't speaking to me. I tried to reach Nasty from Rome. Her phone was disconnected – I had that effect on phones.

On site, the press room was a minefield. The ladies that ran the room did so with military precision. Despite them being fluent in English, only French was spoken. A few minor mishaps, such as me ordering five hundred copies of the rankings instead of fifty, caused consternation. I survived.

**

Brenda caught me looking at the screen where Anastasia's match was supposed to be. She had withdrawn at the last minute and a lucky loser had taken her place.

'Maybe she got knocked up like her mother?' said Brenda as she walked past me.

'What the fuck did you say?'

'Hey, don't look at me, I didn't start the rumour.'

But she did. I knew it the minute she spoke. How could she? What was so wrong with her, that she could do this to a child?

'What's Anastasia ever done to you?'

'Go ask her uncle.'

Click, click, click – that was the sound of my brain attempting to process.

'How the fuck do you know who her uncle is?'

'Oh please, Katie, everyone knows who her uncle is.'

But they didn't. I knew they didn't. It would have come out with the rumours and it didn't. Brenda sidestepped me and exited our cubicle. She had made a mistake. We both knew it, but I didn't know what to do with it. Yet.

Lunch at the players' restaurant was more like a school canteen, complete with queues and trays. Marine and I waited our turn. I had drifted off into nothing land when I felt a sharp shove from behind, pushing me into Marine.

'Get the fuck out of my way.'

I turned to see Nikolai's sister Elena, flanked by her red-faced daughter Nasty. Marine turned, I had to hold her back.

'If you want to go ahead, be my guest,' I said.

'I want nothing from you, bitch.'

It was as if the entire room turned a collective head towards us.

I swallowed hard. 'Nasty, I need to speak to you, but not here.' She did not look at me, but Elena did.

'You are a liar and a monster.' The venom was dripping from her lips.

Nasty grabbed her mother's arm and tugged as hard as she could. She mumbled something in Russian, then in English.

'She's not worth it Mama.'

Elena spat at the floor in front of my feet. A little bit of spit landed on my big toe. I couldn't recoil. I reached out to Nasty, but they were already leaving the room. Leaving Marine at the mercy of the staring hordes, I followed Elena and Nasty.

Weaving through corridors, I found them in a huddle at the bottom of a flight of empty stairs. Nasty was crying in her mother's arms.

'Please, I know you hate me. I didn't do this. I would never hurt you.'

Nasty looked up from her mother's chest. Elena's eyes were glowing radioactive with hate.

'Nasty, is the rumour true? Are you in trouble?'

'None of your fucking business,' screeched Elena, but Nasty was looking at me and she shook her head.

'Oh, thank God, thank God.'

Nothing else mattered. They could hate me forever, but at least Nasty wasn't in trouble.

Elena was on her feet; she had Nasty by the hand and was attempting to pull her up the stairs.

'How does Brenda know Nikolai's your uncle?' I asked.

'She doesn't,' said Nasty.

'She does, and I think she knows more than that.'

'Brenda? Who is that?' Elena's attention was sparked.

'She's from the WTA, Mama. She's the one I told you about. The one who said I was a nobody.' Nasty dropped her head and said, 'Katie, defended me.'

Elena looked to me. 'What exactly did she say?'

I repeated Brenda's words verbatim.

'She will die,' said Elena.

This time, Nasty had no option. They were moving up the stairs at double pace and I was again alone.

* *

I don't know if either of them believed me. I do know something happened with Elena when she heard Brenda's name.

Making my way back to the press room, I imagined smashing Brenda in the

face. She wasn't there; instead, Marine was sitting at her laptop.

'Where's Brenda?' I asked.

'I don't know. She's not answering her walkie-talkie. Anyway, why do you care? Did you catch up with Anastasia?'

'Yep. I think her mother's planning to kill Brenda now. Good riddance.'

Marine screwed up her face in confusion. 'Katie, this is like a bad soap opera. Why is Elena angry with Brenda?'

I told her what I knew. Fragments of the story. I knew Brenda was involved, but I didn't know why. I knew everyone hated me. I sort of knew why.

'Maybe Brenda knew Elena from when she played?' said Marine.

This was a new wrinkle.

'Nasty said her mother played, but I never found any record of her.'

'Ah, but I did. She played as a Petrova, not Topova. She was seventeen when she got pregnant and then she disappeared.'

'Nasty said her mother hates the WTA. Maybe because they didn't support her when she was pregnant. She was a minor.'

'That's possible. But it seems a bit of a minor link between Brenda and Nasty to cause all this drama.'

I had to agree. Something else was hiding under all of this. Hating me couldn't be the only common thread in the story.

**

For the next eight hours we ran around getting players to press and autograph sessions, and writing notes – doing what we were paid for. Brenda was conspicuously absent. I wasn't ready to face her. More pieces of the puzzle were required for a full-on confrontation. At 8.30p.m., I received a text from an unknown number:

**

'Meet me in your hotel room at 9.30p.m. E.'

**

WTF. If the family was anything to go by, this was Elena. How dare she tell me to meet her at my hotel room? At the same time, my curiosity was at fever pitch. The only problem was leaving work and getting across Paris in an hour.

Marine was just as curious. 'Get a car. Go on, go. I'll cover here, the main matches are finished and Brenda will probably show up. Better you're not here for that anyway.'

I opened the door to my room at 9.33p.m. Elena was sitting on my bed. I couldn't fathom whether I was more curious about how she managed to get in or what the hell she was doing here anyway.

'Sit down,' she said, indicating the chair at my desk. *Was I now a bit player in my own life?*

I leant against the dresser in front of her. 'I know Brenda started the rumour,' I said. 'What I don't know is why.'

'She hates you.'

'Sure. I figured that much out. By why hurt Nasty?'

'She hates me.' *Okay, now we were getting somewhere. I had a million questions, but she looked distinctly like she was thinking of what to say next and I didn't want to interrupt her.*

'We used to be friends.'

'When you played on the tour?' *Not sure if this was progress, but I was going to work the mystery out if it killed me.*

'Yes. She was new to the WTA and she looked out for me.' *Hard to imagine Brenda looking out for anyone.*

'What went wrong?'

'I got pregnant and she felt I betrayed her.' *How is getting pregnant betrayal? Unless they were more than...*

'She felt I used her.'

'For a green card?' *Click, click, click. Finally this was making sense.*

'I don't know. I wanted her help. I wanted to get away from Nasty's father.'

'Nikolai said Nasty's father gave you money.'

'Yes, guilty money. He was my sponsor. He supported me on the Tour, until he found out about my friendship with Brenda. It made him angry. He forced himself on me.'

'Did you tell Brenda?'

'I tried. She wouldn't believe me.' *If Nikolai knew what Nasty's father had done, he would kill him. No wonder Elena kept all of this a secret.*

'You have to tell somebody.'

'I just did. And you will tell nobody.'

Her eyes started to water, she looked up and somehow drew the tears back in. I imagined she had been doing this for fourteen years.

'What about telling my boss, Jane? I think Brenda's due for some retribution.'

Elena shook her head.

'Nobody can know. I don't want Nasty or Nikolai ever knowing the truth.'

I knew she was right, but there was a little niggle of an idea in my brain.

'Okay, so not the truth, but maybe just enough to fuck up Brenda?'

This time Elena smiled.

'Perhaps.'

Elena stood to leave. She looked back from the door, hesitating, lingering. Then she spoke, making sure she had my attention.

'He didn't want to believe you did it. He defended you.'

She paused. I wasn't sure if she was waiting for a response. She disengaged eye contact, turned away and added, 'You have his heart.'

She was gone.

**

I rang Marine. My plan to get Brenda was forming. I needed to give Marine enough information to help me, but not enough to betray Elena's trust. My worries were unfounded.

'Marine, you are not going to believe what's happened.' *Okay, so maybe this was too dramatic a start.*

'Brenda's resigned. She's in a car back to the hotel to pack as we speak.' *Holy fuck.*

I barely formed the question. 'What the fuck happened?'

'I confronted her when she came to the office. Told her you knew her game and that Elena was meeting you at the hotel. She completely panicked. Barely said anything. Just got on her laptop, booked a flight home and sent off a resignation letter to Jane. The only thing she said to me was "Fuck you, Marine" as she left. It was quite surreal.'

'You must have been hella convincing.'

'I know, I impressed myself. I certainly wasn't expecting her to fold that easily. I should take up poker.' *She really should.*

'You should.'

'Then Jane came in. She was pretty worked up, wanting to find Brenda and change her mind. Then I told her Brenda had started a rumour about Nasty, pinned it on you and that was the reason for the Russian ban. She literally said, "Fuck her, then." And left.'

'OMG. You've been busy. Taken any players to press?'

'Three, and written the notes. I'm exhausted.'

'Do you want me to come back?'

'No, I'm wrapping up now. It's going to be a busy week. Ricardo's flying in tomorrow to help us. Get some sleep.'

I texted Elena – short but sweet:

**

'Brenda's resigned and on a flight back to the USA tonight. Secrets all safe.'

**

Six minutes later, at 10.45p.m., Elena responded:

**

'Nikolai would like to meet you for a late supper at George V. Meet him at 11p.m.'

**

Okay – they were obviously together or in close contact. I considered the time, the fact that the next two weeks were going to be manic, and then remembered that if I didn't get this whole thing done with, Marine and Ricardo were going to have to cover *all* the Russians.

**

Touching up my makeup in the lift and dropping the compulsory Visine in my eyes in the cab, I was on my way – with more than a few fingers crossed.

Nikolai was at our table. He smiled when he saw me and stood as I approached the table. He kissed me on both cheeks and beat the waiter to pull out my chair. I sat. We watched each other for several minutes. Neither of us spoke. I couldn't hold back my question any longer.

'How could you think I would do that to Nasty?'

I had hit a nerve. The nerve. His answer came out in flood of words and emotion. 'I didn't want to believe it. They told me for days you did it. I refused to believe it. Mario said he had proof. He showed me the emails that morning in Indian Wells.'

'What emails?'

'The ones from you to the journalist at Babushka.' *OMG that's the publication that set up Katarinkova.*

'I never wrote any emails.'

'I know that now. But they were signed like you sign emails…cheers, Katie.' *That fucking bitch hacked my emails. Thank God my social media sites were down.*

'I never write "cheers" to journalists. Always "regards".'

'I didn't know that.' *There's a lot you don't know.*

My shock was disturbed by the arrival of the waiter. We simultaneously ordered steak frites. *Even as hurt as I was, it was impossible for me not to love this man.*

The waiter left us and Nikolai pulled something out of his jacket. It was the iPod I recorded for him for Christmas. 'I found this under the bed.'

I blushed and played with my napkin. 'Have you listened to it?' I asked, continuing to look down.

'Every day,' he said, and I looked up.

'I hate this, Nikolai.'

'I hate it too.'

'Do you think we can get on with our lives and stop hurting each other?'

'I never wanted to hurt you. I know I scared you. I never would have…'

'Are you sure? I'm not so sure. You scared the life out of me. That's not normal and it's *not* okay.' He looked down and nodded.

'Will you hit with me tonight?'

'I don't think that's a good idea.'

'Why? It relaxes me.'

'We both need closure.'

'One last practice together – for luck?'

'Just us, no one watching?'

He nodded and I agreed.

We ate our steak frites. Although Nikolai left the frites on the side of the plate. He smiled as he ate. I was famished. After the scuffle with Nasty and Elena in the canteen today, I left empty. No food since breakfast this morning.

When we were finished, the waiter cleared our plates and delivered the bill. I swiped it before Nikolai had the chance to pay. He didn't protest.

We took a cab to my hotel, he waited in the car while I ran upstairs, changed, and picked up my racquet. I went down the fire stairs and snuck through the lobby with my head down. For once, everyone was preoccupied and I made it to the cab unnoticed. By 1a.m., we were on the indoor court furthest away from prying eyes.

I whiffed the first ball.

'Move your feet,' he shouted at me.

I could only smile and got on my toes. The ready position dance I'd learnt at one of the countless kids' clinics came in handy, jolting my body into action – I was moving.

The rallies intensified as I got a rhythm going. Far from our initial hits in Moscow, the balls were coming cleanly off my racquet. I hit a fantastic down-the-line passing shot, which Nikolai managed to reach at full stretch and win the point. He clapped his hand to his racquet in appreciation. We kept going.

After twenty minutes, I had worked up a sweat. Probably a full steak dinner was not the ideal warm-up. I grabbed an elastic band, pulled my hair back and got into position. We continued. Finally the moment every woman dreams of, I hit a winner past him. 'Move your arse, Petrov,' I shouted, before I could stop myself. He stopped dead, stared at me, and then doubled over laughing so hard I thought we might need a medic.

I walked to the net; he met me there, still laughing.

'Ready to concede?' I said offering my hand to shake. He nodded, but instead of shaking my hand, he initiated the high five. We slapped hands and hugged over the net, which surprised us both. Laughing, we picked up our gear and walked back to transport.

'We should get separate cars,' I said.

His face fell.

'Good luck this week,' I said.

'Thanks, Katie. Good luck to you too.'

He leant down and kissed me on the cheek, lingering a little. The car was ready and I jumped in. It was time for me to get some sleep.

As I rode back to the hotel, I knew I had done the right thing. I felt no sadness leaving him, only happiness that we were in a good place.

#Jinx, #CrisisNQOver

At breakfast, I told Marine of our practice session.

'Did he lift the ban?' she asked.

'We didn't talk about it,' I said.

'Are you fucking kidding me. How are we going to manage this week?' Marine was really getting too comfortable with the f-word.

'We'll manage.'

She shook her head and mumbled something unintelligible.

'Everything's going to be all right, Marine. I have a good feeling.'

'Whatever.' She dumped a huge slab of jam onto her croissant.

Our breakfast was interrupted when Russian player Svetlana Korolova walked up to our table. She addressed Marine.

'What time is the kids' clinic today?'

Marine told her 10a.m..

'Thank you. I will see you then.' Then she turned and faced me, ensuring eye contact and said with a huge grin, 'Have a good breakfast, Katie.'

Marine and I stared wide-eyed at one another as we started coughing. My toast and her croissant had gone down the wrong way. Svetlana turned and left, having achieved the desired result.

When we recovered, I managed a 'Holy fuck, I'm back in the game.' We slapped a discreet low five under the table. Time to get back to work.

#MoveYourArse, #CrisisNQOver

All morning, everywhere I went, Russians were going out of their way to acknowledge me. 'Hi Katie, how are you today?' They were making a point and I was grateful. Rebuilding friendships could start later. Today, it was about getting my career out of neutral. My WTA comrades (including Jane) expressed relief. It was more than about time.

Nikolai took the court at high noon. He was scheduled on the Philippe Chatrier stadium court. After all, he was the Australian Open champion, plus the French Federation were no doubt concerned this may be his only outing. There were no empty seats.

I kept a close eye on the match whilst going about my business. After a few minutes, it was apparent he was in trouble. Going down 0-3 in ten minutes, all the telltale signs of an implosion, followed by an explosion were emerging. Sign 1: shoulders hunched, head down. Sign 2: exaggerated shaking of the head and looking to the sky. Sign 3: ever louder mumbling to himself. It would not take an experienced lip reader to identify the foul language. Sign 4: aggressively scraping his racquet across the court, leaving divots in the clay surface. The umpire had already issued him a warning for racquet abuse. The next stop was a point penalty and I had no doubt that would send him spiralling in the direction of a default. OMG. Indian Wells revisited.

I wanted to do something, but couldn't work out how to get in his face without someone seeing me. If I went into the photographers' pit, they'd snap it up, literally. Then I remembered my secret weapons – Elena and Nasty had made the overt gesture of sitting in Nikolai's player box. It seemed everyone was over with pretense and hiding today. I could use them to communicate with Nikolai.

I pillaged a large sheet of cardboard from the press team and, using my Sharpie, penned a single thought. Texting Elena, I asked Nasty to meet me at the entrance to the players' box at the next change, she responded in the affirmative.

I gave the sign to Nasty – she hugged me. We held on a little too long. How could she have thought I would hurt her?

When we broke apart, she looked at the now slightly crumpled sign and tilted her head.

'Don't worry, he'll understand,' I said.

She shrugged and went back to the box. In the dying seconds of the change of ends, Nikolai looked at his box, Nasty held up the sign and, much to the amusement and surprise of the crowd, he grinned. As his grin widened, his body relaxed. He walked to the court to begin his service game and, with racquet in hand, he blew a huge kiss to the sky. I caught it in my hand.

With the first set lost, Nikolai went back on with the job of building success point by point. He won that first service game after Nasty held up my sign. Not easily, but he won it. They traded serves until 4-3, when a lucky net cord gave him the break. Nikolai jumped on this luck and served out the set. On even ground and believing luck was now with him instead of against him, Nikolai's confidence grew. It took over three hours, but Nikolai won the match. In press, they asked him about the sign, which read: 'Move your arse Petrov'. He smiled and said, 'My arse is very stubborn sometimes. Lucky today it woke up in time.' 'Stubborn Arse' memes were all over the internet within hours. My favourite was a collation of images of Nikolai's butt wiggling on court. Those shorts don't leave much to the imagination. Lucky for me I have memories instead of fantasies.

The ban was lifted and Nikolai had broken his losing streak. Regardless, Marine, Ricardo and I had to get seventy female players to press. I did not stop running. At 7p.m., I realised I had not eaten, drunk or even visited the toilet all day. The toilet was imperative. Marine was in the stall opposite me; we managed some exhausted laughter when we saw each other at the basins.

'First time today?' I asked.

'Yes, not drinking and eating has some advantages,' she said.

'I owe you a drink – Buddha-Bar?' I offered.

'Talk to me in ten days,' was her response. We both ran off in separate directions.

Time raced and the week came to a close. Petrov won his second, third and fourth match. His comeback had drawn the gamblers wrath. Marine showed me his public Facebook feed, as I couldn't access it since cutting off my accounts. It was littered with abhorrent comments from bullies who trolled players who had upset their financial applecart. Apparently, this was the new thing players had to deal with. For some of the players who managed their own social media, it meant dealing with this kind of trolling every time they had a good win. Australia's John Millman was massacred after beating Federer at the US Open in 2018.

Meanwhile, I built the infrastructure for bridges with players and got on with the job. The second week of a Grand Slam is when the atmosphere gets serious. The remaining players are chasing history and a fat pay cheque. The media are hungry for unique angles and the sponsors want their piece of the action. The communications team are trying to place jigsaw pieces together. Occasionally we are required to bash pieces into submission, as a last resort.

In the men's quarterfinals, Petrov was to face Novak Djokovic. In a match that lasted a smidge over five hours, with fortunes changing with hand-wringing regularity, Nikolai kept his cool. He fought like a lion, proud and strong before falling 12-10 in the fifth set. The crowd united in a standing ovation for both players. Nikolai left the court with his head high.

Nikolai was gracious in defeat, completing all his obligations with a new-found serenity. I stood back, but wanted to see him before he left Paris. Two hours after his match finished, I received a text from an unknown number:

**

'Do you have a minute to say goodbye? I'm at transport. N.'

**

Access to his new number no less. I texted: 'Yes', and went to meet him.

When he saw me, he left the throngs of hangers on. We moved to a quiet spot in the lounge, aware, but uninterested in the onlookers. Nikolai kissed me on both cheeks.

'I love you, Katie,' he said. I was holding back tears, determined not to cry. 'But this time is for my career.'

'For mine too,' I said and then added, 'I love you too, Nikolai.' We kissed gently and embraced. He held me tight, those bear-like arms squeezing life in and out of me at the same time. Then he was gone.

#DeservedChampion, #CrisisNQOver

After finding her feet in Rome, Nadia Katarinkova's confidence was high and she made it to the Roland Garros women's singles final. This was her first Grand Slam final. Her task was to defeat Simona Halep.

A victory by either would be good for women's tennis. With Nadia and I on solid ground again, I was assigned to manage her, win or lose. If she lost, I would commiserate with her; if she won, I would manage the champion's press and photo tour. I had some ideas and, as much as I admired Simona, was rooting for a Russian win.

The sun lit up Paris like a movie set. Shadows fell to dramatic effect and monuments shone. This is the city of lights – even during the daytime.

The match was worthy of the setting. Taking three hours and one minute, Nadia prevailed. While the ceremony unfolded on centre court, I unveiled my plan. Nadia's trophy shoot would not be the traditional photo of the champion on a bridge over the river Seine with the Eiffel Tower in the background. I would take her back to Montmartre with the Russian flag, to recreate the superhero shoot from last year.

Nadia delivered her speech in French with a touch of Russian and English thrown in, charming the crowd and officials. She kissed the trophy and held it high above her head, dancing around as if she were a child hoisting a new toy for all to see.

Nadia's press conference overflowed with good will. She was a media darling, a first time Grand Slam champion. Her win was the entire story. Well, maybe not the entire story, but nobody dared raise that photo to her face.

As she bounced off to the locker room, I handed her a t-shirt. 'Wear this,' I said. She nodded, no questions asked.

Sue, the physio, was Nadia's friend and had taken to guarding the shower stall so that Nadia could comfortably shower and change on site. Sue held her clothes and towel and I wouldn't be surprised if she was packing heat. This woman was not allowing anyone to exploit our girl.

In the press director's office, a highly fuelled conversation was taking place. Jane was on speaker-phone fighting for my cause. 'La Tradition,' they exclaimed, wanting their Eiffel Tower shot.

I pushed for my proposal. 'The photo will showcase all of Paris, including the Tower,' I said.

The discussion went to the heights of the French Tennis Federation. Meanwhile Nadia celebrated with her ever-growing support crew. She took call after call, giggling and gushing with delight. Her crew followed her to the press conference and on-site TV studio visits: first French TV, then Russian, then ESPN. An hour passed; she finished her press rounds. Only the champion's photo shoot remained.

'When are we going to do the photo?' she asked.

'Soon, I hope. I'm trying to do something a little different.'

'As long as it's quick,' Nadia said, wearing her 'I love Paris' t-shirt supplied by yours truly. I explained my idea, telling her that it would garner ten times the coverage of the traditional shoot. We were just waiting for approval. The giggling, happy teenager disappeared and a sullen child took her place.

'I'm tired. I want to do something fast and easy. Stop making everything so difficult.'

'This photo will be your legacy. This is your first Grand Slam win. You need to commemorate it with something special. You can rest after the shoot.'

'There is no rest for me. I have to play in Nottingham on grass in two days.'

She stormed out of the locker room into the waiting arms of her trainer and coach. She wailed to them in Russian. They nodded in what I assumed were the right places. After a few minutes she returned to the locker room.

'I will get a massage, while I wait for you to fix the photo, Katie.'

I smiled and continued to type up notes on my laptop. About thirty minutes later, the press director entered the locker room. She did not speak, simply summoning me with her come-here finger, no doubt considering another gesture.

She led me to a room with WTA and French Tennis Federation hierarchy wearing serious expressions. 'This photo should be in the best taste,' said an emissary of the Federation's president. I nodded. That was it. My shot was approved and we were on our way.

Marine helped me mobilise the press corps. Once on board, the press director, Emily, was an enormous asset. She suggested a portrait with the artists at Montmartre – I loved it.

First, we travelled to the top of the stairs in front of the beautiful Sacré-Coeur. Nadia, now beaming, held the trophy, wore her new t-shirt and the Russian flag cape, which flew to tremendous effect for the hundreds of cameras and phones, both professional and amateur, that lined up to capture the moment.

Then we moved to the Place de Tertre where the press director had set a classic scene. Nadia was seated with the trophy, her back to the square and twenty artists with their easels in a semi-circle sketching her. The cameras shot and filmed from behind. The old and the new in perfect harmony. The sketching took less than fifteen minutes. The French Tennis Federation bought all twenty portraits and Nadia signed each one. She was given one, one was for the FFT walls and the rest would go to sponsors. The media had photos of her simulating flight over the city, posing for portraits and signing them. Everyone was thrilled. Emily kissed me on both cheeks and presented me with one of the sketches. 'You're not so bad,' she said and winked.

#CharlesDeGaulle, #Reboot

I sat in the lounge at Charles de Gaulle airport. It was the day after the final and social, newspapers and TV carried stories and, importantly, images of Nadia's victory shoot. They weren't the only images published, the world isn't that nice a place and the internet never forgets – but at least now she was building a portfolio of images to be proud of. I received an email from Jane:

**

Hi Katie,

Good work in Paris. Your vision for Nadia's photo has had enormous global impact with the images reaching across a wide audience. Well done sticking to your guns and making this happen. I look forward to catching up at Wimbledon.

Jane

**

With Jane's permission – I barely go to the toilet without that now – I reinstated my social media accounts. My first post was an image of Nadia and me with her Roland Garros trophy. A modest one hundred and fifty likes/loves and shares – perfect.

My flight would board in thirty minutes. It would take nearly twenty-six hours to reach home via Bangkok. I forced my eyes to remain open. The past year on tour, with all its triumphs and disasters, flitted through my memory bank. I think Jennifer Lawrence would be ideal to play Katie Cook in my self-titled movie. In the meantime, with Wimbledon two weeks away, I had time to go home, sleep and hit refresh.

My Instagram username @NQ30Love had proved to be a self-fulfilling prophecy. On the other hand, I had been on thirty-seven flights in twelve months and had seen many airports, including this one, several times. My passport was filling fast; I would need to have pages added – a badge of honour. FitBit wanted me to know that I had run 6,116 kilometres.

My spot on the tour was secured with blood, sweat, tears and air miles. My email account now had several levels of encrypted passwords. Was it all worth it? #GirlsAreHerosToo.

Acknowledgements

As an avid reader, I never understood how many revisions and decisions go into writing a complete novel. I am in awe of my writing colleagues who produce such masterpieces. There are many people to thank. People who have been generous and offered advice and thoughts, even things not easy to hear. From the tennis world, Adam Lincoln has been a great sounding board and reader. Stephen Duckitt, Nicola Arzani, Mitzi Ingram-Evans, Alison Lee and Vivienne Christie have all contributed. Speaking of inspiration, the 'real Marine', Veronique Beaujardin is truly No.1. My former tennis colleagues, (you know who you are), you have all been part of this journey – thank you.

James Worner from UTS (my alma Mata) has been an inspiration, reader, adviser, editor and friend throughout.

Anne Lawler has been a reader, advisor and friend, thank you Anne.

Joel Naoum and Writing NSW, thank you for helping me along the self-publishing journey.

To Danja dog, the ultimate writing companion, thank you for your presence, for the missed walks when I was in the zone, and for the inspiration seeking walks when I was stuck. I hope we have at least one more book in us!

For my parents who always say 'go for it' and to my sister, Lisa, a reader of early drafts, thank you.

Lastly to my partner Nicole. Stephen King in his book *On Writing*, talks about finding your 'ideal reader'. This is the person a writer writes FOR. The person they're trying to make laugh, cry or impress. You are forever mine.

Author's Notes

The cities and tournaments in this book are based on real tennis tournaments – although all the characters and incidents/events are fictitious.

The scandals in this book are not base on real events, they are from my imagination. The news agencies mentioned, *Pravda*, *Paris Match* and various other news outlets are real media organisations, but none of the characters or policies are based on real people or decision making guidelines/policies.

The WTA, ATP and Tennis Australia are also real organisations. None of the characters portraying employees are based on real people. The decisions made, policies, reference to training manuals are also entirely fictitious.

Any mention of real athletes is used in a fictitious manner.

Milton Keynes UK
Ingram Content Group UK Ltd.
UKHW040711120324
439192UK00001B/157